Timepiece:

A Steampunk Time-Travel Adventure

Book 1 of the Keeping Time Trilogy

by Heather Albano

FOREWORD BY KENNETH SCHNEYER

Stillpoint/Prometheus

Stillpoint/Prometheus
Stillpoint Digital Press
Mill Valley California USA

FIRST PAPERBACK EDITION
First ebook edition published in 2011

Foreword copyright © 2016 by Kenneth Schneyer

Special Hardcover ISBN 978-1-938808-44-9
Paperback ISBN 978-1-938808-35-7
Ebook ISBN 978-1-938808-39-5
version 1.1

The dingbat font used throughout is Nymphette, designed by Lauren Thompson, and the decorative fonts are Steampunk, designed by Marta von Eck, and Octant by Catharsis Fonts. All are used with permission.

Merçi beaucoup à Sharon Mann, Reine de Paris.

❦

BY HEATHER ALBANO
Fiction:
Timepiece
Timekeeper (Summer, 2017)
Timebound (Winter, 2018)

Games (Choice of Games):
A Study in Steampunk
Choice of Broadsides (with Adam Strong-Morse and Dan Fabulich)
Choice of Zombies (with Richard Jackson)
Affairs of the Court trilogy (with Adam Strong-Morse and Dan Fabulich)

❦

INTERESTED IN SPECULATIVE FICTION?
SIGN UP FOR NEWS, GIVEAWAYS, AND MORE AT
stillpointdigital.com/prometheus/news

For Mom, Dad, Molly, and Richard
and with thanks to Anise,
who let me have McLevy's pocket watch in the first place

Foreword

f course time travel represents an inversion of the way we experience the world. The arrow of entropy is reversed. People gain knowledge of the consequences of their actions before they take them. In this, it resembles both the prophecy story and the flashback: more than one author has imagined Tiresias and Cassandra as time travelers.

But there is another, more obvious yet subtle discontinuity: the time traveler finds herself in a place and time when and where her social instincts do not serve her. She experiences not culture shock, but past or future shock. The protagonist is a stranger in her own land.

Yet the form of the narrative has not often reflected this particular cognitive dissonance: H. G. Wells's time traveler wrote like a Victorian, although he was catapulted into the future. David Gerrold's Daniel Eakins spoke like a hip 1970s TV writer, though he was all over history. Even Connie Willis's historian time travelers, who certainly experience social discomfort in the past, experience it as a late 20th or early 21st-century person would. True, some literary time travelers seem to be simply crazy or otherworldly because of their experiences, but their craziness isn't that of another era, or at least not one that really happened.

In the novel before you, Heather Albano has capitalized on this literary quirk. Her time travelers are not contemporary or futuristic folk trying to sort themselves out in the Glorious Revolution. Instead they are Regency characters unexpectedly transported into a Victorian steampunk reality. In shorthand, they are Jane Austen characters in an H. G. Wells situation (or to be precise, an H. G. Wells and Mary Shelley situation!).

This provides Albano with an opportunity she clearly relishes, to critique Victorian values (as any responsible artist who writes steampunk must do) not from our oh-so-advanced 21st-century perspective but from the earlier (and perhaps more sensible?) viewpoint of the Napoleonic wars. At the same time, her protagonists see how the steampunk reality allows them some liberties that their Regency background would not. It is a textured and complex comparison of time periods. For this social conversation alone, the novel would be worth reading.

It also allows Albano to mess around delightfully with the literary conventions we have unconsciously absorbed. We're used to thinking of the comedy of manners as arising out of the romance genre, where the wrong word or gesture means so much. In action-adventure tales, we expect our heroes to speak in broader, plainer terms, or else to wax poetic about their heroics, or to be grim and silent as in Hemingway. Only a few authors, such as Ellen Kushner in her "melodrama of manners" *Swordspoint*, manage to interpolate such interpersonal subtleties in to blood-and-guts action. But this book, as I have implied, is an H. G. Wells adventure that thinks it's a Jane Austen novel. The violence, intrigue, and horror are often subordinated to the characters' relationships and their difficulties understanding one another. I like this not only out of sheer perverse delight, but also because of the surprising note of realism it sounds. People don't stop having social interactions, don't stop being unnecessarily hurt or embarrassed by little things, just because they're in the middle of a war and monsters are coming to get them.

Another treat is Albano's use of "interludes" between chapters, out-of-sequence and sometimes seeming to involve utterly unrelated characters. Apart from the puzzle-solving fun they provide, they inspire meditation on the subjective nature of time travel. Just as Princess Irulan's regular, infuriating propaganda-from-the-future in Frank Herbert's *Dune* forces the reader to experience the chaos of Muad'Dib's prophetic mind, Albano's interludes invite the reader's subjectivity into the sensation of having one's ordinary flow of experience interrupted by the past or the future.

I could go on. I could gush about the exquisite research that has gone into the historical scenes, or the wry winks to various works probably familiar to the reader. I could talk about the serious philosophical conflict between the personal and the global, the private hurt and the public evil. But you have the book in your hands; the feast is before you. Savor every bite, and don't forget I told you so.

Kenneth Schneyer is a Nebula-nominated author whose first collection, *The Law & the Heart*, was released by Stillpoint/Prometheus in 2014. He is also Professor of Humanities at Johnson & Wales University.

Timepiece

Prologue

John Freemantle felt every burst from the cannon as a jolt through his breastbone. At least the blasts no longer tore through his eardrums; his ears had been ringing for hours now, muting the roar into something almost manageable. His horse, a big bay possessed of considerably more battlefield experience than its rider, bore the noise stolidly, with no more sign of discomfort than the occasional twitching of an ear.

The British and their Belgian allies had been under heavy fire for most of the afternoon. In Freemantle's opinion, "heavy fire" made it sound more civilized than it really was. The term did not adequately convey the experience of facing down cannonade while enormous iron balls ripped through the ranks, leaving bloody pieces of men wherever they struck. The senior officers seemed unfazed by the carnage, but John Freemantle, only twenty-five, had not long served as aide-de-camp to the Duke of Wellington, and it was all he could do to feign calm.

The pounding crashed to a halt, and Freemantle would have stumbled if he had not been mounted. The battlefield was not quiet, not by any means, but the relative silence was as abrupt as being doused by cold water.

"Prepare to receive cavalry!" came the shout, and Freemantle, wrenching his nerves back under control, looked about for the Duke. His Grace was for once near at hand, and moreover actually headed toward the position of relative safety his rank demanded he assume. Freemantle spurred to his side and the square slammed closed around them, infantrymen three ranks thick. The outermost rank knelt with bayonets at the ready. A bugle call pierced Freemantle's ringing ears, and then the square was surrounded by the thunderous rush of men on horseback. The wave crashed against the infantry squares. The ground shook under Freemantle's feet.

And the charge broke, as it had broken eleven times before. Horses could not be made to leap into bayonets. The men within the square, Wellington and his aides-de-camp, were as safe as it was possible to be on the battlefield of Waterloo. For a long time afterward, the only sounds outside the square were of swords clashing and men screaming. Then the French cavalry retreated for the twelfth time, and the artillery resumed.

Wellington swatted aside the broad red infantry backs at once, ignoring the entreaties of the aides who wished he would not so expose his person to danger. No one could possibly replace him, as his subordinates pointed out again and again, but the Duke paid no more attention on this occasion than he had on any other. He was invariably to be found riding along the lines, demonstrating to the men his calmness and composure, giving terse orders and the rare word of encouragement. Wellington was not a demonstrative man and had not the gift of inspiring his troops with words—but he was right there with them, in the thick of the fight, and his men respected his courage as they did his skill. Sometimes, Freemantle reflected, that respect went farther toward encouraging battle-weary soldiers than warm words would have done. He did appreciate why Wellington so publically scorned attempts to keep him safe.

He judged the men to be in need of Wellington's encouragement at the present moment. The British force had never been strong to begin with—"my infamous army," Wellington had once said bitterly in Freemantle's hearing—and after the day's pounding by Napoleon's troops, they were in a sorry state indeed. Between injuries, deaths, and desertion, the line along the ridge was stretched nearly to breaking. An entire Belgian brigade had fled in panic, the British cavalry had destroyed itself in a useless charge on the French line, and General Blücher's Prussian reinforcements, promised the night before and sorely needed, were still nowhere to be seen.

Freemantle followed the Duke back onto the open field as other aides emerged from their own infantry squares. Wellington's staff re-gathered itself around him, eyeing the battlefield and shaking their heads.

"If the Prussians do not come, there is no way we can hold until nightfall," Canning muttered, and Freemantle gave his fellow aide-de-camp a startled glance. No one had dared say it quite so bluntly before now.

"They will come soon." General Muffling spoke unhappily. He somehow managed to appear at Wellington's side, like a drooping-mustached Greek chorus, whenever anyone raised the question of the missing reinforcements. Muffling was Blücher's liaison to Wellington, and he had been predicting the imminent appearance of said reinforcements since first light, over and over in almost exactly the same phrasing, while the sun rose high and men died under fire and the hopes of their comrades dwindled. "General Blücher attacks the Emperor's flank down in the village, but once that skirmish is won, then...then, surely..."

He trailed off. No one nearby gave him any aid in completing his sentence.

"Well, gentlemen," the Duke said, as though offering commentary upon an inconvenient rain shower, "they are hammering us hard, but we will see—" He stopped, attention arrested by a sight in the distance. Freemantle turned to follow his gaze, and saw a British officer on a black horse tearing down the ridgeline, mud spraying from each striking hoof. The officer waved as he rode, screaming something over the sound of cannonade, words no one could possibly hear. The Duke raised a hand in acknowledgment.

The black charger skidded to a halt, and the rider nearly fell from the saddle as he saluted. Freemantle recognized him, though his face was drawn and splattered with mud: a staff officer named Kennedy.

"My lord," he gasped. "La Haye Sainte—the farm—fallen. Overrun. The French pursued our men—engaged Von Ompteda's battalion—destroyed it. The whole battalion, my lord. Gap in the center of the line."

Wellington did not hesitate. "I shall order the Brunswick troops to the spot. Go and get all the German troops you can and all the guns you can find." Kennedy saluted and wheeled his horse, and the Duke swung to his aides. "Canning, my compliments to Colonel von Butlar, and the Brunswick Corps is to advance to the center immediately. I shall join them there. Gordon, my compliments to Major Norcott, and I wish a small detachment of the 95th to go into the forest and retrieve those Belgians who retreated so precipitously a short time ago, as their presence is desired to reinforce the center. Freemantle!" Freemantle barely had the chance to touch his heels to his horse's side before Wellington was galloping away from him.

~

Gun smoke hung thick over the crossroads that had once been defended by Van Ompteda's battalion, and Freemantle winced to see the pitiful stratagems being employed to fill the gap in the line. As Wellington rode up, officers from all over the ridge made for him, and their reports were identical to a man. The center had suffered the heaviest of Napoleon's heavy fire since early that day, and so many of their men were now dead or injured that, even with the Brunswick troops supporting them, they would be unable to hold their positions in the event of another French attack. And the French would attack; it was only a matter of time.

"The Prussians *must* come," someone muttered. "If they do not—"

"I am not saying *I* mean to retreat," another officer said, speaking the word aloud for the first time, "but the line may break, and we must decide what to do if it does…"

Wellington ignored that, turning to greet yet another officer stumbling toward him. "How do you get on, Halket?"

"My lord, we are dreadfully cut up," the man said simply. "Can you not relieve us for a little while?"

Wellington paused one beat. "I fear I have no one to send."

"Surely," Muffling said weakly, "surely it cannot be much longer before General Blücher…"

"But until that time," Wellington said, "it is impossible."

There was silence among his officers. Even the noise of the artillery seemed to be faltering. Freemantle strained his ears—everyone was straining their ears—trying to discern if there were drumbeats mixed in with the musket fire. Was the French infantry preparing to march?

"Very well, my lord," General Halket said. "Then we will stand until the last man falls." He turned to gaze where everyone was gazing, at the crossroads hidden from sight by swirling dust and smoke, from which a column of French troops would doubtless shortly appear.

"Damn me," Wellington said softly. Freemantle gaped at him, for that was more emotion than anyone had ever seen the "Iron Duke" betray, on the battlefield or off it. Wellington stared into the smoke, heedless of Freemantle's eyes, lips moving slightly as though working out a complicated sum in his head. He reached the solution, examined it for a moment with distaste, then nodded once. When he turned to Freemantle, any trace of uncertainty had vanished from his face. "My compliments to General Burnley, Lieutenant Colonel. Tell him if you please that I am in desperate want of troops not yet battle-weary, who can join the fight upon the left so that I may move some of my men to plug the gaps in the center. It would seem the Prussians are delayed, and therefore—" He paused only for a fraction of a second. It would scarcely have been noticeable to anyone who knew him less well than did an aide-de-camp. "—therefore the General is ordered to bring up his special battalion."

"Yes, sir!" Freemantle snapped a salute, clapped his heels to his horse's side, and clung tight.

The animal shot away from the ridgeline, up the Louvain road and toward the Forest of Soignes, and Freemantle did everything possible to encourage its speed, making good use of good road while he had it. To enter the forest, he must turn off the road and slow the horse to a saner pace. Maddening, but if the animal broke a leg on the uneven ground, the rider would be lost, and thus also the message, the battle, the war, the kingdom—

The forest closed over his head like a shroud. The ground still shook from the artillery a couple miles off, but it was a dull, meaningless sound under these thick green branches. He might have entered an entirely different world.

The special battalion was encamped a good way into the forest, an inconvenient distance at the present moment, but it would have been worse to have them nearer by. They could not be trusted to restrain themselves with a battle clashing before them and would turn on their allies if lacking other prey. The Duke had made it plain that he did not intend to use them unless he had absolutely no other choice and that, in the meantime, they were to be kept sufficiently far away that the rest of his army would not be hampered in the execution of its duty. It was particularly important to keep them from frightening the cavalry and thereby reducing its effectiveness. Horses did not like the members of the special battalion.

Few of Wellington's generals or aides-de-camp liked them either. Wellington himself liked them least of all, considering them to be the most infamous part of the infamous army with which he had been provided. His Grace would have far rather relied on the Prussians, Freemantle thought, and wished the Prussians had come in time.

The bay stumbled and Freemantle lurched forward, narrowly avoiding being thrown headfirst over its neck. The horse snorted and plunged, but regained its balance before it fell to its knees. "Easy," Freemantle said, "easy, whoa—" The horse stopped its forward stagger and stood, quietly enough but trembling.

Freemantle swung out of the saddle, heart pounding. No rabbit holes met his swiftly searching eyes. Thank God for that at least, but what had caused the stumble?

He ran a hand first down one foreleg and then the other, listening with all his might to the wood that surrounded him, trying to hear anything nearer than the distant rumble of cannon. Were there enemy here? Had someone hit his mount with a missile meant for him? He could find no sign of actual injury to the bay.

He picked up the animal's left foreleg, and saw the problem at once: a stone wedged between shoe and hoof. Freemantle fumbled for a knife. His heart hammered with the need for haste, but for that very reason, he could not grudge the delay to pry out the pebble, or he would be forced to race the sands of time on an increasingly lame mount.

With every instinct screaming at him to hurry, and the forest all around watching him with cold intent eyes, he set to work. Carefully, taking care not to damage the tender hoof any further, he probed with the blade.

The stone hopped out. The bay blew a breath. Freemantle led it forward a few steps and it put its feet down strongly. No lasting damage, thank heaven. Freemantle swung himself back up into the saddle, and the horse moved forward without hesitation or complaint. Freemantle, still unable to shake the sensation of eyes watching from the shadows beneath the trees, set his mount trotting once more.

The bay kept the pace easily until they were nearly upon the clearing where the special battalion was encamped—and then it checked again, shaking its head and snorting. Freemantle fought the animal's fear with both hands tight on the reins, keeping its head pointed toward Burnley's camp through the exertion of every muscle in his body. The horse shook and reared and struggled. Cannon fire could not disturb its calm, but it shrank from the unnatural things beyond the trees.

A few moments later, Freemantle could smell them, too—an odor more like a swamp than a stable—and at that moment, a red-coated sentry stepped out to challenge him. "From the Duke," Freemantle said. "Message for General Burnley." The sentry at once stepped aside, pointing to a man in officer's livery who stood a short distance away. Behind him stretched crudely cleared swathes of forest, trees cut down to make and to make room for three enormous corrals with slatted fences ten feet high.

The smell grew, and it took something perilously close to cruelty to keep the horse from bolting. Here actual eyes of actual monsters watched through the slats of the corrals, and the bay knew it. General Burnley looked up, saw Freemantle's struggles, and raised his voice in an effortless bellow for men to come and hold the Colonel's mount. Actual men rather than special battalion members came running in response to the order, Freemantle was glad to see. One grabbed the horse's bridle and the other two tried to calm it as it reared in ragged circles.

Freemantle did not dismount so much as fall from the saddle. He turned the slide into something that at least landed him on his feet, and Burnley did not seem disposed to comment on his lack of grace. "What news, Colonel?"

"It goes badly," Freemantle said, and rapped out the rest of Wellington's message.

General Burnley whipped around, calling for aides and shouting orders. "All right, lad," he added, "you'd better get back, and tell His Grace I'll have them there directly." It took two men to hold the horse still enough for Freemantle to get himself back in the saddle, and the bay shot away from the clearing like a bullet from a rifle.

Freemantle was only too glad to put the unnatural air of the special battalion behind him. He gave the horse its head and damned the consequences. Brush flew by in a streak of muddy green, and tree branches whipped at him from all sides, but the bay somehow managed to make it out of the forest without snapping a bone on any of the obstacles within. It burst onto the road with a leap, and pounded toward the ridge and the bellowing cannons as though making for the place it most wanted to be.

Freemantle found himself plagued by nightmare visions of what he would find on the other side of the ridgeline. He imagined cresting the hill to find the line broken and his countrymen slaughtered, a line of French infantry bayoneting the last few who could no longer offer any defense. The scene etched itself so plainly before his eyes that he was almost surprised to find it untrue when he reached the ridge. The French infantry had not yet advanced. The British were still holding. Wellington was where Freemantle had left him, and the Iron Duke swung to look at him with no more than a mildly inquiring expression.

"They're coming," Freemantle said.

Wellington nodded once, as though the conversation concerned a dinner invitation.

The French guns roared, paused, roared again. Freemantle, following Wellington as the Duke rode from the center to the left, thought he could catch in the moments of relative silence a faint drumbeat carried in the air behind him. He turned, straining his ears, straining his eyes.

He was not imagining it. The drumbeat from the Forest of Soignes grew louder, more distinct, resolved itself into a definite infantry beat.

And they came.

Out of the wood, through the trees, and down the road, huge slavering things marched in something approximating formation. The flesh of their faces hung slack off the bone, and drool trailed from the corner of the mouths they could not completely close. Their overlong arms and thrust-forward necks strained at the fabric of a simplified private soldier's uniform. A mockery of the uniform, it had been called by some.

Most of them carried muskets. It was in fact easy enough to train them to fire, for they had proven not much more stupid than the average raw recruit. None, however, bore a saber or bayonet. Their primary weapon was instead a large battle-axe, two-headed and spiked like something salvaged from Britain's savage past, for the special battalion was at its best in close combat. Its members were resistant to discipline and incapable of learning sophisticated tactics, but they could be taught to slaughter anyone not wearing a red uniform and to mostly refrain from slaughtering anyone who did.

General Burnley led them on foot, but managed to preserve a certain grim dignity even while marching like a common soldier. The special battalion was coming up on the left flank. Wellington turned and barked an order to get the remnants of the cavalry out of there.

The cavalry went to reinforce the desperate men at the center crossroads. Wellington followed their progress through a spyglass, and his lips turned upward just slightly at the corners. He slapped the spyglass into Freemantle's hand and moved to give another order. Freemantle lifted it to his own eye, curious to see what Wellington had seen.

It was astonishing how much the set of a man's shoulders and the tilt of his head could tell you. Even with the spyglass, Freemantle could not read anything as specific as expressions, but he saw the shift in posture move from man to man, all along the center of the ridge as the cavalry came to reinforce the position. The men in the center had considered themselves under an inevitable sentence of death a moment ago. Now they glanced over their shoulders at the horses and straightened as though they still had a fight left in them after all.

The reaction of the men on the left was even more dramatic. Positioned as they were, they could not see what manner of reinforcements approached from their rear, but they heard the drums and the marching feet, and some caught a glimpse of the flag. The words ran through the ranks of exhausted men like wind through a field of rye: "Reinforcements have come."

The French artillery chose that moment to crash to a stop. The relative silence rang in Freemantle's ears, more deafening than the noise. He made out a drumbeat, slightly out of cadence with the British one behind him. The French infantry advance.

He heard his name in the Duke's distinctive bark, and hastily kneed his horse to follow Wellington higher up onto the ridge. The Duke put out his hand for the spyglass, and Freemantle handed it over.

Even without it, Freemantle could see clearly enough. This high up, the visibility almost qualified as good, and even through the powder smoke that still hung densely over the valley Freemantle could discern precisely which French troops were marching over the churned mud. The Emperor, expecting imminent victory, had sent in the Garde.

The Imperial Garde was the elite of the elite of Napoleon's troops, distinctive by their height and the bearskins that were part of their campaigning uniforms, usually held in reserve until the moment of victory and partially for that reason never defeated. The day was traditionally as good as won when the Garde took the field, and certainly the rest of the French troops assumed this would be the case at Waterloo as it had been so often before. They cheered as the tight columns passed, a wave of sound that started faint but grew into a crescendo from every part of the valley.

The monsters of the special battalion were not particularly suited to defensive fighting. No one, including Freemantle, had expected them to *hold* the left flank, and they did not. But they came screeching over the ridge instead, howling and brandishing axes as tall as men, and the French Garde—said to know how to die, but not how to surrender—took one look at this terrible vision and broke.

"The Garde is retreating!" It was shouted all over the battlefield, in triumph by the British and in horror by the French. The rest of Napoleon's infantry stopped, gaped, then turned and likewise fled for their lives. The French cavalry squealed and trampled, trying to get away from the horrible things advancing on them. The monsters pounded in pursuit, huge and bloodthirsty and completely unfatigued, leaving gore and destruction wherever they passed.

Leaving, too, some fair bit of consternation in the British ranks behind them. It took fast talking and firm handling to keep the British troops who had gotten a good look at their new allies from sprinting away in the opposite direction. No one but the Iron Duke could have managed it, and for a moment Freemantle feared it would be beyond even his powers. But Wellington rode hard up and down the lines, visible and shouting, and soon enough had his men organized to join the monsters' pursuit of the French. By then some isolated fire had resumed from the French side, but Wellington acted as though he did not care. "Forward and complete your victory, my lads!" His voice pierced the chaos. "Look, they fly before us! See them off our land!"

"For God's sake!" Freemantle heard someone else shout in exasperation. "Don't expose yourself so!" He turned his head in time to see another horseman come pounding past. The man reined up beside Wellington, and Freemantle saw that it was Lord Uxbridge, the Duke's second in command. Uxbridge's words were lost in the surrounding noise, but his gestures suggested he was attempting to persuade the Duke of the need for some caution. Wellington shrugged him off, as he had shrugged off all other similar arguments that day. Uxbridge persisted, and Wellington seemed to answer tersely, then made an obvious gesture of impatience and drew his mount an exaggerated step backward. He turned from Uxbridge to continue the coordination of the pursuit.

A sound like the snapping of a tree branch hit Freemantle's ears, and he looked over just in time to see the red stain blossom and spread fast on the white cloth of Uxbridge's trousers. Wellington swung around in the saddle, catching his second before he could slide to the ground, holding him with one arm as Freemantle struggled through the press toward them. Uxbridge's face had gone the color of whey. "By God—" he said in hoarse surprise as Freemantle reached them. "I've lost my leg."

White fragments of bone poked from the mangled hole that had been his knee, stark against the dark blood. "By God," Wellington said, "so you have." Uxbridge's eyes fluttered closed. "Freemantle—" the Duke commanded, and Freemantle reached to take his limp burden. "See to him," Wellington said, already turning to the job still to be finished. "Get him behind the lines."

Freemantle summoned a couple of soldiers with a snap of his fingers and with their aid managed to ease Uxbridge off his mount. As they turned for the relatively safe ground where the wounded were being tended, he paused to take one last look at the battlefield. The road that led out of the valley, the route back to France, was choked with a sickening swarm of fleeing humanity. Nightmarish things pressed close at their rear, hacking through their back ranks.

❧

It was well into the evening and the light was fading before General Blücher's long-promised Prussian reinforcements emerged from the red setting sun.

But Wellington's troops no longer had any need of their aid. By the time the Prussians arrived on the ridge, the French army was thoroughly routed, and England's monsters were observed making for a steadfast square of Gardes who put up such a passionate defense that they must surely be guarding something worth capture—the Emperor himself, perhaps, or at least the Imperial Eagles.

Freemantle, now returned to Wellington's side, watched the special battalion at its work and supposed he ought to be thanking God for its presence. Somehow, the words would not come to his lips. Wellington turned abruptly from the massacre, and for the second time that day Freemantle could read his expression. Only for a moment: then the helm of the Iron Duke came down.

Chapter I

The pocket watch arrived on a day when nothing much else was engaging Elizabeth's attention: no parties or social calls to prepare for or recover from, nothing but gardening or letter-writing to occupy a young lady's morning. Or fancy-work, of course, but Elizabeth avoided needles and embroidery frames whenever she could.

Truth be told, she did not much care for letter-writing either. To her mother's despair, she had no liking at all for any occupation that required her to sit still. She went for long walks every day an optimistic outlook could deem the weather fine; she climbed trees as frequently as she thought she could get away with it; she spent as much time as possible gardening or dancing, for those were the only two activities vigorous enough to please her while still being proper enough to please her mother. As recent days had been rather full of conflict with her mother over her chosen pastimes and as there was no ball conveniently available, Elizabeth had elected to spend this particular morning in the garden and thereby avoid a quarrel. When Bronson brought her the parcel, she was pruning roses and only a little bored by the fine June day.

More accurately, she was bored by the rose garden. The day pleased her greatly, for it was of the sort whose fineness no one could dispute. No more than a handful of fluffy clouds marred the sky, the sunshine was not so very hot, and Elizabeth therefore expected to have no need of the usual coaxing or subterfuge to obtain permission to go walking later. But the canopies and marble statues of the garden could not long hold her interest when she had observed them so many times before, and the high hedges prevented her from seeing anything that lay beyond. She might *know* that her father's house nestled among rolling hills, that it was possible to glimpse the sea from the top of the tallest, that the second-tallest was covered with a sweep of white-blossomed apple trees, and that beyond the orchard lay the estate of Mr. Carrington—but she could *see* none of these things. For all her five senses could inform her, the entire world might have been made up of hedgerows, fencing, and rose blossoms.

Elizabeth was lost enough in her daydreams of sea and hills to clip the head off a perfectly healthy rose. She muttered in vexation, bending to scatter the petals lest she add yet *another* complaint to her mother's ever-growing list. A shadow fell over her, and she straightened quickly, stepping to one side to hide the evidence of her mistake.

But it was neither her mother nor her aunt who had pursued her into the garden. Instead, she found herself face-to-face with Bronson, the elderly butler. His eyes glanced down at the scattered petals as though he knew exactly what she had been doing, but he said merely, "This came for you, Miss Elizabeth," and handed her a parcel wrapped in brown paper.

It was about six inches square, and not particularly heavy. The direction was written in a clear, bold hand. There was nothing remotely remarkable about it—except its presence, for Elizabeth could not think of anyone who was likely to be sending her a parcel. No one of her close family was traveling. Nor was there an imminent occasion that merited a gift, Christmas being more than six months away and her birthday only three months gone. She had the irritable feeling that this was going to be one of those transgressions against decorum that sent her family into fits of agitation over her behavior. Even though she had not sought this particular impropriety. Elizabeth sighed.

"Has my mother seen this?" she asked.

"No, miss," Bronson replied in a tone so neutral no one but Elizabeth could have heard the faint humor in it. "I took the liberty of bringing it straight to you, without acquainting Mrs. Barton of its arrival. I thought it might perhaps be from a young gentleman."

"Undoubtedly that is it," Elizabeth replied. She reminded herself that she must not speak as though she had tasted curdled milk. A normal young lady of seventeen years did not react so to a mention of her presumptive suitors. She thought she managed the correct tone when she added, "Thank you," for Bronson's eyes twinkled. He bowed and turned back for the house. Elizabeth, frowning once he was out of sight, used the pruning shears to attack the twine.

The plain brown paper proved to cover an equally plain brown box. Within the box was a small bag of red velvet. Elizabeth could not help but marvel at the quality of the material, even as her fingers hastened to undo the drawstring mouth.

The velvet bag contained a gold pocket watch, complete with a chain and fob. Elizabeth stared at it. Then she turned the brown paper over, to confirm that it was indeed her name written there. It was; but that only made her confusion worse. There was no note included, so she was no further along in discovering the sender. And to this question had been added another: who in the world would send her a gentleman's watch?

It wasn't new, but the gold of the casing and chain was well-polished and well-cared-for. By looking closely she could see a few small scratches, but she could tell they were honorable wounds, signs of long service. Engraved on the casing were intricate vines, flowers, hourglasses, birds, something that she thought might be the sun, and some other marks that appeared to be only abstract etchings. The fob was not engraved, but the chain felt pleasingly solid as she ran it through her fingers.

The watch itself, Elizabeth reflected, also had a strangely weighty feel. Now that she had it in her hands, it seemed heavier than it ought, and for that matter, considerably larger than was customary. Its ticking was somehow discordant, as well. Was it too fast, perhaps? Elizabeth opened the watch to see if it was keeping proper time.

And almost dropped it. The inside of this pocket watch was like the inside of no other she had ever seen. Instead of one face, it had four small ones, two crowded on one side and two on the other. One of these did look like a proper watch face, though its hands were not moving. The second had both an inner and an outer dial, with miniscule numbers running all around it. The third face was even more complicated, comprised of eight dials nesting within each other. And the fourth—Elizabeth stifled a gasp and brought the watch closer to her eyes. Could she possibly be seeing this? The fourth displayed tiny images—and they *moved*, flickering in and out of sight even as she stared at them.

"Elizabeth!"

That was her mother's voice, piercing the air like a particularly shrill gull, and her mother's figure followed the sound, visible through a gap in the hedge as she hastened over the lawn to the rose garden. Elizabeth clutched the pocket watch to her breast, then cast about for a better hiding place.

"Elizabeth!"

The querulous note in Mrs. Barton's voice seemed more pronounced than was customary, and she was moving at an unusually quick pace. Elizabeth had not a moment to lose. She snatched off her bonnet, shoved the pocket watch and its velvet bag inside, and kicked the brown paper under the nearest rosebush. "Coming, Mamma!" she called. Catching up the pruning shears with her free hand, she went to meet her mother as a good daughter should.

Mrs. Barton did not seem to notice the unusual courtesy. "I have been looking all over for you, and here you are out in this hot sun—and without your bonnet! You will ruin your complexion, I declare you will."

"I only thought to feel the wind in my hair, Mamma," Elizabeth soothed. "I am finished in the garden and was just returning inside." To her relief, Mrs. Barton turned to accompany her back toward the house and away from the telltale brown paper.

"Your hair will be a fright by the time you get there; do you never think of these things, Elizabeth? Have you forgotten that Mrs. Wilton is to call this morning? And that she brings her husband's nephew?"

Elizabeth bit back a sound of annoyance. "I am sorry, Mamma. I *had* forgotten, or I would not have been gardening." This was true. If she had remembered Mrs. Wilton's incipient visit, she would have taken care to be out walking, as far from home as she could reasonably get.

"Well, go and tidy yourself now, at once. Put on your new muslin and I shall send Sarah in to do your hair. Make haste, child, make haste!"

"Yes, Mamma." Elizabeth chose to interpret this instruction as permission to run in an unladylike manner. She darted into the house, ignoring her mother's despairing wail about her hoydenish ways, and clutching her bonnet to her so that Mrs. Barton would not notice how it bulged.

Elizabeth thanked her stars that she chanced to encounter Bronson as she pounded up the stairs. He stepped smoothly aside, and she paused to stop and whisper, "I have left the wrapping paper in the garden. Will you please go and tidy it, and please, Bronson, do not tell—"

"Leave it to me, miss," Bronson assured her, and Elizabeth flashed him a smile and ran up the second flight of stairs to her bedchamber.

She had barely enough time to hide the pocket watch in the drawer containing winter underclothing before Sarah arrived to assist her in changing her gown. A mud-splattered morning dress would never do to wear before company, of course—even Elizabeth had to admit that—but she grudged the time it took to don her new white muslin. She supposed she should be grateful that it was of a simple enough line not to require a long corset and the fuss that entailed, but even so she had to fight to keep from betraying her impatience at every step. When the muslin was donned, she must sit still while Sarah combed and arranged her unruly curls. She had hoped for a few minutes between the maid's departure and the guests' arrival to examine the pocket watch again, but she heard voices below while Sarah was pinning up the last lock of hair.

Elizabeth made her way down the stairs as sedately as a young lady ought. Whether her stately pace was due to reluctance to walk away from the pocket watch and its secrets or to reluctance to enter Mrs. Wilton's company, she could not have said. She opened the door to the drawing room just as Mrs. Wilton and her nephew were invited to sit, which at least gave her mother and aunt no opportunity to criticize her appearance or caution her regarding deportment. But it also meant that all heads swiveled to watch her as she entered, and her chances for playing an unobtrusive role in the conversation were reduced to nothing.

Mrs. Wilton's nephew rose. The ladies remained seated. Elizabeth made a curtsy to the room as a whole. "Forgive me for keeping you waiting," she said.

"Miss Elizabeth," Mrs. Wilton greeted her, without any discernable warmth.

Something in the tone stiffened Elizabeth's back. Mrs. Wilton might have been addressing a child, which Elizabeth certainly was not. She was of an age to be "Miss Barton," in fact, but her father's sister lived with the family and indeed was in the room, so it was she who claimed that title. Still, that did not give Mrs. Wilton the right to say "Miss Elizabeth" as though speaking to a schoolgirl.

"It is a pleasure to see you, ma'am," Elizabeth replied as politely as she could. "I hope you are well."

Mrs. Wilton sniffed. "Tolerably so, Miss Elizabeth, thank you. Perhaps you remember my nephew Charles?"

Elizabeth turned obediently to the young man who had risen and made a second curtsy. He bowed in a manner more theatrical than correct. As he straightened, she was able to observe the dashing cut of his blue coat and the dazzling starched whiteness of his cravat. He had folded it into that most complicated design known as the ballroom—indicating that either he had taken the time to become proficient at executing such a piece of nonsense, or that he had attempted the fold on numerous cravats that morning before getting one right. Mr. Wilton saw the direction of her gaze, assumed her approval, and beamed. Elizabeth stifled a sigh.

"Indeed, Mr. Wilton, it has been too long," she said, and moved to take a seat.

"Allow me." Mr. Wilton swung around, took a chair from the small table, and set it with a flourish beside his own. Elizabeth looked with longing at the far corner of the sofa, but seated herself in the chair.

"Since my nephew has recently attained his majority," Mrs. Wilton said, "his uncle and I thought it time he favor us with a proper visit. He is to inherit, you know." Indeed, that was something everyone knew, all three parts of it, for Mrs. Wilton had mentioned it in every conversation for six months. "We are paying calls throughout the neighborhood. It is only right that my nephew becomes acquainted with my neighbors, since they will one day be *his* neighbors."

Which meant, Elizabeth interpreted, that Mrs. Wilton and her nephew were making the rounds of every family who had a daughter approaching marriageable age, to decide if there were any worthy of being offered an alliance with the House of Wilton.

From her corner, Elizabeth's aunt spoke with her usual grimness. "Are you finding your visit to the country congenial, Mr. Wilton, after the dissipations of Town?"

"Indeed yes, Miss Barton," Charles Wilton assured her. "I am finding the company in Hartwich even more charming than I remember from my boyhood visits." He looked significantly at Elizabeth as he spoke, and she kept herself from rolling her eyes by an extreme force of will. Two floors above nestled a mysterious pocket watch in a plush velvet bag. For that matter, outside the window birds chirped and a soft breeze blew. And here she was trapped in a drawing room without even the consolation of interesting conversation.

"That is very kind of you to say, sir," she said. Her mother looked at her sharply.

"But—if I may ask, Miss Elizabeth—why do I have the good fortune to meet you here? Why is a lovely young lady such as you not making her curtsy to Society?"

"I am not yet of an age to do so, Mr. Wilton," Elizabeth replied, keeping her eyes cast down. Let him strike her off his list as too young, and thene could go about interviewing other eligible young ladies and she could go back to the pocket watch.

"My daughter is only just seventeen, sir," her mother explained. "We did think of this year's Season, but next year, her cousin Lily will be of an age to join us, and it will be merry indeed for the girls to have each other's companionship. Unless, of course..." Mrs. Barton trailed off innocently, and Elizabeth gritted her teeth.

The conversation chirped along around her, and she returned her thoughts to the pocket watch, trying to construct from memory what the picture on the fourth face had been. A dark street, overlaid with fog...and within the fog, a shape moving...what sort of shape? Something quite large, she thought, and...

"Miss Elizabeth?"

Elizabeth jerked herself back to the drawing room and lifted her eyes to Charles Wilton's. "I beg your pardon, sir?"

"I said, it must be very quiet here for a jolly young girl such as yourself. Town will make your head spin next year."

"Indeed, sir, I am certain it will," Elizabeth said. Her mother cleared her throat.

"Only, I suppose, if you are fond of diversions," Mr. Wilton went on, a little uncertainly. "Perhaps you are one of those studious young ladies who do not care for dancing...?" He glanced toward Elizabeth's aunt, obviously a studious old lady who did not care for dancing.

"Elizabeth? Studious?" Her mother laughed. "Oh, but that is a very good joke, sir. She is a most lively girl indeed, and likes nothing better than to dance. *Do you not*, Elizabeth?"

Elizabeth said, "Indeed, sir, I do enjoy a dance."

"Perhaps I can prevail upon my aunt and uncle to give a ball," Charles Wilton said, leaning toward her, "and perhaps you will consent to dance with me upon that occasion?"

"I would be most happy to, sir." Elizabeth shifted to avoid the tickle of his breath on her neck. "It is very kind of you." During her campaign to convince her mother to delay her entrance into Society one final year—and she was still rather surprised Mrs. Barton had fallen for the argument that Elizabeth wished to wait for Lily; Elizabeth and Lily were not so great friends as all that—she had thought of the reprieve as representing twelve additional months of freedom. It had not occurred to her that her mother would not wait for a triviality such as her presentation in London to commence a search for an eligible young man. But Mrs. Barton was not one to deny herself any of the fun accorded to a mother with a marriageable daughter, and Elizabeth had therefore spent many tedious mornings since her seventeenth birthday trapped in a drawing room with some coxcomb or another. Now, nodding her head without listening to the anecdote Mr. Wilton was telling, she had to repress a shudder at the idea of an entire Season *surrounded* by men like him. And *then* what? Decades upon decades of drawing rooms and embroidery stretched out before her.

Mr. Wilton paused, looking at her with eyes like a good-humored dog. Elizabeth inferred it was time to make some reply. "How diverting, sir," she said.

"I am glad you think so!" Mr. Wilton leaned forward. "That's nothing compared to what happened to a man I know out in Surrey"

Elizabeth had a sudden savage wish that she had been born to a family of good breeding but no fortune, so she might be reduced to marrying a second or third son, a soldier who would whisk her off to foreign places. To the East Indies, say—or the West Indies, she wasn't particular. But her thirty thousand pounds restrained her as effectively as a butterfly in a net, and Charles Wilton laid out before her all the details concerning his friend's recent purchase of a horse.

"And what do you think of that, Miss Elizabeth?"

"Very droll indeed, sir."

Perhaps when she did enter Society next year—if she got that far, if she could dodge the advances of her mamma's parade for that long—she might contrive to entangle herself with such a young officer. It could not be very hard to do; she had read of such things in novels. Or to be precise, she had not read them herself. It was one unladylike habit her mother did not need to worry over. Her elder cousin Mirabelle had read them out loud and Elizabeth and Lily had listened. It had been, Elizabeth thought, preferable to attempting *conversation* with Mirabelle. Hearing all the novels meant she knew how the story went. A young lady goes to London for her first Season and is swept off her feet by a dashing young man, but he proves faithless or disreputable or both, and sometimes the young lady is ruined. Or sometimes she merely makes an "unfortunate alliance." Elizabeth thought an unfortunate alliance a perfectly acceptable price to pay for the chance to see something more of the world than the walled-in gardens of fine houses.

"*Elizabeth*," her aunt said in a freezing whisper, "Mrs. Wilton asked you a question."

Elizabeth started. "Oh, I beg your pardon. I...I cannot think what is causing my mind to wander so. It must be the heat, or perhaps I am coming over poorly..."

No one in the room was fooled. Well, Charles Wilton, perhaps; Elizabeth sensed it wouldn't take much to fool him. But her mother and aunt knew she never took ill, and Mrs. Wilton's lips pursed as she repeated, "I wondered if you would join your mother and your aunt when they take tea with me on Friday."

"Thank you, ma'am, I should be most happy to." Elizabeth attempted to give the impression of enthusiasm, but there was not much that could be done to repair the tatters of the visit. Elizabeth was of two minds on that. She was in many ways relieved to have Mrs. Wilton taking her departure, and if she had shaken off Mr. Wilton's interest, so much the better. But as she took note of the agitation on her mother's face and the anger in her aunt's eyes, she became abruptly uncertain if the victory won over the Wiltons was worth the punishment she was sure to catch once they were gone.

Her aunt waited only until the sound of the closing outer door proclaimed the Wiltons to be out of earshot. "Your manners, Miss Elizabeth Barton, do no credit to your family."

"I am sorry, ma'am," Elizabeth replied as evenly as she could. "I am unaccountably distracted today."

"A fine day you have picked for it," her mother exclaimed. "Before Mrs. Wilton, of all people! She is a force to be reckoned with in this neighborhood, as you very well know! She pays us the compliment of bringing her nephew to meet you—and he is to inherit, Elizabeth, you know that! You could hardly find any better match! Here close to home, too! But no, you must go and be sulky and probably you have put him off for all time!"

Elizabeth devoutly hoped so. She wished her mother would have done with the scolding and move on to the punishment, so that she could escape to her room.

"I never heard of such an inconsiderate girl! You have no regard for my feelings at all!"

"I do beg your pardon, Mamma," Elizabeth said, steadily still. "I did not mean to insult you. Or Mrs. Wilton. I find my mind wandering today. Perhaps I had better lie down before dinner..."

"I am certain your time could be more usefully occupied," her aunt said crisply. "In such a way as might train it to keep attention where attention belongs. Sit with me, Elizabeth, and read to me while I wind yarn. That will be much better for you than lazing about your bedchamber." She resumed her seat, took up Hannah More's *Practical Piety*, and held it out. "Now, miss."

There was no escape to be had. Elizabeth, longing to be anywhere else, resumed her seat in the hard chair and opened the book. Her aunt took up a skein of gray yarn and began to wind it. Bees droned against the window.

And *this* was her other option. Either she married some handsome featherhead like Charles Wilton and spent her days making insipid conversation as the mistress of his house, or she declined all suitors until Society deemed her "on the shelf" and thereafter wound yarn year upon year. She fixed her mind on the thought of the disreputable and dashing young officer, resolving to borrow Mirabelle's novels at the first opportunity, so that she would be well versed in the techniques used to secure such a man when the opportunity presented itself. It was the only escape route she could discern.

Her aunt allowed her to cease reading only when it became time for dinner. Elizabeth followed her to the dining room with downcast eyes and an outward show of meekness, and sat down to endure the interminable courses and still more maddening conversation—the latter mostly conducted mostly by her mother and her aunt, with her father occasionally interjecting comments that showed him to have not been listening. Elizabeth managed to keep her tongue in check until the chairs were at last pushed back and the family made ready to remove to the drawing room. Then, taking care to speak politely, she announced her intention of enjoying the remainder of the day out of doors.

Her aunt sniffed. "Mind you keep to the path, Elizabeth, and do not run about. You'll disgrace us all if Mrs. Carrington or Lady Anderson sees you with mud on your ankles and your face red like a farm girl's. Really, John—" She turned to her brother. "—I do not see why the girl should be permitted to run wild like this. There is no need for her to be gadding over the countryside; she ought to take her exercise nearer home. When I was a girl, a turn in the garden was enough for me, as you very well know, and I never stayed out of doors above half an hour. I would be ashamed to tan my skin in the sun and wind—" Elizabeth backed through the door before either of her parents could command her to restrict her movements to the garden, ran upstairs to snatch her bonnet and reticule and the pocket watch in its bag, and escaped for the orchard.

Chapter 2

O n the other side of the orchard, conversation over port had thus far dwelt exclusively upon hunting and the business of estate management. Understandable enough, William Carrington thought, as the three participants other than himself—which was to say, the three participants who were indeed participating—consisted of an elderly gentleman with an extensive estate, a middle-aged gentleman with a great love of hunting and an extensive estate, and a young gentlemen with a great love of hunting who would someday inherit an extensive estate. William had little to contribute on either topic, for he was not himself in line to inherit anything, and he had never been overly fond of the hunt even before he lost the use of his arm. In any case, there was room in his thoughts for only one subject. He kept waiting for his father, his brother, or his brother-in-law to broach it, but they did not. Apparently, it did not interest them.

Or perhaps they avoided the word "Belgium" deliberately, out of some misplaced sense of delicacy. If that were the case, he ought to introduce the topic himself, but he couldn't be sure, and moreover, he rather thought he had made enough of a fool of himself for one day. He had pounced upon his brother-in-law almost before Sir Henry had descended from his carriage to ask if there were news in the London papers from the Continent. There was not—or at least, no news more recent than that which had already filtered into Kent—and Sir Henry had raised his eyebrows at William's urgency.

"Well." William's father set aside his napkin, setting aside with it the problem of roof repair upon which he had been expounding. "Perhaps we ought to join the ladies, hey?" He scraped back his chair, and his son George and son-in-law Henry followed suit. William trailed behind them across the passageway and to the drawing room.

He entered to hear his sister Caroline's voice raised in a complaint. "And the Duchess is giving a ball! Has given it, by now, for that notice in the paper was many days old. I really do not see why I should not have accompanied Christopher to Belgium. I should have enjoyed myself greatly with all the other officers' wives."

"Will you have some coffee, William?" Mary cut in, rather obviously passing over her father and her husband to distract William's mind from the subject of Belgium. She held the coffee cup toward his right hand, and he reached without comment to take it with his left. Mary flushed and looked away.

Mary was Lady Anderson, wife of Sir Henry Anderson, and Caroline was Mrs. Palmer, wife of Lieutenant Christopher Palmer. Before William Carrington and Christopher Palmer had been brothers-in-law, they had been brother officers; but the Lieutenant had returned with their regiment to the Continent when Bonaparte escaped from exile, and William, who had left the Peninsula with his right arm dangling as limply as the sleeve that encased it, had not.

There was no hope of discussing openly the happenings on the Continent with Caroline in the room, for she was in delicate condition and must not be upset with worry over her husband. William therefore took his coffee cup over to the window and out of the circle of conversation. His father's estate spread before him, green and golden-brown against the dark blue sky.

He tried to focus his attention on the richness of those colors. On the taste of real coffee, sweetened with cream. On the smell of earth wafting through the open window. On the soft-voiced conversation behind him, concerning the everyday trivialities of country life. Under the brass-hot Spanish sun, he had dreamed about this. He had wanted nothing but to make it back to this. He ought now to devote at least a portion of his attention to this, rather than allowing his thoughts to always wander back to the battlefield.

But perhaps he could be forgiven for considering the battlefield the only matter of any real importance. Napoleon had burst the bonds of his prison. The monster who had cast a shadow across William's childhood was once again on the march. When news of his escape had reached the shores of Britain back in early spring, William had only just surfaced from his latest relapse, and to his fever-drenched mind it seemed to him inevitable that Bonaparte should have escaped. Bonaparte was like nothing so much as one of those menacing dark things out of a country tale, the sort that haunted the wood and followed in your footsteps and could not be killed. A few days later, William had shaken his head sternly at himself for even entertaining such nonsense, but supposed it was an understandable delusion for a man in the grip of fever. After all, he could literally not remember a time when Bonaparte's name had not stood for everything Britain must fear.

William had been only two years old when Napoleon seized power in France, and he remembered his boyhood as being conducted to the beat of the war drums on the Continent. Napoleon had gobbled France, Italy, Germany, and the Hapsburg Empire; stripped lands from Prussian and Austrian control; waged a bloody invasion in Spain; and left at last only Britain standing fast against him, alone and with the knowledge that the tyrant schemed to cross the water and hang the tricolored flag on the Tower of London as well. William had always known that Napoleon plotted the destruction of England; and William had always known that at sixteen, he would enter the Army and help bring about the madman's downfall.

Well, he had entered the Army. But he had not seen so very much combat on the Peninsula before receiving the wound that ended his military career, and though Napoleon had indeed been defeated not long after, William had not been present to aid in the defeat. Worse, Britain's victory had not lasted even a year, and Napoleon now again held France in the palm of his hand. He had marched into Paris three months ago without firing a single shot. Without *needing* to fire a shot, because not one Frenchman lifted a hand in opposition. Since then, he had reassembled most of the force that had allowed him to conquer Europe before.

William tightened his left hand around the coffee cup, then forced himself to relax it. His scarlet-coated brothers and their Dutch and Prussian allies would face Bonaparte's fanatic French in a drawn battle sometime soon. Sometime very soon. Indeed, the cannons might be firing even now. But William Carrington, worn and weak from his winter's illness, strength gone forever from his right arm, could do nothing but sip coffee in a drawing room and beg his London brother-in-law for news.

The ladies behind him on from balls in Belgium to social matters nearer home. "Charles Wilton has come to visit at last?" Lady Anderson said. "I do hope to catch a glimpse of him at some Assembly or another. I declare I had begun to doubt his existence, all these years we have heard of him and never seen his face."

"Mrs. Wilton pledged to bring him to call one morning this week," Mrs. Carrington said. "We must be content to wait our turn, of course. With all my daughters so advantageously married, there is not so much to interest him here as there might be elsewhere." William could not see her, but he could tell from her voice that she was smiling first upon Mary, then upon Caroline, and then at the portrait of Frances.

"Has he been long in the neighborhood?" Mary asked.

"He only arrived yesterday," Mrs. Carrington said. "Today his aunt took him to call upon the Bartons at Westerfield."

"Better him than me," George muttered, suddenly close beside William. "From all I hear of that young dandy, he'll find something to like in Elizabeth Barton, and perhaps then her mother will cease foisting the chit on the rest of us. You'd think she was some cottager's brat, the way she romps about."

"Does she?" William said without much interest. He had only recently grown well enough to be dragged into company, and he could not remember Elizabeth Barton doing anything so very noteworthy at last week's Assembly. "I hadn't noticed."

"Well, you haven't been obliged to dance with her, now have you? Pretty enough, I grant you, but I assure you the elegance goes no deeper than her skin." There was a pause. "Thirty thousand pounds, of course," George added, in an overly hearty tone. "There is that." He appeared to have belatedly remembered that he ought to be encouraging his brother to meet young ladies.

William tried to clench his right hand again, but of course could not manage it. The fingers would curl a little, but most of their dexterity was gone. He had not been obliged to dance with Elizabeth Barton or anyone else because he could not manipulate his right arm sufficiently to dance a quadrille.

There was in any case no point in clenching anything, for George was right. George would inherit the estate and Thomas had the family living. The girls were all provided for. And a soldier unable to soldier had best find an heiress to marry. All three of his sisters had offered to have him visit their establishments, that he might meet new young ladies at their local Assemblies. Mary had indeed spent the entirety of dinner insisting that he come along when she and Henry and the children departed Hartwich after their annual visit. William found himself unable to imagine an heiress willing to marry a third son without a profession, an easy jesting manner, or the ability to lead her onto a dance floor, but he also found himself lacking the energy to make much of an argument. He had made noncommittal replies instead, until Mary mercifully dropped the subject.

He was now saved from answering George by their mother's voice proposing a game of cards. The party commenced a debate concerning the merits of lanterloo versus speculation, and William excused himself.

❧

He ended up wandering through the orchard more because he had picked a direction at random than because he found within himself any great interest in apple trees. He ought to be interested, he thought. It was the finest sort of summer day; he ought therefore to be charmed by the cloudless sky and the scent of grass and earth. He tried to summon the appropriate feelings of appreciation, but they would not come. It was as though there were swaths of gauze bandage layered between his skin and the rest of the world, making it impossible for anything of that world to actually touch him.

After a while he stopped trying, and gave in to the images that never ceased to haunt his mind's eye: dust and blinding sun and troops drawn into formation. British troops might be formed into ranks even now. They might be facing the French across a Belgian battlefield even now. The cannon might be booming even now...He was so far lost in thoughts of Spain and Belgium that the white streak at the corner of his vision startled him badly, and he jumped to face it.

It proved to be nothing more alarming than Elizabeth Barton flying down the hillside, skirt held up above her knees with both hands, bonnet hanging by its strings down her back and curls streaming out behind her, reticule looped over her wrist and swinging from side to side. Perhaps the ballroom elegance was indeed only skin-deep. He smiled at the sight—then stopped, surprised at the odd feel of that expression upon his lips. He couldn't remember the last time he had smiled out of genuine amusement rather than politeness. The swaths of gauze seemed to shift slightly, allowing an instant's gust of wind to touch his skin.

He watched Elizabeth skid to a stop, plump herself down on a fallen tree, jump up again, shake a shawl from her shoulders, and spread it out underneath her before resuming her seat. She loosened the strings of her reticule and pulled out a man's pocket watch, and the swaths dropped back into place. A love token? Most likely. William sighed to himself and turned away.

A branch snapped under his foot, and Elizabeth's head came up like a deer's. "William!" Then she colored. "I mean, Ensign Carrington."

He had been intending to lift his hat and walk on, but this greeting startled him so much that he answered without considering the demands of proper manners. "William, if you like. It was 'William' and 'Elizabeth' before I left."

Now why had he said that? It was true in one sense—they had indeed called each other "William" and "Elizabeth" once—but that had been before he left for Eton, not before he left for the Continent.

Quite a long time ago, back when childhood manners were still acceptable. They had not had much occasion to see each other since, so what on earth had possessed him? Any other young lady would have been offended at his presumption.

But then, no other young lady would have started the conversation by using his Christian name in the first place. He supposed it should be therefore no surprise that Elizabeth smiled at his offer, looking both relieved and pleased. "William and Elizabeth, then."

"I apologize for startling you," he added.

"Oh, it's no matter." He noticed that she kept her eyes on his. Not on his limp arm, not deliberately everywhere else but his arm, and not modestly cast down. For a moment he wondered at that, Then he realized that although her china-blue eyes were wide and innocent, her hands were moving, and he understood that she was trying to hold his gaze so he would not notice her tucking the pocket watch back into her reticule.

He tried to think of something else to say and ended up taking refuge in commonplaces. "I hope you and your family are in good health?"

"Yes, thank you," she said, "and you?" She had gotten hold of the wrong corner of the reticule, and was carefully easing the timepiece into fold of cloth that was not actually the mouth of the bag. He contemplated telling her that, but wasn't quite sure how to phrase it.

"Well enough, thank you," he said instead.

"That's good," Elizabeth said. "Does that mean we shall have the pleasure of your company in the Assembly rooms the next time there is a ball? You came so rarely into company this spring, and we should all be glad if your health had sufficiently recovered to allow you to—"

The pocket watch slipped through the loop of cloth, landing rather obviously on the path at her feet. She scrambled at once to catch it up, face very red now, but William's fingers closed over it first. He straightened, forcing a smile and hoping it looked genial. "What's this, then, Miss Elizabeth? The token of some admirer?"

"Er," Elizabeth said, cheeks the color of the scarlet coat that hung in William's wardrobe. Which seemed to rather conclusively answer that question, at least until he held the watch out to her and it fell open in his hand.

William stood still in the sunlight, staring at it.

He realized later that those minutes were the longest time he had spent *not* preoccupied with thoughts of Napoleon since March and the longest time he had gone without thinking of his arm since he had first woken after the battle. For the moment, he was oblivious to Elizabeth

Barton's presence as well, able to focus on nothing but the impossibility in his hand. He came back to himself when she laughed at his gape-mouthed expression.

"That's more or less how I reacted also," she said.

"Forgive me." He handed it back to her. "What on earth?"

"I've no idea," she said. "Someone sent it to me by post, and I don't know who or why or what it is. You've…you've never seen anything like it either, then? Not in London, or on the Continent?"

"No." He shook his head.

"It was even more extraordinary a little while ago," she said. "This face here had images in it. Pictures that moved. Truly."

He stepped around to see better, but the face she indicated was dark and lifeless. Still, the watch was extraordinary enough without that detail. He stared at the quiescent faces, focusing after a moment on the one that looked most like it belonged to a watch. "Does the timekeeping part of it work? I mean, can it be wound and set?"

"I don't know yet." Elizabeth flashed him a smile and dug through her reticule. She pulled out a velvet bag. "The watch came in this," she said. "Perhaps there's a key?" But there proved not to be. There was no keyhole in the watch, either.

"There must be some way to set it," William said, and, looking back on the scene later, he rather thought that was the moment when he had sat down beside her, so enraptured by the puzzle in her hands that he forgot how terribly he would compromise her reputation if anyone came upon the two of them sitting close enough to touch in a secluded corner of the orchard.

Elizabeth turned the watch over and over, examining it from all directions, running her fingertips over the etched vines and flowers. "Oh," she said in tones of surprise. "Here." She showed him dials running along the inside of the casing, tiny things that she could only just manage to turn with her fingernail. Turning them made the hands on the timekeeping face move, but it did not make them start telling time. Nor did pressing down the ornate stem above the 12, nor the plain stem beside the 3. Similar dials changed the nested wheels on the second and third faces, but similarly failed to set the wheels moving or deliver any clue as to what they might be measuring. William found himself reminded of the wheels of the water-driven mill he had seen at Cheshire, but that was hardly a helpful comparison.

The fourth face had remained blank all this while, no matter what they did. Elizabeth continued to insist it had displayed images a short time before, and William tried to believe her, an effort that became abruptly much easier when the watch lit up in his hand.

"Look!" Elizabeth said, leaning so eagerly forward that her curls brushed his shoulder. "That's what I meant."

The fourth face displayed a fog-bound city street, with carriages rattling to and fro in the foreground. A gas-lamp burned through the fog, casting just enough light that William fancied he could see shapes moving behind the carriages. Large shapes. Indistinct, but somehow menacing.

Just as he thought the words, the scene changed. Elizabeth exclaimed in surprise, and William hastily shook his vision clear to study the new picture. This one was less complicated, consisting of a meadow by a brook, with clouds and grasses reflected in the water. It was a scene that could be from any estate in the English countryside, and William was about to comment to that effect when the image changed again. Now it was a castle perched upon the crags of a mountaintop. A narrow winding trail led down into the forest below, tiny specs of color moving along it.

"Could those be men on horseback?" Elizabeth asked, and William squinted, holding the watch close to his eye.

"I believe they are," he said slowly. "Elizabeth, I believe they are knights in *armor*."

"Truly?" She leaned in again, and as he moved the watch so that she could see, the mountaintop became an embattled ship, dodging blasts of cannon-fire and riding heaving waves so realistic his insides lurched. As they stared at the ship, the fourth face flickered and went dark. Elizabeth shook her head, blinking. William brought the watch closer to his eye to study it more carefully. A painful burst of light seared his eye as the fourth face came back to life. William flinched, fumbling his hold on the watch case, and it slipped from his grasp. He and Elizabeth grabbed for it at the same time, and his fingers brushed her knuckles at the same moment her palm touched the watch. She managed not to drop it, but it was a near thing; she caught it by closing her hand around it. Her thumb bumped the top stem, depressing it briefly and then letting it spring back as she shifted her grip.

The world had seemed to hold its breath for that moment. The air had been momentarily colder, and the sunlight had dimmed as though covered by a sudden cloud. William looked up in reflex, but there was not a cloud to be seen. For an instant he had not heard birds singing either, but he heard them now.

Elizabeth Barton stared at him with wide eyes. "Did you feel that?" she whispered.

If she had not asked the question, he would have thought it the first wave of a fever dream breaking over his head. He was not sure whether to be relieved that this was in fact not another relapse, but rather something perceptible to those outside his own mind. "Yes," he said, voice catching slightly in his throat, "I did."

She looked back down at the watch and got slowly to her feet, thumb brushing over the top stem.

"Wait," he said, rising with her, reaching to lay a restraining hand on her wrist. "Don't. I don't think we should—"

But she paid him no heed whatsoever. All her attention was for the watch. He had never seen anything to match the delight in her face as she fixed her eyes on the timepiece and pressed the top stem all the way in.

And the bright June day turned into night.

Chapter 3

For a moment, Elizabeth thought she was in a thunderstorm, though no rain fell. Lightning lit up the sky in a flash of blue-white, then was gone. It was followed by a crash of thunder, deafening, just overhead. A sudden cold wind sprang up and rushed over her, tugging her breath along with it.

"*William—*" she gasped.

"Here—" The wind tore the word away from her ears, as it had torn the breath from her throat. But he was right beside her, a vague source of warmth, and then a definite one as he pulled her closer. "I'm right here."

But where was *here*? They were no longer in the orchard. The lightning flash had shown her not trees, but high brick walls. The wind carried with it not leaves, but sheets of paper. They tumbled against Elizabeth's skirt.

There was no second flash of lightning, but there was a second boom of thunder. It shook the ground under Elizabeth's feet.

And it shook the ground again.

She couldn't see, no matter how hard she tried, but she knew that there was something enormous coming toward her. It took another stomping, earsplitting step. For the first time in her life, Elizabeth was too frightened to move. Beside her, William drew a breath to say what she knew would be "Run!" and tensed to drag her with him—

Something grabbed her arm and tore her from William's grasp.

Her shoes scrabbled for purchase, but found none on the slick surface beneath her, and she went down hard, onto bruising cobblestone. She couldn't catch her breath or find her footing. She couldn't do anything except fumble in the slippery muck. There was someone above her, looming over her. Farther away, William called her name in a tone of desperation, while the ground all around them shook, and shook again, as something immense passed them by. The jolts grew fainter and less frequent as the thing, whatever it was, moved away.

A light flared, dazzling in the darkness.

"Get away from her!" William shouted, and flung himself forward. The flame went out. "Unhand her at once, sir!"

"I don't want to hurt you!" a second voice snapped, but William did not wait for explanations. There was a brief scuffle that Elizabeth could feel and hear but could not see. She had just time enough to think again of gathering herself and struggling upright when the fracas before her ended in a "oof" of pain. From William, she realized with a jolt of sickness. The flame flared alight again, a blinding glare that set Elizabeth's eyes tearing before it settled into a larger, duller gleam. A lantern. "I'm not trying to hurt her!" the voice behind the light repeated. It was an old man's voice—it had the crotchety, creaking sound of an exasperated old man. "I'm trying to save you both, you young fool! What on *earth* possessed you to go wandering about after curfew? And what the devil were you doing standing in the middle of the street?" The voice and the lantern moved closer to Elizabeth, and the owner of the lantern crouched down beside her. "You could both have been killed!" he continued. "Don't you know enough to get out of their...?" The lantern shone full on her face then, and the words broke off.

"...way," he finished after a moment. "Well. Well, I imagine...I imagine you don't, in that case. I...presume this is your first foray."

"What?" was all Elizabeth could manage.

"I have one too," the man said. He transferred the lantern to his left hand, and withdrew his right into the darkness beyond the spill of light. He fumbled at his waistcoat and then the right hand reappeared, holding for her inspection an overly large golden pocket watch. Lantern light gleamed softly in the crevices of etching and scratches.

From the darkness behind the old man, something screamed.

Elizabeth jerked and kicked and somehow got enough purchase against mud and cobblestones to lurch upright. Her outflung arm struck something warm and solid, and William pulled her the rest of the way up. The swinging circle of lantern-light told her the old man was on his feet now too. He slammed down the lantern's shutter, dropping inky blackness over them all, and then his hand met her shoulder with almost the same force.

The brick wall bruised her back and knocked the breath from her lungs for a second time, and between that and his hand over her mouth, she could not possibly scream. "Hush," he commanded, his lips close to her ear. "Both of you." Still pressing Elizabeth to the wall with his body, he took his hand off her mouth long enough to reach out and pull William to huddle with them. "It will come back this way, and it mustn't find us."

The shriek came out of the darkness again, somewhere in front of Elizabeth and to her right, a cross between a man in pain and a bull enraged. There was one moment of awful silence, then from the left came another crash that shook the ground. Elizabeth, pinioned by the old man's surprising strength, found herself as frozen and helpless as in any nightmare.

Blue lightning seared her eyes again, and this time did not fade. A white-tinged half-light lit the sky above the buildings—tall buildings; she could see them plainly now; her earlier brief impression had been correct. They *were* in a city. Around her was a city street or more precisely an alleyway, strewn with broken things and filth. Over the old man's shoulder, she could see the entrance to the proper street and a bit of the street itself, wider and cleaner and more evenly cobblestoned. The sobbing roar had come from there, but she could not see who or what had made the sound. Her view was cut off by the dilapidated walls that rose all around her, more than three stories high with chimneys even higher, their stacks straggling unevenly against the sickly colored sky.

Above the chimneys, the nightmare came. It came in the shape of a man, a giant out of a fairytale—except the giant Jack found up a beanstalk had been made of flesh and blood and so could be killed, and this giant's skin shone copper like a teakettle. It moved with heavy, jerking motions, and each time its foot drove into the cobblestones, a jolt ran through them and Elizabeth's teeth chattered in her head. This monster would not even feel a tumble down a beanstalk.

It took another step forward and Elizabeth could see its face. She bit her lip to keep from crying out in horror. It had no mouth or nose, and somehow the blank impassive countenance was worse than the ponderous thundering feet. From its eyes streamed blue-white light, not unlike a lantern in some ways, but so much colder and more remote, and strong enough to light the whole sky.

"Shh," the old man murmured. His hands trembled as he held her against the wall.

From the street came another howl. Pain, Elizabeth thought, it sounded like pain. She had been nearby when one of the men who worked Mr. Carrington's estate had broken his leg, a bad break, ugly, the bones poking through the skin. She remembered that two of his fellows had held him down for the apothecary, and she remembered how he had screamed. She remembered how heads had poked out of nearby windows in response to the screams. The windows of these decrepit buildings were lighting up now, pale yellow squares that could not compete with the giant's streaming light.

The wall pressed cold and rough through the thin fabric of her gown. William was a solid source of warmth beside her, and the old man stood before them both, cloak spread out as though he was trying to shelter them under his wings, keeping them out of the monster's sight or shielding their eyes from whatever horror played out in the street. But Elizabeth could see a small piece of that street, over the old man's shoulder and around a fold of his cloak. She could see the white-lit sky and the giant's impassive face, and she could not bear to hide her eyes and not know.

So when the thing that had howled scrambled to its feet and darted forward, she had a clear view of it. It was more like a man than the great copper giant, but it was bigger than any man had a right to be, with limbs mismatched to its height like the drawing of a gorilla Elizabeth had once seen. The yellowy-white flesh of its face drooped as though too large for the bones. It was dressed in what looked like grave-clothes, with long matted hair swinging over its shoulders. It lurched toward the alleyway, dragging behind it something that might have been an enormous bundle of rags or perhaps another creature like itself.

Then the entire sky blazed with a riot of light and noise and fireworks, and the beast jerked, swayed, and fell in a heap at the mouth of the alley.

"—*now!*" the old man hissed, jerking her by the arm, and Elizabeth stumbled after him, ears ringing with horror and the sound of cannon.

❧

They ran straight into blackness, with neither caution nor a speck of light to guide their way. Behind them the sky flashed and the air shook with a noise that seemed to pierce straight into Elizabeth's brain, driving away all rational thought. She skidded on the muck, stumbled against piles of refuse, tripped on the hem of her gown, and could not even put out her hands to steady herself, for the old man had one of them and William the other. To a degree, this state of affairs was useful, in that it did help keep her upright, but when she slipped or one of them did, the twisting of her wrists made her eyes well with pain.

The old man stopped so abruptly that Elizabeth stumbled against him and William stumbled against her, like actors in a particularly uninventive farce. "It's all right," the old man breathed. "Safe now." He reached toward one of the buildings that loomed on either side, and knocked briskly: twice, and twice again.

The door jerked open so violently that Elizabeth's heart jumped all over again. "Thank God," a hoarse voice muttered from the entryway. "We were about to send out a search party."

"That would have been imprudent." The old man hustled Elizabeth and William over the threshold and into the dark and dank entryway, and the doorkeeper fell back with a hiss of surprise. "No, it's all right," the old man said, "it's safe. They're safe." He shut the door behind himself with an air of frank relief, and the sudden relative silence rang in Elizabeth's ears. "It's safe," he repeated, speaking to her now. "Come inside."

He led them down a corridor whose floor was nothing but bare boards, whose walls were whitewashed and had seen better days, and whose only light came from a single wavering candle shoved into an old and battered sconce. Behind them, echoing in the pauses between the muted thunder-claps outside, came the sounds of a great many bolts shooting home. Then the flickering candle-flame followed them, as the doorkeeper took it from the sconce and brought it along. A cool draft rushed from a passageway to the left, carrying with it a suggestion of a large open space. The old man led them to the right, to a smaller room.

It seemed to be the sort of one-room living space that housed the poorest of Mr. Carrington's tenants, and it was in a state of disorder that would have shamed any of those hardworking souls. Dust and grime lay thick on the floor, and cobwebs stretched unhindered in the corners of the doorframe. The only furniture in the room appeared to be four straight-backed chairs surrounding a rickety table. The tabletop would probably also have been dusty and grimy, had it been visible, but it was cluttered with dirty crockery and half-burnt candles—as well as, oddly, a few things that looked like blacksmith's tools. There was a bookcase immediately beside the entryway, also piled with tools and boasting only two books. The scant space between it and the table was taken up by empty crates stacked one on top of the other.

Elizabeth took all this in, her heart hammering hard in her ears, and then her knees gave way.

When her vision cleared, she was sitting in one of the straight-backed chairs, bent forward and with someone's hand heavy on the back of her neck. She could see the skirt of her slime-coated gown, and the top of her mud-encrusted shoes. As well as the thin and unsteady black leg of a table she was certain she had never encountered before today and was therefore unlikely to be dreaming into existence.

Voices washed over her.

"…haven't any brandy," the old man said.

"There's gin," a woman's voice replied, "but that hardly seems appropriate."

"No, it does not. Perhaps tea?"

"All right, very well, I'll wash these up and make some."

"And I'll get the blanket off my bed," the old man said. His footsteps moved away, out the door and heavily up a stairway. Crockery clinked near Elizabeth's ear, but she kept her eyes closed until that sound moved away as well and the sound of splashing water began somewhere farther off.

Then Elizabeth straightened against the pressure on her neck, and it withdrew instantly. She lifted her head and looked into William's brown eyes, and his face went slack with relief.

"I'm glad you're still here," she whispered.

"I don't think it is possible for us to both be having the *same* dream," he said in agreement. "If we are both still here, it must truly be happening. Are you feeling better?"

"Yes," Elizabeth said in embarrassment, "yes, I'm fine, my knees just went wobbly for a moment."

"A not uncommon reaction to one's first encounter with artillery," he said, and she noticed for the first time how strained he looked about the eyes and mouth.

"Artillery?" she repeated. "What could—"

"Who the devil are you?"

Elizabeth jerked her head around and William sprang to his feet, fumbling with his left hand to catch up one of the tools on the table.

The voice had come from the doorway, and its owner proved to be a tall, thin, hawk-nosed man of perhaps thirty-five. He was dressed like a farm laborer in nothing but trousers and a shirt, both much-worn, much-patched, and very dirty, but he regarded them with a mixture of amazement and annoyance that Elizabeth did not find in the least respectful.

"Don't be touching that," he added, gesturing to the tool in William's hand. "Put it down." His speech had a slight sing-song intonation that did not sound respectful either. He took a step toward them, and William, instead of putting the tool down, brandished it like a weapon—which it was, or at any rate the closest thing they had.

The hawk-nosed man ignored him completely. "Is that Maxwell's watch?" he demanded, pointing with a grimy finger at the timepiece that lay on the table, next to Elizabeth's chair.

"No," Elizabeth retorted, finding herself all at once more angry than frightened. "It's mine. Who—"

"Ohhh," the man said, looking from one of them to the other. "I see. Would this be your first journey, then?" At their blank expressions, he clarified impatiently, "What year was it when you awoke this morning?"

"*What?*"

Footsteps on creaking stairs heralded the old man's hasty return. "Mr. Trevelyan—!"

"What in blazes have you been about, Max?" Trevelyan swung to meet him. "Bringing home guests at a time like this? I thought you were after something more important out there."

"I was, and I got them for you, and here they are." The old man drew a packet from within his coat and handed it to Trevelyan. "I encountered these two young people on the way back, and I could not leave them to be stomped on by constructs."

Trevelyan made a derisive sound as he pulled a multiplex knife from his pocket and slit the parcel's wrapping paper. "Top on the list of things we do not have time for just now—"

"That may well be, but it doesn't matter, as they are here whether we choose it or not—"

"*Excuse me,*" William said firmly, beating Elizabeth to it by about half a second.

Both men turned, and the one Trevelyan had addressed as Max came forward, with a reassuring if hastily donned smile. He started to say something, but William spoke over him.

"Who are you? And where have you brought us?"

"My name is Maxwell." Now that Elizabeth saw him in better light, she could tell that he was not, in fact, so very old. His hair was white, to be sure, but thick; his face was mostly unlined; his brown eyes shone fiercely alert. He did not move like an old man, nor had he during the run through the alleyway. Energy radiated from him with an intensity that almost hurt the eye. If anything, he seemed fuller of life than the supercilious Mr. Trevelyan at his shoulder. "And you, sir?"

After the briefest of pauses, William took refuge in the formula. "William Carrington. And this is Miss Barton."

"Are you feeling better, Miss Barton?" Mr. Maxwell transferred his attention to Elizabeth, regarding her concern. "I have brought you a blanket, if the shock has—"

"No, I'm fine," Elizabeth said impatiently. "I mean, no thank you, sir, I appreciate your concern, but I am quite recovered. Where *are* we?"

"London," Trevelyan said, without looking up from the box in his hands.

"*London?*"

"London." With a delicacy of touch somewhat surprising for such dirty fingers, Trevelyan extracted a small glinting thing and held it critically up to the nearest candle.

"Will they do?" Maxwell asked him, distracted from his concern over Elizabeth's comfort.

"Indeed they will," Trevelyan said with satisfaction.

"There are monsters in London?" Elizabeth demanded.

"Indeed there are." Trevelyan raised his eyebrows as though enjoying her confusion. "You haven't asked the right question."

"This is my colleague, Mr. Trevelyan," Maxwell broke in before Elizabeth could answer, "who possesses a genius for mechanical things and rather less of one with regard to social courtesies. I apologize for his manners."

"I haven't asked the right question?" Elizabeth repeated, instead of acting like a well-bred young lady and accepting the apology. "What, pray, is the right question? Does it regard this, perhaps?" She held up the pocket watch. "What is it? Where does it come from?"

"I found mine in a garret," Maxwell said. "I'm afraid no one knows where they originated."

"But you know what it is?"

"I know what it *does*." Maxwell hooked a finger on the chain in his waistcoat. It was an oddly tailored waistcoat, Elizabeth noticed for the first time, extending over the waistband of his breeches in elongated triangle points—and they were not breeches, either, but something closer to Cossack trousers—She shook her head impatiently at herself and redirected her attention from the strangeness of the clothing to the strangeness of the watch, which was clearly of some actual importance.

Maxwell drew it out in exactly the manner of a gentleman wishing to consult the time, detached the chain, and set the watch on the table beside Elizabeth's. As far as she could tell under the light of three guttering candles, they were identical as to engravings, though not of course as to scratches. Maxwell popped open both lids. They were identical inside as well, with dials and faces such as never belonged to any proper gentleman's pocket watch.

Maxwell indicated each dial in turn. "This sets the date to which you wish to travel—year, month, day. This allows you to give a precise location, by latitude and longitude, if you know it. You set these dials, and then depress the side button twice and top once. But that isn't what you did, is it? For this is neither today's date nor our current location. You must have done it the other way. When the image displayed in this face is one that seems attractive, press the side button once and the top one twice, and the watch takes you there."

"This was hardly the best selection for your first adventure," Trevelyan observed from the doorway. "That nice babbling brook would have been a much better choice."

"Knights in armor," William said, stunned. "The watch lets one... journey to the past?"

"And the future." Maxwell smiled at him in a fatherly sort of way. "What year *was* it, when you woke this morning? Eighteen hundred ten? Or twelve? Thereabouts?"

"The...the year of Our Lord eighteen hundred and fifteen," William answered after a pause.

"I was close," Maxwell said. He looked at Elizabeth with the same fondness. "I knew you were a traveler like me as soon as I saw the watch, but truthfully, I would have been able to tell anyway. Your gown is becoming, but not at all the current fashion. My mother had one very like it."

"So we are in London," Elizabeth repeated. "But where we are is not the important question." She understood what Trevelyan meant now. "What is the year?"

"The year of Our Lord eighteen hundred and eighty-five," Maxwell said. "You are seeing a future that will not take place until after your death."

Interlude

It had been what might be mildly termed a trying day, and the message set the final spark to George Brown's always explosive temper. "There's a *what?*"

His aide winced. The boy would never make a soldier, Brown thought disapprovingly. He shied like a rabbit at every little thing. He would have liked to run like a rabbit rather than face his general's displeasure—Brown could tell by the faint twitching of the muscles under the jawline—but at least he was not such a coward as to actually do it. Instead he repeated, almost steadily, "There is a government observer here to see you, sir."

"Here? Now? *Tonight?*" Brown flung a hand at the tent flap, meaning to indicate the camp beyond it and the valley beyond that. "Ridiculous. You've been taken in, boy. It's a reporter. A 'war correspondent,' here to compete with that milksop Russell."

"No, sir." The boy shook his head. "He's white-haired, sir, not a young man. And he's not dressed like a reporter. He says he's come from the government offices at Whitehall, and his credentials look right. I mean, so far's I can tell, and they must've to the others or he could never have gotten so far within the camp—"

"A 'government observer.'" Brown snorted. "You tell him I am conducting a God-damned battle and haven't time to hold his little hand."

"He said—" The aide cleared his throat, looking truly miserable. "Sir, he said I was to tell you he is happy to swap tales with Mr. Russell for as long as you are otherwise engaged."

Brown felt his collar constrict around his throat. Damn government observers. Damn William Howard Russell, and damn the God-damned *Times*. "Is he waiting outside?"

"Er," the aide said. "He went at once to Mr. Russell's campfire. Mr. Russell offered him a drink."

Of course he had. Brown damned Russell and *The Times* again, out loud this time, before tossing the dirty paper at the nearest brazier.

"Bring him in here." He sank onto the chair behind the desk. "Then clear out. But stay close; we've a war to fight once I finish talking with whatever pretty-boy Whitehall's inflicted on us this time."

The aide saluted and backed away, and General Brown stared at the flame licking along the edge of the grime-streaked paper. Damn Russell. Damn Delane of *The Times,* who had sent his young report-er to bivouac with Her Majesty's Army in Scotland and send home first-hand accounts of the monster war. Russell was a soft little snivel-ing man whose accounts dwelt heavily on the "inhumanity" of Army practices and Army discipline. The soft and sniveling British public had reacted with predictable horror, and now London was awash in a public outcry over the treatment of its soldiers. As a result, the officials who ran the country from their Whitehall offices had inflicted more than one government observer upon Brown. Each was more damnably annoying than the last, tugging upon Brown's sleeve and bleating plat-itudes while Brown was trying to win a war.

A war that was all Whitehall's fault in the first place, for it was Whitehall that had created the Wellington monsters. A proper Army of proper Englishmen hadn't been good enough for the office clerks who ran the government. Blasted penny-pinchers had decided they would rather not give honest pay for honest work, and instead focused their efforts on *creating*—through confoundedly unnatural means—regi-ments of monsters that didn't have to be paid and could stand even worse food and shelter than a human soldier.

Perhaps the first "special battalion" had been a necessity, Brown admitted grudgingly in the privacy of his thoughts. Perhaps Wel-lington would not have managed to defeat old Boney without them, though Wellington had been heard to say that his brave lads would have won Waterloo even without monstrous help. Brown further con-ceded that once Britain had at its disposal a battalion of enormous ape-men wielding battle axes, it would have been foolish not to put them to use. Similarly, once the secret of their creation had been mastered, it was tactically sound to increase their numbers. But the idea of sending them to places too dangerous for the average British soldier chafed Brown like an ill-fitted boot. There should be no place considered too dangerous for the average British soldier. And the credit for victory obtained in those dangerous places ought to *go* to brave British soldiers, not to Wellington's unnatural battalions.

But it was the unnatural battalions—now they were unnatural regiments—who had been awarded credit for the grand victory over the Russians in the Crimea and then for settling what might have been a nasty rebellion in India. *The Times* had trumpeted both victories to the skies, and "Wellington's monsters" had become the nation's heroes. It was rumored among the higher echelons of the Army that Wellington himself had disliked the term, but that was a fact kept secret from the public. Attaching the name of Waterloo's hero to the creatures conferred upon them a sort of legitimacy, a faint cast-off gleam from the Iron Duke's halo. Each year since Waterloo Whitehall had reduced the funds needed to pay the wages of human soldiers and diverted that money to the creation and upkeep of more and more Wellington monsters. There was even a secret training camp far north in the Scottish Highlands—the sort of secret that most Army officers knew, though none discussed out loud. In the thirty-seven years following their first victory, the monsters had been taught steadily more complex maneuvers and armed with steadily more impressive weaponry. They never needed leave or salary or improvement in living conditions; they rarely sickened and recovered quickly from injuries; they were rotated like clockwork between the ever-expanding perimeter of the Empire and the training grounds in the Highlands. They were an effective and easily maintained dream come true.

Then three years ago, they had rebelled, turning the dream into a nightmare. They had killed their human officers and taken over the training camp so smoothly and quietly that it was some days before anyone suspected anything amiss. Whereupon Brown and his Light Division had been hastily collected and dispatched north to restore order with only the sketchiest and most misleading of information as to what they would face. Human soldiers and Wellington monsters did not customarily fight alongside one another, and Brown and his men had no way of knowing how dangerous an enemy awaited them. Damn Whitehall. Not only were the things enormous and fast and capable of seeing in the dark, but they also handled the muskets and artillery that had been part of the training camp with the facility of the very well-trained. After two days of staggering losses, Brown had pulled his men back to a defensible perimeter and wired to London for reinforcements.

The copyboys at Whitehall had shuffled their feet and twiddled their thumbs and finally declared themselves unwilling to recall any of the monster regiments stationed abroad, for fear their members might join rather than oppose their fellows. Instead they retrieved the much sparser regiments of human soldiers and dispatched them north to aid Brown in returning the monsters to their cages. By then, of course, it was far too late.

The monsters had access to the finest light weaponry in Britain. They were skilled at Spanish-style guerilla warfare and had been given time to entrench themselves in the Highlands, an ideal ground for employing such tactics. No one at Whitehall had apparently considered the possibility that they could do more than follow the orders they were given, but it transpired that at least some of their number were capable of formulating strategies and commanding others in their execution. Before the end of the first year, they held Fort William. Before the end of the second, they held most of Scotland in a grip no one had managed since the Jacobite rebels of 1745.

And Brown wondered sometimes if he should have continued the attack, that night in 1852. If he had tried and been annihilated doing it, might the news have galvanized London into action? Might it have galvanized Wellington into action? Might purpose have extended Wellington's life? Brown was irritably aware that Russell's precious *Times* daily compared him to Boney's late vanquisher and daily found him wanting. He'd like to see any of those paper-pushing nancy-boys do better.

"Right this way, sir," he heard his aide's voice pipe, and he straightened in the chair, glaring at the tent flap and the government busybody who would step through it.

The government busybody wore gray, an oddly-styled tweed splattered with mud. His thick white hair fell untidily over his brow, and a bruise high on his left cheekbone gave him a particularly rakish look. "General Brown, sir?" he said at once. "Forgive the tactics, but it was most necessary I see you. I bring urgent intelligence and orders from London."

The fire in the brazier snapped and popped.

The man in gray crossed to the desk in one stride, whipping a map from his pocket. "You're here," he said, pointing. "They're there. Your scouts have reported to you that the monsters hold the high ground across the valley, is that not so? So you are planning accordingly, delaying your attack until General Moore brings his regiment up to join you? But your intelligence is wrong, General."

"The monsters do not hold the high ground?"

"They do not hold it securely. There are fewer of them on that hill than it seems, and their reinforcements will not arrive until mid-morning tomorrow. You have men enough to roll right over them if you attack at first light. And then you will *hold* the hill when the reinforcements arrive. You can crush two small waves of monsters, one after the other. But wait any longer than dawn and the ground is theirs."

"How do you know this?" Brown demanded.

"I told you," the man said, "Whitehall sent me with urgent—"

"Whitehall knew the disposition of the monster troops a month in advance?"

"Whitehall arranged for a covert scouting force," the man said, "deployed a month ago, under my command. This morning they reported to me your status and that of the monsters. I have the vantage to see more of the chessboard than you, General."

It was odd, but not altogether implausible. Certainly Brown had been outraged before now by the aspects of this war Whitehall chose to keep from him. And the "government observer's" reply came smoothly and unhesitatingly, as though it were the truth.

But Brown knew something of how to read men, and even in the flickering light of the brazier, he saw the telltale twitches of falsehood on the face of the man opposite him. Could it be possible that the monsters had subverted an Englishman to their side? Brown was hard-pressed to keep his disgust to himself.

Instead, he circled behind the man as though to better see the his map. "From which direction do the monsters' reinforcements advance?"

The man in gray started to reply, bending over the map to point, and Brown used his pistol to strike the traitor hard on the back of the skull.

~⌒~

At dawn, they told him that the man had spent all night struggling against his bonds and begging to see the General, over and over, until his voice was hoarse. Brown treated this information with the contempt it deserved. He was occupied with far more important matters.

When Moore's regiment arrived at noon, Brown sent his combined troops to take the hill.

He watched the rippling red line of infantrymen cross the valley, start the climb. A cannonball whistled through the air and crashed through the ranks. Then another. Then they flew in earnest. The line shuddered, but did not pause in its advance. Brown nodded to himself. Russell could bleat about "harsh discipline" all he liked. Russell was an idiot. Harsh discipline was what made men unafraid of cannonballs. They were taking heavy casualties, but they still pressed forward.

Before very long, the monsters had spent all the cannonballs in their possession, and the line moved faster, impeded now only by small-arms fire from behind rocks. Brown saw each shot as a pin-prick of flame against the gray-green hill. He heard each sharp pop a disconcerting few seconds later. The infantry paused, took aim, and sent a ringing volley back, filling the air with gunpowder smoke that briefly obscured Brown's vision. The smoke cleared in time for Brown to see them follow their volley with a sweeping charge, and they gained a few more paces of ground before the monsters reloaded and the pin-pricks of fire started up again from among the rocks.

Brown expected to observe fewer pin-pricks this time—but disconcertingly, there were just as many. How much ammunition did they *have* back there? For the first time, he felt a chill, but he was damned if he'd pull his men back now.

By the time Brown's men closed upon the summit, there were fewer of them than he would have liked, and the hill that sloped down behind them was littered with the corpses of their brethren. Still, though, they were close now. One more push, and—

Then the monsters erupted from behind the rocks in a counter-charge.

They should not be able to move so gracefully. He had thought that before now. The thrusting heads and swinging arms should overbalance them, pull them pitching forward, but they poured around the rocks with an economy of motion that put him in mind of India's quiet leaping tigers. They swung battle-axes as though the things were part of their arms, and they howled fit to freeze the blood of any lesser man than a British solider.

But Brown's men held. They fired, reloaded, fired again in a wave of popping flame. Some of the monsters took bullets, but as far as Brown could make out, none of them fell. The infantry line switched to bayonets. Then the monsters were among them, laying left and right with enormous curved axe-heads. Brown could see what he thought might be limbs flying about. He saw monsters reeling back, only slightly impeded by bayonets pierced through them. Bloody tough, bloody fast, bloody well-trained—the only way to bring Wellington's sodding creatures down was to overwhelm them with numbers and bullets.

And Brown, watching through his spyglass, came to the unwelcome conclusion that he had too few of either.

⌒

The Battle of Carron Valley was to capture the British imagination as thoroughly as had the Battle of Waterloo, though in a very different way. William Howard Russell's stirring account of the tragedy, written up that very night and sent to *The Times* a few days later, was largely responsible for its fame. The phrase "the thin red line," used by Russell to refer to the outnumbered scarlet-coated soldiers slaughtered as they struggled up the hill, gained instant popularity. Within a month soon-to-be-famous poetry was written, commemorating the heroic last charge of Brown's men into "the valley of death" and up the hill on the other side.

Perhaps fortunately for him, Brown was killed by a sniper's bullet during the attack. Some in the higher ranks of the Army muttered that otherwise, he would have been court-martialed; but falling as he did with his men, he became a tragic hero, his praises now sung by the very same people who had the week before condemned his harshness. If only Brown had lived, ran popular opinion, he would have won the war.

In later years, military historians were to call this nonsense and maintain that the war had been lost as soon as it began back in 1852. But at the time, responsibility for the defeat was laid squarely upon the shoulders of Brown's replacement, John Moore. Moore was a cautious man by nature, new to command, slow and methodical and by-the-book in his maneuvers. By the time he had gotten himself well-sorted and his Army functioning to his liking, it was spring, and the monsters were once more entrenched in all the lovely bits of high ground so characteristic of the Highlands. Moore sent infantry waves marching across a variety of valleys, in perfect formation, under heavy fire, in pursuit of ground that could not be taken, until at last the attrition became too much for Whitehall to bear. Construction on Moore's Wall began in late 1856, and Whitehall abandoned Scotland to the monsters.

Chapter 4

"Eighteen hundred and eighty-five," Elizabeth repeated in a whisper, and then could not come up with anything else to say. William, too, seemed stunned, staring at Maxwell with lips slightly parted but with no words falling from them. Maxwell waited, posture courteous, for one of them to ask another question or offer another comment. In the doorway, Trevelyan studied his trinket, faint sardonic amusement at the corners of his mouth. The silence lay like a blanket of fog.

A female voice broke it, in tones of amusement. "Was it something I said?"

Elizabeth looked up with a start, having forgotten the woman who had gone to make tea. She stood now in the darkened doorway, mostly hidden by Trevelyan's angular shadow, the candlelight revealing only suggestions of her appearance: a coil of black hair, skin like cream, a high cheekbone and a raised eyebrow. The tea tray might have been floating on disembodied hands, as the candle had earlier. Where, Elizabeth wondered suddenly, had the doorkeeper gone?

"No," Maxwell said, a note in his voice answering the dry humor in hers. "You have merely chosen an auspicious moment to return with the refreshment. Here, allow me." He came to meet her and took the tea-tray from her hands. Both of them had to duck around Trevelyan, who stayed where the light shone most strongly on the bauble in his fingertips, without any apparent recognition that it was also where he would most effectively block the doorway.

"Why, thank you, Maxwell," the woman said, with her head turned toward Trevelyan. "How very thoughtful of you." Trevelyan paid no attention.

She had an unexpectedly deep voice for a woman, rich and warm and throaty, and Elizabeth suddenly suspected the doorkeeper had gone nowhere at all. Maxwell set the tea-tray on the shaky-legged table and the woman came into the light. Now Elizabeth was sure it had been she who had answered the door.

She wore breeches. Between that and her voice, the mistake was a natural one, but seen with time to consider, she was obviously a woman. Those thick coils of glossy hair, so black that the candle-light struck no spark in it, could never have belonged to a man. And though her legs were indeed clad in dark brown breeches and high-legged boots such as a man might wear riding, the top half of her attire left her gender in no doubt, for she wore a blouse covered by a tightly laced bodice. Elizabeth had time to wonder if she might be a gypsy and to consider whether that might explain the outfit as well as the dark hair and eyes. Then she caught her breath as the other explanation occurred to her. *Your gown is becoming, but not at all the current fashion.* Was it now fashionable for women to wear breeches? For the woman was staring at her in turn, and with equal surprise, as if Elizabeth's simple white muslin were the inappropriate apparel.

The woman took a breath, but Mr. Maxwell spoke over her. "Katarina, I have just met these two young people outside. They are time travelers like myself, and possess a watch very similar to my own. As you can see from the young lady's gown, they have come to us from the early part of the century. I was saying to her that I remember my mother wearing just such a frock."

The dark-haired woman said slowly, "I…see."

"May I present Miss Elizabeth Barton and Mr. William Carrington. Miss Barton, Mr. Carrington, Madame Katarina Rasmirovna."

William bowed and Elizabeth nodded at the same moment the woman held out her hand. Straight out, as a man would; moreover, as a man would to a close friend, never to a new acquaintance. Elizabeth, safe behind the table, did not have to decide what to do, but William was caught. He hesitated. Then the woman's dark eyes went to his arm, the skin around them tightened in a faint wince, and she put her hand behind her back and inclined her head instead.

"A pleasure to meet you, Mr. Carrington. I am glad to see you are recovered from your fright, Miss Elizabeth; our London must be quite a shock to someone from your background."

"Is that tea?" Trevelyan said, coming out of his reverie with a start.

Katarina lifted her eyes to the ceiling. "Yes, dear," she said in a voice too dulcet to be entirely convincing. "Sit and have some?"

"No." Trevelyan was already reaching around her for the pot. "I'll take a cup with me. Max got me what I need, so I'll press on."

"You intend to sleep eventually, I hope?"

"I'll sleep after it rains," Trevelyan said, and turned for the corridor, slurping from the teacup as he went. At the doorway he paused, obviously as an afterthought. "I...do thank you, Max."

Maxwell nodded. "Just get it working."

Elizabeth became aware that the sounds of battle outside had died down at some point in the last few minutes. As if in response to her thought, Katarina cocked her head. "It's finally gone quiet out there," she said, pouring tea into a collection of chipped and mismatched cups. "It sounded like Waterloo revisited while it lasted, though. Did you see what all the fuss was about, Max?"

"As far as I could tell, it was about absolutely nothing," Maxwell replied with deliberate irony. "In fact, I'll wager anything you like it was a staged hunt. A handful of foxes and an army of hounds. I don't think there are as many as twelve Wellingtons left free in all of England; six of them have certainly not been hiding out in the East End of London."

"They were hunting *Wellingtons?*" Katarina repeated, handing Elizabeth a pale blue teacup with a crack running ominously down one side. She did not look at Elizabeth as she did it, keeping her eyes on Maxwell instead. "Oh, I see," she said then, apparently reading something from his expression. "Released by Seward's empire of crime, I suppose."

"The newspapers will doubtless tell us so tomorrow," Maxwell agreed in the same tone. "Even if they don't blame Seward, they'll report in glowing words how the constructs kept us all safe from the most recent unnatural threat. Lest Seward's crusade start sounding sensible."

"Do you mean to say that the activity we just witnessed is a commonplace occurrence?" William demanded.

"Tonight was somewhat livelier than usual," Katarina said, "but yes, common enough."

"Then in the year 1885, London is a warfront?" William shook his head at the teacup she offered him. "We have to get out of here. I have to get Miss Barton safely home."

"I would like nothing better than for you to do just that," Maxwell said, before Elizabeth could contribute her thoughts on the matter, "but I fear it is impossible for the moment. It's one of the disadvantages of traveling by pocket watch. After the watch is used, it takes twenty-four hours to recharge before it can be used again."

Elizabeth had never heard the word "recharge" before, but she understood all the other words, and her mouth went dry. "We'll be—we'll be away from home a day and a night?" It came out in a squeak, and she took a hasty sip from her cracked teacup. The tea was lukewarm and bitter as wormwood, but she took a second swallow anyway, trying to steady herself. Well, that was one sure way to put an end to all the matchmaking. If she were known to have been missing from home for a day and a night, no respectable man would *want* to marry her.

"No," Maxwell said, "I ought to be able to get you back within a few minutes of your departure. But you will be living this life for twenty-four hours, and that does not please me at all. It is dangerous here, and you have no way of knowing how to navigate it. One of our monsters cherishes a hatred for mankind, and the other cares nothing for who stands in its path. England no longer bears much resemblance to the green haven of your childhood."

"You should take them back to that green haven yourself, Max," Katarina said, husky voice gone unexpectedly gentle.

"I can't do that. You know I can't. I may not be able to return here once I leave, and I have to see this through with you."

William looked from one of them to the other. "Why should we be able to get back to where we have come from, if you cannot?"

"I can get back to where I came from," Maxwell said. "Just as you can. What neither of us can do is leave a time that is not ours and have any certainty of returning to it. You can't be in the same place twice, you see; the watch won't allow it. The watch doesn't allow you to get anywhere close, in fact. It doesn't let you affect the same junction more than once."

The sudden hammering on the outside door made them all jump. Elizabeth choked on her swallow, and the convulsive jerk of her fingers sent a wave of lukewarm tea cascading down the front of her frock. Maxwell stood up so fast he knocked over his chair and nearly sent the table following, and the liquid in all the vessels on its surface sloshed.

Katarina was already on her feet, hands absolutely steady as she checked the priming of the smallest pistol Elizabeth had ever seen. Where it had been the moment before, or how Katarina had gotten it so quickly into her hands, Elizabeth could not fathom. Katarina's eyes went to Maxwell's. "Better take them to the laboratory," she said, tilting her head toward William and Elizabeth. "I'll—"

The knocking came again, but this time in groups of two. Twice, and twice again, and twice once more. Maxwell and Katarina both went momentarily limp, but Katarina's shoulders stiffened again almost at once. "It might still be a trap instead of someone too scared to remember the code," she said. "Stay here. Keep quiet. I'll deal with it."

Maxwell took a step following her. "Hadn't you better let me—"

"Not when you're dressed like that, Max," Katarina said, walking away. "We've been through this before. There's no imaginable reason for a gentleman to open the door of a place like this. Besides—" She paused to toss an unexpected grin over her shoulder. "I'm the better shot." With that, she disappeared down the corridor.

Maxwell moved fast then, but silently and not in pursuit. He pulled a second tiny pistol from the clutter on the bookshelf, keeping his eyes on the doorframe as he fumbled behind him in a gesture Elizabeth could not immediately interpret. What was it he wanted her to do? She looked in the direction he was pointing, thought she understood, and seized her pocket watch from the table just as William came to a different conclusion and caught hold of her arm with his left hand. He pulled her with him to the darkest corner the room had to offer.

Elizabeth heard the snap and thump of all the various bolts being drawn back, and the cracking open of the heavy door. Then came Katarina's voice, words inaudible but tone relieved, and a babble of higher-pitched voices answering, and the door closing again. "Max?" Katarina called. Maxwell pocketed the pistol at once and left the room.

Elizabeth stirred to follow, at least far enough to hear what was going on, but William tightened his grip and shook his head. She frowned at him, and he leaned in to put his lips close to her ear. "They don't want the visitor to know about us," he whispered. "Or Madame Katrina would have brought him in."

Voices overlapped out in the entryway, the high-pitched ones explaining something with frantic haste, Katarina's elaborating and clarifying, Maxwell's expressing some hesitation. After a moment two sets footsteps came back down the corridor, but they did not enter the parlor where William and Elizabeth hid.

"You have to go," Katarina's voice said, low but close enough to be heard. It seemed she had drawn Maxwell aside for a private consultation.

"Under other circumstances, perhaps, but as it is …" Maxwell left the sentence eloquently unfinished.

"Don't worry about—about this other matter," Katarina said. "I can see to it. To them. You *know* that's true, Max. I can keep them safe just as well as you can—better, maybe—but no one can fetch one of our foot soldiers out of quod except a gentleman, so for all the same reasons you shouldn't have gone to the door just now—"

"A gentleman wouldn't walk the streets for another hour or two," Maxwell said. "It would be more natural to wait a bit."

"Yes, but you don't want Ernie and that lot coming in to see our guests in their vintage Regency fashions, do you?"

"Well…" Maxwell surrendered. "You're right, of course. Take care of them, Katarina. Be very careful with them."

"I understand," Katarina said. In a different tone of voice, she added, "Here, take a latchkey with you. Trevelyan made ones for the new lock while he was waiting for you to return. Saves you knocking later." Their footsteps returned to the entryway. The door creaked open, Maxwell and the owners of the high-pitched voices went through it, and Katarina did up all the bolts again before returning to the parlor.

"All's well," she said to the corner where Elizabeth and William still stood, flicking a catch on her pistol and casting it onto the dining table. "Nothing to fear. Max has gone to…see to something that requires his particular talents, but I can look after the two of you well enough, and he'll be back well before the twenty-four hours have passed." She reached for a cup without a handle and took a long swallow of tea. Then she grimaced at the taste, took the cup to the bookshelf, and filled it from what Elizabeth could only assume to be a gin bottle. Katarina tossed back the entire cupful in exactly the manner of a man recovering from a shock and needing a restorative—but nothing else about her appearance gave that impression, Elizabeth thought. There was not the slightest quiver in her hands or quaver in her voice, though she had clearly thought them all in some danger not two minutes before.

Elizabeth found herself staring at the gin bottle and the pistol, and felt a smile tugging at the corners of her mouth. She had heard of adventuresses, but only vaguely, from cryptic mentions in the society papers that her aunt snatched out of her sight before she could properly absorb them. She had never actually met an adventuress or received a precise description of what it was one did. And of course there was that song about the girl who had cut her hair and pretended to be a boy and fought at Trafalgar—but that was a song. It had never occurred to Elizabeth, not imaginatively, to consider what such a woman must actually be like. Was *this* fashionable now, too?

If it were…The tugging smile grew into something unrestrained and giddy. How wonderful that would be. Even with monsters, what a wonderful world this must be. *I wonder,* Elizabeth thought, *if I must go home after all?*

She looked up to find William's grave brown eyes upon her, regarding her as though he could read her thoughts. She blushed a little, more from being caught than from shame at the shape of them, and his lips drew into a thin, disapproving line.

She looked away and found that Katarina was watching her too, but with something like amusement, or possibly understanding. "As a first step toward looking after you," the dark-haired woman said, "perhaps I had better find you something to wear that isn't soaked with mud and tea, and then we can see about getting the stains out of that before they set. Come with me, Miss Elizabeth."

Chapter 5

The air of the stairway was thick and black, and grew hotter and heavier with each step. Katarina's candle burned in a sullen sort of way and seemed likely to sigh out of existence at any moment, so Elizabeth kept her hand pressed tight to the plaster wall to be sure of her footing. "We divided the warehouse attic into bedchambers," Katarina explained. "That's Maxwell's room, to the left there, and I sleep here."

She turned to the right, drawing aside a thick red curtain that smelled strongly of mold. Elizabeth ducked underneath it, trying not to inhale too deeply as she did so, and Katarina came after, letting the curtain fall behind them. Elizabeth looked around as best she could by the candle's guttering light.

The tiny chamber was as simply furnished and badly kept as the living room downstairs. The bed was only a mattress on the floor, unmade, pillows and coverlet lying limp and slovenly. Against the far wall sat two chests, one with the lid open and one closed. Katarina went and knelt in front of the closed one, setting her candle on the floor as she undid the clasp. The spill of candlelight showed quite clearly the layer of grime on the floorboards, as well as the dust cloud that rose in response to Katarina's rummaging. Elizabeth stifled a cough.

Katarina turned and beckoned. "Come here. I think this will fit." Elizabeth crossed to her, skirting the tangled blanket that hung off the edge of the mattress, and Katarina held up a blouse of some sort, looking critically from it to Elizabeth and back.

"Well, it will have to do." Katarina rose. "I haven't anything more appropriate, I'm afraid, but it's only for today." She handed Elizabeth the blouse—and a pair of breeches. Elizabeth swallowed a wild flutter in her throat and tried to accept the gift with some semblance of dignity. She clearly didn't manage it, for Katarina's eyes crinkled again. But the older woman said only, "Here, let me have your dress, and I'll see what I can do about the stains."

"*Is* there something you can do?" Elizabeth squirmed to undo the buttons down her back. Katarina had not even thought to ask if she would need help—well, obviously not if Katarina were used to wearing breeches—so it was perhaps just as well that Elizabeth was often too impatient to wait for her maid and had therefore perfected the art of undoing her own buttons without snapping any of them off. And that she almost never wore stays. "Is that something else that's changed? In my—" She took a breath, and said the ridiculous and wonderful words. "In my time, we only brush gowns."

"We could wait for the mud to dry, and brush that," Katarina agreed, taking the soaked and muddy garment from Elizabeth's hands. "What do you do for tea-stains, though? Or grass-stains?"

"I get a frightful scolding," Elizabeth admitted, and Katarina chuckled.

"I can only imagine," she said, and bent to examine the damage. "Well—it's muslin. It will hold up to hot water or it won't. At least it's white and there's no pattern to worry over, so I can use kerosene for the tea. Do you want to risk it?"

"I think I have to," Elizabeth said. "Kerosene?"

"My mother used it for grass stains. *After* she gave me a frightful scolding. It worked more often than not."

"Is there grass to stain your skirt, in London?" Elizabeth wondered.

Katarina chuckled again, though now it was a hard sound, without humor. "Not hardly. I spent my childhood in Devon."

"Oh," Elizabeth said. She seemed to have walked right into something, though she could not imagine what. She hesitated, then fell back on tea-time manners, as ludicrous as those were when standing in one's chemise in a strange woman's bedchamber. "That's said to be such a pretty place, isn't it?"

"Once," Katarina said, shortly, but not unkindly. "Right, then. I'll be downstairs. Bring your shift once you've changed." Without waiting for a reply, she was gone, crossing the room in a few long strides and hardly disturbing the curtain as she slipped around it.

Elizabeth let out a sigh.

She looked at the blouse and breeches, then set them down beside the candle. She wriggled out of her chemise—easy enough, no buttons to confound her fingers—and lifted it over her head. Naked except for shoes and stockings, she spent the time it took to draw two long breaths looking around at the dirty room and the unbelievable situation in which she found herself.

Then she picked up the blouse. It was of a coarser material than her chemise, rougher against her skin than she was accustomed to, but it hung loosely and so did not overly trouble her. The breeches were rougher yet, and Elizabeth hesitated before pulling them on—then noticed something that had been tucked between them and the shirt. She examined the white garment, deduced what it was for, and stepped into it. It was also too large, but it tied around the waist. Elizabeth knotted it firmly, then pulled the breeches on over it.

The cuffs hung past her ankles, and she nearly tripped trying to take her first step. She caught herself, biting back a giggle that was probably incipient hysteria. Well, that wouldn't do. She thought about it for a moment, then sat down gingerly on the edge of Katarina's chest. She reached under one floppy leg, undid the garter that held her stockings in place, and re-tied it over breech leg and stocking, hopefully securing both. She did the same with the other leg, and stood to inspect her handiwork. It looked ridiculous. She wanted to laugh out loud.

Katarina had left a final garment on top of the chest, another bodice such as gypsy women wore. Elizabeth avoided stays whenever possible, and even her mother admitted she was too slight to have any great need for them, but this once she thought she might prefer something extra between her person and the eyes that might light upon it. She laced it as modestly as possible, and though it would have been easy to tug down the blouse the way Katarina wore it, she was careful not to do so.

Only then did she realize that the breeches had *pockets,* and scooped up her watch with a barely smothered trill of delight. She could keep it. She needn't give it to anyone else to hold. She could tuck it into her pocket just exactly as a young man would, and fasten the chain to her bodice—yes, just so. Elizabeth looked about for a glass in which to examine the effect, but there was none.

She gathered up her chemise, turned for the candle, and almost tripped over something left abandoned in the shadow. Righting herself, she reached curious fingers to investigate. A boot. She drew it closer. A man's work boot.

Kicked off and left by the side of the bed.

Oh.

Elizabeth picked up the candle and stretched it toward the open chest. She saw a suit of man's winter underthings, darned and patched. A shirt, much bigger than the one she had on and the twin to what Trevelyan had been wearing downstairs. Two handkerchiefs and a cravat, all of which looked as though they had been used as cleaning rags at some point in the recent past.

She looked over at the unmade bed. *Pillows,* plural. Each with a depression where a head was accustomed to rest.

Elizabeth cast her mind back, but she had not seen any glint of a ring on Katarina's left hand. More to the point, she was "Madame Katarina Rasmirovna," not "Mrs. Trevelyan."

A pocket watch pulls me into the future, there are monsters on the street outside, and it's consorting with a fallen woman that shocks me? Elizabeth asked herself sardonically. Not that she was shocked, not exactly, only surprised. She had never actually met a fallen woman before, any more than an adventuress. *But perhaps that's considered acceptable now as well?* And then, with another suppressed giggle, *In any case, it looks to be great fun.*

She swallowed the third giggle and headed back for the stairs. These she took with great care, well able to envision the disaster of tripping with a candle and an armful of cloth. At least her garters seemed to be up to the task of holding the breeches in place. At the bottom of the stairs, she turned for the living room, hesitantly testing the length of her stride, slowly finding the rhythm of it.

The room was empty. The cold remnants of the tea sat abandoned in half-empty cups on the little table, but no one was there to drink them. Elizabeth poked her head around into the scullery and found it, too, uninhabited. Leaving her chemise draped over a chair that looked barely strong enough to support its weight, she ventured into the corridor.

It was filled with a humming sound. Or—not a sound, not exactly; she couldn't hear it so much as taste it. She pressed her tongue against her teeth and the hum seemed to vibrate in all the bones of her face. In her hand, the candle-flame shivered.

She took a step toward the passageway fork that had seemed to lead to someplace large and hollow. The hum grew stronger. Had it been here before, and she just not aware of it between the artillery outside and the threat of violence inside? All of a sudden it was unnerving to stand in the dark with the almost-taste on her tongue, and she hurried forward. Her outstretched fingers touched a thick door, closed but unlatched. She pushed it open. On its other side was a hall absolutely unlike anything she had ever seen.

It was *bright*, blindingly so, as bright as a farmer's field under midday sun. The ceiling seemed as high as the sky would be over that field, and she couldn't imagine where the light was coming from. Squinting, she made out globes of lamps hanging from beams part-way up—but the globes brought tears and flashing colors to her eyes so that she had to look away.

The hum was a rumble now, a rhythmic rattling. It came from the far end of the hall, from a contraption that looked like—Elizabeth put her head to one side, studied it as best she could through her spotted vision, and decided it still looked like an enormous spinning wheel attached to a loom. Behind it glowed the red coals of what appeared to be a blacksmith's forge. Tables lined two of the other three walls and boasted the most amazing assortment of litter on their surfaces—paper covered in sketches, models built out of wood, odd pieces of metal and the occasional tool.

In the middle of the floor sat something large and ominous, something halfway between a cannon and a rifle. Trevelyan crouched beside it, long-nosed tongs in one hand and eyes on the silver barrel, appearing to give it his full attention. Very angry attention it was too, Elizabeth thought, until she got closer and realized firstly that Katarina stood just behind Trevelyan and secondly that they were arguing.

"Well, they can't stay here," Trevelyan said, voice raised to be heard above the clatter. "I can't be bothered childminding. I have work to do if we're to—"

"Were you suggesting *I* ought to be childminding?" Katarina folded her arms and stared at the back of Trevelyan's head, but he did not turn to look at her. "I have my own work to do to ensure tonight's success."

Trevelyan straightened from the contraption and reached to exchange his tongs for an even more unlikely looking tool. "Take them with you."

Katarina rolled her eyes. "Oh, yes, *that* will be inconspicuous."

Elizabeth shifted from one foot to the other. They hadn't seemed to notice her yet. Perhaps she ought to back away and then make a bit of noise as she walked toward them? Although it didn't seem to worry them to be having this conversation in William's earshot—was he not here? She glanced around for him.

He stood where the bright lights fell away into shadows, holding a scribbled-over piece of paper in his hands and pretending to read it, but—judging by the stiffness of his posture—actually listening to Trevelyan and Katarina discuss his care as though he were a pet dog inconveniently left on their doorstep. Elizabeth was sure she did not make any noise, but just then William looked up as though he had heard her. He opened his mouth in what she presumed was intended to be a greeting, then took in what she was wearing and choked.

It was, she supposed, the effect achieved by those fast young ladies who were said to dampen their muslins. Certainly William could never have seen so much of her lower half before, and so perhaps it was understandable that he turned the color of lobster and redirected his eyes hastily to the paper in his hand. But Elizabeth felt her own face grow hot at his disapproval. Well, perhaps it *wasn't* modest, but it *was* wonderfully easy to move in and eminently practical, and he must know she didn't mean anything *harmful* by it.

"Oh, good," Katarina's voice said dryly, and Elizabeth saw she was looking at William rather than at herself. "It fits."

Trevelyan flicked a look upward. "Oh, good," he echoed. "Another distraction. Take the children out of here, Katarina, I have work to do."

"I assure you, sir," William said stiffly, "we have no intention of disturbing you. Miss Barton and I can wait in the outer room until Madame Katarina and Mr. Maxwell return from their—"

"You're going out?" Elizabeth blurted, taking a step forward. William stared at her, but she didn't care. She kept her eyes fixed on Katarina's. "May I come? Please?"

"Elizabeth," William said, "have you gone *mad?* We were almost stepped on by a metal giant *firing artillery.* London is in the middle of a—"

"But they've stopped fighting for the moment," Elizabeth said. "It's safe enough for Mr. Maxwell and Madame Katarina to go out, so it's safe enough for someone to be with them. I'd stay close," she promised, turning back to Katarina. "I wouldn't go running off, and if something happened, well, you have that pistol. You said you were a good shot with it. *Please.* I just want to go for a bit of a walk and see—"

"Dressed like that?" William demanded. Katarina looked at him, and the flush reappeared on his cheekbones. "Er," he began. "I didn't quite mean—"

"Yes, you did," Katarina informed him dryly. "But times have changed, Mr. Carrington. It isn't quite so scandalous as it would have been in your time, for two women dressed in trousers to go walking alone. At least, not in this part of the city."

"And that's the point," Elizabeth persisted. "I'm dressed like you. I'll look like I belong here. I won't do anything you say is unsafe, I promise. I just want to see it. This is the only new place I've ever been, and the only new place I ever *will* be where I *can* just go walking without a chaperone and dressed in trousers, and I—I need to—I just want to—"

"See the world down the rabbit hole?" Katarina supplied, looking amused. Elizabeth furrowed her brows. "Alice in—" Katarina started to explain, and stopped. "Never mind, it would have been after your time. A book I had as a child. 'This brave new world,' then, how about that?"

"Yes," Elizabeth said. "This brave new world."

Katarina studied her with eyes that seemed to strip away her skin and peer inside. "All right," she said abruptly. "Very well. You can come."

"Then I shall accompany you also," William said.

"No, Mr. Carrington, I'm afraid I can't permit that." Katarina's voice was cream-smooth. "We've no men's clothing that will fit you, and your coat is seventy years out of date. You'll attract too much attention. But I assure you I can do everything needful to keep Miss Barton safe. I am, as she points out, an excellent shot."

"That's not the point," William said. "I have a responsibility to—"

"I understand, but there is truly nothing you can do. We haven't another pistol here to lend you, even if—"

There was an instant's worth of terrible pause.

"Even if I could prime it," William finished for her. "Which I can't. Of course. Forgive my presumption, Madame Katarina; I am sure you have the situation well in hand." He turned his back and plucked a sheet of paper at random off the nearest pile.

Katarina stood still. "I didn't mean that," she said.

William barely glanced up. "Yes, you did. Why should you not? You said nothing untrue. There is nothing I can do to aid you, and you are perfectly capable of seeing to Miss Barton's safety. I should doubtless only distract you."

"The lot of you," Trevelyan growled, "should stop distracting *me* this instant if there's to be any chance of testing tonight. Katarina—"

"Yes, of course." Katarina glanced once more at William before turning for the door. "Come, Miss Elizabeth."

Elizabeth hesitated. She wanted to say something—anything—to mend matters with William, but she had no notion what words would be suitable to the task. She wanted to meet his eyes at least, but William did not look up from the scribbled diagram clenched in his fist. Katarina was not slowing her steps, and in another instant the opportunity she represented would be gone for good. Elizabeth turned and ran after her, out into the brave new world.

Chapter 6

The air was as thick and acrid as though a fire had broken out somewhere near. Elizabeth coughed as it struck her throat, but Katarina seemed to notice nothing amiss, only glancing quickly up and down the street before she drew the door shut after her. Elizabeth could not imagine why she bothered to look about. It was not yet sunrise, and between the dim light and the smoky cloud, visibility was uncertain at best.

"It's hard to breathe," she ventured.

Katarina nodded absently. "I thought we'd be in for a bit of fog this morning. It's always like this before a storm. We're frankly lucky it's no worse. In a real London particular, you couldn't see your hand before your face."

"Fog?" Elizabeth was familiar with fog, a cool friendly gray thing that rolled in off the sea when the weather was right. If this was fog, the phenomenon had changed some in seventy years.

"Have you never been to London?" Katarina asked, surprised. "I should think, even in your time—" She broke off in response to Elizabeth's headshake.

"I don't come out until next year."

"You've never even been to your London?" Katarina repeated. "Aren't you in for an education then. Right, well, there won't be much reason for you to say anything at all, but if anyone asks, you've…just come up from the country. From Kent. No reason to invent more than you must. We work together, and I'm showing you about."

"What, ah…" Elizabeth thought about novels, and naughtier tales of which she was supposed to know nothing. How in the world did one ask the question? "What sort of work?"

Katarina gave her a sardonic look. "Singing. I sing in a music hall. So do you." She turned and led the way down the fog-bound alley.

Elizabeth scurried after her. "On a stage?"

Katarina flicked the look at her again. "Yes, on a stage. Where did you think?"

"I only meant...is it a respectable...I mean...I'm not trying to offend you. I just wondered if things had changed. Like the breeches. Is it a respectable profession for a respectable woman, performing on a stage?"

"Not really."

"Oh."

The fog around them whined with the same muted rat-tat-tat that characterized the corridor outside Trevelyan's workshop. Elizabeth felt it like an itch in her eardrums, an incipient headache behind her eyes. She looked about, trying to find the source of the sound, but the mist stymied her. A few wisps blew aside long enough for her to make out tall brick buildings, leaning forward as though watching her pass, but she saw nothing else before the curtain fell again.

Then the ground shivered under her feet, and a familiar ponderous thunder cut through drone and fog and straight to the marrow of her bones. She froze, looking in all directions—*Where is it?*

"It's all right," Katarina said, hand on her arm, drawing her along. "We're in no danger so long as we stay out of their way. We're not breaking curfew once the sun is up."

Elizabeth took a breath, almost choking as the heavy air hit the back of her throat. She grimaced and coughed. "Madame Katarina, there are a great many questions I—"

"Not just now," Katarina cut her off. They turned the corner.

The air smelled different here, something salty and fishy underlying the smokiness. The fog wafting against Elizabeth's face went cool, almost fresh, *almost* what she expected fog to be like. She sensed wide open space in front of her, though on either side looming buildings seemed to still watch her every move. Shouts of men and cries of gulls reverberated through the mist. And there was something else. Lapping water?

The scene before her came gradually into focus. She made out the masts of the ships first, then the ships themselves—huge, lean, beautiful things, wood gleaming and brass glittering wherever the fog parted enough to allow light to touch, much bigger and much sleeker than the ships she had seen in her own time, and with much larger sails. Finally she made out the lines of the docks and the men walking to and fro along them, unloading cargo from a particularly large ship whose figurehead was a snarling lion.

The breeze changed direction, now carrying a smell of rotting fish. Katarina advanced through the last line of warehouses and into the open, and Elizabeth followed. The men unloading cargo were dressed like laborers, like Trevelyan, but their shoulders slumped in a way

Trevelyan's had not. They gave Elizabeth and Katarina one sidelong glance each, then returned their eyes to the work at hand.

They moved in a rhythm, as though somewhere a drum Elizabeth could not hear beat out a cadence over the ever-present hum—not fast, but unfaltering. Four of them were positioned on the gangplank of one of the great ships, passing cargo hand to hand down its length to the dock, where six more walked in a ragged circle between the plank and a nearby warehouse. Whenever a piece of cargo reached the end of the gangplank, there was a man there to take hold of it. He walked it to the warehouse with measured steps, disappeared inside with it, and shortly afterward reappeared for the next load. No one hurried. No one missed a beat. The only thing they did out of rhythm was to cough, wet strangled sounds that overlapped each other.

Until one pleasant-faced young fellow glanced at them as he left the warehouse, and stumbled to a halt. Elizabeth nearly stumbled herself, so clear had the nonexistent drumbeat seemed to her ears. The young man smiled a bit, gap-toothed beneath his freckles. "Katarina!" he said and hurried over to them, pulling off his cap. The cap was nearly black with grime, as was the face it had shielded and the hand that held it, and the mouse-colored hair beneath was dull and lank and greasy. But he had a pleasant voice as well as a pleasant face, Elizabeth thought, and certainly his admiration seemed sincere. "Been a while, love," he said, smiling at Katarina. "Missed hearing you sing."

"Well, come by the hall, then, what's stopping you?" Katarina countered, and Elizabeth started. The low, melodic voice was gone, replaced by something higher, common-accented, almost a guttersnipe sound.

"Don't let you in for free, do they?" the man said. "Not last time I checked, leastaways. But I've got myself some work now, as you can see. So tonight, maybe?"

"You might not want to go out tonight," Katarina said. "There's a storm coming."

The man looked at her. "Is there?"

"Can't you feel it, and you a dockworker?"

The man nodded, glancing out at the oily surface of the river. "I suppose I can, now you mention it. Tonight, you think? In that case... it might well be a good night to stay in. I'll come see you another time."

"I'm not going anywhere," Katarina said, putting her head to one side to smile at him.

The man nodded again, but as though he hardly heard her. His eyes flicked to Elizabeth. "And who's—"

"Hey!" The bellow from the dockside made all three of them jump. A broadly built figure strode down the gangplank and onto the dock, and the rhythm crashed to a stop as he barreled through it. But it had been fragmenting even before he shouted, Elizabeth thought. She had been vaguely aware of the dissolution, though she could not have said why. Then she realized. Katarina's admirer had disordered the pattern as subtly and thoroughly as any couple sneaking away from a quadrille at a country dance.

The big man stopped in the middle of the paused workers, stabbing a finger toward his delinquent dancer. "Stop wasting your time with the ladies, Johnson, and get your arse back here!"

Johnson grimaced a farewell at Katarina. "Coming, sir!" he called, and turned on his heel. Before his boot had struck the pavement more than twice, the others had begun to reconstruct the rhythm. Before Elizabeth could have counted to five, it was as flawless as though it had never been disordered.

At Elizabeth's side, Katarina dipped her fingers into the hollow formed by the top lacing of her bodice, and came up with a tiny watch on a chain. "We'll be able to catch most of the others as they head for work or come back from it," she said. "The shift change whistle doesn't blow until six." Without any further explanation, she led Elizabeth away from the docks and back into the narrow, pinched rabbit warren of warehouses. It did not take very long for the squawk of gulls to be subsumed beneath the distant, unceasing rattle and the occasional thunder of giant feet.

❧

William stalked through the laboratory door with all the dignity he could muster, choosing at the last moment not to slam it, mentally adding one more item to the list of things he could not do. One, protect England from the French. Two, dance a quadrille. Three, protect Elizabeth Barton from 1885. Four, serve as an assistant to a Welsh laborer.

He didn't know the names of the tools, of course, nor which were likely to be needed for the accomplishment of any particular task. His masters at Eton had not instructed him on such matters. Nor was his right hand capable of holding anything steady, and when he attempted the feat with his clumsy left, the item in question had slipped through his fingers and wedged itself into the mechanism below. It was really no surprise that Trevelyan had responded by inviting him to remove himself, though the form of the invitation made William's ears burn.

He stood now in the living room, staring at the litter of tools and grime on every available surface, annoyed with himself for not at least gleaning more knowledge from the encounter. That Trevelyan was building a weapon was obvious enough, and the drawings on the walls—of metal giants, or pieces of metal giants, or pieces of metal giants with the metallic skin missing and the interior workings shown—indicated against which of London's two monsters the weapon was intended to be used. But William was no further along in discovering the parameters of the conflict than that, and Trevelyan had flatly refused to answer questions.

Very well, then, perhaps this room would tell him something. William considered the empty crates, the half-filled cups of cold tea, and the scattering of tools whose names he did not know. Then he made for the bookshelf. He had never seen one so devoid of reading material—only two volumes, and those two textbooks on machinery that assumed a grounding in subjects also not taught at Eton. William set them aside and only then noticed a third tome, hidden by shadows from the casual glance. He drew it out, raising a cloud of dust.

This one was a scrapbook. William took it over to the table, used it to push the dirty crockery aside, and opened it. Each page contained a pasted-in clipping from a newspaper, most only headlines, a few with the article following, none with any annotation or commentary. None with any of the dates preserved either, so it was hard to tell how old this news might be. Still, it was news—it was history—and William settled in to read. Any illumination shone on this mad new world would be more than he currently had. He turned the pages quickly, running his eye over the headline and initial words of each cutting.

LORD SEWARD ATTACKS PILOT BILL, read the first. Below, in smaller text, appeared the words, *Peer Gives Impassioned Speech to House of Lords.*

PILOT BILL PASSES, read the second.

INGLEHAM WAREHOUSE DESTROYED IN FIRE; ARSON SUSPECTED

PHILATHROPIST ENDOWS CHARITY FOR THOSE LEFT JOBLESS AFTER INGLEHAM FIRE Some of the article appeared below this one: *Lord Seward today announced the formation of the Ingleham Fire Charity, for the relief of those whose livelihoods were destroyed by the conflagration ...*

BOILER EXPLOSION ABOARD THE ALICIA BELL, read the fifth headline. *CARGO LOST, ALL HANDS SAFE.*

LANFORD AND SONS FAILS Lanford and Sons today closed its doors, citing the loss of its three largest ships to freak accidents over the past year...

TRAIN ROBBER TRIAL OPENS; ROBERTSON TESTIFIES AGAINST CLAYBOURNE

SURPRISE CLAYBOURNE WITNESS Lord Seward today took the stand as principle witness for the defense, speaking to Jonathan Claybourne's character...

CLAYBOURNE ACQUITTED

FACTORY REFORM BILL FAILS IN HOUSE OF LORDS VOTE

ANONYMOUS TIP AVERTS SABOTAGE Acting on anonymous information, Inspector John Barnes arrived at Murchinson Matchworks in time to arrest five men preparing to engage in acts of sabotage ...

MURCHINSON SABOTEUR CLAIMS TO HAVE BEEN HIRED BY "ROBERT LOCKSLEY" In exchange for a reduced prison sentence, Murchinson saboteur Frank Turner today testified that he was offered twenty pounds for said act of sabotage by a man identifying himself as "Robert Locksley"...

WHITEHALL BREACHED; AERIAL PLANS STOLEN The explosion that rocked Pall Mall in the early hours of Friday morning was said to have caused nothing but property damage. However, The Times has learned—through an exclusive interview with a minor government official—that when the smoke cleared, plans for an experimental new Aerial Defense System were found to have been abstracted from the government office in which they were kept. Whitehall clerk Richard Courtland, missing since the morning of the bombing, is suspected of a connection with this appalling theft...

AERIAL PLAN TRAITOR RUMORED TO BE IN FRANCE It is unknown how Mr. Courtland could have escaped this country without the knowledge of the port officials, but ...

The next clipping, incongruously, appeared to be from the Society page:

Despite his generous donation, Lord Seward was not present at the opening, having departed for the Riviera on Friday.

The final clipping was a letter to the editor—a long and rather rambling one.

Dear Sir,

As the police are not interested in my discoveries, I bring them to you in the hope that you may communicate them to the world. Only if we are forearmed with knowledge have we any chance of withstanding the forces working to destroy our Empire from within.

For some years now I have noticed a certain similarity among various crimes of robbery, forgery, espionage, and sabotage—a certain flair to their preparation that could never have belonged to the fools arrested for their execution, signs of an intelligence working behind the scenes, an immense organizing power moving agents like pieces on a chess-board and throwing its shield over those apprehended by the law. I am certain now that what I have suspected is the truth. He sits motionless, a spider in the center of a web that covers all London and extends throughout the country and even farther. His pawns may be caught, arrested, punished, but the spider is never so much as suspected. The spider has a name, and it is Locksley.

Locksley! Locksley! The word is on the lips of half those arrested for arson or forgery or robbery. It whispers like the wind through grass in the stews of the East End. He has built a kingdom for himself in that seething mass of vice, and it is dedicated to nothing less than the overthrow of the Empire. Unless it is discovered who wears the mask of Locksley, he will succeed in reducing this city and then all of England to chaos. Every man, woman, and child is in danger until this monster is apprehended...

The letter might have continued, but the cutting ended there, with no name given. William sat back, closed the scrapbook, and stared at the scratches running along the faded green cover.

In the year 1885, he thought, *London is a warfront. More: in the year 1885, London is occupied. Someone has imposed a curfew on the city, enforcing it with metal giants that fire weapons second-cousin to artillery.*

These newspaper clippings show a weakening of various institutions of government and industry. Arson, ships sunk, military documents stolen. At least one person thinks it all deliberate. Could that all have happened first, and then been followed by a coup d'état? He thought of the guerilla warfare he had seen in Spain. One weakened the pillars of the temple whenever possible, before bringing it down with a frontal assault. He was mixing metaphors almost as badly as the writer of that letter, but he didn't bother to rephrase the thought to himself.

He read through the letter again, more slowly. The writer did not sound overly reliable, but assuming he had stumbled onto something true, "Locksley" might have been a foreign agent. Perhaps French? Sent to weaken key pillars in government and trade? He wished the clippings had contained dates, so he could understand how long ago this happened. Perhaps the government had been overthrown and the Crown was now in exile, like the House of Bourbon had once been? He thought he had identified Trevelyan's role in all of this now. The mantle of guerilla soldier fit Trevelyan's shoulders very well. Developing a weapon against the metal giants? Perhaps in the service of the Crown-in-exile?

But why the clippings about the philanthropist Seward? William re-opened the book and read them over again, frowning. He couldn't say for certain without more information.

There was one obvious way to obtain more information, to test the theories he had formed. William glanced in the direction of Trevelyan's laboratory, weighing approaches. Trevelyan respected competence, which William had not been demonstrating earlier; hence Trevelyan's impatience. But if he returned and ambushed the tinkerer with competence now, he might just startle some answers out of the fellow.

He picked up the scrapbook and took it to Trevelyan's laboratory, wedging it under his right arm and using his left hand to open the door. Trevelyan was now standing at the workbench just inside the room, flipping through the mess of paper on its surface, fingers moving so fast through the sketches that they seemed to be juggling shadows. William stood obviously in the doorway, but Trevelyan did not look up.

"So then," William said, a little louder than necessary to be heard over the racket. "Your weapon is intended to bring down Locksley's metal monsters? How many people know Locksley is Lord Seward?"

And then Trevelyan's startled eyes came level with his own.

Interlude

Pendoylan, Wales, May 18, 1872

"Ah, Miss Evans! Good afternoon to you." Mrs. Pritchard waddled up to the counter like an amiable partridge. "Here for your letters, are you?"

That was generally what took a person into a post office, but uttering such a waspish response did not even cross Brenda Evans' mind. "Good afternoon, Mrs. Pritchard. Yes, I am."

"You're in luck today!" Mrs. Pritchard turned, sorting through the pigeon-holes behind her with as much eagerness as though the luck had been hers. "There's a letter come for you from your Gavin. He'll be home for the summer holidays before very long, won't he?"

"Next week." Brenda knew she was turning pink with pleasure, but saw no reason to hide it. A letter from Gavin did indeed make it a lucky day. She took it from Mrs. Pritchard, smiling at the distinctive bold script on the envelope. "Then home for good and all this time next year."

"And that'll be lovely, won't it?" Mrs. Pritchard sighed with sympathetic happiness. "No other letters for you, dearie, just the paper for your dad. Awful news up north, isn't it?" She clucked her tongue at the headline, and Brenda murmured agreement without really looking at it. There *was* always awful news from north of Moore's Wall. Nearly every year, the English sent a troop of soldiers over the Wall to try to take back the Highlands. Nearly every year, they made some small progress at first, but then the wild monster clans rose in force and drove them back. This had been going on for as long as Brenda could remember, and she did not find it very interesting to read about.

The bell over the door jingled, and Mrs. Pritchard turned her attention to her new customer. "Ah, Mrs. Jones! Here for your letters, are you? My best to your mum, Miss Evans, and tell her I'll be seeing her at the Ladies' Aid tomorrow." Mrs. Jones held the door, and Brenda slipped around her and outside.

The loveliest sort of evening was coming on, cool clean air and soft blue sky. Spring had finally taken hold, with little green shoots visible in gardens and wildflowers clustered by the side of the path Brenda took home from the village. It was time she got back to help her mother put tea on the table, but she lingered for just a moment, admiring the sparkle of sunlight through green leaves. Between the pleasant weather, the newly trimmed hat on her head, and the letter from Gavin in her pocket, Miss Brenda Evans was very close to perfectly happy.

Not that she was in truth "Miss Evans." She and Gavin had been married very quietly the year before—everyone hereabouts knew that, and the plain gold band on her finger would have told them even if they hadn't. She ought to have been "missus." But they wouldn't be able to set up housekeeping until he took his degree next spring. She lived still in her father's house, and mostly the same as she had done before the wedding; and so most folk tended to forget, as a day-to-day matter. As far as the neighbors were concerned, she was "Miss Evans," and she generally thought of herself that way too. It was still something of a surprise to see her married name on an envelope, in Gavin's forcible scrawl. He was the only one who used it, and it made her feel warm to think of him proudly writing it out.

Theirs was an unusual situation, to be sure. A few of the folk who said "Miss Evans" did so with a meaningful pause before the title to indicate their disapproval. Brenda knew, but could not bring herself to mind. Her parents did not disapprove, so what else mattered? It was unusual to agree to a marriage between one's daughter and a man who could not yet support a wife—a betrothal would have been the more routine arrangement—but Gavin's prospects were excellent. His parents were dead, but a seafaring uncle had left him a legacy in trust to pay school fees and the part of university not covered by scholarship, the principle to come to him when he turned twenty-one. Even had there been no principle, the university degree catapulted Gavin straight to the status of "excellent match." When he took his degree, he was almost certain to obtain a government-sponsored engineering post in Cardiff or London. Brenda's mother hoped for Cardiff, which wasn't too far off for a week-end visit; Brenda herself was excited by the idea of living in London.

Though she had been told London was smelly and noisy, and if Gavin decided to settle there, she would doubtless miss this placid green peace and the smell of freshly turned earth. It was therefore only sensible to store up memories of walking in the countryside at twilight, in case she needed them for comfort later on. So that was a good reason—well, no, it wasn't really; truthfully, it was being naughty, but she could *pretend* it was a good reason—to go home the long way, by the Davies'.

This time of day, their duck pond was perfect mirror of the sky, flat as glass with pink-tinged clouds floating through it. Brenda peeped at her own reflection, admiring all over again the pink ribbons with which she had trimmed last year's hat. The ribbons had been a birthday gift from Gavin, all the way from London, and no other girl in the village had ones so fine.

A duck sailed through her reflected face, and Brenda had to laugh at herself for vanity. She lingered another moment, watching the duck flip itself upside-down in its search for food and listening to a bird trilling in a nearby tree. Before her stretched the Davies' fields, brown and fresh and homely and everything that was spring. Up above them rose the green hills and low mountains that made South Wales so distinctively beautiful. Brenda had never travelled farther than Cardiff, but she was sure there was nothing in England or any other part of the wide world to compare.

From here it was only just possible to see how the tops of those mountains were scarred by coal mines. It wasn't possible at all to see the barracks used to house the tame Wellingtons who worked them. When the mines had first opened, years ago, the miners had been Welsh—men, women, and even tiny children, toiling away in the darkness below the ground from the age of six or even younger. Brenda shuddered at the thought, and drew a breath of fresh air with particular pleasure. How inhuman, to treat children that way. It was much better for Wales to have the monsters work the mines, leaving human families free to farm in the fresh air.

Free to go off to Cardiff and work in the factories, too, of course. Many young men and some young women did just that, and that work was hard and the hours long, but at least those who went were old enough to choose for themselves, not tiny mites. Much better to have the monsters do the truly dangerous work, particularly as they were bred to it and it did them no harm. They were mostly contented with their lives, Brenda understood, not like the nasty wild ones in Scotland. It was the difference between a housecat and the *cath pulag* out of the old tale of Pa Gwr, so people said, and you only had to look at the newspaper's headline to see the truth of that. *THE NORTH IS BURNING,* it said, and it went on to tell of horrible things done to English soldiers by the wild monsters. Brenda thought it would be much better if the English would stop with their attempts to retake the Highlands, just retreat to their side of Moore's Wall and have done, but she supposed they must have some reason to keep trying. She glanced through the first few words of the article, then shuddered and turned her eyes back to the sky above the duck pond. It was a waste of a lovely evening to fret over far off things she could do nothing about. She was glad that she did not live there and never would, and even gladder that her husband was an educated man and not a soldier, so he would never have to go there either.

She couldn't wait a moment longer. She pulled out Gavin's letter and settled down on a rock right there by the duck pond to read it. It would hardly make her any tardier returning home than she already was, for Gavin's letters were never very long. He was brilliant at anything having to do with numbers or carpentry or what they taught at university, but rubbish at putting words to paper in any sort of eloquent manner. Brenda didn't care. She wouldn't have wanted a long poetic letter, for a long poetic letter wouldn't have been the least like Gavin.

Nor had he sent one. His scrawl covered only a sheet and spoke mostly about some work he was doing with a professor, work that seemed likely to lead to a post after he took his degree. The post, if he got it, would keep him in London, but perhaps they might contrive to take lodgings outside the city—somewhere pleasant—and he could take the train in every morning. Just exactly like a gentleman with business in the city! Should she like that? He was very much looking forward to talking it over with her next week. "Yours ever, G."

She was reading it over for the third time, feeling the air cool around her and thinking that she really ought to be getting home to help her mother with tea, when a hand dropped onto her shoulder and she jumped nearly out of her skin.

"Oh, I'm sorry!" a deep voice said as she squirmed around. "My dear young lady, I am so sorry. I did not mean to startle you."

His back was to the sun and she could see nothing of his face. For that moment, he was only a black, broad-shouldered figure outlined in flame, and every tale she had ever heard of things one might meet in the wood flashed through her mind.

Then he shifted to one side, and Brenda scolded herself for a goose. He was nothing fearful, only an ordinary looking man of middle age, broad-shouldered and white-haired, with an agreeable, unremarkable face. An Englishman by his speech—and a wealthy one, for his sleek black coat was like nothing she had ever seen in her life. It must, she thought, be the latest London fashion.

His hand was still on her shoulder. She tried to shrug out from underneath it and rise, but he was standing in such a way that she could not easily get her feet underneath her. "Miss Evans, isn't it?" he said pleasantly.

"Yes, sir," Brenda said. Her initial alarm had been banished by his ordinariness, but now it came creeping back. The stranger smiled at her, but only with his lips and not his eyes, and it occurred to her that the duck pond was somewhat isolated, that no one had passed by in all the time she had spent daydreaming, that the afternoon had faded into the hour when most folk retreated behind doors for their tea…

"I have the honor to count your husband among my friends," the white-haired man explained. "I have seen the little miniature he keeps by him; I would know you anywhere. Though it scarcely does you justice, of course, madam."

She would have been charmed by the compliment had it been delivered in a roomful of other people, in daylight. Alone in the wood it pressed itself ominously against her, like the fingers on her shoulder-blade.

"It is a piece of luck to find you here," the stranger went on. "I was going to call upon you, was just now seeking my way to your parents' house. I saw your husband in London yesterday, you see, and he asked me to bring you a message since I was traveling this way."

Gavin's letter crackled as Brenda's hand tightened on it. Gavin's letter, written only the day before, conspicuously omitting any introduction of a friend. "Indeed," she said, trying not to let her voice quaver. "How fortunate, Mr.—?"

"Jones," the man said with no hesitation at all, but Brenda didn't believe him for a moment. It was a Welsh name, and there was nothing of Wales in his speech.

"Mr. Jones." She took a deep breath, trying to act as though nothing troubled her. "I'm always pleased to know a friend of Gavin's. And—and I'm sure my parents would invite you to tea. We'd, ah—" She took another breath. "—we'd best start walking that way. I'm quite late already, and they're bound to come looking for me if I'm not back soon."

He didn't step back to allow her to rise. He didn't take his hand from her shoulder. Brenda ducked her head, trying to wriggle upright and through the slender gap between the man's looming figure and the rock on which she sat. She wasn't sure if she would have chanced running had she been able to get away from him; but as it was, she stumbled on her skirt, twisting her ankle, and the stranger caught her by her upper arms.

They stood there frozen for a moment, face to face, his fingers biting into her arms and his eyes burning as he studied her.

"Thank you," she said, and tried to pull away. "Thank you, sir, I'm fine, there's no need —" *Let me go,* she meant, *let me go,* she wanted to say, but she feared to betray her distrust. What would happen after she did? "—I'm fine, thank you."

He released her at last, but still stood looking down at her, blocking the path that led home. To one side was the duck pond, to the other a great open pasture. Behind her snaked the road back to the village. Nobody would be walking it this time of day. All the men would be crossing fields to their own homes. If she screamed, would anyone hear her?

"Listen to me," the stranger said abruptly. "Gavin sent me to take you and your mother and father away from here. Just for a day or two. You're in danger. You need to come away somewhere safe."

"What?" Brenda stared at him.

He nodded. "It's true. Your life is in danger, Miss Evans. You need to come away from here. I have money enough for train fares—"

"*Train* fares?"

"—you can spend a day or so in London. I'll take you up to Gavin in London, and you can surprise him."

"I can surprise him? Who are you?" The stranger didn't answer. Brenda backed away, crumpling her letter between her sweating hands. "I had a letter from Gavin this very day. He didn't mention any danger, and he didn't mention anything about you, Mr. Jones. I don't know who you are, or what kind of joke you're having with me, but it's not a very funny one. Now go away. I have to get home for tea." He was still blocking her path. His eyes burned with intensity, but the rest of his face sagged in a way that looked so very tired. "My father will come looking for me if I'm not home directly," she said. He still didn't step aside to let her pass. She stood trembling for one moment. Then she darted for the pasture fence at the same time he dove for her.

His hand snapped in the air just above her arm. She twisted and eluded him and ran two steps before he seized a fistful of her gown. She writhed in his grip, but his arm across her chest was like iron. "Help me!" she shrieked. "Mr. Davies! Johnny! Help—"

The stranger's calloused palm clapped over her mouth like a blow, with enough force to rattle her teeth. "I shan't hurt you," he breathed in her ear as she thrashed against him. "I'm here to see to it nothing happens to you. I've gone about this all wrong, Brenda, and I'm sorry, but I only mean to—*oof!*"

Her boot heel connected with his knee, a strike more of luck and desperation than cunning, but it was enough to free her mouth for an instant. "*Help!*" she cried again, lunging from his arms in the direction of the pasture. It was a large field, but she could see the Davies' house. Surely someone there would hear.

He really struck her that time, hard enough that her head snapped back and she reeled with the shock of it. She could summon no resistance for a moment or two, and he dragged her away from the fence and the safety beyond it. He was holding her only with the one arm, she realized dimly. The hand that had been over her mouth, the hand he had used to strike her, was fumbling at his waistcoat pocket. Brenda felt sick. She was a married woman, after all, with enough experience to guess what he wanted. One heard of fearful stories of girls gone to cities in search of work—but those things happened in *cities*, not villages—

Head spinning, she threw herself against his restraining arm. *"Help me!"*

She couldn't get her vision clear. The field before her seemed to tilt and wobble and tilt again. But there were spots in the middle of it. Moving spots. People. Running toward her.

The stranger jerked something from his pocket—*Oh God*, Brenda thought, *a pistol?* But no. It was something else. She couldn't see what, but the stranger was fiddling with something he held in his left hand as Johnny Davies leapt the fence and struck him with a spade.

✐

They put him in a holding cell in the village, one that had never before had the honor of containing anything more interesting than a drunkard. Constable James, who had also never had the honor of looking after anything more interesting than a drunkard, settled stolidly in to guard him until a sergeant could be fetched down from Cardiff.

The stranger talked with scarcely a pause for breath, staring at James with pleading eyes. "I'm sorry I scared her," he said. "But she is in danger. It doesn't matter what you do to me, but you've got to send her away from here."

James carefully noted down all the wild words, but did not reply.

"You're all in danger!" the man said suddenly. "The monsters in the coal mines are at the point of bursting their bonds! They will break free tonight, they will swarm down from the mountains and take what they want from this village—food, money, women, revenge—you are *all* in danger. You have to find a safe place for everyone to gather, a place you can defend. Pendoylan will be burning by midnight."

James noted those words as well. The man kept repeating them, with only slight variations and in an increasingly hoarse voice, for hours. Every time he came up with a new phrase, James wrote it down.

For the rest of the time, the constable kept his eyes fixed on the wall above the stranger's head and gave him no encouragement.

❦

Brenda's mother had fed her brandy and then tucked her into bed with the extra blankets and the hot water bottle that shock and distress required. Despite them, Brenda had felt chilled through. Her mother had sat in the rocking chair, singing her lullabies as she had done at bedtimes long ago, and somewhere in the middle of them, Brenda had dropped off to sleep.

She woke with a jump, to find her bedchamber lit by a red glow.

The hands of the little clock at her bedside pointed to a quarter past two, and she had the sense of having just woken from a nightmare. The red glow was real, however. It came from the window, from a gap in the curtains. It was not unlike the blue moonlight that sometimes bathed the room—but this was the wrong week for that. The moon had been only the slenderest crescent the night before, and besides, the color was wrong...? Wondering dazedly if something had *happened* to the moon, Brenda got out of the bed and went to the window.

She saw a halo of orange and red blazing from the peak of the mountaintop, stretching high into the sky. Smaller orange blotches shimmered here and there on the side, wending their way downward, toward Pendoylan.

❦

The Evans' house was the one nearest the mountain; they never had a chance. Brenda had only just convinced her parents that she had *not* been dreaming, that they must come and look from her window, when the first monster broke down the kitchen door. He was followed by a swarm of others. They left the family dead and the house in flames.

Nearby dwellings fared almost as badly, though there were some survivors who streamed away from the holocaust of their homes. By the time the monsters reached the village proper, the alarm had been given and the men were organized with fowling pieces. Fewer people died after that point, but the damage to homes and farms was considerable.

The man in the cell shouted all night for someone to let him out, in tones piercing enough to be heard outside the prison. He fell silent as the sun rose, however, and spoke no word afterward. When Constable James, burnt and bloodied from the night's fighting, stumbled back to his post around midday, he found the cell empty and the lock still fastened. His prisoner had somehow managed to vanish from behind the bars. No one in Pendoylan or out of it ever looked into solving the mystery, however. The "tame" monsters had burst their bonds all over the countryside, and Wales had bigger problems to occupy its attention. The south was burning.

Chapter 7

The fog pressed hot and choking, worse every minute. Elizabeth cleared her throat again and again, but could not get rid of the tickling almost-need to cough. Walls of black-smeared brick and weather-worn wood pressed close on either side, so close that she could have stretched out her arms and spanned the alleyway had she wanted to trail her fingers through the layer of soot that coated them. The ever-present rattling drone bothered her less now, but the thunder that heralded the approach of the metal giants still made her jump, and still left her ears ringing when it passed. She craned her head upward each time it broke upon her, and had twice caught a glimpse of a sapphire-and-copper head through gaps in the buildings and breaks in the fog, but had not yet managed anything like a good look at the things. The second time she gave up the attempt and turned her eyes back to the alley before her, it was to find that Katarina had vanished.

Elizabeth caught her breath and darted forward. Panicking would be foolish, of course; she would not panic. Katarina could not be more than a few steps ahead, must be only briefly concealed by fog, surely would not intend to leave Elizabeth behind. But between the mist obscuring her vision and the ringing in her ears, Elizabeth felt as though all connection to the world around her had slipped away. Katarina was the only touchstone she had, the only proof that she was not marooned in a blizzard or an Arabian sandstorm or possibly fairyland. She was *not* panicking, but she was very relieved indeed to see Katarina's coil of black hair come back into view—of course no more than a few steps ahead, of course having suffered no graver fate than to be hidden by fog. Katarina turned a corner, and Elizabeth scuttled after her, only just managing not to plow into the older woman when Katarina suddenly stopped.

They stood at the entrance to a courtyard of sorts, filled to the brim with jostling humanity. Slump-shouldered men in laborers' clothing wandered about, smoking tiny cigars. Over their heads, laundry hung in straggling lines between buildings that sagged toward each other as though the linen was too great a burden for their frames. Two women in skirts and caps stood still, holding bawled conversations with upper-story windows, and two others—younger, their faces brightly painted—sat on what looked to be damp and uncomfortable ground, their backs to a wall, and passed a bottle from hand to hand. One of the latter wore a cheap-looking gown that appeared to have been made for her before she reached womanhood: the skirt fluttered above her knees and her bosom strained against the bodice. Her companion wore breeches and a blouse pulled low, and Elizabeth felt an uncomfortable suspicion regarding the costume she had so eagerly adopted.

There were children running about everywhere and other adults whose situation in life Elizabeth could not categorize, and all along the walls, piles of rubbish and great dark sacks. At first Elizabeth paid no attention to the sacks. She was absorbed in studying the girls with the bottle, for they were the first women of easy virtue she had ever personally encountered, and they did not appear to be deriving as much enjoyment from their role as Katarina seemed to derive from hers. Then one of the sacks *moved*, and Elizabeth jumped back from it. Looking at it more closely, she saw that it had matted hair and a bearded face and a mouth open in a yawn that turned into a racking cough. For a terrified moment, she thought it one of the dead-faced, droop-skinned monsters from the night before, but no. This face was drawn and lined, but human.

"Men whose health has broken down such that they cannot work," Katarina supplied in a low voice, and then clarified, "Ones who didn't scrape up enough yesterday for a night's lodging."

A pair of children appeared out of nowhere, careening into Elizabeth and knocking her backward a step. Katarina caught her arm and the children dashed past without a pause or apology.

"Where—?" Elizabeth's eyes were still on the man who was neither a monster nor a sack, and she couldn't manage more than the one word.

"The children? Headed for their work," Katarina said. "Everyone here will be, before very long. It's nearly that time."

Indeed, the mass of figures in the courtyard had begun to drift toward the alleyway. Even some of the dark heaps on the ground began to stir themselves, and one or two joined the shuffling exodus.

"I thought you said they couldn't—?"

"They can't work in the factories. They can make a few pennies begging, and the businessmen who come on the early trains are a good mark for that. The children do a variety of jobs. Or they pick pockets when there are no odd jobs to be found." The painted ladies had gotten to their feet, leaving the now-empty bottle abandoned on its side, and were heading for a water pump at the far enough of the courtyard. Katarina followed Elizabeth's glance in their direction. "Those two will be off to catch factory workers headed home from the night shift. They're hoping for the price of a meal and then a place to sleep."

Elizabeth swallowed. "Isn't there somewhere...charity from the parish, or ..."

"There are places." Katarina's voice was flat. "They're not places you want to see the inside of, if you've any choice in the matter."

The mob had thinned considerably by now, but a knot of laborers still stood at the far end of the courtyard, smoking their little cigars and watching the wanton girls wet their hair with water and use their fingers to style it into frizzy curls. The two women in caps were still engaged in their screeching parley with the occupants of the upstairs windows. Each woman carried a mop and a pail, Elizabeth could see now, and their overlapping conversations seemed to be with offspring. "You stay right where you are!" the taller of the two concluded. "I don't want to come back and find you've stirred a step, not with those nasty Wellingtons hunting last night!"

"And don't let the baby fall from the window!" finished the other, and both turned for the alley.

Elizabeth dodged out of the way that time. Katarina stood her ground. The taller woman shouldered past her without a comment, but the other stopped. "Madame Katarina!"

"Mrs. Thompson," Katarina answered. "How do you find yourself today?"

"Here, Thompson, look who's here!" the woman called over her shoulder, and one of the laborers leaning against the wall by the water pump looked up. He stared a moment, then pushed himself upright and hastened over the cobblestones, his fellows peering after. Katarina took a step to meet him, but not more than that, and Elizabeth wondered if there were some etiquette about guests not entering the courtyard.

"Madame Katarina, here's a surprise," Thompson said, and raised a finger to his cap. "You're up early."

"She's not been home to bed yet!" the girl in the too-short gown called from the pump.

"True, as far as it goes," Katarina said pleasantly. She spoke less like a guttersnipe now, but still not quite in the voice she had used in the warehouse. Something in the vowels suggested a kinship with these ragged folk. "I'm not yet so high at the Shoreditch that I don't have to take my turn at cleaning, and if the cleaning goes late, well, then I'm stuck there for the night, aren't I? I can't be walking about after curfew."

"You *shouldn't* be," a voice said from just outside the courtyard. It belonged to the taller of the two women possessed of mop and pail, who had apparently not gone on her way after pushing past Katarina. Her emphasis said plainly both that Katarina was often out after curfew and that everyone knew it. "There was a pack of Wellingtons out last night," the tall woman added with relish. "Who knows what devilry they were about before the coppers brought them down. They'll eat you sure, if you don't take more care." With these words she took her departure, and no one appeared to care enough for her company to call her back.

"How would you know what happened last night unless you broke curfew yourself?" Katarina asked the air, and there were some appreciative chuckles from her audience. Quite a crowd had gathered, Elizabeth noticed: most of the laborers, both of the painted girls, and the remaining woman carrying a mop.

"Just come to say hello on your way home, then?" Thompson asked.

"Just so."

"Have a gasper?" He offered her one of the tiny cigars, and Katarina took it. Thompson's eyes slid to Elizabeth. "And one for your friend?"

"I think she'd choke on it," Katarina said, amused. "She's only just up from Kent, hasn't had time to learn city ways. Give her a day or so." She slipped the cigar between her lips and leaned forward, and one of the other men produced a tiny box. He fumbled with it, and with a snap flame appeared between his fingers. Elizabeth stared as he touched the little wooden stick to Katarina's cigar. A matchstick, was it? She had heard of the things, invented by a Frenchman and considered to be quite clever, but too dangerous and too expensive to be widely popular. They appeared to be less expensive now, to judge by the surroundings in which this one was being used. She hoped they were similarly less inclined to explode.

"Is it true what those wicked paper-boys were saying last night?" the woman with the mop demanded. "About Lord Seward being taken by the coppers?"

"Quite true, I'm afraid."

"Wicked," the woman proclaimed, and the men nodded, looking grimly at each other. "I was hoping it wasn't true, so I was, but if you say so—"

"I heard the papers said he was doing terrible things." The man with the matchsticks looked at Katarina. "They said he had a pack of Wellingtons under his control, and—"

"Wicked lies, those papers print," the woman said. "Why, he's given away more to charity than, well, than I'll ever see in a lifetime! Saved us from being thrown into the street, he did, when Thompson lost his work in the Ingleham fire. You didn't see Mr. Ingleham putting himself out, did you? The idea of Lord Seward doing anything he oughtn't. Wicked lies."

"His honor'll be all right, a rich man like him," a third man said, words catching around a soft Irish brogue. "Even if someone's printed lies about him. Won't he?"

"Oh, no doubt of it," Katarina said. "I'm sure it's all a mistake. Tempers run high when the heat is so horrid, after all."

"No doubt it's that," Thompson said, watching her as narrowly as Johnson had back at the docks.

"And I can't think but that it'll break soon," Katarina went on. "There's a storm coming tonight, I shouldn't wonder."

"Tonight?" the Irishman said.

"Oh, I think so." Katarina waved a hand. "Can't you feel it?"

"I can, and a blessing it'll be if it brings a breath of clean air with it," the Irishman said.

Somewhere nearby, a church bell tolled out the three-quarter chime.

"A'right, lads." Thompson tugged his cap more firmly over his ears. "Shift-change whistle's about to blow, better be stepping. Hope you're right about the weather, Madame Katarina."

"Tell the others," Katarina said. "See what they think."

"We'll be doing that," the Irishman promised. He touched his cap to her and joined the men already filing out of the courtyard. Mrs. Thompson and her mop brought up the rear. Within minutes, the courtyard was filled only with half-grown children, dark sack-like shapes huddled against the walls, and an old woman Elizabeth had not previously noticed, slumped on a step in a drunken stupor.

"We can't do better than follow them," Katarina said. "We'll be at the factory gates when the whistle blows, catch those going home. Just on the off-chance."

"On the off-chance of what?" Elizabeth hastened to follow her, but received no answer.

Katarina led her at a brisk walk in the direction where fog had already swallowed Thompson and his companions. Along the way, they passed small groups of similarly dressed men. Many of these nodded to Katarina in a friendly manner. Some asked after Lord Seward. To them all, Katarina mentioned a coming storm.

The drone in the air grew more insistent, and then loud enough to be called a clatter. It clanked rhythmically, like Trevelyan's loom. *Da-*

da-da-DUM, it said, over and over, increasing in volume with every step they took closer to it.

Behind them, a church bell began to faintly toll six o'clock, and over it, through it, screeched a sound that made Elizabeth duck her head and clap her hands to her ears. When she looked up, the fog ahead cleared enough for her to see where the sound had originated, and she stood still to stare at it.

Great black wrought-iron gates, larger than any she had ever seen surrounding a country estate, rose up before her. Behind them was a building of tired-looking brick that might well compare with a country house in size—not so wide, perhaps, but taller, and with space cleared respectfully all around it. At its very top were the largest chimneystacks Elizabeth had ever seen, belching great clouds of black smoke into the thick gray air. On either side, dwarfing the crowd, heads nearly level with the chimney stacks, stood two of the copper giants she had run from the night before.

She tensed, but glanced at Katarina and inferred there was no reason to run now. Katarina did not return her look, but the older woman's fingertips brushed her wrist—unobtrusive, comforting. Elizabeth tried to breathe.

The giants did not look as though they were planning to stomp forward and offer harm to her or anyone else. They stood quiescent, heads unmoving—though their eyes, Elizabeth noticed suddenly, swiveled in their sockets, rolling first one way and then another. She watched the eyes of the one nearest to her as it sought restlessly in all directions. No blue-white light shone from them now; perhaps there was no need of it in daylight. Those eyes could see, she thought. But the head had no other features, neither mouth nor nose nor ears.

She couldn't keep looking at the wrongness of that blank, staring face. She looked elsewhere instead. Seen with time to consider, the giant's red-gold body reminded her even more strongly of a teakettle—or perhaps a coffee urn—a long cylinder, dully gleaming. The legs were slimmer cylinders, with knee joints like a man's and feet that looked as though they could crush anything in their path. The arms—

Elizabeth found herself shivering at the wrongness again. The arms looked like arms up until the elbow joint. But then the left one ended in a gaping cannon-mouth, and the right one in a collection of smaller rifle-mouths gathered in a circle. Between the enormous arms, four evenly spaced bolts the size of Elizabeth's hand held a square plate to the creature's chest.

Below the giants' watchful gazes, close enough that they could have struck the metallic legs as they passed, a line of men stumped through one side of the iron gates toward the building. From the other side stumped a second, identical line, headed from the building. Some exchanged greetings, brief enough not to mar the rhythm of marching feet.

Katarina positioned herself where she could speak with a few of the exiting men, casually, and once they were sufficiently far outside the gates that they might pause without causing others to pile into them from behind. Elizabeth did not try to overhear. She was too busy staring at the building and the copper creatures.

"Never seen the like, have you, love?"

The voice spoke at her elbow, and Elizabeth jerked around. The boy standing there was nice-looking enough, though terribly dirty. He grinned at her. "New to London, are you?"

"Yes," Elizabeth managed. "I've—I've just come up from Kent. What is this place?"

"This here," the boy said with pride, "is the factory what makes coppers for the Empire. The constructs," he clarified in response to her confusion, and pointed at the giants. "Them great big stompy things keeping the monsters away."

"You…" Elizabeth cleared her throat. "You make them, do you?"

"I do," the boy said. "I screw in parts now, but someday I'll be a supervisor or something grander."

"Do you like it?"

"It's not so bad," he said, with affected carelessness. "Better than drudging on a farm, at least. What's your line of work, love?" His eyes ran down her trouser-clad legs. "Music hall?"

"Yes," Elizabeth said. "I've, ah, I've just been engaged."

"Have you? Lovely bit of costume they've given you." He reached out to finger Elizabeth's sleeve. Smudges appeared at once on the shabby linen. Elizabeth glanced at her own fingers and saw a sift of black dust clinging to them as well. She hadn't even touched anything, not that she could remember; this was only from walking about outdoors. "Whereabouts do you sing?" the boy asked, leaning closer.

"The Shoreditch Empire," Katarina's voice said crisply behind them. "There's shows every night, young sir, we'd be delighted to see you. Now, now—" She plucked his hand off Elizabeth's arm. "When you can pay us a penny, you can have a proper look, but until then, we've other business to be about. Come along, then," she added, and Elizabeth was only too glad of the excuse to follow. The boy, though he protested, abandoned pursuit soon enough; but the staring blank eyes of the constructs seemed to bore into her back for a long time.

Machinery clattered and groaned in deafening orchestrations as Trevelyan stared at William. "How did you—?" he started. Then his eye fell on the scrapbook. "Oh."

He put his hand out for it, and William gave it to him. Trevelyan turned without a change in expression and walked to the back of the room. He dropped the book into the forge, and it went up in a whoosh of flames. "Seems Max was right," he commented, returning to where William stood. "Too great a risk to leave that lying about. I didn't think anyone but him could figure it out from those clues, and he already knew."

"Anyone but he and you, you mean," William said.

"Anyone but him and me," Trevelyan agreed, mouth twitching slightly at the corner.

William folded his arms across his chest, using the fingers of the left to coax the right into position. "So I'm cleverer than you thought? I'm right, aren't I?"

"As it happens, you're wrong, but you got closer than I would have liked from that information. Not that it matters any longer, but we've been burning anything we don't absolutely need, in case they burst in here."

There were a number of interesting tidbits in that statement. William bypassed the implication that the snowstorm of papers still in the laboratory were all absolutely necessary, and decided against asking outright how close he had in fact gotten. Instead he repeated, "'Not that it matters any longer'?"

Trevelyan sighed. "Yes," he said, "Seward is Locksley. The world knows this now; Seward was arrested for treason the night before last. The constructs do not belong to Seward, however. They belong to the Prime Minister, whom Seward opposes. Seward is *Locksley*, Mr. Carrington, the clue is in the name."

"Then the monsters—the Wellingtons? Those belong to Seward?"

"No."

"There's a third faction?" William guessed.

"Not exactly."

The temptation to shout was growing overwhelming, but William didn't think shouting would succeed in impressing or intimidating the man in front of him. "If you wish me to be any help at all," he said calmly, "perhaps you could spend five minutes laying out what the devil is going on?"

Trevelyan reached for a rag to wipe his hands. "I suppose I have five minutes. And it's probably better you know the truth than act from supposition. You will likely find it entertaining, Mr. Carrington," he went on, mockery creeping into his voice. "It's quite a Celtic ballad, really. The tale of two students. 'Twas the best of times and the worst of times—"

He glanced at William, so obviously expecting an impatient reaction that William resolved to give him nothing of the kind. Trevelyan smiled a little and dropped the theatrical tone into something closer to normalcy. "It was, though, truly. It was the best of times, and a rich young student who had all he could desire strove for one thing more. He wished to make life from death, and he did; he set a torch to the world he knew by creating a monster from dead flesh, for no better reason than to amuse himself. And then—later, in the worst of times—when the children of that monster ran free and destroyed everything in their path, a poor young student who had nothing but the love of one lass lost her. He built a new monster, this one out of metal and gearshifts and clockwork, and turned Britain into a funeral pyre for a woman he loved."

William digested this. "And Locksley?"

"Seward is trying to dismantle the funeral pyre, but can't while the constructs guard it. He needs a weapon that can bring them down." Trevelyan indicated the workroom. "You might consider him my patron."

"I...see," William said, and he did, at least in part.

He heard a slam from the far end of the corridor, and recognized it as the front door opening with some violence. "Elizabeth!" he said, drenched in relief, and turned to welcome the two women back.

It was not, however, Elizabeth and Katarina returned. It was instead Maxwell, whose fingers had frozen on the locks at William's exclamation. "No," he said, turning, his tone flat and dangerous. "Not Elizabeth, just me. Is she not *here?*"

"Er," William said, wondering how he could possibly defend the moment of pique that had allowed this circumstance to occur, "no. She went out with Madame Katarina to—"

"She *what?*" Maxwell's face went the color of chalk. "Elizabeth Barton is wandering about out there? Trevelyan, have you lost your *mind?*" He looked ill—physically nauseated—and more afraid than angry. William felt his stomach settle somewhere in the vicinity of his boots.

Chapter 8

"Who is this Lord Seward?" Elizabeth asked, and got at least part of her answer from the flash of pain that crossed Katarina's face. "A friend?"

"It would be presumptuous of me to call him so," Katarina said after a pause. "He is a philanthropist. He does great good throughout the city using his personal fortune and aims to do more good still with his Parliament seat. Aimed to do more, at least."

"Before he was arrested," Elizabeth said.

"Yes."

"What crime did he commit?"

Katarina did not answer.

The fog had grown lighter but hotter, a searing humid miasma. It had also grown considerably more crowded. Drab shapes appeared out of it without warning, shouldered past Elizabeth, disappeared again. Voices rose and fell, murmuring and calling and weirdly echoing, and over them the clanking pounded out a monotonous rhythm. That sound came from too many directions to originate just from the one factory they had visited. Might there be many factories, on all sides? Katarina stopped at a bakery, a fishmonger's, and a tobacconist's shop, where she purchased nothing and spoke to the proprietors about the weather.

They emerged from the tobacconist's and Katarina stood for a moment on the street, glancing up and down it before choosing a direction and setting off. "I need you to keep quiet for a bit," she said, though Elizabeth had been listening far more than talking all along. Before Elizabeth could agree or argue or defend herself, Katarina turned sharply to the left, leading the way into an alleyway so narrow Elizabeth thought she might suffocate from the closeness of the buildings.

The path wended and twisted like a knotted rope, and Elizabeth followed Katarina down numerous left- and right-hand branchings for what felt like a long time. The clank of the factories faded back into a drone that was almost possible to ignore. The fog seemed to be really thinning as well, for a particularly sharp turn brought Elizabeth suddenly within sight of the alleyway's exit, and she could actually see a little bit of the street upon which it opened. Katarina led her to within a few feet of the exit, then stopped. Elizabeth drew breath for a question, forgetting that she wasn't supposed to talk—and the breath caught in her chest as heavy footsteps shook the street.

She looked up and could see the red-gold head of the construct over the high brick buildings on either side. In a moment she could see the thick legs and feet as the metallic man stomped down the cross-street a few feet away. Katarina waited until the head was out of sight—waited longer until the ground ceased shaking—and then took Elizabeth's hand and drew her out of the alleyway.

The fog was definitely sparser here and the street was wider, smoother, largely free of rubbish piles. "Made it!" Katarina murmured in a tone of satisfaction. "The disadvantage of a regular patrol. I've never been able to determine whether they think we can't count, or—" She glanced over, took note of the blankness on Elizabeth's face, and actually offered an explanation. "Spitalfields, where the warehouse is, is the oldest part of the city and possesses many streets too narrow to allow the constructs to traverse them. They patrol what they can, but they know their surveillance is imperfect, so they are all the more careful to guard the edges of the stews. They patrol with great care the streets just outside, drawing a ring around us, trying to keep us penned in. But they walk a beat to do it, and there's one very specific disadvantage to having a routine like that: people like me can figure out what it is. If that copper had seen us cross into a respectable neighborhood from Spitalfields—dressed like this, no less—there would have been questions. But until they actually build that fence they're talking of, it's easy enough to slip through the alleys when their backs are turned. At least for those of us who can count."

Elizabeth almost understood. They walked through a better neighborhood now, she could tell that. The buildings stood straight-backed rather than bent with age, and horse-drawn carriages clopped along the smooth cobblestone between them. There was plenty of foot-traffic in between the carriages, but no shoving as there had been in the streets of Spitalfields. The voices from this crowd were not so shrill.

Two young gentlemen passed close by them, arm in arm, talking in low tones of something that sounded important. They were dressed more like Maxwell than Trevelyan, so they were not laborers. They might be barristers or office clerks. Discussing business concerns, perhaps. The nearer one glanced at Elizabeth, then looked her up and down in a way that confirmed her suspicion about the significance of breeches. *If we had crossed into a respectable neighborhood dressed like this,* Katarina had said. The other man was staring now too; the two breech-clad women were attracting attention. Katarina would have attracted attention even had Elizabeth not accompanied her. What were they *doing* here?

Katarina, apparently oblivious to the stares, drew the tiny timepiece pendant from her bodice and consulted it. The gentlemen moved on. Katarina leaned against the closest piece of brick wall, folded her arms, and fixed her eyes on a door opposite.

"We are waiting for someone?" Elizabeth asked.

"We are."

"So you can discuss the weather?"

Katarina smiled but did not otherwise reply.

The door in question opened a few minutes later, and a young woman exited, very obviously a lady by her dress and bearing, though something in the drab beige shade of her costume made Elizabeth think not a wealthy one. Katarina pushed off the wall at once and crossed the street to her. "Beg pardon, miss?"

The young lady turned her head. Elizabeth saw fair hair gathered into a knot under the drab hat, large hazel eyes, a plain countenance. She was closer to Katarina's age than Elizabeth's. Her eyes passed over the two of them, and she made as if to walk away. "This is a respectable neighborhood," she said. The heads of respectable people were turning all over the street, watching the breech-clad woman and the gown-clad lady.

"I mean no harm," Katarina said, the guttersnipe whine twining through her words. "Please, miss, just a moment of your time? My friend and me, we're in a bad way, we just need a bit of help ..."

The woman was walking away now, but not quickly, and Katarina's long legs kept pace with her easily. There was no way the woman could outdistance Katarina wearing that gown, Elizabeth thought. It was more like a cage than any garment she had ever seen. It seemed the fashions of the previous century had returned, and with a vengeance, for the top half of the dress pinched close around a waist whose incredible narrowness could have only been achieved by a long corset full of whale-bone, and that savagely tight-laced. The bulging bottom half was so stiff it must be held in place by a metal frame in the shape of a skirt rather than anything soft like a petticoat. Not that the last century's underskirts had been so very comfortable, but this seemed to be worse; the sight of it made Elizabeth feel lightheaded in sympathy with the woman's little puffing breaths. It must be as difficult to sit in such a gown as it was to breathe. It must be as difficult to stand upright, with the weight of all that metal and cloth tugging at the lower back, as it was to take more than a mincing step. The inconveniences inherent in her own simple frock, now drying in the warehouse scullery, seemed tame by comparison.

"—we've nowhere to sleep, and there's a storm coming tonight—"

"Is there?" The woman turned her head at that, eyes meeting Katarina's for a bare instant before she dropped them and resumed the performance. "I am sorry to hear it, but I cannot—"

Katarina had not ceased talking. "—even a penny or two would help."

"Is this person bothering you, miss?" a gentleman's voice asked, raised to be heard about the thundering construct footsteps that shook the street. Elizabeth looked up to see a man dressed as Maxwell had been, hovering before their little tableau.

"No." The woman in the cage-dress likewise raised her voice, though her accent stayed genteel. "No, there's no trouble; I'm sure she was just leaving—"

The tremors in the cobblestones did not subside as they should have, and Elizabeth looked around for the construct. Of course, in this part of the city, with wider streets, it could come closer …

It slammed around the corner as Elizabeth thought the words, standing still for an instant and blocking all view of the cross-street with its bulk. Then it paced deliberately forward, one pounding step at a time. The street shook even after it had stopped moving. Elizabeth jerked her head to look behind her. From the other side came a second one, likewise blocking the way to the cross-street, likewise moving in. Behind each construct filed a line of half a dozen men, wearing black uniforms trimmed with copper and helmets that somehow echoed the lines of the constructs' smooth expressionless heads. They were all carrying muskets.

A voice came from the mouthless head of the first construct, seeming to set the street shaking all on its own. "Miss Temple?"

The woman's face went gray. Katarina's had already drained of color, and the gentleman had disappeared. "Oh my God," Miss Temple whispered. Katarina grabbed Elizabeth's hand and dragged her at a run back into the alleyway.

"Miss Rachel Temple of the *Gazette*?" the voice repeated behind them.

Katarina was pulling her deeper into the alleyway, or trying to, but Elizabeth set her feet and twisted her wrist against Katarina's sweat-slick palm. It was like the moment under Maxwell's coat the night before; she couldn't bear to be shielded and not know, and her promise to avoid anything dangerous was momentarily the farthest thing from her mind. She wrenched free and got most of the way around before Katarina caught hold of her again.

Elizabeth had an instant's plain view of the woman in the drab beige dress, standing framed by two walls of brick, looking up at the construct who had just asked her a question.

"Yes," the woman said hoarsely.

"Miss Temple, we have some questions for you regarding your friend Lord Seward. Please come with us."

There was a moment of absolute stillness. Then Rachel Temple made a mad dash for the alleyway.

Elizabeth knew what was going to happen the instant before it did. She had seen it the night before. But she was still shrieking a denial, struggling against Katarina's grip to run forward and somehow stop it, when her vision was dazzled by blue fireworks and Miss Temple fell in a bloodied pile on the cobblestones. It was a metal frame holding her skirts out, after all.

"Be quiet," Katarina was hissing, "Elizabeth, be *quiet*, you will draw their attention, now come away, come away from this—" But Elizabeth could make no proper sense of the words, could hardly hear them over the sound she only later realized was her own sobbing voice. Katarina tried to pull her into an embrace, less perhaps to comfort than to smother the sobs, but Elizabeth fought blindly against her. She wrenched free a second time by using her nails like some mad cat and ran back through the twisting alleyway and as far from the body on the cobblestones as she could get.

⁓

She stumbled as though through a nightmare, down a path that twisted and turned and offered no way out. Bricks bruised her hands as she tripped and fell and caught herself, and she must have drawn the attention of the constructs after all, for she could hear them keeping pace on the broader streets to either side. She gave a little gasping moan and tried to run faster, but caught her foot and pitched forward, fetching up against an iron fence twice her height and wrought into ornate flower-shapes.

A short distance away stood a building like nothing so much as a great crystal palace out of a fairytale, but there was no time to scale the fence and hide there. She could hear the constructs. They had circled around somehow and were in front of her. They were coming. She could hear them, but why could she not see them? The fog had broken finally. She ought to be able to see them—where were they?

The sound was higher-pitched and faster than she had been expecting, and she still could not see a construct anywhere. A burst of sulfur struck the back of her throat and set her coughing. The noise was now distinctly a clatter rather than a stomp, and even as she thought this, it grew rapidly into a roar. Clouds of black smoke poured down the street in front of her, enveloping her in a brimstone embrace, and she stumbled away from the iron fence. Someone caught her—Katarina caught her, murmuring reassuring and senseless words. Elizabeth watched something enormous and black hurtle into the space between the iron fence and the crystal palace, and her teeth chattered with the force of the jolting ground beneath her feet. The thing rushed along the fence line, seemingly without end.

It squealed to a stop finally, with one last shriek and then a series of shudders. A flash of white smoke split the black clouds and a shrill whistle screamed in reply. Then the worst was over. Elizabeth, peering through the fog and smoke, could see a door in the side of the thing swing open and a man in green uniform descend from it. It was a conveyance. A carriage? Or a great many carriages, strung together? A wave of people poured out of it, and a different wave of people hurried and jostled toward it.

Katarina turned her around and held her, right hand gripping firmly enough that Elizabeth knew she would not be able to escape a third time, but left hand rubbing comforting circles on Elizabeth's back. "It's all right," Katarina said. "It's all right. This one's nothing to worry over. I didn't think to warn you. Of course you've never seen a locomotive."

Elizabeth jerked away from the soothing fingers. "We should have helped her! We should have done *something*. But you ran away!"

"Because there was nothing I could do for her," Katarina said, dark eyes steady, voice unwavering, hand still firm on Elizabeth's arm. "Not one thing. And there are other people I can still help, but only if I'm alive to do it."

"But they shot her—a woman—they killed her in the street, and no one did anything! What could she have possibly done, to deserve—?"

"She was a reporter for the *London Gazette*. She wrote what they did not want to have read. And she was a friend of Lord Seward's. A close friend." Katarina sighed. "She did nothing to deserve it. I didn't say I liked it, Elizabeth! God, I *knew* her, I've known her for two years, we— But there wasn't anything we could do for her. There are things I can fix, but that wasn't one of them." On the other side of the wrought-iron flowers, the crowd went about its business, women in dresses like cages and men in tailored suits with loose trousers and too-long coats, paying no attention to the two wanton women quarrelling and crying in the alleyway. Elizabeth watched the parade of hats and boots and brass-tipped umbrellas, feeling vaguely sick. And then more than vaguely, and then she found herself crouched over and vomiting while Katarina rubbed her back.

"I did that too, after the first day I walked through London," Katarina murmured. "And again the first time I saw someone die. You'd think I'd learn to carry gin on me, but I'm afraid I haven't any."

Elizabeth slumped against the wall, not even pausing to consider how filthy the ground must be. She accepted Katarina's handkerchief to wipe her face, and then she closed her eyes.

She jumped when the great iron monstrosity behind her gave its piercing whistle again. "What—" She cleared her throat. "What did you say that was?"

"A locomotive. A steam-train, actually. The locomotive is the part on the front that makes it go."

"It's not a construct." Elizabeth felt the need for pedantic clarification. "Nor a monster. It's a third thing."

"A third thing," Katarina agreed. "Not dangerous unless you stand in front of it. The first locomotive was demonstrated in, oh, 1830-something, if I recall correctly. It caught on very quickly, and now there's scarcely a hamlet in Britain where the train lines don't run. Every morning gentlemen come up from fine country houses to transact their business in the City. At night, they go home again. Yes, every day," she added, though Elizabeth had not spoken. Her throaty voice was calm, soothing, slightly sing-song in a way that evoked Trevelyan's Welsh accent or a lullaby. Elizabeth felt herself relaxing, almost unwillingly, in response to the easy tone. She closed her eyes again and listened. It sounded like a bedtime story, a fairytale of a fairy kingdom. "There isn't any place in England you can't get to by train in a day or less," Katarina said. "I don't remember a time when it was any other way, but Lord Seward spoke of the journey to London being a long slow one by coach, when his father was a boy. He said that the folk who lived in on his father's estate never left it their whole lives. Now there's hardly a coach to be found—private carriages, yes, but not public coaches—and it's commonplace to take a weekend trip to the seashore or a day trip to London."

She fell silent then, and after a time Elizabeth opened her eyes. Katarina was watching her. "Do you realize," Elizabeth said, mumbling a little, feeling that the words came from a long distance, "that I myself have hardly ever been out of Hartwich?"

"I know," Katarina said. "The old folks do say the railway changed the world as surely as the constructs did. Not so destructively, though. As I said, it can't hurt you unless you stand in front of it."

"Because it can't think for itself," Elizabeth said.

Katarina gave her a surprised look. "The constructs can't either. I thought you realized. It takes three men each to make them go. Each one has a pilot inside driving it, a second managing the fuel, and a third—" She broke off.

"—firing the artillery," Elizabeth said.

"Yes." Katarina's mouth twisted. "Makes it worse, doesn't it?"

"Who are they?"

"Englishmen." Katarina sighed. "Which makes it worst of all."

Behind them, the steam-train shrilled again, and began the ear-piercing business of getting itself underway. There was a long while where the sound of jerking wheels and squealing metal and cumbersome moving weight made conversation impossible. Finally the clickety-clack noise resumed, and the train sped away from them, belching out a last burst of black as it went.

Elizabeth licked her lips and started to speak, but stopped when she heard a child's voice raised. Craning around, she made him out, standing on the other side of the gate, on the other side of the track where the train had sat, in front of the crystal palace. He was waving a folded paper and chanting in a voice nearly as shrill as the train whistle, "Lord Seward arrested for treason! Read about it in *The Times!*"

A gentleman handed the boy a coin and took a paper. The crowd that had arrived by steam-train had now mostly streamed out of the street and onward to whatever business brought them to London. In the aftermath of their departure, the people who remained were so comparatively few that true silence might as well have descended.

"Seward plotting to bring down Parliament! Read about it in *The Times!*"

Elizabeth turned back to Katarina, who was still crouched and watching her. Her eyes had an odd luminous quality in the shadows. Elizabeth took a breath. "Was Lord Seward really going to bring down the House of Parliament? Like…like Guy Fawkes?"

"Not exactly like Guy Fawkes," Katarina said, but her tone had the quality of "yes" rather than "no."

"What good would that have done, if he had succeeded? Would it have fixed—" Elizabeth gestured. "—all this?"

"No," Katarina said, sighing. "In the short term, it probably would have made things worse. But no one can dislodge this government from power, you see. The constructs work for the Prime Minister, enforce his authority, and, well, you saw what happens to those who oppose him. If we could ease his grip on the country's throat, then the reformers would have a fighting chance to change the laws that need changing. They could speak, write, agitate, pressure Members of Parliament, and not fear reprisal."

Elizabeth nodded. "'We.' So you are part of Lord Seward's...conspiracy? You and Mr. Maxwell and Mr. Trevelyan."

"Yes." Katarina watched her. "Are you going to give me away, Miss Elizabeth?" She didn't seem to find it likely, but there was a certain tension in her posture as she asked the question. "Throw your lot in with—" She gestured at the train and the paper-boy, then back down the alley. "—them?"

"No," Elizabeth answered slowly. "But...but I need to understand it, and I don't. You need to tell me more about Lord Seward. And all the rest of it."

"I will," Katarina promised. "There's one more place we need to go first, and then we'll talk."

Chapter 9

Their last visit was to a part of London that proved surprisingly pleasant—fine houses, wide streets, even a bit of green in the form of a park. At one end of the park rose a marble arch, the entrance to something a signpost proclaimed to be the Zoological Gardens. The hollow beneath the arch was comfortably large, with pillars spaced around it, and the sound of machinery had muted back into a drone. *One would never know Spitalfields was half a mile away,* Elizabeth reflected, and felt sick at the thought.

A cluster of men in neat suits, plus two women in cage-dresses, stood before the arch. Each of them held a notebook and a pencil, and they were engaged in calling questions to a young man with curly dark hair and overalls embroidered with the words *LONDON ZOO.*

"...can assure you ours is safe in his cage where he belongs," the young man said in cheerful Cockney tones as Katarina and Elizabeth reached the back of the crowd. "What happened last night is no failure of the London Zoo."

"Do you have any idea where Seward got the monsters that terrorized the East End?" one of the women asked.

"Haven't a notion, ma'am. They do say he's a dreadful wicked man, but it wasn't from here he got his monsters. And I'd be pleased to prove it to you. Step right this way, and you can see the Wellie in his cage. On the house, just this once, for members of the Empire's news-agents only. Right down that path there, sir, ma'am, and turn to the left." He waited until the last of them had filed past them before he looked over to where Elizabeth and her guide still stood. " 'Afternoon, Madame Katarina," he said then. "Surprised to see you here."

"Missed me?" Katarina asked, turning a dazzling smile upon him as she crossed the lawn.

He chuckled. "Every day, love. But it's not every day I have the pleasure of seeing you, even if I am missing you. Long walk from the Shoreditch. Why today?"

"This is Elizabeth," Katarina said. "She's just joined us, up from the country. Don't suppose you could let us slip in and have a peek at the animals?"

He choked on the chuckle. "In the middle of the afternoon? Beg pardon, sweetheart," he added to Elizabeth. "Bill Ellis, at your service. Come back when you've a night off, and I'll—"

"Oh, come," Katarina coaxed, "just one peek? You're taking that lot to the monster house, aren't you? Can't we tag along just that far?"

"I …" Ellis looked at the finely dressed crowd, which had nearly reached the bend in the path, and then snatched a glance over his other shoulder. Elizabeth followed his eyes to where a sour-faced old crone sat, hemmed in on all sides by the metal of a small enclosure with a window. She was taking the shillings of a pair of school-aged children and seemed to be lecturing them against misbehavior as she did so. "Oh, all right, Meacham's not looking. Come on, now. Quiet, or you'll get me the sack." He hustled Katarina and Elizabeth under the arch, keeping his body between them and the curdled-looking woman.

It was easier to breathe than it had been all day, Elizabeth reflected. Perhaps the grass and trees unclenched the iron fist that had been forming around her insides. Katarina had taken Ellis' right arm, so Elizabeth took his left, waiting for Katarina to say something about storms.

Beyond the arch, the path was lined with small buildings formed of brick and iron bars, and the first sight of them clenched the fist tight again before Elizabeth realized what she was looking at and what this place must be. She had heard of the Tower Menagerie, of course, but she had never visited it, and this was clearly a much larger establishment. "Bengal tiger," Mr. Ellis murmured, directing Elizabeth's attention to a cage with a nod. "Just about the thrillingest thing we have here." The great striped beast lifted its head as they passed, fixing Elizabeth with its tawny eyes, then got to its feet in one smooth movement and came to the bars to investigate. Elizabeth found herself wanting both to sink her fingers into its thick fur and to retreat as expeditiously as possible. Fortunately, Mr. Ellis and Katarina were already walking on, so she did not have to choose.

They passed an equally fearsome lion from Africa and a dromedary from the Arabian deserts, and Katarina still did not say anything about the weather. As they reached the bend in the path, Ellis detached her hand from his arm with an apologetic half-smile. "Got my job to do," he said and strode around to face the well-dressed crowd he had been shepherding. "So you can see it for yourself, ladies and gents, and I do hope as how you'll tell your readers there's nothing for them to fear from the London Zoo. Got our Wellie locked up tight where he can make no trouble, safe as houses." The monster house sat a little ways away from the rest of the cages, surrounded by white columns like a Grecian temple. "The other beasts don't care for the Wellington," Mr. Ellis explained. "So we have to keep him separate. We've only got the one, can't have no more, or they fight. Or worse yet, they plot together, and we here at the Zoo wouldn't risk the safety of our guests. So there's only the one, and him safe behind a wall and a moat, as you can plainly see for yourself. Couldn't get out even if he could bend the bars, which he can't do neither. Right then, when you've seen all you like, I'm to invite you to the refreshment area. Our own Mr. Chelton will be there to meet you, him that runs the office part of the Zoo, and he'll be pleased to answer any other questions you might have. Oh, it was my pleasure, ma'am, and thank *you* kindly for setting the record straight about us here. Thank you, sir. Ma'am. A good day to you, sir...Have a peep," he added in an undertone to Elizabeth as the crowd filtered away, "and then the both of you better cut back to the Shoreditch before someone here notices you never bought tickets."

Elizabeth hesitated.

"It's a'right," Ellis reassured her. "It's Gospel truth what I said, he can't hurt you. You go right up to the wall and have a good look."

Elizabeth went up to the brick wall. It came about to her waist, and she could rest her hands comfortably against it. But the other side dropped down sharply into a pit twelve feet deep—a moat, as Ellis had said. On the other side of the moat rose an island upon which the white stone monster house sat, surrounded by Grecian columns and iron bars. Behind the bars stood a creature with a dead face, looking back at her.

She'd had no opportunity for careful examination the night before. Seen in daylight rather than in lightning flashes, the face was less fearsome, though no less repulsive. Elizabeth shuddered at the overlong limbs, the slack and drooping skin, the thrust-forward head, the nonsensically moving lips. But the longer she studied the face, the more she thought she could discern an expression, and the more the expression looked to her like sorrow. She could not help but remember how one of them had tried to drag another out from under the feet of a construct.

"It doesn't look so fearful," she murmured.

"I expect you're too young to remember," the keeper said, "a little slip of a girl like you, but I mind the days when they were the terror of the countryside. No joke, they weren't then. And it wouldn't have been a joke if that Robert Locksley had let his whole pack loose on us, either.

Lucky he was caught before he could." Ellis shivered a little, not an act. "I mind those days," he said. "They were awful."

"They were," Katarina said softly. "I remember them too."

"Before Her Majesty sent the constructs to save us," Ellis said.

Katarina murmured an agreement. And did not say anything about storms.

⁊

"You wanted me to see the monster," Elizabeth said. "That's why we went to the zoo." Katarina looked up, met her eyes, and nodded.

They were back within the alleyways and courtyards of Spitalfields, not far from the warehouse, or so Katarina said at least, and Elizabeth had no reason to doubt her word, though she could not tell for herself. The little watch pendent that hung around Katarina's neck proclaimed that it was now late afternoon. Elizabeth similarly was obliged to take the timepiece's word for it, having no way to verify for herself. It was not possible to tell the time from a sun one could not see—the fog had thickened again the closer they got to the stews—and any internal instinct Elizabeth might possess was badly confused. She had been awake nearly a day and a night by now and was thoroughly undecided as to whether she ought to have been eating breakfast or dinner.

It was not until she found herself phrasing it that way in her thoughts that Elizabeth realized she was hungry, despite the periodic clenching in her middle. Small wonder, really. She'd had nothing but a few mouthfuls of watery tea since dining with her family some…she tried to work out how long ago. Twelve hours? Seventy years and twelve hours? She felt a momentary return of the hysterical desire to laugh mingle with the raspy air tormenting the back of her throat. Now that she was thinking about it, rather than having all her attention focused on outside things that were bizarre or horrific or both, she found that her legs had begun to tremble with weariness and the bottoms of her feet felt bruised with standing on cobblestone.

Katarina had glanced over at her as those thoughts occurred, and seemed to read them. "Suppose we get a bite to eat on our way home." She changed direction abruptly, and Elizabeth almost stumbled trying to keep up with her. "There's a fish and chips shop this way."

The newspaper-wrapped cone Katarina put into her hands was slick with grease, and the breaded and fried contents glistened like the surface of the Thames, but Elizabeth was too hungry to care. She did wonder how and where they were to eat the food it contained, before Katarina answered the unasked questions by picking a chip out of her cone with her fingers. It seemed one ate fish and chips without the aid of knife or fork. While walking.

Katarina ate neatly, with no overt enjoyment but no apparent disgust. Elizabeth watched her sideways, tasting the fish and the potatoes and the lard they had been fried in and the bitterness of the air. She turned the events of the morning over in her mind as she chewed and slowly came to a realization. "You wanted me to see the monster," she said, and Katarina admitted that this was so.

Elizabeth took another chip from the wrapping and considered further. "You wanted me to see all of this," she said. "That's why you let me come with you."

Katarina gave her another long look from her luminous eyes. "Yes."

"So that I would understand why you want to bring it all down?"

"In part, yes."

"I could have betrayed you to the authorities."

"You could have," Katarina agreed, "but I didn't think you would."

"How can you know what to think?" Elizabeth demanded. "You don't know anything about me!"

Katarina only smiled and took another chip.

Elizabeth returned her attention to the fish. After a long while, she went on, "You said 'in part.' Why else?"

"Because it hasn't happened yet," Katarina said, in a voice gone suddenly dark with passion. "I am ..." Her mouth twisted a little, and she went on with a deliberately theatrical wave of one hand. "I am the Spirit of Christmas Yet To Come, and these are the shadows of things that *may* be, only. Men's courses will foreshadow certain ends, but if those courses be departed from, the ends must change...But you have no idea what I am quoting, do you? That tale must not be quite as old as I thought it was...Never mind."

"You think I can prevent this happening?" Elizabeth said, stopping. "You think *I* can? My—my life isn't— You have no idea how different my life is from yours. I'm not even permitted to walk unaccompanied through— I'm not like you!"

"No," Katarina said, "you're not. I'm the natural daughter of an opera singer. I grew up in poverty and disgrace and I can't do better than sing in a music hall. I've barely a coin to my name and no way to make anyone listen to me. You're a gentleman's daughter, you'll be a gentleman's wife, you live in a time when it hasn't happened yet, and you have a pocket watch like Max's. Do you *truly* think you are powerless, compared to me?"

The air hung hot and heavy between them. Finally Elizabeth looked down at the last soggy piece of fish in its soaked newspaper wrapping. "Well," she said. "When you put it that way …" She looked back up. "You'll have to tell me everything. I have to know what happened…what will happen."

Katarina nodded, and they started walking again. "Ask me whatever you like."

"Is it a…a cipher, what you've been saying about a storm coming tonight? What does it mean?"

Katarina smiled. "It is a message, but not a cipher. It *is* going to storm tonight." That was true enough; Elizabeth could feel the humid fog press against her lungs. "Mr. Trevelyan has invented a device to be used against the constructs, and it needs a lightning storm to be tested. Our friends will be providing distractions in other parts of the city while the test proceeds."

"Then you'll have a weapon, is that it? The Prime Minister will still have the constructs, but you'll have something just as good."

"Then we'll have *a* weapon," Katarina said. "If it works, we can move on to the step of getting someone to create many of them. *Then* the field will be level."

"Oh." Elizabeth took a breath. "This was all Lord Seward's idea?"

"Lord Seward is behind it, yes." Katarina twisted the newspaper between her hands. "The problem with a venture of this kind is financing it. Lord Seward is a rich man—family money of course, and richer all the time for investing it in industry. Only someone of his wealth and position could have diverted the funds we needed. He pays the wages and other bills of a non-existent factory, and he hired Trevelyan to use that money to build him a weapon. He could have found no one better," she added. "Trevelyan…lives for this cause. No one hates the constructs or their creators more than he. And he's truly a genius. Seward is another one, in a different way. This was far from his lordship's only iron in the fire. I don't know what they all were, even. He *did* have an empire of…Well. He had many irons in many fires, let's just leave it there. It was one of the others that brought him down—I don't know which, and the newspapers haven't yet said—and it doesn't matter. What does matter is that…that I believe he would have founded his 'criminal empire' even if Max hadn't shown up on his doorstep and told him what was destined to happen. He would have tried to bring it all down either way, and I think Max knew that. I think that's why Max stayed to see it through with us. Because he thinks we can win."

Elizabeth took another breath. "But now Lord Seward has been arrested."

The skin around Katarina's eyes tightened in a wince as they had the night before. "Yes." She took a breath of her own. "It makes it harder," she said after a pause, "but we were prepared for the possibility that we might have to flee London anyway, depending how the test goes tonight. It's simply more likely now."

Elizabeth found that she was twisting her newspaper cone also, digging her fingers into it so fiercely her knuckles were white. She unclenched them, trying to think what else she should ask. "Where did the constructs come from?"

Katarina sighed, and looked off into the distance. "They were created with a good purpose, that's the hell— the worst of it. They *were* created to protect us from the monsters. They *did* protect us. Mr. Ellis wasn't exaggerating; I remember when the monsters terrorized the countryside to the west. I remember when the constructs came to us from London. They seemed like angels come to deliver us from harm. They *did* deliver us from harm. It was only later that other uses were found for them." She smiled wryly. "It is as if we bred Bengal tigers to exterminate...well, not rats. Wolves, perhaps. Now the wolves are gone, and we are still riding the tigers."

"And what of the wolves? The monsters, I mean. Where did they come from?"

"A brilliant young student, a Genevese. A hundred years ago, he set himself to discover a means by which dead flesh could be brought to life."

Elizabeth's skin prickled. "He raised a man from the dead?"

"Worse," Katarina said. "He acquired freshly deceased body parts and stitched them together, making one monster out of many men. Then he infused that creature with life."

Elizabeth swallowed, thinking of the stitches and the clothes that had reminded her of burial garments.

"Later, he brought the creature to England. He made himself a laboratory on the smallest island off the Orkneys—an isolated place, far away from everything—as far north as one can get and still be on British soil. There he created a female creature, to be the wife and the companion of his monster. And they...were fruitful, and multiplied, and their offspring became a terror to the Scottish Highlands. They broke into homes, took food...committed outrages upon women... killed any who tried to thwart them. The King sent soldiers. The soldiers did not eradicate the problem, but they did succeed in scaring the monsters farther north, out of civilized areas, and they brought one monster back as a captive.

"This was in 1800. The Genevese was dead by then, but some of his notes had been entrusted to a collaborator in London and were found. With the living creature and the notes, naturalists working for the Royal Academy of Sciences learned to do what the Genevese had done. To create full-grown creatures in the likeness of the first. They created a great many, and when England feared Napoleon's invasion—"

"Katarina!"

The shout came from behind them—a woman's voice, choked. Katarina spun around, hand dropping to her hip pocket. As soon as she saw the woman running toward them from the cross-street, she relaxed. "Annie! What in the world—"

The woman was older than Katarina, face lined and fair hair going gray. She wore a skirt and blouse and cap, dingy but modest, and on her face was an expression that made Katarina go very still. Elizabeth could almost feel the air shift as the older woman drew into herself. "What's happened?" Katarina asked quietly.

"Meg," Annie croaked, coughing, stumbling to a halt. "It's Meg. I was just coming to the warehouse to look for you—"

Katarina's voice was still quiet and steady. "What's happened to Meg?"

"That woman," Annie said. "That old bitch of a—" She took a desperate wheezing breath, and Katarina put a hand on her arm, to steady her or comfort her or both. "I was gone because I was *working*. She knew that. She knew. I was behind on the rent, but I'd gotten work, I'd gotten—" Another gulping breath. "—a chance to work on some wedding clothes wanted in a great rush. I've been at the milliner's warehouse these three days. They didn't let us leave, you know how it is, Katarina, you know." Katarina nodded, thumb smoothing the woman's threadbare sleeve, everything else about her motionless and held ready. "She knew it, too, old Martha Hewitt. I was working, and Meg was fine alone a day or two, and I have the money, I've come back with the—" She started to sob again.

Elizabeth saw Katarina's hand tighten into a fist, saw Katarina carefully unclench it and return it to the job of stroking the sleeve. "What's Martha Hewitt done, Annie? Where's Meg?"

"Murchinson's," Annie choked through her tears. "Martha sold her."

Katarina shut her eyes for a moment.

"—because I'd left her—I *didn't*, Katarina, I *wouldn't*, not like that—"

"Of course you didn't," Katarina murmured to her. "Of course you wouldn't."

"I have rent money now, but what good—" Annie choked back a sob.

"How long ago?" Katarina asked her. "You were only gone three days, is that what you said? Meg can't have been at Murchinson's very long."

"This morning," Annie said. "Half a day, not long at all. That's why I was coming to look for you. That man you go about with sometimes, the white-haired gent. I thought maybe he could go, maybe they'd listen to him—"

"Yes." Katarina looked up and down the street, brows drawn in thought. "I'll ask him. He'll go, I'm sure he will. If he gets there before sundown, it will be easy for them to believe it was a mistake or a malicious joke, and likely they'd just as soon have the money for her anyhow."

"Here." Annie started fumbling in her pockets. "Take it."

"No, no, there won't be any need of that. He has money. You'll need it to find better rooms for you and Meg when we've got her safe back to you."

"But just in case," Annie said. "I don't want him to think I can't take care of her, because I *can*, don't you see? I don't want him to think any different. Take it. Take some of it, at least."

"All right," Katarina soothed her. "All right. I'll take…half, how's that? We'll only use it if we need to, and we'll give you back anything we don't need. I'll go and find Max right now." She turned and scanned the buildings looming over them. "I oughtn't take you back to the warehouse with me, though. It's…not a good day for it. Are any of your neighbors more human than that old crone? Can you stay with one of them?"

Annie's lips trembled. "Not one of them stopped her."

"Then to hell with them." Katarina took her by the arm again and turned her gently about. "I'll take you to a place where I have friends."

"Don't worry about me. Just go and—"

"I shall." Katarina was guiding the woman back the way they had come. With a jerk of her chin, she gestured for Elizabeth to follow. "The place I'm thinking of is barely a step out of my way. I'm losing no time taking you there, and I need to know you're somewhere safe, you and that money you need to care for your daughter."

The place Katarina had in mind proved to be the first courtyard in which they had stopped that morning. So they were very close indeed to Trevelyan's warehouse, though Elizabeth still could not have found it on her own. Katarina instructed her to wait in the courtyard while she took Annie into one of the domiciles. Elizabeth thought it was the one belonging to the Thompsons, so Mrs. Thompson must be home from her work. Katarina reappeared five minutes later, without Annie and without any gentleness at all on her face.

"Come. Hurry." She led the way at a rapid walk in the direction Elizabeth could only assume was Trevelyan's warehouse. Once out of the courtyard, Katarina's face grew even grimmer. "I'd kill that old bizzom, except it wouldn't do anyone any good now."

"She ..." Elizabeth swallowed. "She...sold a child?"

"Miss Elizabeth," Katarina said, "that happens in your time too. Families with too many mouths to feed sell their extra children to chimney sweeps. Or to whorehouses. Or to other places where the children may starve more slowly than they would at home. This is nothing *new*. Murchinson and Sons have merely...formalized the arrangement."

Elizabeth didn't say anything. After a moment, Katarina sighed between her teeth and seemed to make an effort to reign in her temper. "I'm sorry. It's only that I know some people who grew up there, members of Seward's conspiracy, as it happens. Few of Murchinson's children live to adulthood, and those who do are...marked by it. The place is worse than the workhouses, as there's no one even pretending to keep watch over what goes on behind its walls."

"What does go on there?" Elizabeth ventured after a pause.

"A child who cannot be cared for or who has been found abandoned may be brought to the Murchinson orphanage. Murchinson's gives a small consideration to the one who brings the child, then undertakes to care for it." Katarina almost spat the last. "Sounds lovely, doesn't it? But children's clever fingers are big enough to make matches, and if they are yours, living in your orphanage, well, you need not pay them even a pittance, and that increases profits significantly. A one-time payment to acquire the child in the first place is much more economical. And the fact that they *pay* for the children has led to some, shall we say, irregularities in the procurement of said children, which neither Murchinson's nor the bobbies seem to find it worth their while to investigate. No one would have checked Martha's assertion that Annie had abandoned the child. And indeed, Annie had been gone three days. That it was working a seamstress' job for rent money...well, what does that matter?"

"We have to stop this," Elizabeth said.

"We will. This one we *can* do something about."

"Not just this one thing. All of it. We have to stop it."

Katarina turned to meet her eyes again. "Yes. We do." She half-smiled, and Elizabeth thought it was genuine, though it did not do anything to mitigate the fierceness in her eyes. "I am pleased you see it that way. Welcome to the resistance, Miss Elizabeth."

Interlude

Even as a child, Genevieve Ramsey had been ill-suited to life in a small Devonshire village. Sir Charles Buford once compared her to an exotic bird trying to nest among wrens and swallows, a spot of color among all the grays and browns. As Sir Charles had spent half his life in South Africa and was therefore the only person in the vicinity of Tavisford with firsthand knowledge of exotic birds, Genevieve's neighbors presumed the comparison to be apt. He missed the point when he spoke of color, however. It would have been more accurate to say she was an exotic songbird attempting to blend into a chorus of starlings.

Her father, a widowed country doctor with a threadbare practice, could never have managed to afford the kind of training her voice called for, but Sir Charles knew people who knew people. He did not offer to pay the fees himself—he had too much respect for the doctor's pride—but he arranged for an audition, and Genevieve won a scholarship and departed to study on the Continent. Tavisford did not see her face for years thereafter, though she wrote often to her father and each letter caused quite a nine-days' wonder in the village. She climbed as high as the La Scala opera house in Milan the year before the doctor died, and her father managed one trip abroad to hear her. On the journey home, he contracted the illness that eventually turned to pneumonia and carried him off.

Two years later, Genevieve retired abruptly from the stage and returned to Tavisford heavy with child. She claimed marriage to a now-deceased foreign nobleman and the name "Rasmirov," but the tongues clacked behind her back even so. Her savings were enough for the purchase of a small cottage, and Sir Charles advised her on the investment of the rest. He would have gladly been of more service to her, but she would take no more from him than his advice. At first she tried to supplement her tiny income with music lessons, but when it became apparent that no one from Tavisford would entrust their daughters to her care, she swallowed her pride and took in sewing.

Her thirteen-year-old daughter could not remember a time when she had not known all this, most of it from her mother's lips, the rest from the background murmur of village gossip. She had never asked her mother to confirm or deny the more uncharitable parts of the gossip for the simple reason that Genevieve would have answered her honestly, and in lieu of an honest answer there was still the chance that he had married her, that he had been a nobleman, that he had loved her, that he had not in fact been some gypsy stagehand. By thirteen, Katherine was no longer certain she believed in the fairytale of the handsome Russian lord, but she was more comfortable with the uncertainty than she would have been with banishing it.

She was still going by "Katherine" then. Her mother called her "Katarina," but everyone else said "Katherine," and she introduced herself that way, as though a foreign *name* were the reason she, too, failed to blend into the grays and browns, as though fitting into Tavisford were not an utterly lost cause. In later years, she would come to embrace her exotic appearance, exaggerating it with every means at her disposal, cultivating every possible alluring mannerism, bartering foreign charm for the things she needed, but in 1876, the year the constructs came to save Tavisford from the monsters on the moor, she was still calling herself Katherine and still trying to pretend she was as Devonshire as the rest of them.

She was outside the stockade on that cold March morning, making the journey to the train station to retrieve a package for her mother. She knew Genevieve didn't like to let her go alone, but her mother prided herself on being a rational and well-educated woman, and the Wellingtons had never once attacked during the day or when they lacked fog to use as cover. It was therefore safe for Katherine to make the short journey on her own, and irrational to dissuade her.

Katherine had been nine when the walls went up and so remembered the days before them, when farms stretched green under the Devon sky and anyone able to read the weather could cross the moor in perfect safety—but she increasingly felt as though she were remembering a story someone had told her rather than a life she had lived herself. Now no one left the Tavisford stockade after dark for any reason. And most Tavisford adults, hard at work in the factory that had grown up to take the place of the monster-ruined farmland, had no reason to leave during the day either. The older Katherine grew, the more the walls of the stockade oppressed her, like the fashion for increasingly tight-laced corsets. Sometimes she felt like one of the boilers in the factory, heated from all sides until steam hissed under her skin in search of any means of escape. She practiced piano and sang under her mother's tutelage and helped with the sewing, and wanted all the time to scream loud and long. Or run somewhere. Anywhere.

Surely, *surely* the stockade was not necessary the way it had been in 1872? Katherine remembered the year the tin-mine Wellingtons had broken their bonds—she remembered that first night sheltering in Buford Hall, the screams of men under the surgeon's knife, blood on her mother's hands and apron, Sir Charles shouting orders as though back on a South African ranch—and she acknowledged the building of the stockade had been necessary then. But since 1874? Since Sir Charles liquidated half of the Buford family heirlooms to finance the building of the factory?

The factory required enormous quantities of peat, and between the scars of large-scale peat cutting on the moor and the huge clouds of smoke belched into the air, the monsters seemed to find the area around Tavisford a less attractive place to raid. Once Tavisford came to display the typical disadvantages of a city—dead farmland and a military presence—the monsters ceased raiding entirely, shifting their efforts elsewhere. So why could precautions not be relaxed a little?

Katherine arrived the station, clean and empty as it always was. The trains ran again now, but very few people dared to travel. She greeted the station master politely, acquired her mother's parcel of needles, bade the station master an equally polite goodbye, and started for home. The road between the station and the stockade stretched out as empty as it always did. Sometimes men came from London to inspect the factory or visit with Sir Charles, but never very many or very often.

Katherine rounded a bend in the road—and froze as brush rustled ahead.

There had never been a Wellington attack in broad daylight, on a clear day. Never once.

Never before.

If there were Wellingtons up ahead, she was lost. They could outrun her; they could track her if she tried to hide. The safety of the stockade might as well have been a hundred miles away. Katherine eased one step back, trying to blend into the brown-gray of a tree trunk, too frightened to even think of the irony.

It wasn't a Wellington.

The man who stepped onto the road was dressed like a Londoner, in a sleek suit with a top hat and gloves. Despite his gray hair, the way he moved made Katherine think him younger than her mother. He glanced perfunctorily right and left—unlike a Wellington, he did not have the perception required to distinguish her from the tree trunk—

took a moment to dust off his clothing, and then set off at a purposeful pace in the direction of the factory's belching smokestack.

Sometimes men came from London to inspect the factory and talk with Sir Charles. They wore suits like this gentleman; they carried valises. They came by train, and usually Sir Charles sent Toby with the dog-cart to meet them at the station, but sometimes they walked. This man was walking toward the factory as though he had come by train.

But he hadn't.

Every nerve prickling, Katherine followed him.

She watched from a distance as he walked up to the factory gates, watched him introduce himself to the guards, watched them peruse the letter he handed over. They opened the gates at once and escorted him within, so the letter must be in order, but…but…

Katherine ran for Buford Hall.

❧

"**H**e had an explosive," Sir Charles told her later, gravely. "He was stopped barely in time. Without your warning, we would have reached him too late. He escaped arrest—but that's no matter. He ran off onto the moor, so he won't live out the night. We've doubled the guard force around the factory. All will be well. Thanks to you, my brave girl."

Her mother took Sir Charles aside to ask him something in a voice too low for Katherine to make out.

"No," Sir Charles said at once. "Not possible. Unthinkable. A man could never turn against his own kind and aid those savage creatures. It is corporate espionage, nothing worse."

"You once said it would be unthinkable for the Wellingtons to turn against us," Genevieve persisted. "Against we who bred and reared them—?"

"I remember saying that." Sir Charles looked troubled. "Well… perhaps I will send Toby to collect the other tenants and have you all sleep inside Buford Hall, just for the next few days. Just in case."

It was not the first time Katherine had slept on a pallet in the old disused ballroom of the Hall. It was quieter now than it had been in those early days of Wellington attacks. Then she had lain wakeful, staring through diamond panes of glass that blurred and warped the twinkling lights outside—the fires on the moor and in the village. Now she stared through the same glass, but there was nothing to see but darkness.

A few mornings later, Katherine stood with her mother just outside the stockade, surrounded by Tavisford factory workers who chuckled with delight at their accomplishment and with relief at finally being permitted to speak of it. Before them on the moor, the thing Sir Charles called a *construct* strode and lunged and showed what it could do.

It was piloted by men inside, Katherine knew that. One of them had stood before the crowd, upright and splendid in his scarlet coat, and had spoken a few words about Queen and country before disappearing through the tall, wide doors of the factory. But even *knowing* he was inside it, *knowing* his hands on a lever were making its knees lift and its arms swing, Katherine could not help but think of the construct as alive. It looked like a man, after all—like a twenty-foot-tall man covered in armor, like one of the Tudor knights in the exquisitely illustrated book in the Buford Hall library. Katherine had fallen hopelessly in love with the book, and had learned the proper names for every piece of armor that protected a knight from buffets in the joust, and she could see them all here. Greaves covered legs thick as tree-trunks. Shining rivets held a breastplate bolted in place. The head had only eyes, no ears or mouth or nose, and so was as closed and anonymous as a visored helm. The whole ensemble shone copper instead of silver, liquid fire against the bright blue sky—but it could still be a knight, couldn't it? Hadn't King Arthur had a Red Knight? Only the creature's arms ruined the illusion of its humanity. No gauntlets covered five-fingered hands. Instead, the arms ended in mouths like those of a cannon, which Sir Charles explained could shoot musket balls of many sizes.

The construct was too large to move fast or gracefully, but it did move steadily and without stumbling on the boggy ground. The crowd outside the village stockade applauded, and the construct gave them a slight but definite bow. Then it turned and pointed with a misshapen cannon-mouthed arm back to the factory.

The crowd turned in time to see a second construct march from between the high doors. And then a third. And then a fourth, a fifth, a sixth. The first half-dozen constructs in Britain were piloted by men who had been working out drills within doors for eighteen months, and it took them very little time to put their theoretical knowledge to practical use. They pranced about the moor before the village gates like show horses on parade. Briefly, that morning, playing to their audience; then seriously and for hours each day thereafter.

On the sixth night after the demonstration before the factory, Katherine lay long awake on her pallet in the Buford Hall ballroom, staring at the swirling patterns in the darkness overhead and listening to the others in the room snore and cough. After she heard the enormous old clock in the main hall strike midnight, she gave up on sleep and rose quietly to her feet. She slipped between the other pallets scattered over the ballroom floor and let herself out into the chilly corridor.

A draft whooshed down the hall and up her legs, bare under her nightdress and dressing-gown. The more nights she spent in this house, the more she understood the old ghost stories; it was draftier than any cottage on the moor. She shivered with the sudden chill, but did not retreat to her bed. There ought to be a candle and lucifers on the table just to her left—and there were. She got the candle lit and headed down the creaking old passage for the library. She would cuddle in a chair there and read something until she felt sleepy. Perhaps she would have a hunt for the King Arthur book, and see if there had been a Red Knight after all.

But someone was in the library before her. Two figures, only just visible by the light of the banked fire, turned from the window as she pushed the door open. After a moment, she recognized the larger one as Sir Charles.

"Katarina?" said her mother's voice from the shadows by Sir Charles' side. "What are you doing here? Put out your candle."

Katherine blew it out. "Is something happening?" she asked.

"Not yet," Sir Charles said.

"But something will?" Katherine felt her way through the room and to the window. A woolly blanket of fog lay over the moor, stretching cold fingers almost to the gates of Buford Hall. There was only the barest sliver of a moon, and not one scrap of light shone from village abode or the factory. Every inhabitant of Tavisford was to all appearances snug in bed. Even the constructs stood quiescent inside the factory gates, looking less like sentries than like men asleep on their feet.

"What's happening?" she asked again.

"Nothing yet," Sir Charles said, "but wouldn't it be a perfect night for the Wellies to try to climb the stockade and get at the constructs?"

Katherine stared at him, trying to make out his face in the darkness. "But they can't. They know they can't. They're not *stupid*. I thought that was the point."

"Perhaps they might have tried a bit of sabotage night before last," Sir Charles offered blandly, "and perhaps we might have acted as though we hadn't noticed."

Katherine stared into the blackness beyond the diamond-pane window. She thought she saw one of the reaching fingers of the fog thicken slightly, but perhaps it was only fancy. Then another seemed to swell briefly, and subside into its original shape. Nothing further happened for a long while, and she had just decided that her tired mind and overstrained eyes must be inventing things, when the fog very definitely distorted its shape, oozing and distending as though it had come to life and meant to swallow in one gulp all of Buford Hall and Buford Factory.

Shafts of blue-white light shattered the darkness as the constructs' eyes flared alight, and the Wellingtons skidded to a stop in the act of bursting from the fog. Pinioned by the beams of light, the advantage of their cat-eyes was negated: they could not see beyond the dazzling circle, and the constructs had light by which to see them plainly. Blue fire burst in flashes from the constructs' arms. A relentless rattling pounded at Katherine's ears. Six of the monsters dropped where they stood.

"What—" Katherine rubbed at her ears; the rapid musket-fire hadn't yet stopped, and it seemed to be burrowing inside her head. "What *is* that? How can a musket possibly fire like that?"

"Because it's not actually a musket, my dear," Sir Charles said, peering out at the fight below. "It's something quite new. An American named Gatling came up with the original design, and a team from the University of London improved upon it. Brilliant."

The other monsters had scattered, were sprinting back toward the fog-bank. The constructs' arms swept through the air, following their paths, and the rattling blue fire dropped another half dozen. The remainder zigzagged faster than the arms could move, and made it to the lip of the fog, past the point where the blue light shone.

The constructs started in pursuit with deliberate, jerking strides, clouds of steam puffing around their heads like breath in the cold March air. Each seemed to be dragging a wagon of some sort behind it, heaped with piles of something Katherine could not see well enough to identify.

"Fuel," Sir Charles explained, seeing her squint at it. "We don't know long the chase will take. There's a new design being tested now, and if it works, the next generation of these things will run more efficiently and not need the provision train."

The constructs seemed to have gotten the feel of the moor, for they were moving faster, eating up ground with huge, thunderous strides. Their blue light advanced onto the moor, dwindling into far-off halos, periodically augmented by flashes of gunfire like heat lightning. Buford Hall was awake now, light shining from windows onto the grounds, people shouting and scurrying and calling questions in the corridors outside the library door, but neither Sir Charles nor Katherine's mother turned from the window

"You have done it," Genevieve Rasmirov said, in a voice low and choked with emotion. "You have saved us."

"Others, my dear madam, not me," Sir Charles replied. "I merely offered what small assistance I could with capital and raw materials. I haven't the brains to come up with something like this, but thank heaven that young fellow in London did. Thank heaven for the modern age."

Thank heaven indeed, Katherine thought, watching the lightning flash on the moor. She felt as though someone had cut through her corset-strings. The constructs would scare the monsters off, would chase them back to their dens and make an end of them—and then surely the walls would come down. There would be no need any longer for the stockade or the factory, and life would return to the way it had been in her earliest memories. The moor would bloom green again. Children would run and play on it. Katherine would be able to go to London. She would go to London, and then the Continent, and she would learn how to sing properly, and she would end at La Scala like her mother. The future stretched before her in a grand green vista.

Chapter 10

"Max?" Even as she called, Katarina was pulling the door shut and bolting it, eyes turned to strain down the dim hall, fingers flying unseeing and unerring to snap the latches in place. "Max!"

There was no answer save a few erratic thumps from the direction of Trevelyan's laboratory. Katarina ran toward it, Elizabeth at her heels. The humming corridor was layered in gray shadows, but not nearly as mysterious or treacherous as it had been before sunrise. "Max!"

"He's not here," Trevelyan said without turning his head toward the propped-open door. The Welshman knelt in the center of the room beside the thing that was neither a cannon nor a musket, and the shining silver of the weapon twisted his reflection into something narrow and drawn.

William stood behind him, again—or still—leafing through the drawings on the worktable. He *had* turned in response to Katarina's voice, and his entire body slumped with relief when Elizabeth appeared in the doorway behind her. "Thank God," he said.

Katarina skidded to a stop. "Where is he?"

"Out looking for you and Miss Elizabeth." Trevelyan still didn't look up as he shot out an arm, clamped his fingers down hard, then reached with a spanner in the other hand to more tightly secure a bit of metal. "And if I were you, I'd be glad he didn't succeed. He wasn't best pleased to return and find you gone."

"Damn!" Katarina struck her hands together in frustration.

This time Trevelyan gave her one swift striking moment of his attention. "What's wrong?"

"A child taken to Murchinson's," Katarina said. "The daughter of a friend. I need Max to—"

"Oh, for God's sake, woman, and here I thought we had another problem." Trevelyan reached for another part of the cannon.

"You *thought* we had another problem?" Katarina repeated. "This *is* another problem."

"If it doesn't delay the rain, break the machine, or put our patron in prison, it doesn't signify."

"You really don't qualify as human sometimes." Katarina started to pace. "He didn't tell you when he was likely to return? I can't go and get the child myself, for obvious reasons, and we've got to retrieve her before sunset, for we may not be hereabouts tomorrow—"

Trevelyan stopped his work again—right-hand fingers holding a metal piece precisely positioned, left hand grasping a motionless spanner, gray eyes fixing on Katarina's dark ones. "You're joking, surely."

Katarina stared at him. "I very much am not."

"Right, and here I thought the children from the past were top on the list of things we don't have time for. Seems I was wrong. The *top* thing we do not have time for is haring off after—"

"A *person*," Katarina said. "A person in this city, this beleaguered city we're trying to—"

"—trying to save," Trevelyan said. "We're trying to save them all. If we can get my rifle working tonight, we've a chance, a real one. We haven't time for anything that distracts from that object. If you could for *once* keep your mind on the larger picture, we might actually be able to—"

"Oh, damn you and your larger picture to bloody hell!" Katarina's voice held a trace of the guttersnipe again, a thin, ugly sound. She drew a breath as if to say more—then stopped, rubbed both her hands over face, pushed the breath out hard through her teeth, and turned to face William.

"We got off on the wrong foot earlier," she said, once more in the low, melodic, carefully correct accent. "I was…discourteous because my pride was hurt, and I am sorry. I truly am…and I hope you can forgive me, because there is a child in danger, and I would…I need to…It would be terrible if you were to refuse your aid because it was I who asked it."

Everyone else in the room stared at her. "My aid?" William said.

"I can't get the girl out of Murchinson's any more than her mother can. It's obvious what I am and I haven't any better clothes. I need someone with the look and manners and speech of a gentleman. Please."

"You didn't want to take him with you earlier because his clothing would attract attention," Trevelyan pointed out acidly.

"The stakes were different then."

"No, they weren't. The stakes are precisely the same now as they were a few hours ago."

William looked from one of them to the other. "Might Mr. Maxwell have a coat more the current fashion?"

"He might," Katarina said, "and even if he doesn't, it's worth the gamble. Come upstairs with me. We'll see what Max has left behind, and I'll explain what you need to—"

"*No,*" Trevelyan said, getting to his feet. "You have no right to endanger what I'm trying to do here for the sake of one brat from Spitalfields."

Katarina whirled on him, dark eyes blazing. "Oh, of course not, because we all know one person can't possibly affect the larger picture. Not unless he's a lord or a general or a time-traveler. A girl from Spitalfields couldn't possibly change anything, couldn't possibly put out a hand and change *everything.*" Trevelyan rolled his eyes and turned to get another metal piece from the worktable to his right. And *that,* Elizabeth thought, that unhurried movement, too casual to even bother being contemptuous, was why Katarina took another step toward him and why her voice dropped into a hiss like crackling flames. "A Spitalfields child could never change anything," she repeated, "any more than a bastard from Devon or a nobody London University student. Or a Welsh farmer's daughter—"

Trevelyan slammed the spanner into the worktable so hard the wood cracked underneath it and the air seemed to crack around it. He looked up, his face full for one instant of the anger Katarina had been trying to provoke from him. Then it smoothed over as though it had turned to ice, and the crack spread through the iced-over air between them. Katarina never flinched, but Elizabeth could not breathe.

"At the moment," Trevelyan said without raising his voice, "you are distracting the one person who can change the world today from doing the thing that can change it." He picked up the spanner with a jerk, as though it were a blade and he were yanking it free of the wood, but his eyes never wavered from hers and his voice stayed calm. "Go and waste your time however you like, but do it somewhere else."

⚮

Mr. Maxwell had in fact left an overcoat behind, but it was sufficiently broad in the shoulders to look dubious rather than fashionable on William's trim frame. More to the point, Maxwell had left it behind because the city air was sweltering like a blacksmith's forge; Elizabeth pondered whether an ill-fitting and unseasonable ensemble would not attract more attention than William's smart but seven-decades-out-of-date blue coat. She looked to see what Katarina thought, and realized that although Katarina was gazing at William, lips pursed, her unfocused eyes were studying something other than the young man before her.

After a moment, Katarina blinked, seemed to realize that both Elizabeth and William were waiting for her to speak, and reached out as though to briskly adjust the collar of William's borrowed overcoat. But a tremor ran through her fingers as she touched the cloth. "That's the worst thing I could have possibly said," she commented, almost steadily. "In fact, I can't believe I actually…" She drew her other hand over her eyes, then dropped it with what looked like an attempt to smile. "I suppose I may claim as excuse that I haven't slept since…I think it was Tuesday."

William met her eyes. "Why the worst?" he asked. Quite gently, as though he genuinely wanted to know.

"No one," Katarina said with another strained smile, "talks to Trevelyan about his wife."

"His *wife?*" Elizabeth couldn't stop herself from blurting it out. She was surprised by the sense of betrayal that flooded her. Being a fallen woman was all very well, still retained a tinge of romance even after the squalor of the painted girls, but to do something as sordid as stealing a man from his wife was unworthy of the Katarina she thought she was coming to know. "He's *married?*"

"He was married." Katarina thought about it for half a second, then amended, "No, you had the way of it the first time, he is married. She's dead, but he's still married. He wears her ring on a chain around his neck, and he might as well wear it on his finger."

"'No one hates the constructs or their creators more than he does,'" Elizabeth quoted slowly, trying to put it together. "That's why, then? Was she killed by constructs, and that's why he hates the men who made them, that's why he's devoted his life to finding a way to bring them down?"

Katarina looked at her for a moment as though trying to decide whether to say something, even went so far as to purse her lips briefly. But in the end she only said, "Not quite, but close enough," and turned back toward William. "I think we'll wrap you in Maxwell's coat for the journey and then find an alleyway where you can shrug it off and leave it with me, near the factory. If the coat fit you better, then I'd say… But as it is, it'll do nothing but attract attention. If you just wear your own clothes, you have a chance at pretending to be an Oxford dandy. I'm told there's a romantic fashion for old-styled clothing this year, and although I don't think it quite extends to this level of detail, we may hope that the matrons at Murchinson's don't know one way or the other. There are some tricks of speech and slang terms I can teach you, and we will drill them as we walk, all right?"

"Who am I to be?" Elizabeth asked. "His sister? I should go and see if my gown has dried."

Katarina snapped startled eyes to her. "No, you'll do no such thing. We might just get away with claiming William's clothes to be Oxford dandy fashion, but your gown is simply seventy years wrong, nothing to be done about it."

"I'll just stay hidden with you, then?"

There was a pause. "No," Katarina said, "you'll stay here, Miss Elizabeth. I can't take the risk of bringing both of you."

"Oh, no," Elizabeth protested, "no, wait. You can't show me all that's out there and then not let me *help*."

"The way you can help right now is by staying safe here," Katarina said.

"No," Elizabeth said, "no, you can't do that to me, you can't shut me up again like—like nothing this morning happened, like I'm just a—*William*—" She turned to him. "You don't know what it's like. I can't know it's there and not try to do something about it."

"There isn't anything you can do," Katarina told her. "Nothing useful, at least. All you'll accomplish if you come along is increase the risk we'll be spotted. I'm sorry, but it's true. You need to stay here."

"You cannot lock me up here! You can't give me a taste of what it's like to mend things and then not let me try, you can't *do* that to—"

"This isn't about you!" Katarina snapped. "This isn't a bloody game, Elizabeth. There's a child's life at stake—a real child, so I'll thank you to stop acting like one yourself. There will be things you can do, but this isn't one of them, and that's the end of it. You're staying here and William and I are going."

Elizabeth shot one last look at William. She would have been satisfied with a look of sympathy, even if they must bow to Katarina's wishes, but instead William shook his head. Regretfully perhaps, but with eyebrows raised as though she were indeed the child Katarina had called her. Elizabeth's eyes filled with hot tears.

Chapter 11

The shabby woman fixed red-rimmed eyes on him as though on a fog-beacon, and William found that his heart was pounding harder than it had in well over a year.

"Mr. William Carrington," Katarina's voice said at his elbow, in smooth explanation, "a young relation of Mr. Maxwell, just down from Oxford. Mr. Carrington, Annie Drew."

"Mrs. Drew," he said. He didn't see a ring, but chose the courteous option as being also the simplest. He didn't know how to assess the likelihood that she had pawned it versus the likelihood that she had never possessed one, and he had no attention for the puzzle in any case. He was occupied with thoughts of walking alone through this fantastic battlefield, completely without defense except for the bits of information Katarina had fed him as they walked, bearing sole responsibility for this woman and her child.

For Katarina was not to accompany them to Murchinson's. She said she dared not, with a gesture at her trouser-clad legs that confirmed his earlier suspicion of their significance. She would disappear a street or so away, so that Annie and William could approach the factory gates without a whiff of indecency attending their appearance. She assured William that it would be simplicity itself for him to get inside, as long as he acted as though he had an unassailable right to do so. He was then to tell the matrons that the woman beside him was a friend of his family's cook, victim of a malicious joke, and that they were to return her child directly. He was to use certain slang phrases that Katarina believed would confirm him as a "young Oxford dandy" and would therefore explain his odd clothing. He tried to remember what they all were, and then tried to remember exactly what he had been thinking when he agreed to this task. How the devil was he to explain the arm, if someone noticed?

"Best leave us now, hadn't you, Katarina?" Annie said diffidently. "I mean, I can show Mr. Carrington to Murchinson's."

"I'll walk with you a bit," Katarina overrode her. "I can vanish quick enough once we're closer."

She obviously had no intention of leaving Annie and William alone together a moment longer than necessary. Perhaps because she did not really trust William to successfully maintain the fiction. She was justified in her fear, if so; he had never acted a part in his life. What had he been *thinking?*

"You will want to agree on the name of the cook," Katarina said as though she always thought this way, as though assuming a role was the sort of thing she did every day of the week. It probably was. "May I suggest…" She paused. "…Dora Brewer. Can you both remember that? Otherwise, there is nothing you need agree upon, no need for you to pretend to know each other any better than you do."

"Mrs. Brewer," Annie repeated. "This is…so kind of you, Mr. Carrington."

"Not at all," he said, and then, feeling the flick of Katarina's dark eyes, tried to infuse the tone with the proper drawl and the rest of the sentence with the proper vocabulary. "Jolly pleased I can be of help." He didn't dare turn head to see Katarina's reaction to that, as he was rather afraid it might involve rolling eyes. He had never heard anything quite so unnatural as those words on his tongue.

Katarina left them a street or so later, drawing William into a shadowed alcove that smelled of horse and worse things to slip the overcoat off his shoulders. "They'll stare at your fine Oxford clothes, I'm sure, but there's no help for that. It's not as though a young gentleman such as you belongs in these streets."

He got the point. At least, he thought, it would not be terribly difficult to act the part of someone not from this part of the city who was taken aback at what he found. He clenched and released his left hand, and nodded to Annie to lead the way.

He was a little surprised by the size of the brick building that appeared out of the smog. It might have been a manor house, or even a French castle, with turrets rising on each side of a courtyard. Then he got closer to the great iron gates that separated the yard from the street, and saw that the turrets were chimneys. The right half of the building put him in mind of soldiers' barracks, so he guessed that to be the orphanage and the other side the factory proper. Where to start?

"I dunno …" Annie murmured beside him, answering the thought he had not spoken. He turned to her, startled, and she flushed. "Excuse me, sir, I didn't think of the gates being locked. Maybe we could… maybe there's a servants' entrance, round the back …?"

"Nonsense," he said, making up his mind all at once, trying to sound certain. "We'll enter by the front door." He turned to the left, away from the enormous gates, and headed for a door in the brick wall. He assumed it led to the business office.

It did. The spare, neatly dressed clerk seated at the front desk widened his eyes at the sight of the Oxford dandy's blue coat and brass buttons. They were pale gray eyes; everything else about the man was similarly gray and pale. So were the plaster walls and the papers on the desk. The very wood of the two doors behind the clerk looked faded and worn.

The clerk raised his eyebrows. "May I help you, sir?"

The quality did not come to transact business in this establishment, William inferred. Obviously not; the quality bought their matchsticks in shops elsewhere. Very likely this man handled the accounts between Murchinson's and those shops. "Indeed you may, my good man," he said, trying to drawl it a little, trying to remember the attitudes struck by some of his brother's Oxford friends. "My name is William Carrington, and I'm here on a little commission for my mother. This lady here is cousin to our cook—" Cousin? Had he been meant to say cousin? Might it have been sister, or friend? It didn't matter, he told himself; the detail would never matter, but a noticeable hesitation would, so he plunged forward. "—and it seems someone brought her daughter along here by mistake. The child's name is Margaret Drew. Would you be so good as to fetch her out for us?"

The sparse brows above the pale eyes lifted again. "That is quite impossible, Mr. Carrington. The Murchinson Orphanage takes in children who lose their parents to death or abandonment."

"And very admirable of you," William said, "but in this case, seems a trifling error was made, don't you see. I'm sure it happens even in the best of places—no reflection on you, of course, Mr.—?"

"Perry," the man said through pinched lips.

"Mr. Perry. Just one of those little mistakes that happen now and again, like putting figures in the wrong column or any other little accounting mishap." William waved a hand at the man's ledger book, and only then realized the mistake he had made.

He might not have made it had he been paying attention. The precision of the man's dress, not to mention precision of the numbers in his ledger and the edges of the foolscap stacked on his desk, ought to have informed that Mr. Perry took a certain pride in exactness. But William had been thinking too hard about the lines he must recite to notice the trap until he was in it.

"Accounting errors do not occur in my office, sir," Mr. Perry said coldly.

"Of course not," William stammered, with an inner feeling uncannily like that of missing a step on a darkened stair. He lost the careless drawl in that moment, but tried desperately to recapture it with his next words. "Fact is, Mr. Perry, we think someone was having a, well, a joke with Mrs. Drew here. No need to look too closely at it—wouldn't want to get anyone in trouble when there's no harm done. We'll just take the little girl back and say no more about it. We've no intention of Murchinson's being out the money, of course!" William fumbled in his pocket as though only just then thinking of such sordid and uninteresting concerns as money. "Here we are, then, I believe that's what's fair? I haven't counted carefully; do let me know if I'm short a bit."

Mr. Perry took the drawstring bag William plunked down before him, and pulled it open. It contained about twice the required sum, William happened to know. Katarina's strategy again. She said bribes often worked where an attitude of careless authority failed.

Mr. Perry dropped the bag and shoved it across the desk. "I do not take bribes, sir. I must wish you good afternoon."

Had William taken longer to talk with him first, he might have figured that out too. Had he instead successfully employed the rattling manner, he might have been able to shrug off the *faux pas*. As it was, he hesitated a moment while the clerk's face turned turkey-red and Annie made a miserable little moan behind him.

"Of course it's not a bribe, sir," he said finally, lamely, not at all with the insouciance the moment required. "I was trusting you for the change. Now, the child, if you please?"

Mr. Perry snorted and picked up his pen, and for a moment William thought he had lost. Before he could regroup and try again, though, Perry plunged his hand into the bag, counted out the coins required, and left the bag and the remainder for William to take. He reached and pulled a bell pull, and when a peaky-looking child appeared out of the left hand door, sent the boy for Mrs. Mason.

William exhaled a breath. *That went terribly,* he thought. And then, *But no matter. It worked.*

Mrs. Mason was dressed in an outfit like Annie Drew's—perhaps a shade newer and a shade worse cared-for, but similarly made of cheap stuff with no hope of lasting long. Mr. Perry identified her as the matron of the girls' orphanage and explained to her what was wanted.

"Oh, but we couldn't do that, sir," she said, eyes wide. "You know as well as I do that we only get such children as haven't mothers to care for them, and if this woman's been mistreating her child, surely it's our duty to—"

"I haven't!" Annie burst out, and "She's done no such thing," William said, forgetting the part for the second time and—separately—making his second mistake.

Because the woman's eyes were wide with innocent horror, but he could tell now it was manufactured innocence. She was almost licking her lips as she gazed at William's smart brass buttons. *Here's where a bribe would have worked,* William thought—and, *Damn! Damn, damn, damn! I can't act a part, another bloody thing I can't—*

"I'm sure the gentleman can see we're in no position to take his word," Mrs. Mason said stiffly, drawing herself up. "He might intend a mischief. You read of such things in the papers. No, sir, I'd be remiss in my duties—I certainly can't without I go to Mr. Jorrick first. He'd be that angry with me if I—"

"If you what? What's this about, then?" The big middle-aged man who entered, also from the left-hand door, had the build and hard hands of one accustomed to manual labor. He wore a jacket that didn't quite fit him over a shirt and trousers like Trevelyan's, and his tie was only loosely knotted about his thick neck.

"Mr. Jorrick is the factory overseer," Perry said to William. "Mr. Jorrick, Mr. Carrington."

Mrs. Mason said, "This woman sold her child a while agone, and wants her back."

"Not quite," William said. "This woman is a friend of my family's, and we believe her child was brought here as a malicious joke on the part of a neighbor." The story was right, but he hadn't accomplished the requisite delivery, and Jorrick seemed to notice the mismatch between his speech and his clothing, for the man's small eyes studied him for a disconcerting moment. "The girl's name is Margaret Drew," William repeated, giving up on the drawl and the slang as a lost cause. He picked up the bag of coins. "We've brought the money you would have given for her."

"Come with me to my office, Mr. Carrington," Jorrick said, rousing himself from his study of William's clothing, "and we'll sort this out, eh?"

William followed his sweeping arm, stepping through the right-hand door the man held for him and into a small and untidy cubbyhole. He could hear Annie following, but Jorrick shut the door before she had reached it.

"Have a seat, Mr. Carrington," Jorrick said, motioning to one of the two chairs on either side of a structure that seemed to serve double duty as a desk and a dining table. The big man circled to take the other chair, slapping at his pockets as though searching for something. "I'd offer you a gasper, but I can't seem to find—"

There was an infinitesimal pause, and William knew that etiquette demanded he offer tabacco in his turn, that Jorrick was expecting him to, and that it would be the best thing in the world he could do, for the man was making friendly overtures and a gentleman who did not stand on position would have a better chance of getting the overseer to do what he needed. He knew all this things. He did not have tabacco to offer. Nor could he manipulate his right arm into the required searching, slapping gesture without drawing attention to his deformity. He tried to think what to do instead, what excuse he could make—for the type of man he was pretending to be would surely have smoking material ready to hand—and as he hesitated, Jorrick's eyes hardened and his hands dropped to his sides.

He had interpreted it as a snub. *Damn. Damn, damn, damn.*

"I needn't take much of your time, Mr. Jorrick," William said as pleasantly as he could over the renewed rapid beating of his heart. "This strikes me as a very simple matter."

"Ah, but there are considerations you know nothing of, young sir," Jorrick said. "Rules and regulations. We take good care of all our youngsters, you know, and we've got to be ready to answer to Mr. Murchinson and the law should they inquire. I can't just hand the girl over to you."

William unclenched his teeth. "I've brought with me the money Murchinson's gave for her. Plus a bit extra. If there should be any fine imposed, I should be happy to cover it."

"But it would still be me held to account, wouldn't it?" Jorrick shook his head as if sadly, and leaned against the wall, arms folded. "It's plain you've little experience with men of business, Mr. Carrington— and nor should a young gentleman like yourself, of course. In any case, though, I couldn't disrupt the work shift. The wheels are turning, you know. I'd have to go and find a magistrate to approve the releasing of the child to your custody. Why don't you…ah…leave me with a card, and I'll…be sure to send to you when I've arranged for the legal paperwork."

William had heard enough. He recognized the glint in Jorrick's eye as that of a cat enjoying its power over a mouse. An astutely admin- istered bribe might compel Jorrick's assistance; but then, he might find he preferred power to money. It was too late to try blather, and William had his doubts regarding the efficacy of that tactic in any case. Calm reason wouldn't work at all, nor would pleading. Though both might have with Mr. Perry, Jorrick was cut of different cloth. William knew the cloth, for he had encountered it both at Eton and in the Army.

Fortunately, that meant he also knew at least one sure tactic for defeating it. A young, mild-tempered, slenderly built ensign learns very quickly that he must not be afraid to assert his authority over private soldiers, even those bigger than he is. Especially those bigger than he is.

William stood up sharply enough to knock the chair over, re-calling to mind the techniques for hardening his face as though he had completely lost control of his temper. "That's enough." He looked straight at Jorrick, picturing him as a delinquent private soldier, and Jorrick appeared to abruptly derive less enjoyment from the encounter. "I've no more time for this nonsense. You know as well as I do that it's as much as your position is worth to involve the law, and let me assure you I will not hesitate to do just that if this situation is not instantly resolved. You will take to me to where the child is."

He didn't actually expect instant obedience from a man not drilled to obey an officer's orders, but he didn't give Jorrick the chance to recover himself, turning instead to the door and wrenching it open before Jorrick could see how he fumbled to manage both the coin bag and the doorknob. He would lose if this came to a physical fight; but against so large an opponent, he would have lost even back when he had full use of both his hands, so that hardly mattered. He could only triumph if he acted as though a physical contest were an utter impos-sibility.

He strode into the outer office, and made for the left-hand door. Mrs. Mason fell back a little at his face, and the clerk looked up, sur-prised. William ignored them both. "Come, Mrs. Drew," he said, and led her down the narrow corridor with Jorrick's "Hey, wait!" ringing in the air behind him.

The wave of heat struck him like a blow—not the searing, burn-ing, bright heat of a Spanish summer, but a dull, overbaked staleness, like an oven. He pushed through the dead air as though through a physical obstacle, Annie close on his heels and Jorrick and Mrs. Mason behind her. "You can't—" Jorrick started.

The passage ended abruptly in a room the size of Trevelyan's labo-ratory. Around long trestle tables, half-grown children stood—girls at some, boys at others—fingers moving in steady rhythm. William knew what they were doing; Katarina had shown him matchsticks, and brief-ly explained their manufacture, so that he would not look like a man from an earlier era who had never seen the things. He was prepared for the tables, the boxes, the vats of liquid. He ought to have been prepared for the youth of the workers; he was, after all, there to fetch a child.

What he was not prepared for was their appearance. Too thin and too pale—he had expected that; these were pauper children after all—but with red-rimmed eyes that seemed almost scarlet in contrast to the white skin of their faces. The hands that moved among the sticks and vats were equally red, worse than the mere rawness of a kitchen maid. The faces of the girls closest to him, engaged in packing finished match-books into crates, were horribly swollen, jaws distended with misshapen lumps, cheekbones sunken. Their skin seemed to glow green in the shadowed room. Another girl walked past him, a full crate balanced on her head, and when she set it on a pile of similar ones and turned back, he saw that hair clung to her skull only in occasional chunks.

He felt as though he were choking from the lack of air. He wondered what the attempted sabotage had been, back before Seward's capture. He would have given a great deal right now for a way to bring this whole place down and fetch all of the children out of there.

He drew a long, burning breath, Katarina's argument with Trevelyan ringing in his ears. They were *trying* to bring the whole thing down—Trevelyan with his cannon, Seward with his conspiracy. It was not as though William could do better in a single instant, with no weapons except his educated accent and the brass buttons on his coat. He didn't have a lever long enough to shift this world, and if he tried, he might well put into jeopardy Trevelyan's evening plans. For certain he would endanger Annie. He turned abruptly to her.

"Which?" he snarled through the thickness in his throat. He didn't dare more than the one word for fear of how his voice would shake.

Annie was already moving toward a girl working at a table set against the far wall, already calling her daughter's name. She seized the child's hand, and William turned on his heel, thrust the bag of coins at Jorrick, and shepherded his charges toward the corridor. "I'll have the law on you—" Jorrick blustered behind him.

"Do," William said, opened the door for Annie and Meg, and made sure it slammed behind him.

Chapter 12

Elizabeth stood looking down at the unmade bed for a long time before she loosened the laces of her bodice, unbuckled her shoes, and gingerly lowered herself onto the mattress.

It shifted under her weight, the hay within crackling softly, and she thought a cloud of dust stirred itself briefly. The brown woolen blanket was rough under her fingers, unappealing. At least she did not need to draw it over herself. She was fully clothed, and the garret bedroom sweltering. She put the blanket to one side, and laid her head on the pillow she assumed to be Katarina's.

The other pillow seemed to be staring at the back of her skull.

She tried to ignore it. She had lain down upon Katarina's bed, that was all. She was weary to the bone, and Trevelyan had brusquely ordered her out from under his feet, so she had gone to rest upon her friend's bed. She would forget that it also belonged to a man. She would not think of Katarina lying here at Trevelyan's side, nor of the hurt in Katarina's eyes at Trevelyan's coldness. She wondered what would be worse—to choose for yourself, and choose to love a man who did not love you, or to have a husband like Charles Wilton thrust upon you and know for certain that love was impossible? It was a knotty problem, but in the end the quandary and even the discomfort of the heat were no match for the fatigues of the day. She drifted off into a doze, her last conscious thought to wryly wonder if she would awaken in her own bed.

A door slammed somewhere below, startling her upright.

There was no way to tell how long she had slept. Sweat ran down her face and her heart hammered against her breastbone. The stuffy air pressed like tight-laced stays against her ribs.

A man's voice spoke, angry but indistinct. Elizabeth strained to hear the words. It spoke again, closer, and this time another voice answered. Katarina's.

"What the devil is wrong with you?" Maxwell demanded. His voice came clearly now; they must be approaching the bottom of the stairs. "What were you *thinking,* taking her out into the city?"

"That she was at least as safe under my watchful eye out there as she would have been under Trevelyan's inattentive eye in here," Katarina's voice replied tartly. "Especially when you consider—" She chuckled, but without much humor. "If I understand the young lady's character correctly, she would have been very likely to sneak off on her own and go exploring. At least under my scheme, someone knew where she was."

Elizabeth felt herself growing even hotter.

"And taking William to Murchinson's? What would have happened if he'd drawn attention?"

"Oh, you sound like Trevelyan. I took him because you weren't here and it couldn't wait. There might not have been another chance."

"We cannot risk losing—" Maxwell broke off. There was a pause. He seemed to use it in an attempt to calm himself, for when he went on, his voice was somewhat lowered. "We cannot risk losing people from the past. Their deaths could alter everything that comes after."

There was another pause. "I apologize," Katarina said. "But there's no harm done."

"I suppose not," Maxwell admitted. "But at this stage—with Seward imprisoned—none of us should be taking any risks at all. The whole thing is balanced on a knife's edge, and—"

"Do you think it will work?" Katarina asked quietly.

"I...don't know." From the sound of it, Maxwell had started to pace. "Do I think the weapon will fire? Yes. But it's a long step from one working prototype to an army equipped with them. I do think it's worth trying. I've always thought that."

"And if it doesn't work...?" Katarina's voice trailed off into a question.

Maxwell sighed. "Orkney, the fifteenth of September, 1790. I'll have another try at stopping it before it starts."

"Did you ever...?" Katarina hesitated. "Did you ever think of going to Pendoylan, the eighteenth of May, 1872?"

"Oh, Katarina." Maxwell stopped pacing. "I've already been there. I've already failed there. Katarina...would you really wish for that to be altered?"

"I think...yes, I think I would," Katarina said. "But there's no chance of it?"

"No. I've already been there. And to the University of London the following year. To Geneva in 1788, to Inverness in 1800, to Carron Valley in 1855...to every place I could think of where the outcome trembled on a knife's edge and there was a chance I could affect it."

"And now here," Katarina said.

"And now here. And if we fail here, then to Orkney. To change his course if I can." Maxwell's voice turned grim. "And to shoot him if I cannot. I have grown both brutal and desperate in my old age. We have to stop this. It doesn't matter what tool we use."

"That's why I took William to Murchinson's," Katarina said.

"Yes." Maxwell sighed. "I see that. But we can't risk either of them any further. I'll make sure they're back home before the excitement starts here."

"I do not think the storm intends to cooperate with your timetable," Trevelyan's voice interjected, and his feet came to join them from the direction of the laboratory. "Their watch won't work until, what, three in the morning? I doubt the lightning will hold off so long."

"You're ready for the test, then?" Katarina asked, almost as easily as though there were no harsh words or cold silence between them.

"Indeed I am." Trevelyan spoke with a satisfaction very nearly approaching warmth. "Come and see, the both of you." The voices at the bottom of the stair moved toward the laboratory, and Elizabeth scrambled for her bodice and shoes. She could join them now, pretending that she had just awoken and that she had not heard any of what Maxwell and Katarina clearly had meant to be a private conversation.

Her sweat-damp fingers fumbled the shoe buckles, and then she did the bodice lacings wrong and had to feed them through again. She located Trevelyan's other spare boot by tripping over it as she had its mate, and nearly pitched headlong through the curtain. She caught herself, took a deep breath, and tried for a more sedate pace as she headed downward.

William was waiting for her at the bottom of the stairs. "I'm sorry," he said.

She froze.

He lifted his chin to look straight into her eyes. "I've seen it now. I understand what you meant earlier. I'm sorry."

"Oh, Lord," Elizabeth said, "William." She ran down the last two steps so that she could face him. "You haven't done anything you need apologize for. I shouldn't have—have made such a fuss. I just wanted to—But I shouldn't have, and I'm sorry, for—"

A wave of relief broke over his face. "No," he said, catching one of her hands to stop her talking, "you don't need to apologize either. I told you, I've seen it."

There was another emotion beneath the relief, something grim and hard. She had never seen William's face look like that. He was squeezing her hand tightly, as though using the sensation to remind himself of a world other than the one he had just seen.

She squeezed back. "Did you find the little girl?"

The hardness about his jaw eased. "Yes," he said, relief uppermost again, "thank God. She's safe back with her mother now. At least I could change *something*. I could do one little thing."

"I'm glad you could," Elizabeth said without rancor. "I'm glad one of us could, at least."

"It's a shame your gown would have given you away," he said, "for you would have done the bit at the factory much better than I did. I nearly muffed the whole thing, I was so nervous. I don't think I could have done it at all if I'd had more time to think about it."

She smiled a little. "I want to hear all about it."

"Well, it doesn't do me any credit except that it worked anyhow," he said, "but I'll tell you. Later. Shall we go and have a look at Trevelyan's rifle now? Er—" He seemed to realize for the first time that he was holding her hand, and a flush spread to the tips of his ears. She feared for a moment he would drop it, but after a brief hesitation, he transferred it to his arm instead and led her toward Trevelyan's laboratory as though escorting her into a ballroom.

The worst of the clutter had been cleared or, at least, piled up onto the workbenches, out of the way. Nothing now distracted the eye from the gleaming lines of the weapon that was too small for a cannon and too big for a musket. Elizabeth really could not decide which it was more like. It had a bit that nestled into the shoulder and a trigger at about the length of a man's arm, but surely it was too heavy for one man to lift, and the wooden stand looked like a cannon mount. She looked at Trevelyan. Since he was here, without a hammer poised over something delicate, and possibly even in what passed with him for good humor, she might as well make an attempt at asking.

"How does your rifle work?"

She did not actually expect more than a two-word token answer, if that. To her astonishment, he looked up from the cloth he was using to polish greasy streaks off the barrel, and gave her a full one.

"An ordinary musket ball can't pierce the hide of a construct," he said. "Particularly not the hide right over the boiler, which is the most heavily armored because the boiler is the construct's most vulnerable part. The bullet simply hasn't the force to get through the skin, do you see?" Elizabeth nodded. "So the trick is to increase the force. Steam won't give you the energy you need, nor will tension, nor will gunpowder. Nothing *man*-made—" He smiled a little, a bare twitch of thin lips. "—would serve. That's why we can only test the rifle in a lightning storm. See that rod there?" He pointed with a shrug of one shoulder, and for the first time she noticed the long slender pole running from floor to ceiling. "We'll be extending itout through the roof, and lightning will run down it and be trapped here." He touched the side of the gleaming silver barrel.

"Like a genie in a bottle," Elizabeth murmured.

Trevelyan snorted. "Like lightning in a bottle."

"The rifle will fire lightning?"

"No, no—the lightning will be the power behind the bullets. Which are not the ordinary kind either, but javelins. The barrel of the gun has little rails inside it, and the javelins are pushed along them. Like the cars on the railway, if you saw the railway."

"I did." Elizabeth looked at her own twisted reflection in the barrel, with its wide eyes and tangled hair. "I am all impatience to see it working."

"You will be doing no such thing," Maxwell said, straightening sharply from his examination of the trigger. "It is too dangerous to have you two anywhere near this field test. I am sending you home before we begin."

Trevelyan glanced over his shoulder at a barometer pinned to the wall. "No, Max, I'm not thinking you are. The storm won't hold off until three tomorrow morning."

"Good," Elizabeth said, greatly daring. "You dragged me all over this miserable city, then left me trapped in here and incapable of aiding it. At the very least, I want to see what *you* are going to do with this miraculous—"

"*No,*" Maxwell said, but in the manner of a schoolmaster beginning to lose control of his class. "Absolutely not. Even if I cannot send you back, I will not see you exposed to that danger."

"With all our associates raising hell out there," Trevelyan said, "this is very likely the safest place in the city. Unless you want to take them *completely* elsewhere." He nodded to the watch chain stretched across Maxwell's waistcoat.

Maxwell frowned. "I don't want to leave this juncture unless I must."

"Then just keep them by you," Trevelyan said. "If the plan works as it's meant to, there's nothing to worry about. If not, the three of you can pop out of time." Maxwell started to argue further, but Trevelyan raised one imperious hand. "Did you hear that? Thunder, far off. We've no more time for talking. Let's get ourselves ready."

~

It was not exactly uncomfortable to be dressed in her own clothing, but Elizabeth found it odd after a day spent in breeches. She also felt the absence of the pocket watch like an ache. William had it now, since she had nothing in which to tuck it, and this reversion to the customs of 1815 annoyed Elizabeth even as she acknowledged the need.

The wind annoyed her as well. She had never before particularly noticed wind, not even when it swirled cold in winter, but now she found herself irritably aware of every gust that tangled her skirt against her legs. She wondered how she had ever found it easy to climb trees in a gown.

There had been no tree to climb tonight, only a ladder leading from the attic of the warehouse through a trapdoor and onto its flat roof. Mr. Maxwell had not wanted her to risk even so much, but Elizabeth did not consider it necessary to worry over what Mr. Maxwell wanted. There was, as Katarina assured Maxwell and as Elizabeth thought obvious to any observer, no real danger. She would hardly fall while climbing the ladder. She might, she supposed, fall off the roof, but she would have to try hard in order to manage it. A low wall ran all the way around the edge, easily concealing from the casual observer anyone who sat behind it. "A duck blind," Trevelyan had called it. "Cruder than I'd like, but it's worked so far. No copper's ever noticed anything amiss."

Katarina crouched beside Elizabeth, equipped with what Elizabeth persisted in thinking of as opera-glasses-on-a-stalk, despite Trevelyan's derisive snort when she used the term and his subsequent explanation as to their correct name (periscope field glasses) and design. Elizabeth did not really listen, recognizing Trevelyan's relentless detail as a manifestation of nervousness, though she had no doubt the man himself would have angrily denied any such accusation. The glasses, admittedly too heavy and crude for any opera, were attached to a pole and thereby to another set of lenses that looked out like eyeballs over the wall. Those behind the duck blind could therefore look in any direction without the risk of a lifted head. Katarina did most of the looking herself, but was kind enough to occasionally allow Elizabeth to peep through her glasses. Maxwell likewise occasionally allowed William to look through his. Trevelyan, manning the third pair, dealt with William and Elizabeth's presence by pretending they did not exist.

The city did not sleep the way the country slept—or, at least, the country of 1815, Elizabeth reminded herself, for who knew what the country was like now. But she remembered spending the occasional sleepless night at home looking out of her bedroom window to a view quiet hills and fields and unseen houses. Unseen, for there were no lamps in the windows, no light to mar the soft dark anywhere.

Not so here. Big Ben had tolled two o'clock, but the shadows on the street below still fidgeted with restless movement under the blue-white beams of light thrown by the constructs' patrols, as the enormous feet drove a monotonous beat into the ground. They never came very close to the warehouse, but Elizabeth found "not very close" to be quite sufficiently nerve-wracking for the two or three minutes every half-hour it lasted. During the twenty-seven minutes in between, the shadows were even more restless, an almost-silent scurry of activity as the London underworld engaged in whatever clandestine activity took it out after curfew. "Fools," Trevelyan muttered, with no apparent sense of irony. Once a star gleamed suddenly far below, and Elizabeth stiffened in alarm—before the man's cupped hands brought the star up to his face, held there for a moment, and then waved it out. A matchstick. She followed the faintly glowing red of the cigarette-end until it disappeared around a corner. If *she* could see it, couldn't the construct pilots see it? Fool, indeed. How many such fools did the patrols catch every night? And what happened to them afterward?

There was no doubt that a storm was indeed coming. The wind smelled of clean water, oddly so, for the nearby river was anything but clean. Every draught brought a moment's relief from heavy, breathless air, and Elizabeth gulped each one gladly. In the country, she thought, the leaves would be tossed upside down, the underside proclaiming the advent of thunder. She noticed her skirt attempting to fill that role instead, and impatiently smoothed it down again.

The sky growled. It was symptomatic of Elizabeth's state of mind that her first thought was panic that an off-schedule construct was approaching them. In the next instant, she pulled herself together, recognizing the sound to be the thunder so long sought. It rumbled again, and the sky off toward the river flashed abruptly bright.

The first fat drops of rain splattered against the roof, and Trevelyan abandoned his opera-glasses-on-a-stalk and got to work. There were two trapdoors, the one with the wooden ladder, and another some few feet away, this second one no more than a small round hole with a crude oilskin covering. Trevelyan pulled the oilskin back and weighted it down with a shingle, then headed for the ladder. William followed, backing down the steps carefully, holding on with his left hand.

The creaking sound of a winch started a few minutes later. Elizabeth cringed at the shrillness, thinking it was lucky the thunder drowned out the sound and that there was no one close to hear in any case. The tip of a thin metal rod poked its way through the hole in the roof. As Trevelyan turned the winch below, it extended itself smoothly up and up and up.

Elizabeth did not dare go near the metal rod—"it's safe as houses," Trevelyan had said, "provided you don't *touch* it"—but she peered through the larger trapdoor to see what transpired in the room below. Trevelyan was working with only a dark lantern to aid him, a lanky shadow that ran nervous fingers over the great shiny barrel of the gun. Elizabeth saw the moment when he took a deep breath, took his hands away from his invention and clasped them behind his back, and took two deliberate steps backward to join William.

Lightning lit up everything for one instant—the room below, Trevelyan's set face, the wood grain of the ladder that crossed Elizabeth's field of vision, the patch of sky that formed a background for it all. Elizabeth winced away, eyes dazzled.

When her vision cleared, she noticed the tension in Katarina's shoulders as the older woman pressed her eyes to her opera glasses. Elizabeth squirmed around to look through Trevelyan's abandoned set.

The first thing she saw was a spark of light to the northwest, deep within the maze of buildings that comprised the financial district known as the City of London. It was as bright a star as the momentary match gleam had been, but this one did not instantly vanish. It stayed steady, and then it was joined by another. Then a third. And a fourth. Lanterns, Elizabeth thought.

One of the lanterns flashed hot white in a way that seared her eyes again. The *boom* came to her ears several heartbeats later—or perhaps not, perhaps it was only the wind. "One," Katarina said beside her, voice low and satisfied.

"Where?" Elizabeth asked, not looking away from the opera glasses.

"Bank of England. They'll be chased away by constructs well before they can actually steal anything."

Another white-hot spark flared, farther to the northwest. This one was answered, some few seconds later, by a beam of blue light as a construct stomped to investigate it. "Two," Maxwell said. "A disturbance near Newgate Prison. Men out after curfew, attempting to distract the guards."

Much farther north, though of course they could neither see nor hear it, a pane of glass was breaking in one window of the British

Museum, and stealthy feet were creeping toward a treasure so precious that a threat to it would prompt another rush of protective men and constructs. Three.

Sand in the works, altering the pattern of the night, pulling the constructs away from their usual orbits.

Katarina swiveled her opera glasses around on their stalk. "Four," she said, and Elizabeth tried to follow with hers. From the southwest came a dull red glow. "Arson. Police headquarters. Again, no real cause for worry. They'll have it out before much damage is done."

Then came a *boom* loud enough to rattle the teeth in Elizabeth's head, and Maxwell swung in the direction from which it had come. "Five," he said. "Westley's Steelworks."

The streets shook in discordant arrhythmia as constructs moved farther from their usual routes of patrol, shining their lights away from the docks, going to investigate the disturbances in other parts of the city.

More star-gleams of lantern light lit up the darkness, these due south on the other side of the Thames. "Fighting in the streets," Katarina said. "Outside Bedlam. How *odd;* can't imagine what would cause it. Six," she added as an afterthought.

More beams of blue light pierced the sky. Constructs stomped across the bridges to Southwark, leaving whole swaths of Whitechapel and Spitalfields unobserved.

"Right, then," Katarina said. "The lightning can hit any time it chooses. There's no one here to see it now."

However, the lightning did not immediately oblige. The rain pattered down, and the sky growled, but the lightning forks stayed off in the distance.

Gradually, the sparks of lantern-light and firelight around the city began to go out.

"They've chased off the burglars at the Bank," Katarina said, eyes to the opera glasses.

"It looks as though the fire at police headquarters is coming under control," Maxwell reported a short while later.

Elizabeth swung her glasses to follow the gaze of first one and then the other. A chill clamped around her heart. The constructs were settling the disturbance, the blue beams of light once more freed to go about their patrol.

"Don't worry," Maxwell said to her, without turning his head. "There was no way to do it without raising suspicion. So many disturbances taking place after curfew, all at once—impossible to manage it without it looking contrived."

"So the only thing to be done," Katarina finished for him, "was use the suspicion to our advantage. Their commander doesn't think all this disruption tonight was random. And he knows about the criminal network working for the traitor Seward. Watch."

Some of the constructs were still busy with the fire at the police headquarters, the chase through the streets near the British Museum, and the riots in Southwark. But even those now freed from distraction did not return to their usual patrol routes. They converged toward the northern banks of the Thames instead—uncomfortably close to the docks and the warehouse, as it happened, but it became clear before very long that neither were their goal. They advanced to encircle the Tower of London, where the traitor Seward was being held and from which his criminal empire was no doubt trying to free him, using these citywide disturbances as distraction.

"Bless you, Seward," Maxwell murmured. "You're still working for our victory."

Katarina glanced from her opera glasses and to the sky. "Really, though," she murmured to the lightning. "Anytime you like would be fine."

That time it listened. The next crash of thunder was close enough to make Elizabeth jump, and all at once the rain drove in sideways, piercing her thin gown, raking fingernails down her bare arm, singing through her blood. She had never felt so alive as she did now, under the cold rain that poured like a waterfall, looking down at the wondrous coming together of all those brave people who meant to make a stand against a monster. She wanted to shout, or fly, or—

A fork of lightning leapt with a crash onto the rod, and sizzled all the way down it.

In the room below, Trevelyan let out a fierce, half-choked sound—what in another man might have been a cheer—plainly audible even through the rain and wind and thunder. William's less restrained hurrah echoed it. Elizabeth, smiling at the sound, looked down at him through the trapdoor. She could clearly see both men's faces: exultant, glowing in the red light of the newly charged rail-gun, Trevelyan's transformed by a grin that Elizabeth would have sworn him incapable of the second before. The Welshman spent a bare instant running eyes and hands over the gun barrel, and then swung for the ladder. "Done!" he shouted up to them. *"Done, it's done—"*

Katarina laughed aloud and applauded, and Maxwell sighed as though setting down a load that strained his back. Elizabeth saw William come up behind Trevelyan, offering his left hand in clumsy congratulations, smiling, saying something inaudible but admiring.

Thunder crashed again—deafeningly close, again—and lightning lit up the sky. This time, it did not fade.

Elizabeth looked up in time to be blinded by the sapphire-blue beams of light that swept from the construct's eyes. It was one of those drawn into a ring around the Tower of London, but it had turned to face them. Its head was tilted up and its eyes trained right on their rooftop, and as she watched, it started a deliberate, ground-eating march toward them.

Chapter 13

"It couldn't have seen us," Trevelyan said, wrenching the winch angrily. "Did you stay behind the duck blind? Then it couldn't have seen you. We'll batten down the hatches and stay quiet, and—"

"That won't answer," Katarina said. "We have to leave. It was facing us, Gavin! It saw lightning strike a building no taller than any around it, it saw lightning strike a building and not set it afire, it probably can see the rod as you're lowering it right now, we can't stay here! If we leave now—"

"—and run into the streets so it can spot us easily?" Trevelyan's mouth twisted.

Above their heads, the oilcloth slapped into place, and the indistinct light that had been filtering through the roof hole was gone. The air outside crashed with thunder and the advancing construct's feet. In the laboratory, the rail-gun glowed softly red, but it was no longer a warm light, and Elizabeth no longer found the chilly rain exhilarating. She stood dripping, watching Trevelyan anchor the winch in place.

"Two more coming," Maxwell said, dropping through the trapdoor without using the ladder. Despite the water on the floor, he landed as neatly as a boy jumping from a hayloft, with bent knees and no apparent ill effects. "We're out of here, Trevelyan. Now."

Trevelyan cast one look all around the laboratory and cursed.

Maxwell ignored it, herding Elizabeth and William in front of him toward the laboratory's back door. "Trevelyan, this was always a possibility, we burned those papers for a reason, now let's go! We're headed for London Bridge," he told William and Elizabeth. "There's a submersible waiting for us there. Part of the plan from the beginning, just in case this night went badly."

"A what?" But Elizabeth was not surprised that no one took the time to answer her question. It was hardly the matter most urgently requiring attention. The walls around her shook, and plaster flaked off the ceiling.

Maxwell paused with his hand on the door latch and looked back over Elizabeth's head. Katarina was right behind them, face dark and mouth grim, checking the priming of her tiny pistol. Further back in the laboratory's darkness, there was a sound of groaning metal, and then a hissing breath of effort, and Trevelyan came to join them, staggering a little under the weight of the rail-gun strapped to his back and shoulder.

Maxwell stared at him. "Are you *insane?*"

"I would be insane to leave it for them to find," Trevelyan said. His eyes burned hollowly in the dim light, and the barrel of the gun burned too, smoldering red against the darkness.

Maxwell bit off whatever he had been about to say. He pulled off his overcoat, flung it over Trevelyan's right arm to hide the red gleam, and plunged out of the door and into the rain.

It was like walking into a wall of water. Elizabeth found herself instantly blind as rain pounded sideways against her face. Blue light from high above cut through the droplets, turning them into dazzling rainbows. The wind howled down the alleyway, a hair-raising sound like a monster with a dead face. For the second time in two nights, Elizabeth followed Maxwell in a stumbling run down an alleyway.

Headed the other way, this time. Not into the warren of back streets and alleys, but out into open space, toward the great flat expanse of the docks. The Thames stretched before them, oily rippling freedom. If only they could get there.

They left the shelter of the alleyway and burst onto the main thoroughfare in time to see the construct take the final shuddering step that brought it beside their warehouse. Elizabeth could have hit it with a tossed stone. But it was looking at the rooftop, Elizabeth thought wildly. It was looking at the rooftop; surely it would miss movement at its feet—

Its head swung around. A beam of light from its eyes cut through the lashing rain, and the five of them froze under it—instinctive, stupid, the reaction of mice under the eye of a hawk. Cobblestones shook under Elizabeth's feet as the construct turned away from the building, taking a heavy step and then another toward their huddled group of five. A flash of lightning gave Elizabeth one clear view up the main road: the two other constructs Maxwell had spotted were visible, steadily advancing to the aid of their fellow.

Maxwell took a step as though about to risk it all in a sprint toward the river—and then, as the gun that was the creature's right arm swung to follow his movement, abruptly changed his mind. He caught Elizabeth's hand and darted back the way they had come, into the rabbit warren of alleyways.

"Halt!" came from the copper giant's mouthless head.

Maxwell paid no attention. He pushed Elizabeth in front of him, and William came right behind. The construct followed with deliberate, ear-splitting steps, and each stride pushed the light from its eyes farther into the darkness of the alleyway. Pound. Pound.

Maxwell gained the shadows, paused for an instant. Elizabeth stopped when he did, and William nearly tripped over her. Maxwell steadied them both, staggering just a little under the impact, casting an anxious look over their heads. Elizabeth looked too.

Katarina was still caught in the wash of blue light, running through it, graceful and fluid. Trevelyan came behind her, moving awkwardly, stumbling from the weight of the gun. Above him, the construct loomed, its right arm beginning to take aim.

Trevelyan swung around, ripping away the coat and tossing it aside, setting his feet and his teeth, hauling the barrel upright to bring the giant into its sights—

"Gavin, no!" Maxwell shouted.

—and slamming down a trigger that sent a sharp-tipped javelin hurtling toward the copper torso.

In the one sense, it was an immensely successful field test, for the javelin did in fact pierce the copper hide. The left knee joint buckled with a horrible squeal of wrenched metal, and the copper giant slid slowly sideways, falling to one knee like a wounded man, pulled still farther into helplessness by the weight of the cannon that was its left arm. Trevelyan shifted the barrel of the gun to the falling chest.

The construct's right arm swept down in an arc, shooting as it went, transfixing Trevelyan with a hail of bullets. The impact lifted him off his feet, then flung him aside like a ragdoll. He lost his grip on the rail-gun and it slid from his shoulder, flying wide as he hit the wall and then the ground.

Katarina had not screamed. The scream that echoed in Elizabeth's ear was her own. Katarina made no sound as she ran toward the construct, shooting with the little pistol. *Useless,* Elizabeth thought numbly. The bullets clinked against the copper hide like pebbles. She could accomplish nothing that way—

Nothing save the turning of the great blue-eyed head in her direction. The right arm moved as well, jerkily, trying to fix its aim. Suddenly William was gone from Elizabeth's side. She looked for him wildly, saw Katarina zigzagging through the alleyway, saw Maxwell and William take advantage of the distraction to seize Trevelyan's body and drag it backward. The construct's head turned back to them as they scuttled into the shadows, and Katarina darted for the rail-gun.

She got no closer than a step before the construct's bullets ran her through. She dropped to the ground all in a heap, a marionette with cut strings, and the shadows seemed to swallow her whole.

Elizabeth was unsure if Trevelyan knew. He seemed to be focused elsewhere, his glazing eyes studying something over Maxwell's shoulder as the older man ripped open his soaked red shirt. "Poetic…justice," Trevelyan said to Maxwell, the words coming clumsily around the blood in his mouth. One corner of his thin lips twitched, turning upward in what might have been a smile. "Quite a…Celtic …" And then, with one last burst of energy and bad temper, "Never mind…me, y'fool…*run.*"

Maxwell jumped to his feet, grabbing Elizabeth's arm with one bloodstained hand and hauling her with him, pushing her in front of him and tugging at William, shoving them down the alleyway and away from the crippled metal giant. Elizabeth ran on numb feet, painful blocks of ice that tripped over her skirt with every step.

"Water," Maxwell gasped as they rounded the corner. "River. Quick. This way—"

The ground shook with thunder that was not thunder. The sky shook with lightning that was not lightning. The streets and buildings seemed to tilt in Elizabeth's blurred vision, something out of a kaleidoscope or a nightmare. Somewhere far away, Big Ben tolled out the hour with ominous precision: one, two, three.

They turned left on the next cross-street, heading back toward the docks, toward the river, toward escape. They were more than halfway when an enormous copper body took a sideways stomping step to block the exit. It loomed implacably before them, black against the blue-white sky.

Maxwell stumbled backward into Elizabeth, almost tripping them both—and then all the alleyway's shadows blinked out of existence under a bright shaft of blue light. *"Halt!"* the construct boomed.

Behind them came the sound of running feet. Not stomping feet, not a construct. Men's feet, many of them, pounding on the cobblestones. A voice raised in a shout over the pounding, snapping orders.

Elizabeth looked over her shoulder in time to see three uniformed and helmeted figures block the other end of the alleyway.

Maxwell reached over and yanked the pocket watch out of William's waistcoat.

"Show your hands!" the construct commanded.

"Wait—" Elizabeth said.

Maxwell caught hold of her reaching arm with his left hand, eyes fixed on the pocket watch in his right. He pressed the top stem twice and the side stem once—a warning shot from one of the helmeted men sailed past them—and he pushed her away from him, hard. She collided with William and they both fell toward the wall, the pocket watch sailing out of Maxwell's hand and swinging from its fob at William's waist.

"Keep her safe!" Maxwell said. The world flickered around them. The helmeted men brought their rifles to bear and Maxwell snatched his own watch from his waistcoat pocket.

Elizabeth's last sight of 1885 was of Maxwell fumbling with the dials as men rushed him from one direction and the construct leveled its right arm from the other. Then the world went rainbowy and dark and bright, and she and William landed in a tangle of limbs at the base of a serenely blossoming apple tree in the orderly orchard of his father's estate.

Chapter 14

He had been falling into a crate. He had felt the sharp corner of it against his leg, felt his knee strike it and buckle even as he tried to support Elizabeth's weight and keep her upright. Then the splintery prickle was gone, and he landed sprawled flat on his back on soft earth, and the air all around him was warm and calm and sweet with the scent of apple blossoms.

His left hand still gripped her arm, and his collapse brought her falling with him. For one moment she was all he could see—his entire universe was made up of her dilated eyes and wild brown curls. Some of the water on her face might have been tears. He wasn't sure which of them was gasping. Both, he decided after a moment.

Water droplets bunched on the ends of her curls and fell onto his face, and he would have reeled back from the icy shock of it if he had not already been prone. He was desperately cold, he realized suddenly, fingers numb and teeth chattering, and he could feel shivers running through the length of Elizabeth's body.

Because she was still on top of him. And although propriety was far from foremost in William's mind at the moment, there still seemed to be a number of good reasons why he ought to correct that situation before doing anything else. He shifted his grip so that he was holding her off rather than pulling her close, and eased them both into a sitting position. She went with him, pliant and shuddering. The blue sky above the apple tree tilted around them for a moment, and he didn't let go until it steadied itself and he was sure they would both stay upright.

"Elizabeth?" he started to say, taking his hand from her shoulder so that he could use it for something else—bracing himself, or possibly touching her face, he hadn't quite decided—but her name died in his throat when he saw the red smudges he had left on her white gown.

Because his palm was slick with Gavin Trevelyan's blood.

There was no reason for him to want to vomit. He had been a soldier; he'd had blood on his hands before. He turned his head sharply to one side, closing his eyes against the renewed dizziness, swallowing so hard he thought he would choke. He had to break off the swallow to breathe, but none of the rising bile escaped his throat.

The darkness behind his eyelids seemed full of lashing blue lightning and pumping red blood. He wrenched his eyes open to the sight of white blossoms and made himself turn back to her. Made himself look at her face, not at her shoulder or at his own hand. "Elizabeth?" he said again, and counted himself lucky it came out in a croak rather than a gasp.

She looked at him, but her eyes had an unfocused quality. She was shivering as though she had been drenched in ice water, and so was he—and that wasn't right, he thought. Yes, they were both soaked to the skin, but the air around them was mild; there should be no reason for such desperate, convulsive shuddering. What was it you were supposed to do? Brandy and warm blankets? He didn't have either. He unbuttoned his coat and tried to shrug it off one-handed. It was as soaked as her gown, but it was of a heavier material, so perhaps it would help a little. He couldn't think of anything else to do.

He got the thing off finally and reached to put it around her shoulders. She put a shaking hand to her throat, holding the collar closed. He couldn't tell where his shivers left off and hers began.

"Did he get out?" she whispered. "Did you see?"

William hesitated. "I don't know," he said at last. "We left before he did."

"They killed him."

"Elizabeth …"

"They must have. They were all around him…how could he have possibly…" She shuddered hard. "Because of me. Because I was in his way."

"No," William said. "Because they were fighting a war, because they were doing something dangerous, because their plan went awry. It wasn't a different plan because we were there. We didn't draw the construct's attention or choose the route to the river or tell Trevelyan to fire—"

"He sent us home before he escaped himself," she said. "He told you to keep me safe. It *was* because of me. Not Katarina or Mr. Trevelyan, but Mr. Maxwell—" Tears spilled down her cheeks.

William could see Katarina as clearly as if she had been there in the orchard—freezing in her scramble for the rail-gun, dropping in a heap of limbs. He could see Trevelyan, eyes glazing over as his blood pumped between Maxwell's fingers. He could see Maxwell, looking every way at once at the men who surrounded him as he—

William cut off the unhelpful sequence of thoughts right there.

"Come," he said to Elizabeth, "come with me, come to the brook. A drink of water will help." Hot tea and some blankets would help more, but he didn't want to risk going home or to Westerfield yet. He got very awkwardly to his feet, barely managing minimal assistance as she got to hers. Once they were both upright, he offered her his arm and she took it. He drew her down the path.

"Did it hurt terribly, when you were wounded?" she asked.

He looked at her, startled. "Well—yes, it did, it hurt quite a lot, for a long while after." *Shock,* he thought. *I wish I had brandy to give her.* "Why …?"

"I just wondered. Mr. Trevelyan didn't scream, so I thought maybe …" She took a deep breath. "Maybe it wouldn't hurt right away, maybe Katarina didn't have time to hurt before …"

"She didn't," William said with certainty. At least he could provide reassurance on that point. "I'm sure she didn't. It was too quick."

"She loved Mr. Trevelyan," Elizabeth said. "I mean, she truly did. I don't think he…But maybe it would have come right if there had been time."

She loved him, but she knew it wasn't going to come right, William thought. He knew something about wanting what you could not have, had recognized a particular look on Katarina's face as one he had seen in the glass when contemplating his lost career. Katarina had, however, made peace with her situation in a way he had not; she had at least made an attempt to want something else. On the way back from Murchinson's she had spoken a little about her mother the opera singer, and William had heard enough to be fairly certain her plan for "after the war" had not been to settle down with Trevelyan but rather to make tracks for La Scala.

Not that it mattered what the plan was. She'd had one. It was all wrong that people with future plans should die on battlefields. Particularly when there were so many others who didn't care whether they died or lived. Trevelyan had been one of the latter, William thought, but Katarina's death was a tragedy. And then there was Maxwell, the enigma, the mystery, who didn't easily fit into any category, but who—

"We can't let it happen," Elizabeth said, stopping and pulling her arm free so that she could face him. "We *can't.* We've got to stop it."

"Come here," William said, gesturing in the direction of the water that bubbled just out of view. "No, come, we'll talk about it in a minute, just come and have a drink first."

She followed him. He plunged his left hand into the water, rubbed it against the grass, and managed to get it mostly clean. Then he got her to drink and dab her face with a wet handkerchief, and it seemed to help a little. Water on his own face and down his own throat helped too. Neither of them had completely stopped shivering, but at least he could think more clearly, and Elizabeth's eyes seemed to be focusing.

"He was going to Orkney," she said. William looked over at her, and she clarified, "Maxwell. I heard him tell Katarina that he was bound for Orkney if their plan failed. Orkney in 1790, to stop it all before it started. If he—" She took a deep breath. "—if he died in the alleyway—if he died because of me—then what we saw is going to happen. There will be no one to stop it from coming true."

"That's not necessarily so," William said, trying to marshal his thoughts. "Now the two of us know the future, we can work here to change it." But he knew where she was headed. "You want to go to Orkney in his place?"

"If he can't do it," she said, "and it's because of me that he can't, then …"

"What would we do there?"

"Stop the Genevese," Elizabeth said. "Convince him not to make the first monster. Stop all of this before it starts. Maxwell said he retired to the smallest island off the Orkneys, as far north as you can get and still be on British soil. We could find that. And I know the date. I heard Maxwell tell Katarina. The fifteenth of September, 1790."

William thought about it all for a moment. "We can't," he said.

Her eyes flashed. "William—"

"Not for a full day, we can't." He fumbled in his pocket for his actual watch, nestled next to Elizabeth's uncanny one. He drew it out and popped it open to check the time, which had begun to seem like an odd thing to do with a pocket watch. "The watch won't work again until a quarter to seven tomorrow evening."

Elizabeth scrubbed the wet handkerchief over her face again. "Well, that's plenty of time to consult an atlas."

"Yes." He sighed. "We can't spend a full day in wet clothing," he said. "We have to go home. We'll need to come up with some excuse for why we're both sopping. If I could row, we could say I took you out on the dory and it overturned, but as it is …"

"It wouldn't work in any case," she said absently, as though she were accustomed to concocting creative falsehoods. He was reminded of Katarina outside Murchinson's. "We'd have to actually go to the pond and turn over a dory, and we're sure to be seen by *someone* if we try that." She thought a moment, then sighed. "We'd better say I climbed a tree and fell in the pond and you came in after me."

Even with the images of blood and lightning still dancing before his eyes, he had to smile. "Won't you be in dreadful trouble at home?"

"I'm always in trouble at home," Elizabeth said, and he smiled again.

"Here," he said. "There's...I'm afraid I got blood on your gown. Let me just ..." He reached to smear some dirt over the stains. "I'm sorry. I fear the gown is ruined either way."

She reached in a matter-of-fact manner for a handful of mud, dribbling some along her skirt for good measure. "It's rather small fish, in comparison with—with the last few days. What was it Mr. Trevelyan said? 'Top on the list of things which do not matter'?"

"Something like that." A breeze sprang up, and they both shivered—and that was enough, he decided. It was time to get indoors unless they both wanted to truly fall ill. He got to his feet and stretched out his hand to help her to hers. "I had better see you home. How shall we...? What shall we do tomorrow? Shall I call in the evening?"

Elizabeth frowned. "No. I can't say how much trouble I will be in. They might not let me see company, and they'll certainly not let us be alone. I'd better come and meet you."

"How will you contrive to—"

"I'll manage," Elizabeth said firmly. "Don't worry over that part. Shall we meet at the tree?"

"Yes, that should do." They were well on their way back through the orchard and to her father's house. At some point he had pulled her arm through his, though he did not remember doing so. "Seven tomorrow evening."

⁓

The slap snapped Elizabeth's head around and rattled her teeth, but did not in any deep way surprise her. Her aunt's hand had been metaphorically drawn back for some time now. It didn't scare her, either, though that might have had more to do with the last twenty-four hours than the last seventeen years.

It would not have been quite so bad to face her parents. She had been planning on doing so, had steeled herself for her mother's wailed predictions of imminent death by pneumonia or lingering death by spinsterhood, had expected that the wailing would be followed by an order to the servants to bundle Elizabeth up to bed. Elizabeth had been looking forward to the seclusion of her room, the warmth of dry clothes, and the decadence of a feather bolster. Even the thought of some coddling was not so very unwelcome. Ordinarily she had no patience for it, but after the last day's events, it might have been rather nice.

Not being scolded at all would have been even nicer, and she had not quite given up hope for that outcome as she and William approached Westerfield. She obviously could not keep her ruined gown a secret forever, but there would be less wailing if her mother only heard reports of her dripping and mud-streaked condition rather than observing it first-hand. Elizabeth therefore decided that she and William should approach the kitchen door, where they would be likely to encounter no one save Mrs. Bronson. The kindly old cook was as much Elizabeth's friend as was her husband the butler. Mrs. Bronson would keep a secret if Elizabeth asked it of her.

The plan worked well enough at first. Mrs. Bronson was alone in the kitchen and, though horrified and alarmed, did not react with hysterics. Elizabeth explained about climbing the tree, falling into the pond, and being rescued by William. Mrs. Bronson clucked, shook her head, looked approvingly at the young man, and told Elizabeth to nip upstairs and get out of her wet things as quickly as she could.

William said, "If I can be of no further service, E—ah, Miss Barton, I'll bid you good evening."

Mrs. Bronson might have lifted her eyes to the ceiling as she bustled to make tea. William looked annoyed at his slip. "Sorry," he mouthed to Elizabeth behind Mrs. Bronson's back.

Elizabeth shook her head. "Elizabeth," she mouthed back. He nodded, bowed slightly for Mrs. Bronson's benefit, and squelched his way toward the outside door.

Elizabeth eased the corridor door open, noted with relief the empty passage and staircase, and only then realized she was still clutching his coat around her shoulders. She turned back. "William?"

He looked up in the act of opening the outer door, took conscious note of the coat for the first time, then shook his head a little at himself and came to retrieve it. Elizabeth's hand still held the door open as William took his coat from her and bent to murmur in her ear, "I'll see you tomorrow." Without the coat wrapped about her shoulders, there was nothing at all to conceal the fact that her waterlogged muslin clung to her as closely as had Katarina's skin-tight blouse and breeches. Her aunt came through the drawing room door at that precise moment and saw them in just that position, and Elizabeth had to admit to herself that it did look pretty bad.

t seemed neighbors had come to call, and were currently with Mr. and Mrs. Barton in the drawing room. It further seemed that Elizabeth's aunt was unwilling to have them know of her niece's disgraceful behavior. Overall, Elizabeth thought, a circumstance to regret, for the scene that followed would not have been nearly so bad in front of witnesses. She was later given proof to bolster this belief; the slap had not been delivered until William left the kitchen.

The second slap was even less of a surprise than the first, but it hurt more. Elizabeth grabbed hold of a nearby chair, tears starting in her eyes.

"You'll ruin us all," she heard her aunt saying. "You're just like her, I always said you were, and you will finish what she started. We struck her name from the family Bible, but it didn't matter. After she ran off to flaunt her harlot's ways, no decent man would have me—and no decent girl would have had your father if he had not already been wed to your mother. We hushed it up for your sake, you ungrateful chit, but you're just like her—" She caught hold of herself, with what Elizabeth recognized even through streaming eyes as a visible effort. "Mrs. Bronson. Conduct my niece to her room."

⁓

he was in her room now, alone and in dry clothing, which was a significant improvement. Having a hot drink inside her would be more of an improvement still, and she waited with some impatience for Mrs. Bronson or one of the maids to bring it. She wondered if she might be able to charm something like a nuncheon out of the cook as well. It had been quite a long time since she had eaten a proper meal.

When the door opened, however, it was her aunt who entered. Elizabeth stood up, anger clenching her empty belly, but her aunt only deposited a cup of what turned out to be exceptionally weak tea on the bedside table and left without saying a word. Elizabeth heard the key turn in the lock as soon as the door shut behind her, and no one else came to her room that night. Not even the servants. Not even though she rang for them.

She dropped to sleep out of exhaustion, but slept only fitfully, waking often from dreams of lightning and Katarina falling and Trevelyan facing down a copper giant, standing in the square of light it threw like a black knight on a chessboard.

The third time she woke, the room was lit by morning sun and the housemaid was just withdrawing. "Wait!" Elizabeth said, swinging her legs over the side of the bed. The housemaid flinched away and scurried through the door, looking back once she was safe in the hall.

"No, miss," she said. "Miss Barton said you were ill because of something that happened yesterday, that you had to rest abed all day."

Elizabeth glanced over her shoulder at the tea tray. There was no food on it, and she suspected that cup of tea was dishwater strength as well. "Will you bring up my breakfast, then?" she said, testing the waters.

"Miss Barton said she would order special meals for you," the maid said, looking scared, and shut the door. Elizabeth wasn't quite quick enough to get to it before the key turned again.

There was breakfast later—but not much, more weak tea and a slice of toast. At dinner-time, there was broth. Elizabeth got the point and it only made her angrier. This couldn't last longer than a day—she had heard her mother's voice keening outside, and her aunt explaining that Elizabeth needed rest, that if she was not better by morning they would call the apothecary, now come away, sister, it will only upset you to see her, I'll care for her... So the punishment would be over by morning. But even that was too long.

We struck her name from the family Bible, Elizabeth thought, staring at the sunlight stretched across the floor, *but no decent man would have me.* She thought she could work out what the story had been—it must have occurred before her father took the house in Hartwich, for she had never heard so much as a whisper of it from the neighbors—but she found herself disinclined to spend any time doing so. She simply didn't care. There were too many more important things to care about.

The foremost being, how she was to get out of this room at seven o'clock to go and meet William.

She considered her options. What would Katarina do? Rush past the next maid to bring a tray? Yes, but then do what? Besides, who knew when that would be? Perhaps not until full dark, or they might not bring her supper at all. Elizabeth's stomach rumbled, and she tried to ignore it. Get the lock open from the inside and sneak out? Undoubtedly Katarina would do just that, and Elizabeth thought she could manage the sneaking, but she had no notion as to how to pick a lock. She had very much enjoyed Katarina's story of doing so, but that was not at all the same thing.

Memory of the alleyway hit her like her aunt's open palm, and she breathed hard for a moment.

Katarina is not dead, she told herself. *Not yet. She hasn't even been born yet. They're the shadows of things that may be only, and we'll stop it before it starts.*

Elizabeth got up off the bed. The fast young ladies whose ranks her aunt assumed her to have joined snuck from their windows to elope to Gretna Green, did they not? They did it in Mirabelle's novels, at least, and they did it wearing gowns. It couldn't be that hard. Elizabeth stole to the window and opened the shutters very quietly.

If she recalled Mirabelle's novels correctly, the fast young ladies usually employed a trellis when fleeing their bedchambers. Elizabeth thought she could probably climb down a trellis if there were one, but no ivy ran along the gray and grainy stone under her window. How else did young ladies escape? Elizabeth racked her memory for other stories, and came up with Bluebeard's wife, locked in a tower to avoid her murderous husband's rage, waiting for her brother to come to her rescue. No help there; Elizabeth had no brothers. Anything else? There was the maiden Rapunzel from the collection of German fairytales that had been so talked of two or three years ago—definitely a fast young lady; hadn't it been her dress tightening about her belly that had betrayed her indiscretion to the enchantress? Rapunzel's prince had brought her silk every night to weave into a ladder.

Well, ladders could be woven from material other than a prince's silk. And now that Elizabeth thought about it, she seemed to remember bedsheets figuring in one of those novelized escapes Mirabelle so enjoyed. Elizabeth took the muslin sheets off her bed and found her sewing scissors.

She hesitated for one instant before she made the first cut. If there had been ivy, she might have slipped out and back and no one ever been the wiser. But if she tore up her bedsheets, they would know. She didn't know what they would do in response, but nothing would ever be the same again.

In her mind's eye, constructs thundered through the streets of London and Katarina fell in an alleyway. Elizabeth took up the shears and got to work.

By the time the downstairs clock struck half past six, she had a ladder of sorts, wrapped twice around a post of her heavy bedstead. She looked at it with satisfaction, and went to dress.

She would have given almost anything for a pair of Katarina's breeches. She put on a gown instead, wriggling to fasten as many buttons as possible. It was harder to do them up than to undo them, but she thought she managed enough to keep the thing from gaping. She took her gloves from their drawer. What else? She tried to think what would have been useful in 1885. Something to carry things in. She fetched her reticule. Something to keep off the rain. She fetched a spencer. She added a second gown and a change of stockings to the pile, tied the whole thing up in a bundle, and took it to the window.

She would never be able to climb down with such a bulky parcel under her arm. How did the fast young ladies manage it? She stood frowning down at the drop until a creaking floorboard out in the hall made her jump. Then she froze, listening, but it was not repeated. No one was coming toward her room. Or at least, she didn't think so, but she could be wrong, and there was no more time to waste.

Elizabeth tucked up her skirts, pulled on her gloves, dropped the bundle to the grass below, prayed no one had been near a downstairs window to see it, and scrambled up onto the window ledge.

Climbing down a muslin rope-ladder was harder than climbing up a tree, but it was not much harder than climbing down. She clung to the ledge until her feet found the first knot, then transferred her grip to the bedsheet-ladder. She fancied she felt it strain under her palms. She eased downward, feeling with her feet for the second knot. She shifted her grip and felt for the third.

About halfway down, it became much harder than a tree. Her feet couldn't find a knot to support them. She hung, legs flailing, knowing she wouldn't be able to hold up her own weight for long. Didn't sailors go hand over hand up and down ropes? How? Her knees scraped against the brick of the house.

And then the muslin was slithering through her gloves and she was falling.

She landed with a thump, breath knocked out of her, staring up at the window and the slowly-swinging muslin ladder.

I'm all right, she told herself.

She wasn't completely sure she believed it.

I'm all right. I'm not hurt, only bruised. I need a minute to catch my breath, but I'm all right.

She didn't get even the minute, though. Just then she thought she saw a movement from the other side of the ground-floor window, and she knew she heard a cry of surprise. She scrambled to her feet, grabbing her bundle and running full tilt for the orchard.

William was waiting for her under their tree, a rucksack over his left shoulder. He looked up when he heard her coming, and straightened. She thought he was smiling, but the smile vanished from his face when he got a good look at her expression. "What's happened?"

"Nothing," Elizabeth gasped, breath gone more from the fright of the fall than from running. "I had to—sneak out—is all." She didn't want to tell him how she had done it, how irrevocable a decision she had made. She fumbled to pull her skirts down where they belonged. "I think they saw me."

"Right. Quickly, then." He pulled out the pocket watch.

"Did you—check the—?"

"Latitude and longitude, yes. Ah, frequently." He gave her a self-deprecating half-smile. "About once an hour for the last twenty-three." He was clearly checking it again. "The date too. It's right. Are you—?"

"Ready," Elizabeth said. She reached a hand for his arm. She thought she heard a shout from back toward the house.

"Then one," William said, depressing the side stem. "Two—" He pressed it again. *"Three—"*

Chapter 15

They stood on a rocky shore. The light was fading fast, and there was not enough of it remaining to discern the sea, but Elizabeth could sense it anyway, an amorphous dark menace somewhere off to her left. Waves broke hard upon the shingle, and the echo of them bounced off the rocks, filling the air in every direction with the sense of something encompassing and remorseless. To her right, a cliff rose up, indistinct like an inkblot against the indigo of the sky. William's form was an inkblot also, his features impossible to read.

"Right," he said in a voice not entirely steady. "It worked."

"It worked!" Elizabeth agreed, elation singing through her. For just a moment, she forgot about Katarina and Trevelyan and blue lightning, not to mention rope ladders and windows. It had *worked,* they had *done* it, they were *here,* and she wanted to shout.

"Right," William said again. Letting go of her hand, he swung his pack to the ground and bent over it. "What do you have there?" he asked, and his hands brushed hers as he reached for her bundle. "Likely I can fit it."

She stopped him long enough to disentangle her spencer and layer it hastily over her gown. Salt-flecked wind gusted off the water, piercing straight through to her skin and setting her shivering. She couldn't get the buttons done fast enough.

She could see the William ink-blot struggling to repack the rucksack with his left hand and thought of offering to help. Then she noted the set of his jaw and refrained. He rose at last, swinging the rucksack over his left shoulder and squirming to get it over his right as well. She did not offer to help with this either.

"Right," William said for the third time, once both straps were settled securely. "What do we do now?"

That was a good question. "We go find the Genevese and persuade him not to …" It sounded rather feeble even to her own ears. It was the first time she had given thought to the "how."

"Do you know his name?"

Elizabeth shook her head. "No, but there can't be so very many students from Geneva hiring a cottage here, can there? We should ..." She looked about, seeking inspiration, and spied a gleam from the cliff high above them. "There's a house there—see the lamplight? We should start there and inquire."

William nodded as though he found the plan sensible enough, and turned his attention to the cliff. "One would imagine, with a house so near, there would be a safe path down to the shore," he murmured, and they set about looking for it. But none sprang into view, not even when the sky darkened enough for the gibbous moon to do them some good. They walked the length of the beach and back, stopping at each end to stare at cliffs that dropped sheer into frothing water. The slope in between the endpoints was not much more forgiving. Perhaps at low tide, there was an easy path upward, but it seemed as though the tide was now at its highest ebb.

When they had nearly returned to their starting point for the second time, William suddenly paused. "Well," he said, peering at the jagged rocks nearest to hand, "I suppose that isn't *so* bad." It was a testament to their lack of other options that he said so. They would have otherwise rejected the barely existent path as being far too difficult—in fact, they had already done so twice. "Could you climb this, do you think?"

Elizabeth's answer was to tuck up her skirts again. "I can. At least, I think so. But, er, forgive me—"

"I'll manage," he said, still turned away from her and looking at the path. His voice was grim, but she did not think it was angry. "It's steep, yes, but it's not a sheer drop. I've got one good hand. The problem is, only having one, I won't be able to help you if—"

"I'll manage," she echoed.

She had the oddest sense that he smiled, though she still couldn't see his face. "All right," he said. "Once more unto the breach?"

It was no harder than shimmying down the bedsheet. *I'd give almost anything for breeches,* Elizabeth thought again. Her tucked-up skirts were bunchy and awkward, and the sea-breeze blew numbingly cold on her stocking-clad legs. Three steps in, she revised the thought: *No, never mind. While breeches would be helpful, what I'd really give anything for is better shoes.* The moonlight was a witchy, deceptive sort of thing, making sharp-pointed rocks look like harmless shadows, and hollows look like footholds. Elizabeth found a hollow by putting her foot in it, twisted her ankle, and cast an irritated covetous glance at William's boots.

"All right?" he said.

"Yes. Fine."

Her voice must have been a little sharp, for he stopped moving and turned his head. "Take it slow," he said. "Test with your foot to be sure you've got something firm before you put your whole weight on it. Use your hands between steps. It's all right if it takes longer. We needn't rush."

"No," she agreed, testing the next step with her throbbing ankle. William himself was moving very slowly, feinting each movement before committing to it, putting his left hand down after every step. Not trusting his balance, she thought.

She moved her right foot toward what looked like a rock. It was a rock. She leaned into it, and it shifted. She drew back, tried another angle, found the shifting to be less treacherous this time, and managed to bring her left foot forward.

She looked up to find William watching. He turned his eyes front rather quickly. "Exactly," he said in an approving sort of voice, but it was a little muffled. He braced his feet and reached for another handhold, and it wasn't until she was well into doing the same that she wondered exactly what he had been looking at. Well—no help for it. He had already seen her in breeches, anyway, and with muslin clinging to her skin. It seemed ridiculous to worry over modesty now.

Her eyes came at last level with the crest of the path, where rocks and tufts of grass sat outlined in a weird silver glow. With one last effort and scramble, she made it to the flat ground, and William took two long, carefully balanced strides to stand beside her.

Here the wind blew harder and colder. It whistled in Elizabeth's ears, and she shivered despite the spencer. Some few yards away sat a crofter's cottage—a rude, slant-walled affair with a thatched roof, perched nearly on the edge of one of the cliffs whose base was covered by high-tide water. Behind the cottage was a building that might have once been a barn, before its roof fell in. There was no sign of any living thing anywhere the moon shone, but a light winked through the shutters of one window of the hut.

Well, at least the occupant was awake. Elizabeth pulled down her skirts, strode up to the door, and knocked on it.

There was no response.

She glanced back at William. He lifted his shoulders in a shrug, so she knocked again.

Still nothing. This time she held her breath, listening for movement inside, but could hear none over the sound of the sea and the wind—

—except a thump, a slight one, as though something within had fallen from a shelf.

Then the door shuddered hard before her eyes, to the accompaniment of much louder thump. Elizabeth seized the latch and wrenched the door open.

The room was almost bare of furnishings. Her eyes took in a pallet in the corner by the hearth, a rickety table set against the opposite wall, three brass-bound trunks askew and open, their contents spilling every which way. The sparseness made the room seem cold, despite the fire in the hearth. Or maybe the impression of coldness came from the shadow that loomed over everything.

The figure casting it was frighteningly tall in its own right, of course, seven or eight feet in height. With the light behind it, the shadow it threw was immense. Elizabeth could not see the stitches and scars, but the hunched shoulders and drooping skin of the silhouette left her in no doubt that a Wellington monster cast that shadow—not that she had been in particular doubt in the first place, for it could not have belonged to a normal-sized man. It was bent over a smaller figure, its ham-sized fists clenched around the latter's throat. It slammed the smaller figure for a third time into the wall, and as it did so it shifted just enough to allow light to fall on its victim's face.

Maxwell.

William took a step in front of her, dropping his right shoulder as though to shrug the rucksack off it, but Elizabeth was too frightened to stand still. She ran forward before she had decided what to do, looking in every direction for something—anything—

There was a poker gleaming dully in the fire from the hearth. Elizabeth grabbed it. Even bent over Maxwell's slumping body, the creature's head was higher than she could reach, but she swung at it anyway, hitting its back as hard as she could.

It let out a roar that sounded more like anger than like pain, but at least it dropped Maxwell. Elizabeth was striking out again as it rounded on her. This second blow went wide, barely brushing the creature's ragged sleeve, and the monster swung at her. She tried to dodge, but tripped over something on the floor and then over her skirt, and its heavy hand slammed into the side of her head. She fell, poker flying from her fingers. She heard William shouting something.

For a moment, Elizabeth thought she had hit her head hard enough to see double, for it seemed that two stitched-together faces stared down at her, demonic in the firelight. Then she realized that there actually were two monsters: the one that had struck her, and a smaller one huddled behind it, outlined by a doorway to an inner room that Elizabeth had not previously noticed. A kitchen, most likely.

The larger creature swung away from her, snapping out something…in *French?* It certainly sounded like French. William stumbled over the detritus on the floor to Elizabeth's side, but she was already struggling to her feet. The larger creature seized the arm of the smaller one and hustled it through the inner doorway. Elizabeth grabbed the poker again and ran after, William right behind her.

A blast of cool air struck her face just as she reached the inner doorway, and she knew what that meant before she heard the slam in the darkness. There was a back door to this cottage, and the creatures had escaped through it.

She didn't dare run through the dark kitchen. *They* might be able to see in the dark, but *she* couldn't, and who knew what menaces might be lurking in the shadows? She turned instead and ran the other way, back through the sparse main room and to the front door. She reached the doorway just in time to see the two creatures running through the moonlight and to the cliffside, the larger one dragging the smaller after it.

Their long legs ate up the distance to the cliff before Elizabeth could run more than two steps in their direction. They paused for a bare instant at the precipice. And then they jumped together, hands linked. Two splashes carried clearly to the ears of the watching humans.

There was something dreamlike about the entire scene, Elizabeth thought. The blue-black night, full of sea-sounds. The dark water lapping far below. The moonlight shining in a silver path along the inky waves. One dark shape and then another crossed into the path of the moon, swimming steadily, moving farther and farther out to sea until they became indistinguishable from the water around them.

"Don't ever do that again," William's voice said in her ear. "Good God, you can't just go rushing into—At least give me a moment to—You're not hurt, are you? Are you hurt?"

Elizabeth shook her head, as much in experiment as in answer. No, she decided, she was not hurt. Her cheek still stung—and no surprise; that was the third time in twenty-four hours it had been struck—but her head did not spin. She felt bruised from hitting the floor, but it was no worse than falling from a horse. She reflected, with a strange sense of calm, that either she had gotten the date wrong or Maxwell had, because it was demonstrably too late to stop the Genevese from making the first monster.

Maxwell—

She said his name in a gasp, and whirled back toward the cottage. But he stood on the threshold, disheveled and coatless, shirtsleeves and hair shining blue-silver in the moonlight. He leaned against the doorway for support and he had his other hand pressed to his throat, but he was alive.

"There is—something comforting," he choked out, "—about the statistical—inevitability. Suppose you felt—honor bound? Though for all—th'good I'm doing, you ought—t'have let them kill me." He staggered toward them. "Are either of you hurt?"

"No," Elizabeth said at once, and "No," William said, giving her one last anxious look before shaking his head as though trying to clear it. "Two. There were *two.*"

"Yes." Maxwell looked down at the moonlit waves with an expression of loathing. "I'm too late. Again." He turned back to the cottage, stumbling a little. "Safe enough inside now," he added over his shoulder. "May as well come in."

There was indeed no longer anything alarming in the outer room, though the signs of violent struggle were now clearly visible in the firelight. The pallet had been kicked away from the hearth, the rough brown blanket dragged off it. A stool had once sat beside the rickety table, and now lay broken in two pieces on the floor. The brass-bound trunks—far too grand for their surroundings, Elizabeth noted for the first time—lay all on their sides, contents spilled across the floorboards. Maxwell staggered about, taking candles from the mantelpiece and the table, and lighting them at the hearth. The room gradually grew light enough for Elizabeth to see that just within the kitchen door lay a huddled form, head covered by Maxwell's coat.

"Don't look," Maxwell said quietly behind her. "It's not a pretty sight."

Elizabeth did not go and lift the coat. She did take one of the candles and advance toward the inner room, but she conducted her observations from the doorway.

It had indeed been intended as a kitchen originally, but its current inhabitant had put it to different use. This hearth was cold. The shelves held gleaming copper instruments and things in jars, not herbs or cooking pans. There were no chairs or stools around the table large enough to seat a crofter's family, and the table itself was spread with oil-cloth and had been fitted with…Elizabeth studied it. It had been fitted with irons, like those of the stocks in the village green back home. She looked at the thickness of the irons and the distance between them, and swallowed. Some huge thing had been chained onto this table by its wrists and ankles. She had no trouble guessing what huge thing that might have been.

"It seems," Maxwell said, still in that flat, quiet tone, "that our information was inaccurate." Elizabeth turned back to him. He stood by the unsteady table, gazing down upon it with candle in hand. A thick layer of dust sprang into view in the candlelight, strangely marred by the clear space where a book had sat long open. Maxwell traced his finger around the outlines of the vanished book. "His journal ended with an entry dated September the 16th, saying the work would be completed upon the morrow. Perhaps our young scholar lost track of the days, so far removed from the world." His tone was very mild, but all at once he slammed his hand hard onto the table, and Elizabeth took a startled step back from him.

Maxwell paused only long enough to set down the candle and curl his hand into a fist, and then he hit the wall so hard that the table seemed to shiver from the nearby impact and the candle flame wavered dangerously. He hit the wall again, harder; stumbled against the pieces of the stool and swore as he kicked them away. Elizabeth had retreated several steps more by then, well into the center of the room. William shouldered past her, somehow managing not to trip over the instruments on the floor as he captured Maxwell from behind in a one-armed bear hug.

Maxwell was bigger through the shoulders, but William was taller and younger and quite determined; Maxwell made one halfhearted attempt to throw him off, then gave up and seemed to go limp. "It's all right," William was saying calmly, "it's all right. Come over here where it's warm. Come on now. I've brought brandy. Elizabeth, can you—?" He made quick eye contact as he manhandled Maxwell past her and to the pallet beside the hearth. "It's in my pack." She saw now where he had dropped the rucksack. "And perhaps you could shut the kitchen door."

Shutting the door on the dead body of the Genevese student did indeed seem like the thing to do. Elizabeth did it gladly, then hurried toward the rucksack. She had to set the candle down to get it open, and so had to sort through its contents blind. With chilly fingers she rooted through various pieces of folded cloth, seeking the solid coldness of a flask. She had just grasped it when a noise behind her startled her into dropping it. Then she belatedly recognized the strangled sound as a sob, rather than the breathing of a returning monster, and fished the flask out of the pack again.

She brought it over to William, who had Maxwell seated on the pallet and the rough blanket draped over his shoulders. William stooped and put the flask in the older man's hand. Maxwell stared at it for a moment unblinking before taking it, uncorking it, and gulping down a swallow. And then another. And a third.

William eased away from him. For a moment, he stood watching; then he turned away. He met Elizabeth's eyes as he did—a silent question, *Are you all right?*

She nodded. William went over to the nearest trunk, righted it, closed it, and dragged it one-handed over to the hearthside opposite the pallet. He met her eyes again, gesturing to it, and she came to sit on the seat he had provided for her as he went to fetch another trunk for himself.

"I'm sorry," Maxwell said at last, brokenly. "I am sorry." His shoulders hunched and his head drooped over the flask in his hands. "They were my friends."

"I cannot even imagine," William said quietly, standing just outside the circle of firelight. After a moment, he added, "And you have been doing this all alone for quite some time, haven't you?"

Maxwell leaned back, seeming to make an effort to straighten his shoulders and steady his voice. He looked much smaller than he ever had before, sitting cross-legged on the pallet with the blanket hugged about him. He cleared his throat. "For some time, yes."

William went over to the far wall, retrieved his pack, and brought it back with him into the firelight. He sat down on the trunk he had claimed for himself, and bent to rummage in the rucksack. "How did it begin?"

"How—?" Maxwell cleared his throat again, then waved one hand to indicate the room. "This story?"

"Your story." William's head came up from the pack as his hand drew out a handkerchief-wrapped bundle. He balanced it on his knees and set about working out the knot.

"I…came by it honestly, I suppose." Maxwell's lips twisted a little, not really a smile. "My…my parents were time-travelers. I found their watch after they died, and it seemed I inherited some of their taste for adventure. Some of this story did begin within my lifetime. When I first went forward and encountered the future that was to result, I…" He trailed off. Elizabeth looked up, and he was gazing at the far wall, as though there was a message to be seen in the play of the shadows. "I could not let it stand," he said finally. "Not when I had a way to stop it, or thought I did. I had to try. I have…been trying, ever since. Quite a while now, indeed."

The far wall seemed to be fascinating him, so much that he lost the thread of what he was saying. William frowned at that, even as he set the handkerchief-full of biscuits where they all could reach. He licked his lips and seemed to be looking for another question, something to keep Maxwell talking. He glanced at Elizabeth as though for help.

"The poor man who's in there," she said, nodding toward the kitchen. "That's the Genevese student?"

Maxwell's eyes went to her, startled out of wherever he had sunk into. "Yes, of course."

"I had thought you were coming here to stop him making the first monster? But there were two."

"I've already tried to stop him making the first monster," Maxwell said, and his smile was bitter. "I've failed there already. I was going to stop him creating a wife for the monster…kill him if I had to, if that was the only way to stop him. But I'm too late again."

Elizabeth bit her tongue on, *Why did you not plan to arrive a month ago, so you would have plenty of time?* She settled for, "In twenty-four hours, can you not go back one week ago for another try?"

Maxwell shook his head. "I began to explain this earlier, but I suppose I did not do it properly. The timepiece allows only one journey to each junction. The opportunity to change this moment is forever closed to me."

"'Junction'?"

"The places where the road forks and the story changes. The moments that matter. One cannot dip in the same river twice, or whatever that saying is. The watch does not let you return to a place where you have already been."

"But you could go to one of the other junctions, to stop this?" William asked.

"I've been a part of nearly all of them. I've been in Geneva, trying to steal away the books that first started the young student down this disastrous path. I've been in London, trying to steal the letters sent by his collaborator, the ones that gave the final piece of the puzzle. I created an entire persona and rented a house, so that I could get to know him during his travels, invite him to stay with me, prevent him from coming here …" His voice thickened again.

"So what happens next?" William asked, trying to recapture his attention. "After tonight, what happens, what's the story?"

Maxwell did not answer.

"The first monster takes the female one to wife," Elizabeth said, remembering Katarina's tale. "Their children become a terror to the Highlands, and the King sends soldiers, and the soldiers capture one."

Maxwell looked up, not asking how she knew. "I was there," he commented, almost without inflection. "I was hiding in the heather,

trying to prevent the capture, trying to save my enemy from my King
…"

"But you were unable to," William said, doggedly keeping to the
chronicle of events. "And then?"

"In 1855, I tried to prevent the building of Moore's Wall. I failed.
In 1872, I tried to rescue a Welsh farm girl from the first uprising of the
rebel miners. I failed there too. In 1876, I tried to prevent the constructs
from being built. I failed. In 1885, I tried to assist the man who meant
to forge a weapon capable of bringing down the horror he had created.
And failed again."

The horror he had created. Elizabeth shivered, but realized she did
not feel surprise. William did not look surprised either.

"I had wondered whether Trevelyan was involved," he said.

"He was studying at university when his young wife was killed in
a monster uprising," Maxwell said, with a gesture of helplessness. "It
gave his studies a new goal. He was a genius, truly. They would never
have managed to create the constructs without him." He took another
swallow of the brandy.

William thought about it. "You haven't told us what all the junctions are. What happened between 1800, when a single marauding
creature was captured while you hid in the heather, and 1855, when
there was an army of them in full revolt?"

Maxwell looked at Elizabeth. "What has Katarina already told you?"

"The Royal Academy of Sciences learnt to do what the Genevése
had done," Elizabeth remembered. "She said they created a great many
when England feared Bonaparte's invasion—ten years ago, then? I
mean, ten years ago for us? In 1805?"

Maxwell nodded slowly. "They began work in 1804," he said. "I
cannot fault them for concluding it a prudent thing to do. In 1804,
Bonaparte held the Continent in his hand and had his eyes cast across
the channel. He was heard to say—by the year 1885, it is considered
a matter of historical record—that he had some one hundred thirty
thousand troops and three thousand gunboats *only awaiting a favorable
wind* in order to place the tricolored flag on the Tower of London. A
boast perhaps, but Whitehall considered it sober threat enough to wish
to have a surprise awaiting any Frenchmen who set foot on English
soil. The monsters—the 'special battalion,' they were called—were intended for our defense when the future seemed darkest. As it turned
out, we had no need of them in 1804, and in 1805, Admiral Lord Nel-
son did us proud at Trafalgar and settled by other means the question
of Frenchmen on English soil." He paused. "But the Royal Academy
continued their researches anyway."

William's brow furrowed. "Why?"

"Because there were men in the government interested in seeing the research pursued. Because there were men in the Academy interested in solving the Genevese's riddle." Maxwell shrugged. "Because sometimes the crank turns itself. By 1814, the riddle had been solved and monsters created in great numbers, housed and trained in some secret camp in a barren corner of the Highlands, ready to be deployed to the Peninsula if need be. But then Bonaparte was defeated by mundane means and exiled to Elba. The secret offices of Whitehall debated whether to put the special battalion to some other use—in the Empire's colonies, perhaps? Slaughtering them seemed wasteful, after all...Meanwhile the not-secret offices of Whitehall discharged soldiers and sailors in huge numbers, wartime being over. This you know, of course." His eyes went from Elizabeth to William. "You have lived through it."

"Within the last twelvemonth," William said. "Bonaparte escaped exile in March, and seized Paris again. And the Duke set out to meet him on the Continent, with—" He broke off. "Oh."

"With an army a shadow of its former size and strength," Maxwell said. "Do you understand now?"

"*I* do not," Elizabeth said. "Do you mean to say it was the Duke who did this to us? He took the monsters with him to the Continent? Why not call again to service the English soldiers who fought for him on the Peninsula last year—I mean, in 1814?"

"You do not understand the dangers the Duke faced." Maxwell saw her expression, and added, "I mean you no insult. It is fact. You don't have an appreciation for the situation; you can't."

Elizabeth stared at him. "All right," she said finally. "So explain it to me. What don't I understand?"

Maxwell sighed, resettling himself. "Well, to begin with, you think of Napoleon as a—The word monster has been somewhat over-used of late, so let us say, as the Devil incarnate. He's a fiend in human form; his followers are minions; all good Frenchmen wished to see their King restored, and their righteous souls rejoiced in 1814 when the tyrant was sent to Elba...no? So that is the first thing you do not understand. Because it will not have been widely publicized in England, and certainly, no offense, not among the ballrooms and drawing rooms you frequent, that Napoleon was welcomed back with tears of joy by the soldiers who had once been his." His eyes went to William. "You know this."

"I do," William said. "Those men in his army would follow him to hell."

"Yes," Maxwell said. "Now for the other half of the story. Wellington's force was not 'his' in any meaningful way. They were not the force he had built up between 1808 and 1814, the ones devoted to him personally; those men had been discharged or sent to see to matters in the Colonies. *Some* of the men Wellington commanded in 1815 were veterans, of course, but the rest were supplied from Hanover, Brunswick, Nassau, and the Netherlands, and they and the Duke did not so much as share a common language, let alone common training methods or battlefield experiences. He said he had been given 'an infamous army, very weak and ill equipped, and a very inexperienced staff.'"

"Did you hear this from *him?*" William demanded suddenly. The tone in his voice was one of awe rather than challenge.

Maxwell smiled a little. "No. I have never had the honor. Waterloo is not one of the places I have been. But I have read His Grace's writings on the subject. Lord Seward was an incomparable source of history the British government would as soon be kept quiet."

"Kept quiet?"

"His Grace the war hero was quite critical of the whole special battalion matter, and Whitehall therefore went to some effort to keep his memoirs suppressed. In any case—" Maxwell paused for a mouthful of brandy. "On eighteenth June, 1815, Wellington set out with his motley crew to stand against a force of French veterans."

Elizabeth drew in her breath. "The eighteenth June. But that's now. I mean, then. I mean, when the pocket watch arrived, yesterday, when I was sitting in the garden, the date was the seventeenth June."

"It is happening while you sit in the garden, Miss Elizabeth," Maxwell agreed.

"So what's happening?" Elizabeth said. "What happened?"

"Wellington is not without allies. A Prussian force is nearby, and if the two can join, they can surely stand against the Emperor. But they have not joined yet; the Prussians have unexpectedly met with the right wing of Bonaparte's army and been defeated and forced to retreat north. On the morning of the eighteenth, Wellington faces the French artillery and cavalry alone, though expecting Prussian reinforcements at any moment. He and his men have camped all night in a deluge of rain that made it impossible to sleep and turned the battlefield into mud."

Maxwell took another swallow from the flask, and maneuvered himself around on the pallet until he was facing the hearth. "Look," he said, and taking a handful of soot, arranged it in a line along the hearthstones. "Wellington arranges his men along a ridgeline, facing the French across a valley. In the morning, the French artillery starts shelling the British lines, and the British hold fast, for Prussian reinforcements are expected to arrive at any moment. They do not arrive.

In the afternoon, an entire Belgian brigade breaks, flees, and deserts under the charge of French cavalry, and the British cavalry destroys itself in an attack on the French line." He ran his fingertip along the line of soot he had created until it was half its former thickness. "The British line thins.

"Late in the afternoon, the defenders of La Haye Sainte farm are overrun and slaughtered." He smudged his finger through the line of soot, and Elizabeth found the resultant break curiously unsightly and alarming. She wanted to reach out and mend it. "There is a gap in the line, and the Duke no longer has reserves sufficient to plug it. He pulls men from the left flank to reinforce the center, but now the left flank falters." Maxwell added soot to the gap in the center, then used his thumbnail to create tiny breaks along the left. "A full quarter of the men who stood beside Wellington that morning are dead, dying, fled into the woods, or too hurt to stand. The line will break under the next French charge, or the one after. Evening is approaching, but the line will break before night falls. And the Prussians are still not there.

"And *that* is when he sends a rider for the special battalion." Maxwell looked up at her. His eyes were William's color, she thought, but not warm like William's eyes. They had an intensity, an anxiety to them that William's never had. "It is the sort of heroic tale one tells children: the Duke's aide-de-camp spurring through the woods with his message, the desperate Englishmen staying steadfast as their posts for just that little bit longer, the—" He made a face, tossed back a swallow from the flask, and the timbre of his voice changed. "The army of monsters pouring through the woods and over the ridge, British ingenuity come to triumph over Napoleon. The French Garde breaking at the sight of them, fleeing and leaving the Eagles behind them in the mud. Wellington sends a messenger with those Eagles at once across the Channel, and the man stumbles—with the mud and blood of battle still upon him—into a ballroom where the London *ton* parades in glittering splendor, to drop to one knee and lay the Eagles at the feet of the Prince Regent...And within a fortnight, every single man, woman, and child in the British Isles knows how 'Wellington's monsters' won the Battle of Waterloo and rid the world of the tyrant Napoleon. At that point, there is no chance whatsoever that Britain will turn aside from its wonderful and terrible creation.

"And Wellington—" Maxwell was slurring his words by now, a flush of color high in his cheeks. "—Wellington spends the rest of his life enjoining those around him to call the creatures something else. The older he gets, the more plainly he speaks his dislike that they should be christened after him. The more plainly he speaks his regret that he was forced to engage their services on the battlefield. In the memoirs that were never published, he said that the monsters were unfairly awarded the credit for the Battle of Waterloo, that his brave lads were robbed of accolades that should have been theirs for standing so long against such punishing odds. He wrote that he wished he had never sent for them—that he regretted that victory as he never regretted any defeat—for had he held his hand, his men and Blücher's could have routed Bonaparte. He wrote that the British could have held until sundown, and had he *known* the Prussians would be there by sundown, he would never have sent for the monsters."

"And what do you think?" William asked, quite softly.

Maxwell looked over at him out of glittering, near-feverish eyes. "I think His Grace was never wrong in such matters," he said with the distinctive slurred precision of a man who has indulged in too much brandy. "If he says the British could have held, then they could have held. Had there been no special battalion, brave Englishmen and their allies would still have won the war. We needed no monstrous help at Trafalgar, did we?"

"Then why," Elizabeth said, "are you not at the Battle of Waterloo, preventing the Duke from summoning the special battalion?"

Chapter 16

"I'll go and try," Maxwell said, "because I have to try, but it's unlikely to work. I've attempted to influence battles before. With no success."

The sky had darkened once again to evening blue, changing the color of the waves beneath it from silver to cobalt. They were even higher up this evening than they had been the last, at the top of a green and rocky hillside some distance inland from the Genevese's cottage. They had been here for much of the day, and the argument had been going on for most of that time.

"If you mean Carron Valley, the situations aren't congruent," William said. "Carron Valley was a decisive defeat that led to the losing of that war, but changing its outcome wouldn't have made it a decisive victory. It would have been a small victory at best. Whereas *everything* depends on Waterloo. If Bonaparte is brought down by some other method on the eighteenth of June, 1815, there will never be a need to summon Wellington monsters to do anything, not that day and not any other day. The need for them will be over."

Maxwell turned a cynical eye on him. "I believe you underestimate the ability of the offices of Whitehall to find a war suitable for employing the weapon they have crafted."

"But by that logic, we'd never try to change anything!" Elizabeth said. "We'd sit here and say, 'There is no point, it will all put itself back, would that we could make a difference but we can't, such a pity,' like women twittering over tea back home! Katarina Rasmirovna changed things and Gavin Trevelyan changed things, and why should we be any less—It's the *future*, it hasn't *happened* yet, why isn't it ours to change if we wish to?"

"I keep trying," Maxwell said tightly. "It seems disinclined to change."

"If the problem is stepping into an existing situation as an outsider," William said slowly, thinking it out, "if the problem is that an outsider has limited tools with which to work, perhaps the correct ap-

proach is to allow more time." Exactly what Elizabeth had been thinking the night before, but William was more courteous in his phrasing.
"Don't set the watch for the day of the battle. Set it a week before. A
month before. Years before. Live through the entire campaign with the
principles. Give yourself plenty of time to craft a lever of length sufficient to move the world. Craft *many* such. Would it not then be more
likely that one will work?"

"What did you think I was doing," Maxwell said heavily, "living
the life of a resistance fighter in 1885? The technique served me no
better than the other. I convinced Seward to change the focus of his
conspiracy, and look where it led—the leader of the resistance imprisoned on a treason charge, Gavin Trevelyan and Katarina Rasmirovna
dead in an alleyway. Sometimes I wonder if Time or Fate or some such
is resisting me. That it isn't actually possible for someone like me to
change history." He looked away from the two of them, down to the
Genevese's cottage far below. Their hilltop was a good ways away but
had a clear line of sight, and Maxwell had kept a wary eye on the cottage throughout the day. It was now too dark for him to see anything
of it, but he kept glancing that way still.

According to his recollection of history, the Orkney farmers who
would find the Genevese's body were not due to make their discovery
until tomorrow. However, since Maxwell's information had proven itself faulty before, he was disinclined to take the risk that they might
arrive early and find intruders in the cottage along with the corpse.
As soon as it was light enough to see, he had therefore searched the
Genevese's trunks for anything that might be useful, liberated some
hardtack and dried fish from the lean-to pantry, and led Elizabeth and
William up the mountain. He said he knew of a cave, and indeed he
found it with no trouble, suggesting that some portions of the Genevese's journal were more accurate than others. It was pleasant enough,
as far as caves went, a good place to spend the hours of the shortening
September day. A good place to argue over next steps.

Maxwell studied the darkness as though he could see the cottage.
"I have to say I hope my suspicion is the truth," he muttered. "If I am
actually unable to change any of this, then I may be forgiven for failing
to do so."

"No," Elizabeth said, furious. Maxwell turned toward her, surprised. "No, you may not be forgiven. Not for *surrendering* when there
are avenues still left to pursue. Even if—" She fumbled for an example.
"—even if Napoleon is only awaiting a favorable wind, it's better to
try to fight than to hang the tricolored flag on the Tower yourself. You
said your parents were time travelers. Would they have abandoned—"

"Elizabeth," William said softly, in gentle reproof.

"I *won't* hush. It's an important point. Your parents were time travelers. Did they try to change things? Did they succeed? Did they never tell you how they went about it?"

"I never had the opportunity to discuss the matter with them," Maxwell said in a voice stiff with anger. "But you are—" He took a deep breath. "—you are perhaps correct that they would not have surrendered to Napoleon or anyone else. I find it...admittedly hard to picture."

"At the very least," William said, taking firm hold of the conversational reins, "there is some evidence it is possible to change small things. Unless the child Meg is kidnapped back to Murchinson's again, I had an effect some effect on 1885. It mattered little overall, true, but surely it mattered greatly to her? It was only luck I was there, that Katarina could ask me in your absence, but we did succeed in fixing that small thing..." He trailed off, his own eyes wandering toward the invisible cottage. "Perhaps the moral is that small things are easier to affect than large ones."

"I had already come to that conclusion," Maxwell said. "I have for some time now been trying to change the paths of individual people—the Genevese student, the Welsh farmer's daughter—"

"—trying to find the ones who set larger events in motion, yes, I see," William said. "But that doesn't mean a battle is impossible to affect. A battle is a whole collection of individual moments, decisions by individual people. The ensign who decides only whether to duck to the left or the right while holding regimental colors—" The tone of his voice was too dry to be amusement. "—does nothing to affect the greater picture, true, but the rifleman who decides whether or not to squeeze the trigger when his gun is aimed at the enemy general, or the captain who orders his men to take the high ground, or the private who decides to take this path versus that when bringing a message...The Battle of Waterloo is a collection of these moments, because *every* battle is a collection of these moments. Unless there is some cleaner avenue to pursue—persuading the Genevese to dismantle this madness while it's still only one man's insanity—but you said that option was closed to you—"

"It is," Maxwell said. "I've already tried."

"How do you know which moments are 'junctions' and thus closed, and which stay open?" Elizabeth asked.

"Any moment that matters," Maxwell said, choosing his words carefully, "can only be affected once. Any moment that can be affected more than once does not matter. Think of it this way: if you find you *can* return, there's no point in returning."

William's brows drew down. "I thought you said it isn't possible to ever return."

"I did. It isn't. I—" Maxwell stared at the water far below, searching for words. "One cannot be in two different places at the same time. I cannot ever return to Pendoylan on the eighteenth May of 1872, and try again to save Brenda Evans' life. I cannot spend the eighteenth May of 1872 anywhere else, either."

"I understand that," William said.

"The subtler point is that I also can't go to the *seventeenth* of May 1872 and try to save Brenda Evans' life before the eighteenth dawns. I ought to be able to, logically speaking; it's not as though I'd be attempting to be two places at one time. But the watch won't allow it. I can set the dials, but when I press the buttons, nothing happens."

"Because it's a 'junction,'" Elizabeth said.

"Yes. I can't get anywhere near her. I can't even leave a—a letter in trust for her to open on her sixteenth birthday, or speak to her father before she is born, or anything of the kind. I can't do anything that might conceivably save Brenda Evans, because I've had my chance to do that. Anything I have been able to try twice has proven not to matter, to have no bearing on the unfolding of the larger story. If I can return and try again, there's no point in trying; anything I can affect can only be affected once; and the Battle of Waterloo is almost certainly the former. There are so many decisions made by so many people that form the shape of the day—undoing one is unlikely to divert the whole river."

"Yes," William said, "but what's stopping you from undoing many? If you go with plenty of time before the battle, time enough to find an ally or several allies—people like Trevelyan, like Katarina—actually, I suppose more like Lord Seward—someone who can get you to the Duke—and if you can explain the entire situation to His Grace—"

"—His Grace would have me locked up as a madman and I'd have no chance at all to affect anything. That has happened to me, with variations, twice."

"But surely he wouldn't if you showed him the pocket watch?" Elizabeth said. "If you proved to him—"

Maxwell shook his head. "And then he'd know about it, and who knows what that would do to history? I can't risk it. I wouldn't have risked it with Seward and his band if they hadn't found me out. I won't go and tell Wellington." He paced a few steps. "I'll go and try to divert a stream. Perhaps if Ney had had six horses shot out from underneath him, rather than five, he would have hesitated long enough for the Prussians to come reinforce the English. Or if the men at La Haye

Sainte had been better provided with ammunition, perhaps the farm would not have fallen and opened a gap in the line. Or there's that young aide of Wellington's, the one who rode alone to summon the special battalion—all I'd need do is delay him, and then Wellington would have no choice but to hold until the Prussians arrived—"

"But any one of those things might be corrected by something else," Elizabeth objected. "Even I can see that. If the shape of the day is due to more than one decision, you have to change more than one decision. Divert more than one stream."

"Mr. Maxwell, I really do not think it is possible for you to divert enough of them by yourself," William said, very carefully. "I was able to take your place at Murchinson's, when you could not be in two places at once; I think the lesson to take from Meg's rescue is that is that two people may accomplish something when one cannot. If you allow me to accompany you, I could—"

"Absolutely not," Maxwell said.

"But there's also evidence that a group can be more effective than a single person," William pressed on. "You were working with Seward and Trevelyan and Katarina this last time, and you said you managed to change Seward's conspiracy. Not to the good, but you did change it, you changed something, so perhaps the lesson is that you need more than one person, a team of people, diverting many streams at once."

"You are not coming. Neither of you. It's an unconscionable risk."

"You seem to think," Elizabeth said irritably, "that we *want* to be sent back to the balls and the drawing rooms. I would much rather be doing this with you."

"Which tells me you do not understand what it is actually like."

"I was in that alleyway," Elizabeth said. "I think I understand."

"If you understood, you would want to get back to your drawing rooms while you had the chance. Lord knows I would like nothing better than to escape to that pleasant green haven."

"A pleasant green haven is a cage if you cannot choose to leave it," Elizabeth said sharply.

"An adventure is a torment if you cannot choose to abandon it."

"But you have the chance to *do* something."

"And therefore the duty, and therefore the culpability for all the— If I *do* have the ability to change it, do you have any idea how many deaths there are to my account because I could not stop the turning wheel?" Maxwell got up with a jerk, walking a few paces away and rubbing a hand over his face. He turned, black figure merging with the almost-black sky, face impossible to discern.

"So let us help you," Elizabeth said.

"Absolutely not," Maxwell said again.

Elizabeth scowled at him. "William is a soldier, and I have said I am willing to take the risk. If Katarina Rasmirovna can do it, so can I. Why should our lives be more valuable than yours?"

"It's complicated," Maxwell said, and there was something in his voice that made her look quickly up at him. But the rising moon did not yet provide enough light; she could not see his face. "For one thing," he went on, after a pause and in a noticeably different tone of voice, "even if I were willing to let you anywhere near it, which I am not, the pocket watch itself won't permit it. A person cannot be in a two places at once, and you are already part of eighteenth June, 1815. You are in England, sitting in a garden. Or, I suppose, sneaking out of a garden to come to Orkney. It simply won't be possible for you to also be part of eighteenth June, 1815, in Belgium; your watch won't take you there."

"But if that's the primary objection, then we ought to at least try," William said. Either he had not caught the shift in tone, or he was pretending he had not. "You could be wrong about the way the watch works. At least let us try to come, before you say it's impossible."

"No," Maxwell said. His features were coming clearer as the rising moon spangled the sea and rocks with silver. He pulled his watch out of his waistcoat pocket, tilted it toward the moonlight, and began deftly to set its dials. "I'll go see to Waterloo, and you'll take Miss Barton home."

Elizabeth made a noise of inarticulate protest, but Maxwell acted as though he had not heard her. He checked the watch again, tucked it back into his pocket, and held his hand out toward William. William reluctantly unthreaded the second pocket-watch and handed it over.

Maxwell set these dials expertly as well, with the barest touch of a fingernail. "I am," he said without looking up, in a voice curiously thickened, "very grateful to have had your companionship thus far. It has been…most valuable…to hear your advice, and I thank you for it." He looked up from the watch, at William, and William rose to his feet in response to the solemnity in the older man's voice. "But this isn't yours to worry over," Maxwell said, handing him back the glinting golden orb. "You're not even twenty, either of you—and Mr. Carrington, you've already been injured in service of the Empire. I'm a soldier of sorts as well. Go home and have the rest of your childhood, and let me handle the danger."

"I…" Whatever William saw in the old man's face dried the protest in his throat. He stood a moment meeting Maxwell's eye, then inclined his head. "It's been an honor, sir," William said, meeting formality with formality.

Then Maxwell reached toward Elizabeth, and she let him aid her to her feet.

"Miss Barton," he said, and bent over her hand, brushing her knuckles with his lips. "The honor has been entirely mine." He stepped back, drew his watch back out, and bowed to them both. "On three, then?" he said to William, and William nodded, shifting toward Elizabeth. She laid her fingers on his right arm, and he held the pocket watch ready in his left hand. Maxwell lifted his watch, and the moonlight ran in silver rivulets all over the engravings and scratches. "One," Maxwell said. "Two. Three."

The moonlit rocks shimmered before Elizabeth's eyes. The sounds and smells of the sea receded, the dark sky seeming to take on a certain distant aspect, and she thought she caught a glimpse of evening sun through apple blossoms. As though from a long distance away, she saw Maxwell holding up his pocket watch, fingers closed over the top stem. She barely had time to reach out and grasp his sleeve.

Chapter 17

The last three times, the watch had taken her in the blink of an eye, with no physical effect at all. This time, Elizabeth felt as though some unseen force was trying to rip her tongue out of her mouth, while her lungs attempted to crawl up her throat and something tugged her arms so fiercely she thought they might pop off. All was black before her eyes, and the blackness seemed to scream. She had a handful of cloth gripped in each fist, and she was able to remember that she must keep hold of them both. She dug her fingers in desperately, and howling wind tore at her.

The ripping and tugging suddenly ceased, and the blackness lightened into grayness, but Elizabeth could see nothing clearly and could hear nothing at all. Her ears rang with a shrill shriek like howling wind. She was crouched on her knees, fingers digging into slimy leaves and cold clammy earth, and then Maxwell was shouting almost loud enough to be heard over the roaring in her ears.

"—are you out of your *mind,* you could have gotten us all *killed!*" Suddenly he was kneeling in front of her, his white hair wild and his eyes wilder. He took her by the shoulders and shook her. "The watches aren't meant to be forced that way, Elizabeth, are you out of your *mind?*"

Elizabeth couldn't answer. She could almost see clearly now, but dizziness plagued her. She wrenched away from Maxwell only just in time and was sick all over the twisting roots of a very large tree.

A handkerchief appeared before her tearing eyes. She took it and looked up, expecting to see William. It was Maxwell, who turned away without offering any words of comfort.

With his broad back gone from her field of vision, Elizabeth could see that they had landed in a forest. Trees twisted into fantastical shapes all around them, and where there were not trees, there was undergrowth. William was a few feet away, crouched as she was against a trunk. As she watched, he rose shakily to his feet, very pale and running his tongue over his lips. He started to make a comment to Maxwell, looking down at the watch in his hand—and then froze, eyes fixed on it.

Elizabeth lurched to her feet. "What? What is it?"

William didn't say anything. He looked, in fact, as though he might be incapable of speech. But he took two unsteady steps toward her, and held the watch out for her to see.

It lay in his hand like a dead thing. All four of the faces were cracked. None of the hands moved. No image appeared.

Elizabeth felt sick all over again. "Oh, no. I shouldn't have—I shouldn't have made it—try to go two places at once—"

"No," Maxwell snapped, looking over her shoulder at the watch, "no, you should not have. Nor do I have any notion of how you're to get home again, since you are already *there*. You may well have made it impossible."

"We're there," William said, "but only until seven o'clock on the eighteenth of June. We're not there at quarter past seven—we were in Orkney by then—so wouldn't it let us get to quarter past…?"

He trailed off in response to Maxwell's glare. Maxwell didn't want to hear reasonable and conciliatory solutions, Elizabeth could tell. He wanted to be furious. She felt like that too often herself to feel she possessed any moral high ground, and besides, she knew she deserved his anger. The sight of the inert watch made her feel as though she had killed something helpless.

William cleared his throat. "What day is it now?"

Maxwell held out his own watch without speaking. Elizabeth peered at it, trying to make sense of the dials, trying to remember which was latitude and longitude, which was hour, which was day, month, year—

"Midday, seventeenth June, 1815?" She whirled to confront Maxwell. "I thought we talked about allowing more time!"

"You are *truly* in no position to lecture me," he said, and there was no argument she could make to that. Silence fell between them, cold and uncomfortable.

"Well." William cleared his throat again. "We can't change either of these things. We have the time that we have, and all three of us are here for at least a day. So…we should figure out how three people might best use twenty-four hours."

I f only they had longer, William thought. Even forty-eight hours more would make a difference. Had they arrived on the fifteenth, they might well have been able to wrangle an invitation to the Duchess of Richmond's ball. They might have even had time to scrabble together appropriate clothing. They could have sought Wellington there, spoken to him in private before news of the French incursion into Belgium reached him. And if two days more would have made a difference, two weeks more would have made it easy. They would have had plenty of time to waylay His Grace and explain.

Though two weeks would have also have been more than enough time to be caught, and that was a consideration. William Carrington was, after all, known to some percentage of the officers assembled here—those of his own regiment of course, and those with whom he had attended Eton. Though it was conceivable that a wealthy injured and discharged officer might have returned to the warfront as a spectator, a wealthy ensign was nearly a contradiction in terms. Besides which, William Carrington was at that moment not only known to be in England, but actually there. Two weeks was plenty of time for that inconvenient fact to impede their plans. William understood some of Maxwell's desire for discretion—but at the same time he felt his heart pounding and his mouth dry. Seventeenth June! Twenty-four hours! What in hell could they do with twenty-four hours? The Duke was on the field already. The British were even now making for Waterloo, and very shortly they would be doing it in driving rain. Messages had gone to and fro from Wellington to Blücher; the strategy was decided; the special battalion was encamped and waiting as a last line of defense. The crank was poised and ready to turn itself. He could see history about to crash down on them all like a clockwork-driven construct's foot.

He tried to keep the panic off his face, lest Elizabeth and Maxwell see. The three of them had beaten the oncoming storm—just barely— to a moldy-smelling barn between the Forest of Soignes and the village of Waterloo. The owners of the barn had fled ahead of the approaching armies, and the British officers were likely to be quartered closer to the presumptive battlefield. While they could not count on absolute freedom from discovery anywhere, William had agreed with Maxwell that this hiding place was the best of the available choices. Now he watched the rain pound down, watched the earthen road stream by in slick brown rivulets, and thought about hauling guns and horses and all the impedimenta of a battle through this sea of mud. Men in scarlet coats were doing so right now, not far away. He wondered where his old regiment might be positioned.

He wrenched his mind back to his actual role in the upcoming conflict, took a biscuit from the rucksack—not because he was hungry, but because munching it served as a fine way of feigning calm—and returned to eliciting from Maxwell the details of the following day.

By the time full dark had descended, the three of them had amassed a reasonable list of moments they thought it possible to change. They had also amassed a list of clothing and tools they would need to implement their plans. Maxwell rose and helped himself to a dark lantern left in the corner of the barn, lighting it with matchsticks he had acquired in 1885.

"Pen and ink and paper," he recited, sounding like a country woman preparing to go to market. "One lieutenant's uniform. One sergeant's uniform. Needle and thread to—"

"We have needle and thread," William said. At Maxwell's surprised look, he clarified, "In my rucksack. I thought it might be useful."

He thought the older man looked impressed. "Indeed."

"While you're acquiring the uniforms," Elizabeth said, face a glimmering oval in the lantern light, "perhaps you could also find some boy's clothing. Not a uniform, just something a lad from the village might wear. Also, a cap big enough to hide my hair. I can't do the sorts of things you plan to do," she added in response to their raised eyebrows, an edge to her voice, "but I can't do anything at all dressed like this. As a boy, I could at least linger behind the lines and learn whether your attempts are having an effect."

Maxwell started, "You shouldn't—"

"I am *not* going to sit in the hayloft and wait for you to come back or not come back."

"If you don't get the clothing and the cap," William said, rubbing at a spot between his eyes, "she'll sneak off tomorrow once we're gone and get them herself. I expect you're more experienced at this sort of thing, and less likely to be caught with disastrous consequences. Would you please get boy's clothing and a cap while you're out, sir."

"Was it unclear what I meant, when I said 'keep her safe'?" Maxwell spoke between his teeth.

"Perfectly clear. Have you advice as to how?"

Maxwell started to reply, broke off with a snarl, then jerked open the door and plunged into the black and blowing night.

"He'll come to terms with it eventually," William said into the darkness, and Elizabeth laughed, soft and surprised and delighted.

"Er," she said. "Does that mean you have?"

"Come to terms with the idea that I can't stop you, so any plan had best include you in it? More or less." He had badly wanted to shake her in the first hour following their unexpected diversion to Waterloo, but at the same time, he had been forced to admire the brazenness of it. After all, he had wanted to come as well, but hadn't thought to force the issue by grabbing Maxwell's sleeve.

"I'm sorry about the watch," she whispered.

"It will be all right," he said. "Getting home, I mean. We'll manage. Elizabeth, if we have to, we can take a *ship.*"

She laughed again, surprised. "I hadn't thought of that. But what if we're there?"

"We'll manage," he said again. "Don't worry about it now. One thing at a time." If they *were* forced into taking a ship, he thought, if they returned home after a shipboard voyage, the damage to her reputation and his would be considerable, unless they also . . . .He cut off the thought. One thing at a time.

They were both dozing by the time Maxwell returned. William jumped awake at the creak of the door, blinking in the dazzle from the lantern. "I'm astonished," Maxwell said. "You are both where I told you to stay."

"Were you successful?" Elizabeth asked, ignoring his tone.

"Very." Maxwell opened the pack with the air of a conjurer. "Pen. Ink. Paper. For Mr. Carrington, one lieutenant's uniform—of the 52nd Foot. For me, one sergeant's uniform from the Coldstream Guards."

"How did you—?" William started.

"It's better you don't ask," Maxwell said. "I did not kill anyone to get them, I can at least assure you of that."

"And for me?" Elizabeth demanded.

Maxwell silently handed her shirt, trousers, and cap.

"Thank you."

"We had better see how badly these fit," Maxwell said to William, not acknowledging her thanks, "and improve them as we can."

William needed Maxwell's help to get his limp right arm into the sleeve of the coat. The buttons he could manage himself, if clumsily. "Well," he said, coming to stand where the light of the lantern fell so Elizabeth could see him, "I think it's too big."

That was an understatement. The shoulders drooped, and the sleeves hung past his wrists. Elizabeth frowned, turning the needle over in her fingers. "I may be able to…I'll see what I can do."

"You needn't spend time fussing over the right sleeve," he said, trying to make a joke of it. "We'll tie my arm up in a sling tomorrow. A broken arm is a misfortune that might easily befall a soldier on a battlefield, and it won't look odd." The jesting tone sounded feeble even to his own ears. He looked down at the regimental facings glittering on the scarlet cloth and found himself in the absurd position of needing to swallow hard. He chose not to crane his head to observe the epaulet on his shoulder.

Maxwell had also retreated to the shadows to change his dress. He emerged now looking grim. Also, rather like a sausage stuffed into a uniform as tight as William's was loose. The catch in William's throat turned to a desire to laugh, and he swallowed that too. It was not in fact amusing, not at all. It was a potentially serious problem.

"I may be able to do something about that too," Elizabeth said, surveying him critically in turn. "Move buttons, at least. I hope there's enough thread."

"How well do you think you can do it?" Maxwell asked her bluntly, rolling his shoulders under the tight back of the coat. "It would be worse if it looked obviously altered, and I didn't think you cared for needlework."

"I don't," Elizabeth returned, "but I have been trained in it. I am competent at the art moving buttons and adjusting hems. I'll start with William's coat, as it will be easier, and then I'll see what I can do for you."

She went to try on her new clothing first, and returned to the lantern with a quick step and a smile on her lips. At least hers fit, William thought. The boy's shirt was almost modest, compared to Katarina's blouses. When Elizabeth bound up her hair and hid it under the cap, he thought she would be able to pass well enough.

She came back to him and stood close, examining the length of his sleeves, pinching the fabric at his waist to gauge the fit. For a moment he thought nothing of it; then his face flushed hot at the same time she suddenly turned pink. "Did you happen to bring pins along with a needle and thread?" she asked, determinedly matter-of-fact.

"I did not."

"Well, no matter, I can remember." Her eyes swept him up and down again, then rested on his face. "You do look very smart," she said, rather shyly. "It suits you."

The unmanly sense of choking closed his throat again. *Damn. Damn, damn, damn, so it does, and I shall never*—He coughed hard to clear it. "Why, thank you, Miss Barton."

She was blushing again, shaking her head. "I am sorry. I…didn't think, before I said that."

"No matter," he said. "I made it to Waterloo in a lieutenant's uniform after all, didn't I?"

The alterations to said uniform were quickly completed, and they did help the fit some. William thought he would be able to manage the required deception tomorrow, especially as no one would examine him so very closely in the heat of battle. He sat down with pen and ink to write out his message, talking it through with Maxwell several times before committing words to paper, while opposite them Elizabeth fussed with the sergeant's uniform. Maxwell then took the pen to write a message of his own.

Elizabeth rose and stretched. "Here, Mr. Maxwell, I believe this will suit." She came to stand beside him, coat in hand, and her eye fell quite naturally on the paper before him. Then William saw something flicker over her face.

"What a...clear hand you write," she said. "I don't know that I've ever seen one so bold."

Maxwell looked up at her. "I beg your pardon?"

"Oh...nothing." Elizabeth shook her head. "It was nothing. Try the coat, if you please. I think it will fit better now."

William lay down in the hay and closed his burning eyes, telling himself it was only for a moment and knowing it was a bad idea even as he did it. The rain drummed down on the roof, almost drowning him in soft dark sleep before he jerked himself back into a sitting position.

Maxwell and Elizabeth looked over at him with identical expressions of concern. "You ought to sleep while you can," Maxwell said gently.

William found it difficult to muster any argument. He contented himself with, "So should you, sir," and lay back down. "We'll take it in turns. Wake me in two hours."

Somewhat to his surprise, Maxwell did. The older man dropped into sleep almost immediately afterward, leaving William to sit alone until the early dawn. He listened to the sound of rain fade and watched the blackness lighten into gray, reflecting that a mile or so distant, other men in scarlet coats would soon be doing the same. He stood up, for he had the farthest to go, and tucked his message into his shirt.

He crossed softly over to Elizabeth. She lay huddled in straw, chemise covering her like a blanket, cap beside her, hair mussed and escaping its knot. He put a daring hand to her shoulder, and she blinked up at him. "It's dawn," he said unnecessarily.

She nodded, struggling to sit up. "Here," she said, "your arm—" She tore a strip of cloth from her chemise to fashion into a sling.

"Won't you need—" he began, too late.

"It doesn't matter," she said. There were dark smudges under her eyes, and though she tried to smile as she fashioned the sling, he did not find the attempt convincing. She looked up from her work finally, and swallowed hard. "Good luck," she whispered.

"And to you," he said. "Give Maxwell another hour. Neither of you can do anything until the chaos has well begun, so you may as well let him rest that long. *Take care.* Please." He wanted to say more than that, but now was not the time.

"I'll take care," she promised. He gave her a bow that felt absurdly formal under the circumstances, and then headed off for Placenoit.

❧

The artillery was not due to start until late morning. Elizabeth stayed hidden in the barn until then, knowing that she would, as William said, need chaos to blend into if she wished to overhear anything worth hearing. When the first boom shook the rafters overhead and the ground under her feet, she brushed off the hay and started the walk to the makeshift infirmary at Mont Saint Jean. She had been forced to acknowledge that it was impractical for her to get any closer to Wellington than that, much as she might prefer to. Her source of information as to the Duke's actions would have to be from his injured soldiers and officers.

The path from the village to the farmhouse of Mont Saint Jean took her through the Forest of Soignes. Remembering her first encounter with the forest the afternoon before, Elizabeth resolved to keep close to the road. Getting lost in woods like these was a staple of German fairytales, and now she understood why. The shadowed glades and twisting tree trunks were as menacing as they were confusing, looking capable of concealing absolutely any fantastic thing. Elizabeth stopped herself there and resolved to think no further along those lines. She had enough to worry about as it was: the deafening barrage up ahead, the risk of encountering messengers or deserters if she stayed on the road, the risk of encountering the special battalion if she strayed too far off it. She had more than enough actual dangers to avoid without imagining clawlike fingers and cackling laughter.

The trees thinned finally, and a pleasant white cluster of buildings came into view. This must be Mont Saint Jean, for it matched Maxwell's description perfectly. He must have quite committed the Duke's unpublished memoirs to heart, Elizabeth thought. The farmhouse that was to serve as the main infirmary was hidden from her sight by the rise of the road. This was the moment, then. She took a deep breath, left the shelter of the trees, and crested the hill.

It was horrible. The injured had begun to make their way from the front line to the surgeons, and she had a perfect view of them stumbling through the slimy mud of the road—some supported by comrades, some carried in blankets, a few stumping grimly along unaided.

When she drew closer to the farmhouse, she could hear the screaming within, and she had to clench her hands into fists and force herself to go forward. She peeped through a window, thinking she had better know.

She ought to have realized that the surgeons would set up near the windows, for the sake of the light. But this did not occur to her, and so she was badly startled when she pressed close to the pane just in time to come face to face with the teeth of a saw. There was an arm underneath the blade, there were two men holding down the owner of the arm, and then there was a spurt of blood and a gagging cry. Elizabeth clung to the windowsill.

The surgeon wielding the saw looked up, irritated at the shadow that marred his light, and Elizabeth found herself—in the role of idle village lad—pressed into service as a water-bearer. It was more or less what she had wanted, since it put her in a position to hear the men talk. She could even ask, in carefully French-accented English, how the day went on the field. In between attempts to learn what she could, she went around with a dipper and a bucket, kept her eyes cast down to avoid the sight of mangled limbs and blood, and tried not to think about what could happen to William or Maxwell today.

The worst part was always the waiting, William thought. Having crept into position before the French and Prussians could engage at Placenoit, he could do nothing until late afternoon. So he huddled within a copse of trees, watched the sun move along the earthen floor, and tried to look as much as possible as a British messenger who had been thrown from his horse and knocked insensible. Just in case someone should come upon him before his hour.

The Prussian reinforcements had been delayed by a combination of bad decisions and bad roads. The first division of the four, the one commanded by General Bülow, was only just now approaching. Maxwell said they would come to attack the French flank, and clash with the French in the village of Placenoit. The fighting would be fierce and long—the village would change hands more than once—and there would not be Prussian troops free to actively support the British until evening. By which time Wellington would have bowed to the inevitable and sent for the monsters. But if the Prussians could be hurried… William waited until the nearby gunfire and shouting told him that the French and Prussians had in fact engaged at Placenoit. Then he rose from his hiding place, dirtied his uniform and face with handfuls of mud, and staggered as if dizzy toward the village.

It wasn't much of a role to play this time. Nothing so nerve-wracking as Murchinson's, even though there was significantly more than one child's life dependent on his success. *An entire battle,* he thought, trying out the idea. *The course of history.* It sounded ridiculous, and he thought he might be fortunate that it did. Could he have been fully aware of what he was trying to do, his tongue might have seized in his throat and made the attempt impossible.

As it was, his tongue considered the lines he was to speak to be comprised of eminently ordinary words. He was no kind of actor, but this role was no deception. He had no reason to feign the conventions of the service, for they had settled back into his skin with the scarlet coat's embrace. He *was* a British officer. If he was not one Wellington would have customarily sent as a courier, well, that was a small point. He staggered toward the Prussian line, reminding himself with every step to walk as though dizzy and injured.

"*Le général Bülow?*" he said over and over, to everyone he encountered. "*J'ai une dépêche de Monsieur le Duc de Wellington.*" *I have a message from the Duke of Wellington.* Bizarre in one sense to be asking for his ally in the language of his enemy, but it would not strike a false note. Wellington did not speak German any more than William did, and since few of the German officers spoke English, business was customarily conducted in French.

"*Encore un messager?*" a staff officer responded in surprise.

Another messenger. William's gut clenched. Wellington had of course been sending messages to Blücher and his subordinates all afternoon. That was the point. That was what would enable William's alteration of history to slip in unnoticed. But apparently he was hard upon the heels of a legitimate courier, and oh hell, attracting suspicion would undo—

But the staff officer only jerked his head. "This way," he said, and led William toward Bülow—a man of sixty, handsome despite his narrow face and long nose.

"*Quoi?*" Bülow snapped.

"*De Wellington,*" William said, handing Bülow the message he had forged the night before and doing his best to sway. "*Un officier français a été capturé, et a divulgué leurs stratégie pour cette offensive.*" *From Wellington. A French officer was captured, and gave information about their tactics for this battle.*

Bülow unfolded the paper, and William breathed a sigh of relief. He had delivered the message. Assuming Maxwell's recollection of history was accurate, the note contained enough information about the dispersal of the French troops to enable the Prussians to efficiently finish their business at Placenoit. Assuming Bülow chose to act on it, he would be free to press forward and bring badly needed reinforcements to the British. It might not hasten the Prussians by more than half an hour, but even half an hour could be enough when combined with Maxwell's message.

It took William quite some time to make it to the comparative safety of the British lines, but at last he found himself once more on the road that led away from the ridgeline.

He need only hike back through the forest to find himself at the village of Waterloo and the barn he had slept in the night before. He decided to pause at Mont Saint Jean, for a glimpse of or possibly even a word with Elizabeth.

He crested the hill and stopped. The road before him, the road from the ridge to the infirmary, was crawling with the injured and the dying. They dragged themselves along with their arm over a companion's shoulders. They lay limp in blankets carried between six men. They walked alone until they fell, and then they lay in crumpled heaps of scarlet on the roadside.

His usually numb arm gave one of those ghostly twists of pain that had been a common feature of his early convalescence but had not haunted him for nearly six months. The thought occurred to him, in a rather distant way, that it was too great a risk for him to walk alongside these men, that he had better return to the barn by a more discreet route. But even as he considered this fact, his feet took a step into the road as if not subject to his will.

That man there will lose his leg, whispered a voice in his mind, automatically categorizing what he saw in light of expert knowledge, though he would have much preferred to do otherwise. *That one has a belly wound—he's dead even if he hasn't stopped moving yet. Dear God, how did the one over there get so mangled? Not a cannon ball, or he'd be smashed to pulp—is that what it looks like when the enemy fires bags of horseshoe nails that break apart on impact?* He had heard veterans speak of that particular weapon, but he had never seen it or its horrible effect himself. *That man there might have nothing worse than a broken leg— how did he get that, did a horse perhaps fall—*

"Will?"

He was turning, responding to the bone-deep familiarity of the voice before he had consciously placed it and well before he had time to think that perhaps answering to his name would not serve the purposes of discretion.

His brother-in-law Christopher Palmer lay curled on the side of the road, staring up at him out of glazed, incurious eyes.

The skin of Palmer's face shone sickly white, a stark contrast to the muddy red wool below it. A bandage around his left thigh was soaked through with blood, the same scarlet as his coat. Beside him on the roadside lay a tree branch of length and breadth sufficient to be used as a walking stick. William could read the whole story from those few signs. The wound. The necessity of getting it tended. The refusal to allow anyone else to leave their duties to accompany him. The boast that he could manage perfectly well with a staff to support his weight. The slow stumbling progress toward the infirmary while all the time his beating heart pumped hot red blood onto the road, until the stick slipped from his nerveless fingers and he fell.

Palmer's brows furrowed. "Why're you...here? You're not...here, are you?" He squinted at William's coat. "Not our...regiment..."

William knew that cross-eyed look. He had been on its other side, remembered fighting to make his eyes focus and his tongue untwist while darkness lapped at him. Chris Palmer would be seeing nothing clearly at the moment. William could easily decline acquaintance—"No, sir, you must have mistaken me for someone else"—and Palmer would neither argue with him nor find it an unreasonable fever-dream once he recovered. He might not even remember it once he recovered.

If he recovered. William looked at the soaked bandage and the blood oozing around it.

It was errant madness for him to stay here any longer. At any moment, someone else from his old regiment might happen by, might hail him as Palmer had and cause him and Maxwell no end of trouble. The closer he got to the infirmary, the greater was the risk of such a meeting. He should never have taken this route in the first place, and the longer he lingered with Palmer, the greater the chance of Palmer becoming convinced of William's reality and drawing attention to William's presence. William imagined being waylaid and forced to explain himself; he imagined Maxwell and Elizabeth searching for him; he imagined failure, the looming future, all those lives, the child Meg with her jaw eaten away and her skin glowing green, Katarina falling under a hail of construct bullets.

"Will?" Palmer said again, with even less conviction this time.

I can't carry him, William thought wildly. *I can't even brace him. Surely someone else will come along and help him.*

Surely. The word seemed to echo in his mind.

"You're not here...are you, Will?" Palmer murmured.

William crouched down to eye level. "No, Chris," he said, pitching his voice low so that no one passing would have their attention caught by this ridiculous performance. "I'm not here. I'm home safe in England. You're thinking of me, is all. You're hurt enough to dream while you're awake." Which was, in William's assessment, a true statement. William vaguely remembered a parade of ghosts and delusions from his fevered time in bed after the bullets were dug from his arm, and he did think Palmer was as badly injured.

"Oh." Palmer's eyes slid away from his. "Help me, then?"

"I can't. I'm not here. You have to get up yourself. Your staff is right there. Pick it up, put your weight on it, and get up."

"Tried," Palmer said. "Can't."

"Yes, you can, and you must. You know you must. I'm not here, Chris; where do you think these words are coming from?" William pushed on before he could spend more time contemplating that thought. "You know you must get up. You know you must get home." He was no kind of actor, but he didn't need to be. He knew what would drive Christopher Palmer to his feet. "Your wife needs you. Your son will need you. My sister is with child, you remember that, don't you? Chris, you have to pick up the staff now and you have to get your right leg under you, or the only thing your son will know of you is a portrait and a medal. Chris, the staff, now."

He didn't have to say it the last time. Palmer's hand was already closing over the wood. "Yes," William encouraged. "Now your right foot, flat on the ground. Good. And up." Palmer staggered drunkenly, but managed not to fall.

"Take a step," William ordered, and Palmer obeyed him. "Take another." He thought a couple of heads might have turned nearby, but the sling immobilizing his arm made it plain why he was not offering more direct aid to his companion. Palmer fixed his eyes on the white farmhouse ahead and took one jerky step at a time.

William walked beside him, talking the whole way, reminding him of Caroline, reminding him of the child, reminding him to take a step every time his attention wandered. Behind them the cannons volleyed and thundered, and ahead of them the dying screamed.

❦

John Freemantle felt every burst from the cannon as a jolt through his breastbone. At least the blasts no longer tore through his eardrums; his ears had been ringing for hours now, muting the roar into something almost manageable. His horse, a big bay possessed of considerably more battlefield experience than its rider, bore the noise stolidly, with no more sign of discomfort than the occasional twitching of an ear.

The Duke, Freemantle thought, looked similarly unperturbed, despite the steady worsening of their fortunes over the course of the afternoon. An entire Belgian brigade had fled in panic, the British cavalry had destroyed itself in a useless charge on the French line, and the Prussian reinforcements were hours overdue, but no one would have guessed it from Wellington's face.

"My lord!"

Wellington turned toward the cry, and his aides followed suit. Freemantle thought he recognized the reedy voice, despite the chaos and noise all around them, and an instant later was certain he recognized the slender form. James Warren, the most junior member of the Duke's staff, drove his distinctive roan mount toward Wellington with all the speed he could manage through the mud.

"My lord!" Warren nearly fell from his saddle as he saluted. He pulled a folded piece of paper from his pouch and handed it over. "From General Blücher! He comes, my lord!"

Wellington paused in the act of unfolding the paper, one eyebrow raised.

The boy's face turned crimson. "I don't meant I—I would not have read it if—" He cleared his throat. "This was found on the dead body of a Prussian courier by a sergeant from the Coldstream Guards, my lord. The sergeant recognized its importance and showed it to me, wondering if it ought to be delivered to Your Grace. I agreed it ought, and brought it at once."

"Ah." Wellington looked back down at the paper.

In the pauses between the thunder of the artillery, Freemantle could just distinguish a sound like popping corn. *Skirmishers*, he thought. He looked about, but could not spot them through the cloud of gunsmoke. Skirmishers were a nuisance, using their muskets to distract their enemy rather than to inflict graver damage. Freemantle resolved not to be distracted, and turned back to the Duke.

Wellington was re-reading the note, his brows drawn together. "The Coldstream Guards?" he said.

"Yes, my lord." Warren was almost visibly glowing, clearly proud to have been the bearer of the day's first piece of good news. "I recognized the uniform quite clearly."

"You encountered him where?"

Warren's fair face twitched in confusion. "On—on the left, my lord. I was returning from—"

"The Coldstream Guards are stationed at Hougomount," Wellington said, finally looking up. "On the extreme right. Was this man known to you?"

"N-no, my lord."

A shell sailed rather closely overhead, whistling as it went. Other than automatically moving backward a pace, Wellington ignored it. He kept his eyes on Warren. "Describe him."

"He…he looked like a sergeant, my lord," Warren said helplessly. "He had the uniform of…"

"I said describe him, not his uniform." Another shell whistled, not quite so terrifyingly close. Precise aim was impossible with large cannon, Freemantle knew that. The French gunners could shoot *at* Wellington all they liked, but they would find it nearly impossible to hit him. The thought was comforting in one sense—for if the Duke did not survive this day, all was lost indeed—but nerve-wracking in another. An imprecise weapon was a greater threat to those standing beside the person at whom it was aimed. Freemantle tightened his grip on his rein to keep from pondering that fact too closely, but it did not even occur to him to edge away from the Duke.

"A biggish man," Warren said, eyes shut and body taut with the effort of recall. "Broad-shouldered. White hair. Old enough for his rank; it made sense—"

"How did he speak?"

"Speak?" Warren's eyes flew open. "I…I don't remember noticing, my lord."

A third ball whistled. It found its mark—or at least *a* mark—for men off to the right began to scream. Wellington's eyes flicked once in that direction, then back to James Warren's face. "Like a man from the ranks?"

"I…don't…No, my lord, I don't think so, now that you mention it. He was well-spoken for his station."

Wellington pursed his lips. "I'm sure he was. Now you may tell me about his uniform."

Warren floundered.

"Well looked-after?" Wellington prompted. "Torn? Loose? Tight?"

"Tight," Warren said suddenly. "My lord. Tight in the shoulders; it's what made me remember—"

"It is possible that he might have borrowed a uniform not his own," Wellington said. He took his eyes off Warren now, appearing for the first time to notice the still and listening circle of aides. His voice turned caustic. "Gentlemen, we are somewhat thick on the ground. May I suggest—?" Freemantle, Cathcart, Wotten, and Canning all shifted their horses a sheepish few steps apart, but Warren stayed where he was, horror dawning on his face. Wellington returned his attention to the matter at hand. "It is possible that a Coldstream Guard might have borrowed a uniform not his own," the Duke repeated. "It is possible that one single Coldstream Guard might have been seconded to Best or Kempt on the left." He tapped the note against his palm. "And it is not impossible that Blücher should have sent a message of this kind. However, there is something about all this which smells rather rank." He looked back down at the note. "'Delayed by poor roads this morning,'" he quoted. "Yes, that I already know. 'Attacking Napoleon's flank at Placenoit.' Yes. 'Expect imminent victory, presence at your left within the hour.' Perhaps. I might have believed it, had it come from a more creditable Coldsteam Guard. Napoleon has humbugged me once in this affair; does he try to do it again?"

"You…do not believe the note to be genuine, my lord?" Freemantle asked.

"I do not."

"But who—"

"A spy, perhaps? Wearing a uniform that is almost correct, but not quite, and speaking carefully unaccented English?"

"For what purpose, my lord?" Freemantle asked. "How could it benefit—?"

"A man expecting reinforcements might not retreat when retreat would be otherwise called for," Wellington mused. "He might stay and suffer even greater loss. Not that I consider us close to either eventuality, gentlemen," he added briskly. "We are far from without recourse— much farther than Bonaparte can know." Freemantle knew he meant the special battalion, though the aide suspected Wellington to be reluctant to call in the monsters, and with good reason. The Duke would doubtless far rather believe the note and its promise of an imminent Prussian presence. Freemantle shook his head in admiration. Only Wellington could have maintained the coolness necessary to think past the moment of hope and consider—

A snap somehow pierced through the thunder of the guns, and Warren sagged, blood soaking fast through the shoulder of his coat. Cathcart grabbed for him, catching him before he could pitch off his saddle.

"My lord," Freemantle said, attempting to crowd Wellington backward, "my lord, that was surely meant for you. You must come farther away—"

"Get someone to drive those fellows off!" Wellington told him, waving a hand at the snipers. "Cathcart," he added, "see James taken behind the lines. Wotten, I want you to ride down to Placenoit yourself. Show this note to Blücher and discover if he did indeed—"

Freemantle, riding in search of men to drive off the snipers, heard no more than that. He went about his task feeling numb. What manner of subtle plot was this, to send a false message of hope? Surely that violated the rules of war. He could not fathom all the things it might mean.

At the very least, he reflected, it meant that the British could *not* in fact count on imminent Prussian support. *If they are delayed much longer, will there be anything left of us for them to reinforce? His Grace may need to summon the special battalion after all.* Freemantle grimaced at the idea, but if the Prussians were not coming, the Duke might have no other choice.

∽

William managed to coax Christopher Palmer to nearly the door of the infirmary before the latter's leg crumpled underneath him and he pitched forward in a faint. William couldn't shift position fast enough to break Palmer's fall, but at least they were within easy distance of aid. One of the surgeons' assistants came over, wrapped a fresh cloth around the wound, and dragged Palmer inside, whether to be tended or to join the others waiting to be tended, William could not be sure, but either way, Chris was safe in their hands now. William had done all he could, all that duty and friendship demanded.

He stepped over to the doorway anyway, wishing to have one final look, wishing to assure himself that Chris needed nothing more from him.

The smell of the place almost knocked him down. He knew that odor—blood and urine and feces and misery. His limp arm seized with pain again, and bile rose in his throat. He leaned against the door frame, realizing after a moment that he was giving a very good impression of a man nearly too weak to stand who had dragged himself to the surgeons. Someone paused inquiringly before him, but William managed to wave the man off. "Just a broken arm. I'm fine." He pulled himself straight, willed his swimming vision clear, and decided to leave before he vomited.

One of the water-bearers had snapped a look up at the sound of his voice, and William recognized the face in a distant sort of way as Elizabeth's. She hastened across to him with no thought for discretion, but at least she kept her voice low—and faintly French-accented; it seemed she could not dismiss the affectation all at once. "What are you doing here?" she hissed.

"My sister's husband," William said, gesturing vaguely toward the inner room. "I couldn't leave him."

"Oh—of course." She glanced at the doorway and bit her lip. "Will he be all right?"

"I think so. At least, they'll tend to him." He hardly knew what he was saying. His nostrils were full of the smells of sweat and despair, and he wanted to back out the door and run.

"And—and otherwise?" She looked up at him, and he wondered how anyone in the room was fooled by her ruse. Surely no boy alive had a mouth shaped like that. He, at least, would have known her anywhere and under any disguise. "How—" She took a breath, and tried to resume the performance. "How does it go on the field, sir?"

"Well enough, I think," he said. "At least, I believe I discharged the duty I was given. I could not say how...how all my comrades fared, though."

She nodded. William felt eyes boring into the back of his skull, and turned slightly to see a man in a captain's uniform seated on the floor, back braced against a wall, studying him with eyes only slightly less glazed than Palmer's had been. A chill ran through William, and he shivered. He wondered if he and Elizabeth had been speaking loudly enough to attract attention. But even if they had, surely they had said nothing to arouse suspicion?

The odor had driven most other thoughts from his mind. It took him a moment to realize that a *tête à tête* between a lieutenant and water-bearer was rather odd, more than enough to attract a more senior officer's attention. William thought he had better leave Elizabeth before they drew any further gazes. He said as much, and she nodded. "Don't stay too long," he added, and she nodded again. He stumbled out of the door and turned his steps for the barn.

He was nearly there before his mind cleared enough to realize that the captain had been wearing a uniform of the 52nd. He had doubtless been perplexed by the sight of his regiment's uniform on a young lieutenant unknown to him, and William cursed inside his head, but it was too late to do anything about that. At least the captain was in no position to tell the Prussians and rouse their suspicions about his message. His intelligence ought to have already done its job in any case.

To his profound gratitude, William found their barn still deserted. He loosened the sling, peeled off his uniform coat, and sank into the straw a bare moment before Maxwell opened the doors he had just closed. Maxwell took in his presence with an air of relief, then frowned. "Where is she?"

"At the infirmary, playing at being a water-bearer," William said. "She told me she would come to us shortly."

Maxwell frowned again, but did not comment further. "Did you succeed?"

"I think so," William said. "At least, I delivered the information to General Bülow. Perhaps the Prussians will quickly break through Placenoit, and there will be no need for the monsters. Did *you* succeed?"

"I think so," Maxwell echoed, undoing the straining buttons of his own uniform. "At least, I delivered the paper message to one of Wellington's aides, and I spoke of it to as many other people as I dared. Perhaps His Grace will decide that the Prussians have nearly arrived, and there is no need to send for the monsters. Perhaps this will actually work."

"It didn't work," Elizabeth said, opening the door in a rush. Her face was drawn and pale beneath the boy's cap. "The aide to whom you gave the message—he was brought to the infirmary just after William left, and I heard the one who brought him talking with some of the other injured officers. The Duke did not believe the message. He thinks Napoleon sent it, for some purpose of his own."

Maxwell's face drained of color in its turn, aging him twenty years in an instant. "So he will not delay before summoning the monsters," he said heavily. "He may even summon them sooner, thinking the Prussians removed from the calculation entirely." He looked at William. "I just undid any good you might have managed."

"We're not defeated yet," William said, struggling to his feet. "They're not—" He waved in the direction of the distant artillery. "—so we're not. What other streams can we divert? There must be something. What about the lieutenant colonel who took the message to General Burnley?"

Maxwell closed his eyes in thought. "Yes," he said at last, remembering, and some of the color started to come back to his face. "Yes, I've read his journal as well. He dismounted just inside the forest to remove a stone from his horse's shoe."

Chapter 18

The twelfth charge of the French cavalry surged against the British infantry squares, a wave crashing upon a beachhead. The square in which John Freemantle sheltered with his Duke seemed to tremble under the onslaught, but the broad red backs before him held fast.

After one breathless uncertain moment, the charge broke, as it had broken eleven times before. For a long time afterward, the only sounds outside the square were of swords clashing and men screaming. Then the French cavalry retreated for the twelfth time, the artillery resumed, and Wellington swatted aside the men guarding him. Freemantle followed him back onto the open field as other aides emerged from their own squares, eyeing the battlefield and shaking their heads. Wellington's staff re-gathered itself around him.

"If the Prussians do not come, there is no way we can hold until nightfall," Canning muttered, and Freemantle gave his fellow aide-de-camp a startled glance. No one had dared say it quite so bluntly before now.

"They will come soon." General Muffling spoke unhappily. He somehow managed to appear at Wellington's side, like a drooping-mustached Greek chorus, whenever anyone raised the question of the missing reinforcements. Muffling was Blücher's liaison to Wellington, and he had been predicting the imminent appearance of said reinforcements since first light, over and over in almost exactly the same phrasing, while the sun rose high and men died under fire and the hopes of their comrades dwindled. "Once the skirmish in the village is won…then, surely…"

He trailed off. No one nearby gave him any aid in completing his sentence.

"Well, gentlemen," the Duke said, as though offering commentary upon an inconvenient rain shower, "they are hammering us hard, but we will see—"

He stopped, attention arrested by a sight in the distance. Freemantle turned to follow his gaze, and saw a British officer on a black horse came tearing down the ridgeline, mud spraying from each striking hoof. The officer waved one arm as he rode, screaming something over the sound of cannonade, words no one could possibly hear. The Duke raised a hand in acknowledgment.

The black charger skidded to a halt, and the rider nearly fell from the saddle as he saluted. Freemantle recognized him, though his face was drawn and splattered with mud: a staff officer named Kennedy.

"My lord," he gasped. "La Haye Sainte—the farm—fallen. Overrun. The French pursued our men—engaged Von Ompteda's battalion—destroyed it. The whole battalion, my lord. Gap in the center of the line."

Wellington did not hesitate. "I shall order the Brunswick troops to the spot. Go and get all the German troops you can, and all the guns you can find." Kennedy saluted and wheeled his horse, and the Duke swung to his aides. "Canning, my compliments to Colonel von Butlar, and the Brunswick Corps is to advance to the center immediately. I shall join them there." Canning raced away, and the Duke turned to another aide. "Gordon, my compliments to Major Norcott, and I wish a small detachment of the 95th to go into the forest and retrieve those Belgians who retreated so precipitously a short time ago, as their presence is desired to reinforce the center. Freemantle!" Freemantle barely had the chance to touch his heels to his horse's side before Wellington was galloping away from him.

❧

Gun smoke hung thick over the crossroads that had once been defended by Van Ompteda's battalion, and Freemantle winced to see the pitiful stratagems being employed to fill the gap in the line. As Wellington rode up, officers from all over the ridge made for him, and their reports were identical to a man. The center had suffered the heaviest of Napoleon's heavy fire since early that day, and so many of their men were now dead or injured that, even with the Brunswick troops supporting them, they would be unable to hold their positions in the event of another French attack. And the French would attack; it was only a matter of time.

"The Prussians *must* come," someone muttered. "If they do not—"

"I am not saying *I* mean to retreat," another officer said, speaking the word aloud for the first time, "but the line may break, and we must decide what to do if it does …"

Wellington ignored that, turning to greet yet another officer stumbling toward him. "How do you get on, Halket?"

"My lord, we are dreadfully cut up," the man said simply. "Can you not relieve us for a little while?"

Wellington paused one beat. "I fear I have no one to send."

"Surely," Muffling said weakly, "surely it cannot be much longer before General Blücher ..."

"But until that time," Wellington said, "it is impossible."

There was silence among his officers. Even the noise of the artillery seemed to be faltering. Freemantle strained his ears—everyone was straining their ears—trying to discern if there were drumbeats mixed in with the musket fire. Was the French infantry preparing to march?

"Very well, my lord," General Halket said. "Then we will stand until the last man falls." He turned to gaze where everyone was gazing, at the crossroads hidden from sight by swirling dust and smoke, from which a column of French troops would doubtless shortly appear.

"Damn me," Wellington said softly. Freemantle gaped at him, for that was more emotion than anyone had ever seen the "Iron Duke" betray, on the battlefield or off it. Wellington stared into the smoke, heedless of Freemantle's shock, lips moving slightly as though working out a complicated sum in his head. He reached the solution, examined it for a moment with distaste, then nodded once. When he turned to Freemantle, any trace of uncertainty had vanished from his face. "My compliments to General Burnley, Lieutenant Colonel. Tell him if you please that I am in desperate want of troops not yet battle-weary, who can join the fight upon the left so that I may move some of my men to plug the gaps in the center. It would seem the Prussians are delayed, and therefore—" He paused only for a fraction of a second. It would scarcely have been noticeable to anyone who knew him less well than did an aide-de-camp. "—therefore the General is ordered to bring up his special battalion."

"Yes, sir!" Freemantle snapped a salute, clapped his heels to his horse's side, and clung tight.

The animal shot away from the ridgeline, up the Louvain road and toward the Forest of Soignes, and Freemantle did everything possible to encourage its speed, making good use of good road while he had it. To enter the forest, he must turn off the road, and then he must slow the horse to a saner pace. Maddening, but if the animal broke a leg on the uneven ground, the rider would be lost, and thus also the message, the battle, the war, the kingdom—

The forest closed over his head like a shroud. The ground still shook from the artillery a couple miles off, but it was a dull, meaningless sound under these thick green branches. He might have entered an entirely different world. The special battalion was encamped a good way into the forest—an inconvenient distance at the present moment, but it would have been worse to have them nearer by.

The bay stumbled and Freemantle lurched forward, narrowly avoiding being thrown headfirst over its neck. The horse snorted and plunged, but regained its balance before it fell to its knees. "Easy," Freemantle said, "easy, whoa—" The horse stopped its forward stagger and stood, quietly enough but trembling.

Freemantle swung out of the saddle, heart pounding. No rabbit holes met his swiftly searching eyes. Thank God for that at least, but what had caused the stumble?

He ran a hand first down one foreleg and then the other, listening with all his might to the wood that surrounded him, trying to hear anything nearer than the distant rumble of cannon. Were there enemy here? Had someone hit his mount with a missile meant for him? He could find no sign of actual injury to the bay. He picked up the animal's left foreleg, and the horse allowed it willingly.

He saw the problem at once: a stone wedged between shoe and hoof. Freemantle fumbled for a knife. His heart hammered with the need for haste, but for that very reason, he could not grudge the delay to pry out the pebble, or he would be forced to race the sands of time on an increasingly lame mount. With every instinct screaming at him to hurry and the forest all around watching him with cold eyes, he set to work. Carefully, taking care not to damage the tender hoof any further, he probed with the blade.

So intent was he upon his work that he did not notice the shadow detach itself from the undergrowth behind him. A hand grasped his collar. Another hand slammed a nauseatingly sweet handkerchief over his nose and mouth, and John Freemantle collapsed into darkness.

*

"You're sure he'll wake?" William asked.

"Chloroform is routinely used by surgeons and midwives," Maxwell answered, though he kept eyes fixed on Freemantle's face. "He'll wake."

It was the first coherent thing any of them had said in some time, as it had been difficult to talk while simultaneously attempting to control John Freemantle's horse and drag Freemantle himself away from its lashing hooves. The horse had been trained to accept riders who were not Freemantle, of course, since a battle steed who sat only one man was of little use on the field, but its near-stumble had put its nerves on edge, and it reacted to Maxwell's unfamiliar hands on its reins with a squeal and a rear, dumping Maxwell neatly on his backside and careening away through the wood.

At least it didn't go far. Though spooked, it apparently cared enough about Freemantle's welfare to return to him. It stood now a few feet away, munching at some green undergrowth and eyeing the three of them warily. The better part of valor was clearly to let it alone and hope it wouldn't run off again, or at least not in a direction that would warn Wellington the message had not been delivered. Elizabeth tried to watch the horse and the rise and fall of Freemantle's chest simultaneously.

"What is chloroform exactly?" she asked. "Did you get it from the Genevese's trunks?"

Maxwell shook his head. "From 1885. It hasn't yet been invented, which has the additional benefit of meaning no one will suspect its use." Maxwell took a tiny bottle out of his pocket and passed it to her for inspection. "No, don't sniff it, you little fool, didn't you just see what it does? But his compatriots won't know, won't have any reason to suspect. They'll think he was thrown from his horse." Maxwell closed his eyes as though to picture something. "He has delivered no message to Burnley. Wellington will wait a short while at least, expecting a response, before he sends another messenger. And while he waits, Blücher's reinforcements are advancing. If the sun goes down and we haven't seen a troop of monsters march past, then we've stopped them arriving in time to take the credit for the victory."

"Ought we do something else to ensure that?" William mused. "I am still in uniform. Perhaps I ought to ride to Burnley and tell him to withdraw?"

Maxwell pursed his lips. "No," he said at last. "Burnley knows Wellington's staff in a way Blücher and Bülow do not. It's too easy for you to arouse suspicion—to do exactly what I did in an ill-fitting Coldstream Guards uniform." The faint self-disgust in his voice was there and gone too fast for Elizabeth to comment on it. "We'll just wait here for a bit," Maxwell went on. "And while we wait," he added, "we may as well decide what the deuce we do next. With you. Since you are in two places at once."

Elizabeth felt heat prickling over her face again.

"First we ought to try a quarter past seven on the eighteenth of June, when we are *not* in two places at once," William said. "It seems like it should work. If it doesn't …" He frowned down at Freemantle's body. "We know we can force a watch to take us where we shouldn't be able to go," he said slowly, thinking it out. "At the cost of the watch. So if we had two, and if there were no other option, we could sacrifice one to get back home. Is there anyone who could mend Elizabeth's? Not here and now, obviously, but someone in *some* place and time must know how they work. Someone far in the future, perhaps? Gavin Trevelyan, even. It doesn't seem like there's much Trevelyan can't do. Did he ever get a look at the inside of yours, sir? Oh, but..." Elizabeth looked up at the sudden change in tone. "But he'll be a different Trevelyan. He won't know who we are."

Maxwell smiled a little, sadly. "I hope not."

"How wretched that should be the best possible outcome. What a very odd life you lead, sir. But yes, I have to agree, I too hope he inhabits an utterly different world."

"Could we not ascertain at least something of his world now?" Elizabeth said. "The fourth face on the watch shows images. We got to the year 1885 the first time because we pressed the stem when it showed an image of fog and lightning and a construct in the shadows. If we've delayed Colonel Freemantle enough to change the outcome of this battle, won't the image of 1885 change too? Won't we know the moment we've succeeded?"

Maxwell looked mildly interested, and fished the pocket watch from his waistcoat. "No," he said, holding it out of Elizabeth's reach, "you're indulging in some pleasant dream if you think I'd let you lay hands on this one after what you did to the last. Look if you like, but don't touch." Elizabeth made a face at him, but didn't touch.

The watch seemed to linger with deliberate care upon the reeds of the meadow beside the sun-dappled brook, and then upon the knights in armor wending down the mountainside. Elizabeth kept her lips pressed tight together to refrain from giving voice to her impatience, but the strain was taking a toll on Maxwell too. She knew this when he abruptly jerked the watch closer to his eyes and began to fiddle with the settings.

"What—?" William asked.

"Sometimes it shows an image of the date to which it's set," Maxwell answered. "I don't know why, and I haven't yet identified a pattern as to the circumstances, but perhaps putting 1885 into its head will encourage it."

It did not, as far as Elizabeth could see. The watch showed them heaving waves. Knights on horseback. The meadow again. Heaving waves. It almost seemed as though the confounded thing was deliberately avoiding the image they wanted to see.

Elizabeth tried the word *confounded* in her head, and decided it was insufficiently unladylike as an expression of her current frustration. It almost seemed as though the *bloody* thing was doing it deliberately—

Katarina would have phrased it more like that. Elizabeth wondered if she would ever be able to enunciate such a sentence herself, and the very idea made her suddenly and inappropriately want to giggle. *Hysteria again,* she thought. *Perhaps understandable, given the circumstances.*

It seemed like years before the fourth face of the watch displayed an image she recognized. Lightning zagged through yellow-gray fog, from which an ominous silver form loomed to menace London's streets.

An image she recognized.

Bloody hell.

It was no effort to think the word that time. She looked up, stricken, but William laid a soothing hand on her arm before she could speak. "We're not defeated yet," he said again, though his eyes had begun to take on the same sort of strained look that haunted Maxwell's. "It just means we haven't succeeded yet either. We've stopped the message, but the effect could still be undone. If we leave now, there might still be time for Freemantle to wake, or...or something. We haven't succeeded, nor have we failed. Not yet. Let's see this attempt through to the end before we try something else."

Maxwell nodded, lips tight.

The cannon thundered in the distance and the light changed around them as they watched John Freemantle sleep, Maxwell reapplying the handkerchief to his nose every few minutes. In Maxwell's other hand, the pocket watch flickered its way through its collection of images.

❧

Sunlight slanted diagonally through the branches, filling the wood with a red-gold haze. Freemantle still slept, the horse still cropped grass, and the pocket watch showed its images in turn. Waves. Knights. Meadow. Constructs. Elizabeth shifted, and shifted again, and could not find a position that even approached comfortable. It had been some time since she had been able to think of anything except the aching pressure in her lower abdomen.

At last the discomfort grew until pride could no longer restrain her from doing something about it. It was the disadvantage to being a female adventuress, she thought. Adventuresses presumably had to learn to deal with the inconveniences surrounding a lack of convenience, and had to learn to conquer their embarrassment over such things. At least she wasn't wearing a ballgown.

Though she did not know how in the world she was to manage breeches. She thought about asking for advice. Then she thought she would far rather avoid the conversation and figure out the trousers on her own.

She stood with as much dignity as she could muster. William and Maxwell both looked up, William from the persistently unhelpful pocket watch and Maxwell from Freemantle's face.

Presumably adventuresses also became accustomed to not blushing about this sort of nonsense, even if they *were* embarrassed. "Excuse me for one moment. I'll just be…" She indicated the bushes a short distance away, and both men nodded understanding.

The branches were thick, scratching at her arms as she struggled through them. She found, however, that merely being on their other side was insufficient to alleviate her embarrassment. She picked her way further into the underbrush. It was darker here, the thicker trees screening more of the evening light. Darkness seemed to offer a more complete privacy, or at least the illusion of same. She stopped when she could no longer hear Maxwell and William's quiet conversation, because that meant they could also no longer hear her. Then she went a little farther anyway.

It was, indeed, an inconvenient and annoying business. She found it necessary to remove the breeches completely, and then she found it necessary to devote attention to preventing undergrowth from rasping against skin not usually exposed to such dangers. Elizabeth had her teeth set in thorough irritation by the time she had resumed and resettled her garments. She began to pick her way back through the brush to her companions, toying with imprecations that might best describe her sense of frustration with *this* situation.

Maxwell's voice came to her ears sooner than she expected—that was her first clue as to what lay ahead. The timbre of the voice provided the second, for there was more changed than just the volume. It was deliberately calm, deliberately soothing, overly reasonable. And, Elizabeth realized with a sick spasm in her middle, he was speaking *French*.

Chapter 19

L eaves tickled Elizabeth's cheek, and a sharp weed pierced into the flesh just above her ankle. She held absolutely still, not even breathing, straining her ears to make out words.

"*Vous ne voulez pas le faire,*" Maxwell said calmly. Elizabeth had studied French, of course, had spoken it with governesses and read it in books, but she could not make her brain detangle these sounds. Maxwell's voice told her enough of what she wanted to know, however. It was too calm, a note off from being believably so, a violin expertly played but with one string mis-tuned.

"*Tais-toi!*" That voice was harsher. Louder. A different instrument altogether, Elizabeth thought wildly. A drum, possibly? "*J'en ai assez des bâtards anglais comme vous qui me donnent toujours des ordres.*"

"*Votre désertion ne serait pas puni,*" Maxwell went on, still soothing. "*Mais si vous assailliez des officier britanniques—*"

There was a sound like a branch cracking, and he broke off. Not with a cry, nothing so overt, but all at once and completely—and Elizabeth could guess. The air vibrated with the sound of the snapped violin string.

"*Embarque-le,*" a third voice said. This one was higher-pitched, reedy. "*Ou nous allons te tuer sur le champs. à ce moment. Peut-être que la poudre est mouillée, peut-être pas, eh?*"

"All right," Maxwell said, in a voice shaky with pain. "All right, *d'accord.*"

Elizabeth's heart was hammering so loudly she was half-surprised the men did not hear it, did not plunge through the brush to seize her. But they were making some noise of their own now, rustling and muttering. No one said, "*Y'a quelqu'un?*" or gave any other indication they knew she was there.

She picked up one foot and put it down very gently into the underbrush. *Slow and careful,* she told herself. It sounded almost like Katarina's voice. *No noise. You can't make noise.* She raised her other foot and put it down in turn. *You can't make a speck of noise, or they'll know.*

With great care she lifted her arm and eased a branch out of her way. *If you rustle the brush, they will know you are here. And if they learn you are here...* She shivered at the thought, and knew she ought to keep still—Maxwell would doubtless tell her to keep still—but she didn't see how she possibly could. She had to know what was happening.

One step, and one more, and she was close enough to hear clearly, though she still could not manage to decipher the French. A final step, and a careful parting of branches, and she could see.

A swarthy man in the dark blue coat of the French infantry held William immobile, forced to his knees and with his good arm twisted behind him. William's mussed hair and blackened eye, not to mention the blood leaking from the Frenchman's nose, suggested that William had put up a valiant struggle, but the Frenchman had to outweigh him by three or four stone and had full use of all his limbs. The opportunity for struggle had passed, in any case, for one large brown hand held a knife so that the blade just touched the skin of William's throat. Late afternoon sun struck sparks off the steel, shifting and glinting as though the hand holding it kept tightening with eagerness or nerves.

There were fourteen or fifteen other men similarly attired, all dark-haired and French-looking, most as large as the first, and all armed with blades or muskets. The second one crouched on the forest floor, rummaging through William's rucksack with cheerful abandon. He pulled out one of Elizabeth's gowns and then the other, and whistled through his teeth. "*Pour ta putain, hein?*" he said, and his was the harsh, gravelly voice she had heard before. "*Maintenant, c'est pour ma putain!*"

On the far side of the clearing, a third man searched Freemantle's slumbering body, tearing off decorative trim and ripping open pockets. The remainder stood about, watching the show. Six of them held muskets pointed nonchalantly at Maxwell's head, and perhaps it was that which made Maxwell look so much smaller than usual. Or perhaps the blood running down his face had something to do with it, or maybe it was just the threat to William. Elizabeth could see how Maxwell's eyes kept going to the knife blade at William's throat, even as he retrieved coins and a pocket-knife and a snuff-box from his pockets and handed them over to the little weasel of a man beside him.

Where could the Frenchmen have come from? The Forest of Soignes was well behind British lines. How could French infantrymen have so quickly crossed the disputed valley, marched through the British guns, and eluded the two thin rows of British soldiers upon the ridge? For a moment Elizabeth imagined the worst, but then she listened hard and decided artillery still pounded in the distance. The battle still raged. So she was left with her first question: how could French infantry be here, and why would they be here robbing British officers when there was a battle still to fight?

"*C'est tout?*" the weasel-faced man demanded, reedy voice sharp. This time Elizabeth's brain made the leap—well, no wonder, the words were simple enough. *Is that all?*

"*Oui,*" Maxwell said. *Yes.*

"*Ce n'est pas possible!*" The weasel looked down at the coins in his hands in his disgust. "*Il vaut presque pas la peine!*" It is almost not worth the bother.

"*Et la montre?*" suggested one of the men with the muskets. It took Elizabeth a minute to place that word—*La montre?* What was *montre?*

Watch. The watch.

Oh, no.

The man with the gravel voice looked up from the rucksack at the chain that stretched across William's waistcoat. "*Bien vu,*" he said, "*les montres!*" He reached up and pulled the broken watch free of its fob.

Elizabeth clenched her hands and lips so she would not make a sound. The weasel man raised his eyebrows at Maxwell and held out his hand expectantly.

"No," Maxwell said, "wait. *S'il vous plaît, monsieur. Cette montre n'a pas de valeur.*" Elizabeth found herself able to follow him now. *Please, my watch is not valuable.* "*C'était un cadeau de mon père et c'est tout ce que j'ai de lui.*" It was a gift from my father and all that I have of him. "*Tenez, prenez celle-ci à la place et laissez-moi la montre de mon papa.*" Here, take this instead, and leave me my father's watch. Maxwell slipped his hands inside the collar of his shirt and drew out a locket on a silver chain—a little thing, so finely made that it had hidden unseen all this time beneath his coat and waistcoat. His hands shook as he undid the clasp, and Elizabeth wondered whose face the locket held, what lost love might be commemorated inside it—and in what year the woman might have been born. What a very odd life Maxwell led, indeed...

The weasel snatched the chain with one hand, yanking the pocket watch free from Maxwell's waistcoat with the other. "*Je prendrai les deux!*" he said. *I'll have them both!* "*Allons-y, les gars, on sort d'içi!*" Come, lads, let's get out of here.

It doesn't matter, Elizabeth told herself fiercely. *It doesn't. We'll manage somehow. We'll follow them, or we'll—we'll—something. But it doesn't matter, not even losing the watch matters, not as long as they leave William and Maxwell unharmed...*She held her breath, hoping they would do just that, trying to think what she could do if they made a move to act otherwise. She still had the little bottle of chloroform tucked inside her shirt. Was there anything she could do with that?

"Drop your weapons!" a voice boomed in English from the path that led back to the battlefield, and Elizabeth could have fainted in sheer relief. She saw the musket barrels jerk away from Maxwell as the men whirled in surprise; she saw the eyes of William's captor widen in alarm. "*Vos armes!*" the voice repeated in French with a note of impatience. "*Lâchez vos armes tout de suite!*"

The voice was accompanied by the sound of several rifles cocking in unison. William's captor shoved William hard into the man pawing through the rucksack, and bolted through the trees.

A thump and a cry proclaimed he had not gotten very far, and the others had no chance to even attempt to follow him. Men in dark green jackets were appearing as if from thin air. The hands of the remaining Frenchmen rose in jerky unison, puppets pulled by an unseen thread.

"On your feet! Battalion will form ranks!" the voice continued. "*Serrez les rangs!*" Elizabeth shifted just slightly to one side, in hopes of catching a glimpse of the speaker.

He stood on the path that led back to the field of Waterloo—a thin, sallow man, dark hair shot with gray, arms folded across his chest in an attitude almost of boredom. He might have been calling a group of unruly subordinates to order on a parade ground, rather than facing down an enemy force that outnumbered his own two to one. His hatchet-narrow face was lined and weathered, the texture and color of the tree trunks surrounding him on every side, and his jacket was the same dark green as the pines—so he was a Rifleman, a member of the odd 95th Regiment, the skirmishers and sharpshooters who were so different from the usual red-coated officers. "Sergeant," the man continued briskly, "you will shoot the next man who attempts to flee."

"Yessir," one of the green-coats answered with relish, though the Frenchmen did not look to have flight in mind.

The hatchet-faced man strode forward, steely eyes flicking everywhere at once. "What in the bloody hell is going on here? Not bad enough you gutless bastards had to run and His Grace had to send me to fetch you back, now I find you molesting British officers? On your feet, Sergeant," he added—to Maxwell, Elizabeth realized in a moment. "Lieutenant." Maxwell staggered upright, holding a hand out to William. The hatchet-faced man's cold eyes went to Freemantle, and forbore to issue any orders to a man obviously unconscious. "What were you about in the woods to let these Belgian cowards get the drop on you?"

Belgian. Oh. Elizabeth exhaled. Now it made sense. The robbers were not Frenchmen at all—or, at least, they were, in very meaningful ways, but they were part of the Anglo-Allied army. They must be from the Dutch-Belgian brigade that Maxwell said had deserted. Of course they had run; they were after all more French than anything else; they had been part of the French empire until the year before. Even now, they spoke French rather than Dutch, and still wore uniforms almost indistinguishable from those of the men on the other side of the valley. Elizabeth presumed that not all Belgians were useless as allies, but these men plainly were—dishonorable as well as cowardly. It was a sign of the Duke's desperation, Elizabeth thought, that he had sent Riflemen to round up the runaway Belgians in the hopes of more men to plug the gap in the line.

"I asked you a question, Lieutenant," the Rifleman said sharply.

"You must excuse him, sir," Maxwell interposed. "The Lieutenant was knocked on the head in the scuffle and hasn't quite regained his wits. We—"

"*Ces deux-là ne sont pas ce qu'ils prétendent être,*" the weasel-faced Belgian piped up. *Those two aren't what they seem.*

"Silence." The Rifleman snapped it out in English and without sparing him a glance.

"*C'est vrai,*" the weasel persisted. "*Nous les avons découvert és alors qu'ils attaquaient ce pauvre officier britannique.*" *We came upon them attacking that poor British officer there.*

"That's ridiculous," Maxwell said. "One of them flung a rock that knocked the Lieutenant Colonel from his horse, and then they rushed—"

"*Ils tentaient de l'étouffer.*" *They were trying to smother him.*

"Major, are you going to believe some Belgian riffraff over a sergeant in your own—"

"*Je soupçons qu'ils sont des espions français. Nous avons essayé de les maîtriser, il va de notre devoir.*" *I think they're French spies. We were only subduing them as was our duty.*

The Rifleman's cold eyes swept sideways. "And what call of duty led you to be out here in the wood instead of with your allies on the line? Not another word." But when he looked back at Maxwell and William, it was suspiciously. "Your name and regiment, Lieutenant."

William hesitated a bare instant. "Carrington, sir, from the 52nd Foot."

"And what business has a lieutenant of the 52nd Foot here in the forest, with that regiment stationed far front and on the right? In company with a 'sergeant' who speaks like he went to Eton with the quality?" The steel eyes flicked over them, probably taking in the ill fit of the uniforms. "I heard a rumor of a French spy dressed as a Coldstream

Guard sergeant, and here you are with one of His Grace's aides, conveniently unconscious…No, don't bother answering, I don't want to know. You're something far more interesting than deserters." He raised his voice. "Private Prentiss, bring me those trinkets the Belgians took off these men. Good. Now search them for weapons. Baker and Willis, you will keep your rifles pointed at their heads. Not another word, sir—" That to Maxwell, who was still protesting. "Or I assure you it will be your last. Sergeant, can you spare us a bit of rope? Prentiss, bind their hands. Excellent. Now then. Sergeant, you will take these Belgian cowards to join those of their compatriots we have already located, and see the lot of them back to the line where they belong. My compliments to the Colonel, and tell him I am conveying French spies back to the village, to be held until His Grace is at leisure to interview them. I shall return once I have secured them."

"Yessir, Major Nysell," the Sergeant said. "A'right, lads, you heard the Major."

"Baker, stay with me," Nysell added. "Prentiss, before you go, give me a hand with the Lieutenant Colonel."

Nysell arranged it with what Elizabeth supposed was admirable speed and efficiency. He mounted Freemantle's horse, which submitted to him willingly enough, settling Freemantle's limp body before him on the saddle. William and Maxwell were commanded to walk in front of him, hands tied behind their backs, a length of rope attaching them to each other and its other end looped through Baker's belt. Baker walked between the horse and the prisoners, rifle at the ready, and Nysell was precise in his instructions. "If they make any sudden movements," Nysell said, "or utter so much as a syllable, do not wait for my order. Shoot them dead. Right then, m'sieurs, forward march, double quick!"

They left the clearing in a blur of sound and color. From her hiding place, Elizabeth caught a glimpse of William and Maxwell's white shirts and slumped shoulders, the fluidly moving dark green coat of the Rifleman Baker, the bay flank of Freemantle's horse, Freemantle's lolling fair head. She heard the harness jingle and quickly moving boots stumble over tree roots, and then she was alone in the woods.

Chapter 20

It was all she could do not to dash off after them. She clenched fistfuls of breeches in both hands instead, forcing herself to remain still until they had moved off at least a short distance. She could still hear them, but if she were careful, they would not hear her. She took a deep breath and the first step in pursuit.

It would be better to follow them if she could. She could get to Waterloo from here, following the road, but she didn't know where in Waterloo Nysell was headed. So she would have to follow him, and then…And then what?

It was the first time, *ever,* that she would have had more options dressed as a woman than as a boy. If she could have presented herself to Nysell as an officer's wife—or even mistress—he might have allowed her to nurse Freemantle, and then at least she would be in the same building as William and Maxwell…not to mention the pocket watch …

But maybe she wouldn't be. Maybe Nysell was intending to convey Freemantle to one place and the prisoners somewhere entirely different, and if she were trapped by Freemantle's side, she wouldn't know where. Maybe it *was* better that her female clothing was in the rucksack and she was forced to continue her role as a boy. She could…pretend to have a message for Nysell? What other entrée might be available to a boy who seemed to be from the village? She would have to be careful, for his suspicions were already aroused, and if he thought her another spy—but even that might not be so bad, if they confined her *with* Maxwell and William—

No. Such a circumstance would be acceptable if they had the working pocket watch, but they didn't. She must somehow keep track of both pieces of the puzzle. Of all three, she realized suddenly, for Nysell might order Maxwell and William separated. Of all four, for without Maxwell reapplying the chloroform to Freemantle's nose, he might wake and remember he had a message to deliver. She must keep track of four puzzle pieces, and she must do it dressed as a village boy.

Elizabeth realized with a flash of panic that she could no longer hear rustling ahead of her. She threw caution to the wind and started to run.

Even to her own ears, she sounded like a troop of cavalry crashing through the brush. Bushes and tree roots rose up to trip her, and the thin branch of a sapling hissed as it whipped across her face. She jerked away from it, lost her balance, and came down hard on the side of her foot. She stumbled and fell almost to her knees, and only barely managed to avoid impaling her eye in an inconveniently placed broken tree limb. It seemed the better part of valor to hold still for a moment or two.

Her wild flight had at least brought her to the edge of the forest, where evening-blue sky peeped between the thinning tree branches. She pushed herself to her feet, on the chance she would be able to glimpse something other than sky. Her ankle gave one throb, then subsided—or maybe she only forgot to think about it as she caught sight of Nysell's horse. His cavalcade had crossed perhaps half the green slope between the forest and the village. They were headed directly for the back of the church, which meant they would almost certainly then cross the street to the tavern.

At least it was easier to leave the wood as a boy than as a girl, since there was no reason for a gently born English maiden to be wandering about the Forest of Soignes with a battle taking place on its other side. Elizabeth crossed the expanse of open space as indifferently as she could, fighting the desire to run, feeling very relieved indeed when she fetched up against the back of the town's row of shops. Now she could circle around and walk down the main street toward the tavern as though she had not, in fact, been tracking Nysell through the woods.

She peeped around the corner just as Nysell reined his horse in front of the tavern and dismounted. His subordinate followed suit. Elizabeth gave them another breath or so to get inside and started the walk down Waterloo's mud-slimed main street.

She might have been walking at midnight instead of supper-time, for all the signs of life that greeted her. The people of Waterloo, the inhabitants of these houses and proprietors of these shops, either had prudently gone elsewhere, had been turned out by Wellington's commandeering officers, or were shut up behind barricaded doors until the outcome of the battle should be decided. No one hailed her—there might have been no living soul for miles—but Elizabeth could not quite shake the feeling of eyes watching her. From upstairs windows this time, rather than from shadowed glens. She hoped no one would come out to summon a seemingly local lad to join them in safety. She might be able to put them off by pretending to be English—dressed in Belgian boy's clothing? Why?—but she really did not have time to waste on explanations. She had to get to the inn and find out what Nysell planned to do next.

The green hill and sloping dome of the church rose up on her left side, peaceful and sleepy in the evening light, and across from it sat the coaching inn Wellington had taken for his headquarters. No one seemed to be stirring here either, though at least Nysell and his party must be inside. Elizabeth did not know if the proprietress had fled or had stayed to care for the English soldiers, but if she and her servants were within, they were busy at their work in the back of the house and nowhere near the front door. Should Elizabeth try to get in through the front door? Knock and spin a tale? Or hope it was unlocked and sneak inside?

Trying to make up her mind, Elizabeth spied a third option. The great swinging iron gates that led to the inner courtyard yawned open. Wellington's officers had doubtless put the courtyard to some use this morning, and no one had locked the gates after them, perhaps thinking there no need. Elizabeth nipped through them before anyone could chance to spot her through the front windows.

The evening sun was too low to cast any rays over the high two-storied walls. The cobblestone courtyard was, in consequence, surprisingly cool—the evening air moist, and smelling of mud and horse. But the heat of the day had only recently lessened, and the shutters of every window surrounding the courtyard were open, threadbare white curtains and mint-green leaves of ivy moving lazily in a breath of air too light to really be called a breeze.

A door slammed like the report of a musket, and Elizabeth jumped nearly out of her skin.

There was no one nearby, she realized after a frantic moment of looking in every direction. No one had come out of the inn; no one had seen her; no one threatened her now. The slamming door had come from inside, the sound carried to her through one of the open windows. She tried not to move at all as she craned her head to see from which. On the south wall, she thought, but it was hard to tell, given how sounds echoed in a courtyard. She wondered if holding still would do her any good at all if the slammer of the door did look out. Would her muddied white shirt hide her against the dingy white wood of the inn? She feared it would not. Certainly the rough brown breeches would give her away.

"...leave him here," Nysell's clipped tone came to her ears, and it *was* from one of the windows on the south wall. Wonder of wonders, Elizabeth could actually see him from where she stood—a flash of green coat and profile, no more—but it did tell her which window. He wasn't facing it, at least, so if she did not move and thereby catch his eye, maybe he would not notice her.

"There's no point in taking him to Mont Saint Jean," Nysell's voice went on. "Stacked six deep there, and what can a surgeon do for a man who hit his head falling from a horse? He'll wake or he won't, so best to leave him here." A hard breath, not laughter. "The Colonel won't be needing his room tonight, after all."

An inarticulate rumble in reply. Nysell turned his back to the window, saying something Elizabeth could not catch, and she seized the opportunity to inch her way along the wall, closer to the window. If she were right underneath it, she could hear better. Moreover, he would have to look straight down to see her, and the twining ivy might provide just enough cover. She kept her eyes fixed on the window, waiting for the hook-nosed profile to turn back—and when Nysell did turn, she froze like a rabbit. She hadn't made it far enough, but at least she had stopped before he could see the movement. He didn't seem to notice her.

"I'll leave this nonsense here," Nysell said, and Elizabeth's heart leaped at the clink of metal on wood. "For all we know, some of it is Freemantle's. We'll sort it when we sort the prisoners. Right then." He pivoted. "This is the key to the coal cellar, which you will guard with your life. Give it to no one until I come back myself, or until His Grace returns. Let *no one* let those men out. There's more here than meets the eye, and we'll damned well find out what it is. Otherwise, stay here. Check on Freemantle often. He may wake, and be able to tell us some part of the story."

"And you, sir?" a second voice asked.

"Back to the line. Can't let His Grace think I'm as faithless as those Belgian hounds, can I? Don't worry, he'll know you're doing him a service too. Stand fast, private. I'll see you after sundown."

The sound of a door opening. The sight of an edge of door sweeping into the square frame of the window. Nysell's tall, stiff back walking through it. The squatter form of Nysell's subordinate following him. The sound of a door slamming shut. Elizabeth, expecting it, did not jump so badly this time. And then silence, from all the watching windows with their fluttering leaves and curtains.

Elizabeth thought. There must surely be other people in the inn, but they did not seem to be taking any part in the unfolding drama. If they were soldiers, they would follow orders to leave the prisoners be, and if they were the proprietress and her servants, they would not interfere with the unconscious British officer or the captured spies locked in the coal cellar. Not while there was any chance of the British winning the day, at least. As far as she could tell, no one was watching from any of the windows, and Nysell was safely descending a staircase within.

And she might never have another chance like this.

Elizabeth ran for the trellis. As she had long suspected, it was indeed much easier to climb while wearing breeches than while wearing a skirt. A trivial undertaking, in fact, when one compared it to an Orkney cliffside, or out her bedroom window via a bedsheet. Thinking of one of Mirabelle's novels, she at first tried to hold onto the ivy itself—but Mirabelle's novel must have featured a different sort of ivy, for the leaves of this plant ripped free as soon as she put any weight on them. After that, she used the latticed trellises for handholds as well as footholds, and if some of those creaked ominously, at least none of them broke.

At last she came level with the open window. She reached out with her right hand, and by leaning and straining, managed to wrap her fingers around the wood of the window frame. Then she lifted her right foot from the trellis and extended it through empty space and to the sill.

The lattice under her left foot groaned.

Her heart pounded like the distant guns as she probed with her right foot for the window sill.

Just as her toes touched the sill, the trellis under her left foot snapped.

Her knee struck the sill hard enough to bring tears to her eyes, but she didn't lose her grip on the frame. The filmy curtain molded to her face, half-smothering her, as she fought to draw up her left leg without losing her balance. She did not quite fall into the bedroom, but it was an eminently graceless entrance, seat-first and with a curtain wrapped about her. She caught herself before she could fall with an audible thud and turned, terrified that she had woken the man on the bed.

To her profound relief, Freemantle slept on, fair face slack, mouth open and revealing rabbit teeth. Elizabeth noted nervously that he did shift a little from side to side, hands twitching along the threadbare quilt underneath him. But at least he did not wake.

There was little else in the room beside the bed: a table with a lamp and a jug of washing water set upon it; the kit of whatever officer whose bedroom this had been, stowed neatly in one dark corner; William's rucksack tossed beside it; a chipped mirror above a chest of drawers, on which sat a heap of glinting paraphernalia. Belgian spoils of war, no doubt—coins, rings, lengths of braid, fine lawn handkerchiefs, a golden locket and a silver one, and several pocket watches. Including two familiar ones.

Elizabeth restrained both the cry of satisfaction and the impulse to dash across the room. She stole to the chest of drawers instead, taking great care with each step. *All* she needed now was a creaking board.

Her image appeared in the mirror, twisting and wavering with the flaws in the glass—a boy in a mud-streaked shirt, battered cap pulled down low but not quite concealing the seam down one cheek where the branch had left its mark. She thought of sitting before her own glass the day before yesterday—the seventeenth of June—while Sarah brushed her hair. It might have happened a hundred years ago. She watched her pale, mirror-twisted hand steal out toward the glass and the heap of objects piled before it.

The silver locket was on top. She took it, for Maxwell had seemed pained to let it go. She moved slowly lest it clink, extricating its chain from the chain of the nearest pocket watch, and fastened it around her own neck. Her fingers encountered the lump of chloroform bottle in her breast pocket as she did so, and she drew it out and set it on top of the chest of drawers for the moment. Freemantle stirred again, and she glanced sharply in the reflection. He seemed restless. She would have to hurry. All the time she had her ears strained for a sound on the other side of the door, but none came.

She picked up the pocket watch nearest to hand. A piece of glinting braid came with it, and she pulled it free. She snapped the watch open, and the image face flickered reassuringly at her, waves tossing so realistically that she half-expected salt spray. She tucked it into her right-hand trouser pocket, then took the broken one and tucked it into the left.

Then she took one of the fine white handkerchiefs from the dresser top. A man's, clearly; an officer's, by the quality. Freemantle's? From the bottom of William's rucksack? Stolen from someone else found in the woods?

The little brown bottle was easy enough to uncork. The scent that rose from it had Elizabeth almost wishing for smelling salts. She held it hastily farther away from her face and poured about half its contents onto the handkerchief. She didn't know how much Maxwell had used. She didn't dare be too frugal. She stole across to Freemantle, wondering only her fevered imagination made it seem as though his eyelids were fluttering.

She held the square of cloth to his nose and mouth as Maxwell had done, and watched as his face went slack. It seemed much easier to maintain the faint than cause it, for Freemantle had struggled wildly in Maxwell's strong grip for the three breaths it had taken for the fumes to work.

With that thought, Elizabeth realized the flaw in her plan. She had been thinking to use the chloroform on the guard when the man returned. But she would never be able to hold him still, never, not even for three breaths. She looked around the room. She could slip back out the window and—

No. *No.* He had the key to the cellar. She *had* to get to him, and she had to make him sleep so she could search his pockets. And she had to do it soon. Sundown was coming.

Elizabeth took a strangled breath—and nearly fell over from the force of the fumes. Hastily she rose from Freemantle's side and held the handkerchief as far as possible from her face. That was enough. She couldn't risk more. He looked to be sleeping soundly now anyway.

Now how was she to get the key from the guard?

She considered option after wild option. Pick his pocket? If she only knew how. Seduce him, like an adventuress? If she only knew how. Trick him, as Maxwell was so fond of doing? Well, that was at least within her purview—she was good at making up long consistent falsehoods to cover her various escapades—and it didn't trouble her to lie, as it seemed to trouble William—

But that wouldn't work, it couldn't work, she knew nothing about this guard or this world or what was supposed to happen, nothing that would enable her to enact a ruse such as Maxwell's failed attempt earlier. She didn't know enough. She needed the help of someone who did.

Allies. It was all about allies, wasn't it? Katarina and Trevelyan and Maxwell working together in the future London; she and William and Maxwell working together here. The one time Maxwell had been forced to tell his secret, his unwilling truthfulness had created a team willing to work with him to pursue his goal. And that was the closest he had ever come to success.

Which made sense. Of course one couldn't change the future all on one's own. The future was an awfully big thing to change.

On the bed, Freemantle stirred.

It was a mad risk, she knew that. But William and Maxwell were locked in a cellar, and she could think of no other way to get the key from the guard, and the sun was darker red all the time. The battle would end soon, one way or the other, and His Grace would return and demand to see the French prisoners.

Surely she could convince Freemantle. Surely once he saw the watch, he would understand, and he would choose to help.

Freemantle groaned.

Elizabeth hastily opened her watch, relieved to find the fourth screen awake. She took the cap off and shook her disheveled curls down around her face.

Freemantle's hand came blindly up to rub his forehead.

And when he dropped the hand and opened his eyes, Elizabeth was right beside him. With one hand she held the pocket watch where he could see, and the other she pressed lightly over his mouth—trying to make the motion coquettish—while she shook her head and whispered a plea for silence.

Fortunately, the pocket watch tended to inspire speechlessness. It gave her a few seconds' advantage.

"Please, you must help me," she whispered. "We're both in terrible danger. Please, you musn't make a sound."

Freemantle sat up slowly, palm to his head as though it clanged with pain. He stared at the watch, then at her, then back at the watch.

"I'm—you will scarcely believe this, but I am—" How had Maxwell managed to explain this to Seward and the others and be believed? "I come to you from the Year of Our Lord eighteen hundred and eighty-five. The picture you see here—" The fourth screen luckily choose to change its display just in time to support her dramatic timing. "—is a future that will not take place until after your death."

Honesty. The one time in her life that the honest truth was more unbelievable than any elaborate story, and the one time it was absolutely the right weapon. She plunged on. "It's a terrible place. Great mechanical men roam the streets, and they shoot down any who try to oppose them, and ..." She talked fast, never raising her voice above a whisper, covering all the details she could. "And it all starts here, with you carrying the Duke's message to summon the special brigade."

Freemantle's eyes sprang wide, and he snatched his hand from the watch to touch the back of his head. "You—"

"Yes," Elizabeth said, meeting his eyes. "My friends and I, we stopped you, I'm so sorry, but we had to. It will be all right. His Grace always said the brave men of England could have triumphed without the monsters. So no monsters will come, and England will hold the line without them, and Napoleon will be defeated, and there will be no further danger so severe that England uses them, and all will be well."

"For lack of a message," Freemantle murmured, as though dazed.

"The future is won," Elizabeth said, and couldn't keep the smile off her face.

It seemed to go even further toward convincing him than the watch had done. He believed her joy. Well, and why not? Honesty. What a remarkable weapon.

"The future is won," she said again, "but only if you help me. There is still time, you could likely get the message where it needs to go, you could likely bring the monsters to the Duke's aid—but please don't. Please believe me. Please help me get home."

Freemantle nodded slowly. He looked down at the watch and up at her face. "Help you? How?"

"My friends," Elizabeth said, and explained about the cellar and the guard and the key. "And there's no time to be lost; we can't be caught here."

Freemantle thought. "What was it you gave me?"

She showed him the handkerchief. "But I couldn't possibly hold him still long enough."

"No," Freemantle agreed. He looked from her to the door to the watch, and back to the door again. "I have a plan."

In her hand, the fourth face of the pocket watch changed to display an image she had never seen before. It looked like the London of 1885—but no construct peered through the fog.

∾

The waiting was the hardest part.

Freemantle seemed to think so too. He sat tensely on the edge of the bed, lamp ready in his hand, and Elizabeth waited with equal tension behind the door, holding the chloroform-drenched handkerchief as far away from her face as possible, and they both listened for the returning tread of the guard.

When it came, Freemantle met her eyes for an instant. Then he jumped to his feet and threw the lamp with all his strength.

It sailed neatly to the far corner, crashing to the floor like an entire crockery set smashing, glass flying in so many directions that Elizabeth could see some of the splinters from where she stood. From the other side of the door came a startled oath, and the footsteps broke into a run.

The guard entered the room with his eyes already on the bed, expecting to find a man waking from nightmare or delirious from pain. If he had looked toward the mirror he might have seen a flash of Elizabeth's white shirt in the shadowed corner, but Freemantle gave him no chance to look. He surged forward like a man possessed by a fever dream, and when the guard raised his hands soothingly, Freemantle flung himself at the man like a springing tiger. Together they crashed to the floor, Freemantle making certain the guard's head struck the boards.

It wasn't hard enough to stun him—Elizabeth didn't think, at least, though she didn't really know. But it was hard enough to stagger him for a moment, and that was all she needed. She was there immediately, slamming the handkerchief over his face, pressing her whole hand over his nose and mouth. This had to work. Had to.

One breath, two breaths, three—and a sliver of white showed as his eyes rolled back. His body went limp against her. He wouldn't chase her for a few minutes at least, and that was all she needed. And she couldn't wait, for if there *was* anyone else in the house, they must have heard the racket.

With feverish haste she ran her hands over his uniform coat. A key, a key, where would he have put the key—She undid the buttons and thought she saw his face tighten. She grabbed for the handkerchief again, holding it to his face as she patted his shirtfront with the other hand.

It proved to be in his breast pocket, a worn brass thing that certainly looked right for a coal cellar. Elizabeth almost sprang up, then took an extra second to check his trouser pockets in case he carried more than one key. He didn't.

She scrambled to her feet. "Thank you," she mouthed to Freemantle, not daring even a whisper, lest the guard could hear even in his drugged sleep. She leaned forward with the handkerchief one last time, and Freemantle did not resist. Later he would tell a story of fighting with a man who entered his window, of mistaking the guard for being in league with the intruder, and thereby accidently giving the intruder the opportunity to overpower them both. It would save him from having his loyalty called into question. And between them, they had just saved the Empire.

Elizabeth grabbed William's rucksack and plunged out the door. The passage was narrow and dark and smelled of something moldy. All the fresh air was apparently held on the other side of the closed bedroom doors. She had a moment to notice chalk scribbles on each one, but had no attention to puzzle that out.

South side of the building. So the main stairs would be that way—Elizabeth turned and ran in the other direction. A coal cellar would be at the back of the house. Near the kitchen. Narrow twisting stairs sprang into view and she flung herself down them, clinging for support to a nerve-wrackingly rickety banister. The rucksack swung against her side, delivering a bruising thump in the ribs from what had to be the dark lantern inside it.

She hit the ground floor and stood one moment, trying to look in every direction at once. Which way? She was in a back corridor, all dim wood and shadowed corners. She didn't *hear* anyone pursuing her. Was there no one else in the house? Dared she shout William's name?

She picked a direction and ran. But this was the wrong way—a carpet suddenly sprang into being under her feet—this was the front hall. She turned and ran the other way. She thought she might be detecting kitchen smells, and here was a corridor full of doors. Elizabeth started pulling on handles at random, finding pantries and storerooms.

And eventually, a locked door. She almost dropped the key in her haste, hissing with impatience as her sweating fingers fumbled it once, twice. She finally got it inserted. From somewhere else in the building, she was sure she heard footsteps.

It turned. Thank God. The handle yielded to her, and she wrenched the door open. Stone stairs led downward into blackness.

"William?"

It felt like a year at least before one pale face and then another appeared in the shaft of dim light, two sets of brown eyes looking up at her with identical astonishment.

Elizabeth dropped the key and the rucksack to the ground. Heavy booted feet thundered on the stairs above her head. "Hurry," she said as she yanked the working pocket watch out of her pocket. The chain caught on the cloth. "They're chasing me—"

At the sight of the watch, William laughed aloud and Maxwell swore—in almost exactly the same tone, Elizabeth noted distantly as she detangled the chain. William came running up the steps two at a time, disheveled and dirty, coat gone and shirt streaked with grime, but grinning like a schoolboy. Elizabeth, succeeding only at that instant in getting the pocket watch free, looked up at him just in time to take in the grin. She was so utterly surprised when he pulled the cap off her head and kissed her that she almost dropped the watch.

"Do you think," Maxwell growled, "we could possibly get out of here first and you could do this later?" But it sounded as though there was some affection beneath the usual crustiness.

The booted feet reached the landing just around the corner. There might have been other feet approaching from elsewhere, Elizabeth couldn't be sure. There was, in any case, no time to try to reset the tiny dials. They would have to see if the watch would let them go to an altered 1885. William caught hold of her right arm, and Maxwell seized William's sleeve, grabbing the rucksack with his free hand. Elizabeth pressed the top stem, the top stem, and the side stem, and the world went velvety black.

Chapter 21

nd the rain came down like a waterfall.

Elizabeth yelped and Maxwell swore, but William found that he had been instinctively expecting it, that his shoulders had begun to hunch against it while Elizabeth was still fumbling with the watch. Of course it would be raining when they got to 1885. It had been raining when they left, and what had they done in 1815 that would have any chance of affecting the *weather*?

The wall against his back had the gritty texture of brick. Otherwise the entire universe might have been made up of black rushing water, for all he could tell. He literally could not see his hand before his face and hastily returned the hand to Elizabeth's arm. She shifted a little, but toward him rather than away, and he dared to run his palm down her soaked sleeve until he found her fingers, clasping them and the cold metal of the watch together.

Dared? He had kissed her on the steps of the coal cellar, and she hadn't objected. Surely the touch of his hand was nowhere near so bold, and he might assume it would be welcome if the kiss had been. Though to be fair, she might have been too surprised to resist the kiss, and he might in fact be presuming …

She wriggled her fingers, and his heart momentarily froze. Then she succeeded in extracting the pocket watch from between their palms, and, after the briefest of hesitations—brief, but he still would have been prepared to swear it took a month to resolve—she squeezed his hand back.

His heart resumed beating with a thud, and a foolish grin stretched his mouth wide under cover of the darkness.

He did not think he had ever been so terrified as during that seemingly endless period in the coal cellar—and that included his time on battlefields, under the feet of constructs, and as the prisoner of a grinning, knife-wielding Belgian. In the pitch black chill, he and Maxwell had worked at each other's bonds with grim, sweating desperation—

Maxwell demonstrating that he had done this sort of thing before, and William cursing his clumsy hand in language explicit even for a former soldier—arguing in whispers what they ought to do once they managed to free themselves. Where was she? Had there been more Belgian deserters in the wood? If any came upon her and recognized her for a woman—more, for an Englishwoman—

William could not bear to think of what would happen after that. If Nysell captured her as a third presumed French spy, the possibilities were equally grim. *How are we ever to find her?* William had wondered, staring into the blackness of the cellar. *How are we to find the pocket watch? How can we possibly manage an escape for all three of us before His Grace returns from the field and Nysell discovers our absence?*

It appeared he—to put it mildly—needn't have worried. The remembered sight of her standing at the top of the stairs, watch in hand, made him want to laugh aloud again.

On his other side, Maxwell was muttering imprecations loud enough to be heard over the rain, and twisting himself into an improbable eel-like configuration that William could feel even if he could not see it. "What are you doing, sir?"

"Matchsticks," Maxwell snapped, straightening, and something gossamer-soft and not yet drenched fluttered past William's face.

He understood then, and let go Elizabeth's hand. "Stay still," he told her—reflecting with another private grin that she might, this once, actually obey the instruction—and grabbed for the soft floating thing that was undoubtedly one of her gowns, shoved back into the rucksack by Nysell's men and now being used by Maxwell in an attempt to keep the precious matchsticks dry.

His elbow connected, rather hard, with something rather solid. Maxwell expressed his opinion in one of the military turns of phrase to which William had introduced him a quarter of an hour earlier.

"Come, come, sir," William said mildly. "You really ought to mind your tongue. There's a lady present." He heard Elizabeth bite back a giggle.

"I was planning to use that eye for something, once we got the lantern lit," Maxwell grumbled. That told William where his head was and where the cloth might be best positioned, but it was another of those tasks for which it would have been quite helpful to have two working hands. He and Maxwell got thoroughly tangled in the muslin as he struggled to be of assistance. "Oh, for—" Maxwell snapped, but cut himself off. "Really, Mr. Carrington, it might be better if you *stopped* helping. All right, that'll do." He had succeeded in draping the material over both of their heads and shoulders, sheltering the rucksack and lantern under impromptu tent. "Hold it steady a moment." There was a pause, and William had time to reflect that the fine muslin was hardly the best choice of a garment to ward off rain. It would be soaked in a matter of seconds more, and then the matchsticks would be at risk again. "There," Maxwell said. "Found them. Just hold that still another moment."

A clank of metal latch and a scrape of metal hinge, barely perceptible under the drum of the rain. William did not hear the hiss of the match at all, but he did see Maxwell's hands spring into being in the sudden circle of light. He pressed closer, holding the not-quite-yet useless gown over the flickering little flame. Maxwell maneuvered it through the door of the dark lantern, and the wick caught.

They stood in an alleyway, William saw at once. Dingy brick rose up behind them and not very far in front of them. The ground at their feet was a litter of rubbish and broken crates and a soaked newspaper or two. Maxwell looked at it with a grim expression, unwilling to draw any favorable conclusions from what he saw, but William turned his head to find Elizabeth beaming. Her hair clung lank and streaming to either side of her face, the cap having apparently been left in 1815. Her torn and muddied shirt looked all the worse for its impromptu bath. He thought she had never seemed lovelier. "We are in 1885?" he asked.

"The twenty-eighth of August, 1885!" she said, stretching out her hands to hold the pocket watch within the lantern glow. Rain streamed down its faces, and the light glinted and rainbowed in each drop so that he could not see for himself, but he trusted her. "Ten o'clock in the evening, the day after we left."

"And we're in the right place?"

Maxwell took the watch out of Elizabeth's hands, glancing at the face briefly before clicking it shut and tucking it away in his pocket. "The precise latitude and longitude from which we departed."

"And there's no lightning," Elizabeth said, as though she were singing it. "No thunder."

"No constructs," William agreed, grinning at her. And no signs that anyone had bled to death here last night. His message might have affected Placenoit, then, at least a little. His mind's eye presented him with a vision of the Prussians seizing and holding the village, then marching up to join Wellington's left. He could visualize how the British soldiers would straighten in relief, knowing their reinforcements had come. Wellington would wonder why the monsters had not joined the fight, but it would not matter, for the British and Prussians together would achieve victory over the French. And then everything would be all right. Everything was all right. Meg would be free from Murchinson's, Katarina could go sing at La Scala. "Mr. Maxwell," he said, "I do believe we had an effect. And Miss Elizabeth?"

She glanced up at the unwonted formality before she caught the playfulness of his tone.

"That was beautifully executed. We'd still be in that coal cellar if it hadn't been for you. When we are at more leisure, I think I should like to hear exactly how—"

"We ought to find some form of shelter first," Maxwell interrupted, "before we all perish of pneumonia."

"Yes, and I should give you back your things." Elizabeth extracted the broken watch from her left-hand pocket and handed it to William. Then, to Maxwell's obvious surprise, she reached under her collar and unclasped a silver locket from around her neck.

He did not immediately put his hand out to take it. "You brought my ..."

"It seemed to matter to you," Elizabeth said, when it became evident the end of the sentence had eluded him.

"Yes," Maxwell said. He took the little silver ornament from her hand, then gave her the lantern to hold so that he could manage the clasp. He eased a step backwards as he fastened it around his neck, a movement that might have been casual, but that also very effectively hid his face in shadow. "Did you...happen to open it?"

Elizabeth furrowed her brows at his unseen face. "No. It seemed private. I had no chance in any case."

"We ought to start by trying these doors," Maxwell said, as though they had been having an entirely different conversation. He took the lantern back from her, turning away as soon as his hand closed over it. "There are worse places to spend a rainy night than a cellar."

He began the enterprise at once, lighting his way with the lantern, leaving Elizabeth and William to follow. William let Elizabeth help him settle the rucksack onto his shoulders. Then he offered his arm, and she took it immediately. "I think the rain's easing a bit," William said, to cover the renewed giddy desire to grin like a lunatic. "Just a summer storm, a quick drenching quickly over."

"I don't mind the rain," Elizabeth said, leaning against him. "It's not very cold, after all. And so peaceful. No thundering constructs. We might almost be in the country."

That was true, William thought, suddenly struck by it. It *was* peaceful. Now that the rain pattered rather than drummed, he could hear the silence that blanketed the city. And the night was dark as well as silent, soft black like the nighttime countryside. Granted, it was late on a rainy night, and therefore perfectly understandable that the local inhabitants would choose not to traverse the streets, but oughtn't there be *some* light? Some foot-traffic? William found that he was craning his neck to see down the end of the alleyway, in search of a gas-lit glow from the main street. Or a bobbing lantern light. Or the sound of drunken men walking home from public houses. Or *something.* Maxwell's fruitless investigation took them closer and closer to the main road, and finally to its corner. The rain slackened into almost nothing, and there was still not a speck of light or a sound anywhere. William set his shoulder against the brick wall and strained his eyes trying to see something—anything—anywhere down the main thoroughfare. Were it not for the brick and the evidence of the pocket watch, he might have thought them far from 1885 London indeed, marooned perhaps on a desert island or the surface of the moon.

"Well, this is a fine kettle," Maxwell muttered.

"It must have happened to you before," Elizabeth said, and Maxwell turned on her.

"Indeed it has. But upon those occasions, I had only myself to worry over."

Far down the main street, a single spark of flame flashed into existence. It winked and wavered for a moment, then settled into an easier swinging pattern. A lantern, William thought, either just lit or just come around a corner. The cold fist that had tightened around his heart relaxed its grip. So there was at least one other living creature in Londontown. He had actually feared for an instant that they were utterly alone, as absurd a supposition as that was. He reached to touch Maxwell's arm, to distract him from his argument with Elizabeth and tell him to draw the slide over the—

"Douse that light," a voice snapped from the darkness behind them, and William's blood froze. He had lunged to get between Elizabeth and the stranger, trying to shrug off the straps and ready the rucksack as the best weapon available on short notice, before he realized that something about that voice should have given him pause. Then Maxwell's lantern shone full on the man's face, and William stopped.

"I said *douse your light,*" Gavin Trevelyan hissed as he stepped out of the shadows. "And stop that row. Anyone would think you were *trying* to be caught. What the devil are the lot of you doing out after curfew, anyhow?" Reaching to shutter Maxwell's lantern for him, Trevelyan got a good look at the older man's face. And went still himself.

"Oh," he said. "Mr. Maxwell. In that case, I...suppose I understand what you are doing out after curfew." William tried to collect his scattered thoughts while the sharp eyes went to each of their faces in turn. "It's as you said it would be," Trevelyan said in a tone of wonder. "You two paces from arrest and me with a chance to repay you for the past— Right, then, you'd best come with me. Quick."

"At once," Maxwell agreed, and Trevelyan plunged into the darkness of the alley, away from the main street and the approaching lamp.

They managed to scramble about halfway up the alley before Trevelyan lifted one hand to call for silence and nodded to Maxwell to darken the lantern. The four of them crouched breathless behind crates, waiting. William heard a regular step beneath the soft patter of raindrops, louder and closer every second. A faint flush of light shone somewhere down the main road. The steps grew closer. A lamp appeared at the entryway of the alley—paused one heart-stopping moment—and kept going.

Trevelyan let out a breath. A familiar faint creak came to William's ears, and the Welshman proved to have a dark lantern of his own in his left hand. "We ought to be able to avoid the patrols long enough to get home," he said.

"Lead on," Maxwell said.

As they negotiated the second alleyway, William stepped into the beam of Maxwell's lantern, and the older man glanced at him through the dancing light. "Does this happen to you *often?*" William demanded.

Maxwell did not ask what he meant. "More often than the laws of probability would permit on their own. I have no explanation for it, other than that perhaps the watch knows?"

"Has it ever stung you?" That was the important point. It did not matter who Trevelyan might have been once, in some version of London that had never existed and never would. At the moment, he was nothing more or less than a guide about whom they had no information whatsoever.

"Well," Maxwell answered after a pause. "Twice. But I think we're all right." He added in explanation, "I've never told this one I would need his help."

It took William the rest of the alleyway to work out why this was cause for reassurance rather than alarm.

⁓

The buildings were laid out in a different sort of chaos from the one William had begun to learn during his last sojourn in 1885, and the streets wound in unexpected directions. So it was something of a surprise when Trevelyan led them around a corner that William thought he had seen before, stopping before a door that was very familiar indeed. William looked a question at Maxwell, and Maxwell only shrugged, as untroubled by the second flouting of the laws of probability as he had been by the first.

There were some differences. Trevelyan did not knock twice and twice again, but drew a latchkey from his pocket and unlocked the door himself. It swung soundlessly open, and Trevelyan gestured them to precede him into a shabby corridor of bare boards and dingily white-washed walls. "Hullo?" he called past them, shutting the door and fastening the bolt with nimble fingers. A muted chorus of voices, male and female, answered from somewhere in the darkness ahead.

Trevelyan's lantern showed a small corner table, scored and scratched and burnt, with a battered and empty candle sconce above it. Scuffed white walls led down a narrow hall with a dim light at its very end. Trevelyan doused the lantern and headed for the faint glow, and his guests followed. A draft blew from the left-hand fork in the passageway, suggesting it still led to a great hollow room that might serve as an inventor's laboratory. Trevelyan's lanky form led them to the right and the parlor.

Which had definitely changed. It was still sparsely and cheaply decorated, still boasting only a single table, half-a-dozen straight-backed chairs, and a low bookshelf as its furnishings, but now it was scrupulously clean, as well-swept and well-dusted as any goodwife's cottage. No blacksmith's tools littered the corners or the shelves, and the bookshelf actually boasted three volumes that were not textbooks, bound in tattered red, green, and blue cloth. A smoking lamp sat in the center of the table, concealing rather than illuminating the faces of the two men and the woman who sat playing what looked like a game of lanterloo.

They glanced up as Trevelyan entered—and then dropped their cards at the sight of his guests, the young man and the woman jumping to their feet. "It's all right," Trevelyan said. "Friends of mine from long ago. It's safe."

"You could have said something," the woman chided, and a flash of relieved joy seared William through at the sound of her voice. "You'll kill us all from heart failure, Gavin."

"Madame Katarina," Elizabeth said at William's side, swallowing as though something thickened her throat, "it is so very good to see you again."

Katarina stepped into the light, turning curious eyes in the young-er woman's direction. She looked exactly as William had last seen her, even to the trousers and bodice. "I beg your pardon," she said in the same smooth, low voice, "have we met?"

"Not exactly," Elizabeth admitted. "It's...complicated."

"I will explain," Trevelyan said. "At least, I believe this gentleman and I between us can explain. This is Mr. Maxwell, whom I met some years ago under what you might call peculiar circumstances. And his companions—" He paused interrogatively.

"Miss Elizabeth Barton and Mr. William Carrington," Maxwell said.

Trevelyan gestured to the three who had been playing cards. "May I present Madame Katarina Rasmirovna, whom it seems some of you already know—" Katarina nodded in courteous confusion. "—Mr. Frederick Kent—"

Maxwell snapped his head around. The older of the two men sat in the heaviest shadow, and it seemed Maxwell had not gotten a good look at his face through the lamp's smoke. Now he took an unsteady step forward, hand outstretched, and the seated man took it with an expression of polite surprise. Maxwell looked as though he were trying to keep his movements casual and any show of emotion off his face, but the attempt failed rather badly. "It is indeed a great pleasure," he said, clearing his throat as Elizabeth had, "to see you both well." Kent's eyes went to Katarina's, and she lifted equally puzzled shoulders.

"And Herr Emil Schwieger." The younger of the two men bowed deeply. He was no more than a year or two older than William, with hair so fair as to be almost white and eyes so blue as to be clearly seen even in the inadequate lamplight. William glanced at Maxwell sideways, but there was no indication that Maxwell had ever met Herr Schwieger in the other 1885.

"Oh," Trevelyan added from behind them, "and my wife. This is Mrs. Trevelyan."

Of course, William thought, giddy again, *of course, no monsters, she's alive, she's fine, they're living happily ever after. Everyone should find a woman who suits him and live happily ever after. Oh, but wait*—The giddiness ebbed into confusion. *She's hardly old enough to have been married to him for fourteen years, is she?*

The girl in the doorway, a sweet-faced little slip of a thing with hair hanging down her back in a honey-brown braid, in fact looked no older than Elizabeth. Then she stepped into the light, and William could see lines around her mouth and eyes that proclaimed her to be Gavin Trevelyan's contemporary, despite her girlish-lithe build and girlish-shy manner. The expression on her face wasn't exactly fear, but she drew nearer to her husband than she did to his guests, and Trevelyan shifted his stance to lean toward her. She barely came to his shoulder.

"Miss Barton, Mr. Maxwell, Mr. Carrington," Trevelyan said to her, indicating each of them in turn. "I didn't realize you were there behind me; I thought you had long since gone to bed."

"I never can sleep when you're out past curfew," Mrs. Trevelyan said, but ruefully rather than pettishly. Her voice was as sweet as her face, and the singsong Welsh lilt, much stronger than her husband's, struck William as completely charming. "I gave up trying and thought I might as well come down here. I am so glad to make your acquaintance," she added to the newcomers. "Did I hear Gavin say you knew him in Vienna? Dear me, Miss Barton, you're soaked to the skin! Come with me, won't you, and I'll find you something dry and put the kettle on."

"What's this?" Maxwell demanded.

He had turned from Kent to the bookshelf, as though wishing to have an excuse for looking elsewhere while he regained his composure—but what he found there had undone him completely. There was naked horror on his face now. He had taken up some slips of paper stacked at one end of the shelf, and they shook so in his hands that William could make out nothing about them.

There was a pause.

"You know what it is," Trevelyan said then, speaking carefully, watching Maxwell with wary eyes. "You know my trade. I've a printing press as well as some other tools, in the other room. That particular piece there happens to concern conditions in the mines."

"Who works the mines?" Maxwell's voice sounded strangled.

"The British," Trevelyan said, "who did you think?"

"Not monsters?"

Mrs. Trevelyan took another half step closer to her husband, and Katarina took a half step closer to Maxwell. William could hardly blame them. Max would have sounded mad to him too, if he hadn't known better. But he did know, and he had moreover caught Maxwell's urgency. Trevelyan had run away from a patrol. He had taken them to a hidden place, another warehouse that was not a warehouse. This was a time of curfews and political pamphlets and some desperate struggle. But it was a different 1885; the world outside had been different. Who were they struggling *against,* if not constructs bred to fight monsters?

"Whom are you fighting?" he managed.

"The Empire," Trevelyan said, one hand now in his pocket, shoulder between his wife and the rest of the room. "Who did you think?"

"No monsters," Elizabeth said. "No constructs. What evil is the British Empire guilty of, to make you—?"

"The British Empire?" That was from young Herr Schwieger.

Then William knew. It was only a matter of playing out the final few moves. They must go through the ritual of asking the questions, but he knew what the answers would be. His giddy blood turned to lead, sending him plummeting from a great height, crushing his feet to the floor.

"The French Empire?" Elizabeth whispered, not really a question. "How long?" She cleared her throat. "How long have the French ruled this island?"

"Since 1815," William said, not phrasing it as a question. He was sure. "Since the eighteenth of June, 1815, the day the Seventh Coalition lost at Waterloo."

Trevelyan nodded, brows drawn.

"Oh, my God." Elizabeth turned stricken eyes in William's direction.

"We had an effect," Maxwell said, a note of something like hysteria in his voice.

"We did this," Elizabeth said, the same note in hers.

"We'll fix it," William told her, and took her hand.

Timekeeper

Coming Summer 2017!

Waterloo, Belgium, June 18, 1815

John Freemantle felt every jolt of the cart like an explosion within his skull.

At least, he thought it was a cart. He had reason to think so; he had been carried semi-conscious in a cart once before, and it was not an experience one forgot. The sickening arrhythmic lurches, each one as bone-rattling as it was nauseating, had nothing in common with the plunging deck of a ship or the joggle of a properly sprung carriage. Moreover, each jolt seemed to give rise to a fresh bout of moaning in a variety of registers, from sources surrounding him at close range. Then there was the smell—sweat and blood, vomit and urine. He was becoming more certain every instant that his initial impression had been correct. He was in a cart.

What he could not determine was why. Freemantle cast his mind back, trying to recall some sequence of events that would logically end with his person residing in such a conveyance. The battle had been going badly, he remembered that. The British and their Belgian allies had been under heavy fire from the more numerous French. Between injuries, deaths, and desertion, Wellington's line was stretched almost to breaking, and when the news came that the farm La Haye Sainte had fallen, Wellington had no fresh troops he might move to plug the gap. The promised Prussian reinforcements had still not arrived, and so there was nothing for the Duke to do but—

Freemantle remembered with a jolt worse than anything the cart could throw at him, and jerked upright. Or tried to; he only got halfway before pain spiked through his temples and he sagged back down. The Duke had summoned the special battalion. The Duke had sent him, John Freemantle, to summon the special battalion. But something had ambushed him in the woods. And he could dimly remember, as though recalling a dream, a girl with a minx's face and an impossible pocket watch—

"Battalion," he croaked.

"Easy, John."

Freemantle turned his head toward the voice. The movement seemed to take a long time, and a green blur swooped across his field of vision as he did so. He wasn't sure if he had opened his eyes, or if the sickening haze was present only behind his lids.

He squeezed his eyes hard shut, then forced them open. This time they focused enough to recognize James Warren. Warren was propped upright against the side of the cart, chest and right shoulder bound with blood-soaked bandages, face paper-white except for the dark shadows under his eyes.

"Battalion," Freemantle said again. "Burnley. I was—" The cart jerked underneath him, drowning the faint flicker of memory in a flood of queasiness. Freemantle drew a deep breath, holding it until the worst of the sickness past. "What—happened?"

"You were thrown from your horse," Warren said. He spoke almost without inflection. The gray eyes that regarded Freemantle seemed unnaturally wide, unnaturally steady.

Freemantle made one more effort to sit up, and this time managed it despite the spike of pain through his skull. "The message—"

"Hit your head," Warren added, as though that were the question he had asked. "They took you to the village to recover."

"The message, James. The battalion—"

"Didn't come," Warren said.

"Oh, God." The blur of green crashed over his head like an ocean wave. There had been a girl and a pocket watch and an impossible story, and he had—chosen not to bring the message? But no, that was impossible, that was a fever dream. Surely he could never have chosen to betray Wellington. Surely he was guilty of nothing but failure. "Oh, dear God."

"I wasn't there," Warren said, as though he were talking in his sleep. "Leeches wouldn't let me leave. But I heard. Heard the others talking. They said His Grace was waiting on the battalion. They said it looked like the Prussians might reach us—they were even in sight. But then the infantry broke under the last French charge. The Prussians thought the day lost, and made tracks. It didn't take long after that…"

"But the Duke," Freemantle said, struggling to comprehend it. The girl had said they could win without the special battalion. And because of that, Freemantle had chosen to— He shied away from the memory. "Never beaten—all those times on the Peninsula—conjuring possibilities from thin air—how could the Duke—" He stopped at the look on Warren's face. "Dear God. No."

"He was trying to rally them," Warren said hoarsely. "He was— being conspicuous, the way he always—Lord Uxbridge rode at him, shouting, 'For God's sake, don't expose yourself so!'—and then—A lucky shot, they said. Uxbridge was so close that the Duke's blood— the Duke's blood splattered—" Warren choked. He coughed, and the crimson stain on his bandages darkened and spread.

"Under Uxbridge," Freemantle said. It was the only part of the paragraph he could absorb. The other intelligence was too momentous, as though the universe had been pulled up by the roots, or broken and reformed into something entirely new. He could not comprehend it. He pushed it instead to the back of his throbbing brain. The girl had said that, to save the future, he must not bring the message. And he had believed her, as mad as that seemed now, he had chosen— "We're under Uxbridge. What are we about?" He looked around himself. Bleeding and hastily bandaged comrades-in-arms lay wedged and piled around him, groaning with each fresh lurch of the wheels. Past them, the green haze would not come into focus.

"Retreating," Warren said, still expressionless, eyes still staring. "Bonaparte sent in the Garde. Immortals. Undefeated."

"Retreating," Freemantle repeated. She had said they would win. "Where to? Brussels?"

"In Brussels," Warren said, "they are preparing feasts to welcome home their Emperor."

Of course they were. The Belgians had always been more French than Dutch, had never been likely to stand with Napoleon's enemies in the event of the Emperor's victory. Some had fled the battlefield, and some— Freemantle had an instant's memory of Belgians in the Forest of Soignes, but it fled when he tried to grasp it. The effort struck through his head, a blinding spear of pain. The girl had a handkerchief, and a pocket watch, and a glib tongue, and he had believed her, and he was worse than a traitor, worse than a fool. She must have been a French spy. If she were real at all. Perhaps she wasn't real. He wanted her to not be real.

If she were not real, this was not his fault.

"Bonaparte's done it," Warren said. "Separated us from the Prussians. They retreat across the Rhine, we back to the North Sea while the route home is still open to us. The French pursue, but Uxbridge left a small band of monsters to cover our retreat. He thinks they will be enough. He takes the rest home to garrison our shores. It's too late to use them any other way."

"Too late," Freemantle repeated. The words tasted awful on his tongue, slimy and nauseous.

"Not your fault," Warren said suddenly. But it was. "Even Wotten said so, when he came to fetch me from Mont St. Jean. You hit your head. The Duke oughtn't to have waited. He delayed too long in sending a second courier. He delayed too long in sending for the monsters in the first place."

Freemantle's guts twisted inside him. "No," he said, as the sky throbbed in time with the throbbing in his temples. "It wasn't his fault. Never his fault. It was mine—mine—I failed—I caused—" She had said, The message must not get through, and he had said, I have a plan. His hand had thrown the lamp, struck the guard, misdirected the message, lost the war. "I caused this. Oh, God."

He was no longer wearing his pistols. But a polished-smooth handle still rode on the belt at Warren's hip. Freemantle reached out, and Warren was too drunk on his own injuries and grief to stop him seizing hold of it.

READ THE CONTINUATION OF ELIZABETH, WILLIAM, AND MAXWELL'S ADVENTURE AS THEY TRY TO SET TIME RIGHT...AGAIN

IN

Timekeeper

BOOK 2 IN THE KEEPING TIME TRILOGY

COMING SUMMER, 2017

STILLPOINTDIGITAL.COM/TIMEKEEPER

Keeping Time

It's 1815, and Wellington's badly-outnumbered army stares across the field of Waterloo at Napoleon's forces. Desperate to hold until reinforcements arrive, Wellington calls upon a race of monsters created by a mad scientist 25 years before.

It's 1815, and a discontented young lady sitting in a rose garden receives a mysterious gift: a pocket watch that, when opened, displays scenes from all eras of history. Past…and future.

It's 1885, and a small band of resistance fighters are resorting to increasingly extreme methods in their efforts to overthrow a steampunk Empire whose clockwork gears are slick with its subjects' blood.

ARE THESE EVENTS CONNECTED?

OH, COME NOW. THAT WOULD BE TELLING.

TIMEPIECE
TIMEKEEPER (SUMMER, 2017)
TIMEBOUND (WINTER, 2018)

STILLPOINTDIGITAL.COM/KEEPING-TIME

Stillpoint/Prometheus

HEATHER ALBANO is a storyteller, history geek, and lover of both time-travel tropes and re-imaginings of older stories. In addition to novels, she writes interactive fiction. She finds the line between the two getting fuzzier all the time.

Heather lives in Massachusetts with her husband, two cats, a tankful of fish, and an excessive amount of tea. Learn more about her various projects at heatheralbano.com.

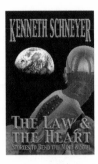

Made in the USA
Middletown, DE
13 August 2019